KILL TIDE

TIMOTHY FAGAN

Fireclay Books

All rights reserved. Published in the United States by Fireclay Books, Winchester, Massachusetts.

www.fireclaybooks.com

Cover design by damonza.com.

ISBN-13: 978-1-7324596-4-9 (paperback)

ISBN-13: 978-1-7324596-5-6 (ebook)

First Edition

01.05.21.123.321

To Karen.

CHAPTER ONE

It was on a wet July afternoon that Pepper Ryan became a hero to pretty much everyone on Cape Cod, except himself.

Pepper was driving through warm rain to the apartment of a woman he thought maybe he loved. He was going there to answer an epic question she'd asked him two days earlier. His hands were shaking, just thinking about it.

His hands were also shaky because he was driving a police SUV which he'd basically stolen a few minutes earlier from the New Albion police station, where he was working that summer as a police cadet.

Pepper was beyond pissed off at his dad, the chief of police, and it had felt like rough justice when he'd swiped the keys. So he hadn't cared that a marked police vehicle was completely off-limits to a lowly cadet. Especially the department's only brand-new Ford Explorer SUV Police Interceptor, with all its bells and whistles.

Including one hell of a sound system.

To drown out the mess of thoughts filling his mind, Pepper cranked up a Kings of Leon song, "Use Somebody," on the SUV's radio. Pepper was only twenty years old back then. He hadn't yet heard that song ten billion times. He sang along, really getting into it. As he neared the woman's apartment, his heart was banging louder than the song's crazy drumbeat. And faster.

So Pepper was cruising a bit too hot-headed and singing a bit too loud as he came down the hill on Rogers Folly Road late on Thursday afternoon. Especially since it had been lightly raining for the past couple of hours—the windshield wipers were squeaking back and forth and the road was shiny black.

He was about a hundred yards short of the intersection with Lower County Road when he saw a brown Chevy cargo van pull onto the road from the grassy strip to the sidewalk. It approached the four-way stop, to Pepper's right, at almost exactly the same time as Pepper.

The cargo van was a dull brown that the rain had darkened to exactly the color of dog poop. Pepper also saw what looked like a white garbage bag in the high grass near where it'd been parked. Had the van driver dumped that trash? But the object was smaller than a kitchen garbage bag. A grocery bag?

The van's right-turn signal was flashing as it approached the stop sign. Pepper saw the driver—a white guy in a green trucker's cap—look left and their eyes crossed for half a moment. The brown van rolled into the intersection and stopped about five feet beyond the little white stop line.

Pepper stopped at his sign a split second later. No turn signal because he was continuing on Rogers Folly Road.

The man looked at Pepper again, spat out his open window, then grinned and drove away straight, despite still having his turn signal on. *What an idiot!*

And that was the moment Pepper got his inspiration. A crazy solution to all his problems that summer. A perfect way out.

Again, Pepper was not a cop. A cadet was half a level up from a boy scout, minus the merit badges and knot-making skills. He had absolutely no authority to do what he was contemplating. He mentally flipped a coin.

Go straight? Or turn left?

The coin came up tails and Pepper didn't think he'd cheated. He turned left to follow the brown van. But as he turned, he thought, *Pepper, you're nuts.* He was about a hundred yards behind the van, which was moving at a slowish pace, probably five miles under the thirty miles per hour speed limit.

Pepper caught up to the van and settled in twenty yards back. Brown paper covered the inside of the van's twin small rear windows. It looked the same as thousands of other work vans all over the Cape. And not really at all like the white van that Pepper's dad and law enforcement had been hunting on Cape Cod that week, in connection with the most notorious crimes on the Cape in many years.

Kings of Leon reached the bitter end of their song and a decent Black Keys tune started up, but Pepper killed the music. Then he turned on the police radio and lifted the mic. First time ever, but he'd seen his dad and others do it for most of his life. Still, he fumbled around, too jacked up with energy.

Then he hit the talk button. "Hello, ah, Dispatch?" he asked.

Pepper's stomach was suddenly in his throat. It was one thing to get a crazy idea. The way people standing near a ledge getting a momentary impulse to jump, which they quickly dismiss, leaving their toes tingling while staying alive. That self-preservation instinct...

The voice of Barbara Buckley, one of New Albion's police dispatchers, crackled over the radio, acknowledging.

Shit. What should he do? It wasn't too late yet to bail out on his idea.

And then it was. "Ah, Dispatch, this is Car Two-Two," said Pepper. "Please send units for, ah, backup. Lower County Road, east of Rogers Folly."

Long silence, then: "Is that you, Pepper? Repeat that—"

Instead, Pepper hung up the mic. He fumbled around the dashboard and eventually found the switch to activate the roof lights and siren. His heart jumped as he flipped it. *Pepper, now you're fucked. Congrats, you're fired for sure.* His right foot didn't belong to him...he barely could feel it, heavy and strange, as it floored the gas. His siren screamed in his ears.

Thirteen minutes later...

Pepper felt a strong hand reach down and shake his shoulder.

It belonged to Lieutenant Donald Eisenhower—his dad's second-in-command on the New Albion police force. And his dad's longtime best friend from way back in their army days. Pepper had never seen Eisenhower's African-American face so pale. Or so close. It was ridiculous.

It registered with Pepper that he was lying on a wet road, looking up at Eisenhower, and his left side from his shoulder down to his hip felt like it was on fire. His hand too. He tried to sit up but couldn't.

"Hey man, what's up?" Pepper asked. He didn't recognize his own voice. Thick. Slurred. Pepper gingerly raised his hand in greeting and saw it was stained blood red.

Thump, thump, thump.

"Hey...you hear that?" asked Pepper.

Lieutenant Eisenhower was bent over at his side and answered him. But Pepper couldn't follow his words very well, because the lieutenant's head was lazily splitting into a mosaic of Eisenhowers. Like Pepper was looking through one of those kaleido-thingamabobs he'd played with as a kid... What was Eisenhower saying?

Pepper tried to wipe the blood off his hand on the wet road. But the blood only smeared. He was in a ton of pain and his hand looked wrong now. Why wasn't the rain washing it clean?

He saw a small group of fuzzy people behind Eisenhower, gawking down at him. The evening sky behind them was a broken shade of gray. Were they civilians? Like what, this was all a goddamn show?

Pepper tried to push himself to a seated position, but his hand landed on someone else. He saw it was a man who was covered in blood too. This man was deathly still. A wet green baseball cap lay in the street at his side.

Eisenhower slapped his cheek, as if to make him focus. But the slaps felt way too feeble. What was wrong with the lieutenant? Was he hurt too?

"What happened, Pepper? What the holy hell did you do?" Lieutenant Eisenhower asked.

Pepper could barely hear him over the *thump, thump, thump*. He tried to clear his head and answer. *I can explain...just give me a second. Please!*

Pepper really tried. But no words came out. And now the many faces above him looked wicked scared. And way too close.

Then Pepper had a thought that gripped him like an icy hand on his neck.

If I die, I'll never get to explain...

Then his world slid to darkness.

CHAPTER TWO

Six days earlier

Pepper Ryan drove through the summer night with his focus on one thing. And it wasn't the road.

Pepper was driving Brad St. John's van back to New Albion from their band's first-ever gig. Pepper should have been happy and relaxed after their successful show, but instead his body was tight and shaking a bit with nervous energy. All because of the woman sitting next to him—their lead singer, Delaney Lynn.

They shared the bench seat with their bass player and fearless leader, Brad, but he was semi-passed out against the front passenger window, snoring. Brad was a lanky white guy with café au lait–colored dreadlocks and a tightly manicured beard which emphasized the angles of his face. He'd drunk too much Wild Turkey bourbon tonight to numb his stage fright. That's why Pepper was driving.

Pepper's best buddy, Angel Cavada, the band's drummer, was crammed in back with the gear. He'd lost the rocks-paper-scissors.

Their band—Brad and the Pitts—had played the

Beachcomber Bar on a rowdy Thursday night out in Wellfleet. And they had killed it. The Beachcomber crowd had loved their classic rock cover tunes, especially the drunks. Delaney had been a fireball on stage, strutting around and belting out song after song, whipping the crowd into a party. They were a brand-new group, but you wouldn't know it if you'd seen them up there on stage.

Pepper thought Brad and the Pitts was a goofy band name, but Brad St. John was the oldest member of the band at twenty-six and he owned the rusty white Dodge van and most of the gig equipment, so he was their self-proclaimed leader. But who cared about that right now? Could life be any better?

Pepper had felt exhilarated and free on stage. So *alive*. He remembered the end of their first song, with fear in his throat during the moment of silence when the song ended. But when the applause of the crowd hit him, Pepper had said to himself, "I've *got* to do more of this."

Pepper noticed Delaney definitely seemed to have slid across the bench seat a little nearer to him. Delaney was a worldly twenty-three with a hint of a southern accent, and Pepper had a hard crush on her. He worried it was too obvious—that his desperation was wafting around the van's cab, invisible but pervasive, like Brad's whiskey breath.

Would Pepper have the guts to ask Delaney out before he dropped her off at her apartment in New Albion? That'd take his night from amazing to perfect.

Pepper snuck a side-eyed peek at Delaney. Her shoulder-length brown hair with blue streaks was now up in a scrunchie. She'd kicked off her low-rise Converses, and her legs were under her and sticking out to the left on the van's bench seat. Her leather skirt was lead-singer short and made her long legs appear even longer. An optical delusion, Angel would have called it. Her toes brushed against Pepper's thigh, tickling him and sending a shiver of electricity up his leg.

Pepper had only known Delaney since joining the band three weeks ago, but he found her pretty and cool and funny, in a sarcastic, street-smart way. Her eyes fascinated him: one blue, one dark hazel. He'd never seen eyes like that before.

And he knew she had words tattooed down her lower back. From a poem or a song, it looked like, from the peekaboo glances Pepper had snuck without looking like a pervert, when she wore a cutoff t-shirt onstage. He hadn't seen enough of the tattoo to make out the words and hadn't worked up the guts to ask her.

So far Pepper had been too intimidated to make a move on her. He was three years younger than Delaney. He couldn't even take her to a bar without a fake ID.

And he was going off to Harvard in less than two months, which no one in the band knew except Angel. He'd soon be a twenty-year-old freshman, which was weird for most students but typical for hockey players (who had to pay their dues for two years in junior hockey before a college coach would give them a spot). If Delaney learned he was underage and disappearing to college, she'd never give him a chance. So how would he navigate that?

Pepper was debating the perfect opening line to charm Delaney without completely embarrassing himself as he exited Route 6 onto Route 28 at the Eastham rotary. He hadn't thought of anything particularly clever, but he promised himself he'd ask her out before they reached the other side of the sleepy little town of Orleans. Which was fast approaching.

Then he rounded a curve and saw the dancing red and blue lights of police cars blocking the road ahead.

Pepper stopped the van at the end of the line of waiting cars as the police lights bounced around inside the van's cab.

"Uh-oh," said Delaney, breaking the silence. "What's up?"

"Maybe an accident?" guessed Pepper. "Or a DUI roadblock?" More likely an accident.

Their van was seven vehicles from the front of the line. A county deputy—looked like a woman—was at the window of the lead car, a little Toyota. She asked them something, looked into the back with a flashlight, then got the driver to pop the trunk. She flashed her light around the Toyota's trunk, then shut the lid and waved the Toyota through.

"You must be exhausted from the gig," Pepper said to Delaney. "I've never seen you this quiet."

Brad was making little snoring noises over against the door. So Pepper kind of felt alone with Delaney.

She laughed. "I am a bit," she admitted. "But I was just thinking about the original song you did: 'Try Me'? That was wild!"

"Hey, sorry about that," he said, attempting to sound casual. "The manager was giving us the stink eye, and Brad was still outside smoking or puking or whatever. I thought we had to get going with the second set."

Delaney looked over at Brad to make sure he was still snoozing, then answered. "No, it was beautiful. You took a chance and killed it."

It'd happened around eleven, at the end of their only break. Brad was in the parking lot by the sand cliff overlooking the beach, chain-smoking like a good rocker should, holding court for a few other smokers. But they really needed to start playing again.

Pepper enjoyed playing cover songs, but he'd also spent a ton of time writing songs that summer. He'd finished a song earlier in the week that he believed was by far his best ever. It was about a guy wanting to kiss the girl of his dreams and her torturing him every step of the way. A simple song, like Eric Clapton did simple...with a touch of John Mayer's playfulness. Wicked romantic. No one had heard him sing it until the Beachcomber crowd that night.

"But you were awesome, the way you jumped in," he said to her. Delaney had listened to the chorus the first time through and then she joined in the second time, harmonizing with Pepper. She'd never listened to the song before, but made it sound easy and practiced. And the song was way better as a duet.

Delaney laughed. "I loved it, Pepper! It was the sexiest thing!"

The Beachcomber crowd had eaten it up, gave them a nice loud round of applause even though it wasn't a Journey or Tom Petty cover.

But for Pepper the highlight had come after the song. "Thank you," he'd said into the mic, trying to sound older and cooler than he was. "That's an original song I wrote myself. It's called 'Try Me.'"

And Delaney smiled at him and said into her mic with her southern drawl, "Anytime."

The magical moment broke when Pepper saw poor old Brad swaying by the edge of the stage, his mouth flapping open and closed like a skinny tuna. He thumped up on stage, with raw fury on his face (and a little speck of what might be puke). Brad gave Pepper a glare like he'd really fucked up.

Then Angel had done the *one, two, three, four* with his drumsticks, and they broke into Guns N' Roses, and Brad and the Pitts were back in the safe comfort of cover songs.

Man, what a rush it'd been.

"Too bad we're just a cover band," Delaney said quietly. "Your song's legit good. You got any more?"

"You bet," he fibbed.

The sheriff's deputy finished talking to a pickup truck and waved it through. Pepper inched the van forward, nervous as he got closer to the front.

He'd had two beers during the show, despite being underage.

He hoped this wasn't a drunk driving checkpoint. Would they be able to smell the beer on him? Would they look at his driver's license and say out loud in front of Delaney that he was only twenty? *Jesus.*

"What did you think of Brad's biker buddy?" Delaney asked.

She meant Dennis Cole, a white guy in his early thirties who'd been at the Beachcomber for their gig. He was Brad's roommate in a small place in New Albion. He was a hard-looking guy in biker clothes with a brown ponytail and pockmarked skin.

Cole came over to congratulate the band as they were packing up. Cole was also buddies with the people who managed the Beachcomber and had helped Brad land this gig.

Cole went on and on about the song Pepper and Delaney performed to open the second set. Telling them how their duet was pretty kick-ass. The real deal. Pepper saw Brad make a sour face at Cole's compliment.

"You Pitts are all right for a cover band," he said to Pepper and Delaney. "But if you two want to do this music thing more seriously, call me. I can help you record your own music, put together a tour, the whole nine yards. I know people in Nashville, Austin, you name it." Cole's voice was soft and warm, a real contrast to his biker look. And his words were flattering. Although he mostly faced Delaney...

Now riding home from the gig, Cole's offer seemed too good to be true.

"It's exactly what I dreamed about," said Delaney. "Performing in some nowhere bar, being discovered, the whole crazy fantasy. Do you think he can help us?"

Before Pepper could answer, the deputy waved them forward to where she stood. Pepper stopped beside an antique red pump in a barrel on the side of the road.

The deputy was a slim white woman in her late twenties, and Pepper thought he might have seen her somewhere before, which wouldn't be surprising. As a deputy in the sheriff's department, her turf covered all of Barnstable County, including the town of New Albion just fifteen minutes farther up the road, where Pepper's dad was chief of police. And where Pepper was serving with no great distinction as a police cadet that summer.

The deputy had one hand on her firearm as she shined her flashlight on each of them. Pepper heard Delaney's skirt squeak as she inched away on the ripped vinyl seat.

Pepper cracked stupid jokes when he was nervous, and he almost made a drive-through order joke to the deputy: *three burgers, fries and three Cokes, please.*

But the deputy's tired, serious face stopped him just in time.

She asked for Pepper's license and registration. Delaney popped the glove compartment and rummaged around for Brad's registration. Brad was awake now and tried to help her, which slowed the process.

Pepper explained to the deputy they were a band and had played tonight at the Beachcomber up in Wellfleet. What was going on?

"Ryan?" she asked, looking at his license. "You one of those New Albion Ryans?"

"Yes, ma'am," he said, then hoping "ma'am" wasn't offensive to a woman of her age.

"I've worked with your dad. Great cop. And I know your brother Jake," she said, and hinted a smile.

Hmm...thought Pepper. "So, what's with the roadblock?"

"Amber alert. A seventeen-year-old girl from Eastham went missing earlier tonight."

Pepper remembered he'd seen a network amber alert text when he checked his phone during their break, but he'd been too focused on the whereabouts of their drunk bass player to give the text much thought.

Maybe she's just out past curfew with a boyfriend, thought

Pepper. He'd been that boyfriend more than once, back in high school..."An amber alert already?" he asked.

"We had a witness. The victim's little brother. He saw her get abducted right in front of their house. The perp dragged her into a light-colored van. Probably white, like yours. The boy's seven, so we don't know much, except this one's for real."

"Oh my God!" whispered Delaney.

Pepper was stunned too. They'd just passed through Eastham and had seen no police activity. "Why isn't this roadblock up on Route 6?"

The deputy sighed. "We've got roadblocks up and down 6 and 28. And the Staties have roadblocks at the Bourne and the Sagamore. Every available car's patrolling the side roads. Big time. Your dad'll have everyone out too."

"What's her name?" asked Delaney, leaning forward to look at the deputy. "The missing girl?"

The deputy's flashlight found Delaney's face. "Emma Bailey. Why, you know her?"

Delaney said no, still looking upset.

When the deputy told Pepper to unlock the back, he warned her their drummer was riding in there with the gear, so she wouldn't accidentally shoot Angel.

Less than a minute later, she slammed the rear door and returned, handing Pepper back his ID. "That guy in back, I think he was flirting with me," she said, shaking her head, then smiled and for a moment the tiredness left her face. "Tell Jake that Karen Tammaro says hey." Then she waved for them to take off.

Pepper drove away. His arms were shaking as he pictured what'd happened. A sudden, violent snatching of a teenage girl on quiet Cape Cod, right in front of her house. *Unreal...*

Brad seemed to have sobered up a bit. Delaney had untucked her legs and slid away to the middle of the seat.

Pepper wasn't thinking anymore about trying to talk her into a date tomorrow night.

No one was thinking about Brad and the Pitts' successful gig anymore, either.

None of them talked. The van's air conditioning wasn't on, since it was one of the many features of the old van which didn't work, but he felt like cold air was blasting on his neck. It seemed ten degrees cooler in the van since the roadblock.

Pepper decided he would call his dad the minute he got home. Hopefully, his dad would say they'd recovered the girl unharmed and arrested her goddamned snatcher. That the emergency was already over.

The rest of their ride along Route 28 had fewer streetlights, and Pepper shifted uncomfortably on his seat, looking left and right, searching shadows for the kidnapper and his white van. He saw nothing.

But he kept his headlights on high beam all the way home.

CHAPTER THREE

Four and a half hours earlier

Trust the plan... Trust the man...

The man in the white cargo van anxiously repeated those thoughts, over and over, as he drove through the summer night with a teenage girl bound by duct tape in the back of his van.

It was all happening. He needed to finish his getaway in the next fifteen minutes. Back to the safe place, back to the Heart. Or the plan (and his life) could go down the toilet with a flash of red and blue lights in his rearview mirror.

No, he would just follow the same route he'd driven so many times. Right at the speed limit. Slower would look suspicious, someone might remember him. Faster would give the police a stupid excuse to stop him. Then his exciting new life would end before it even got started.

The grab in front of the teenager's house had gone fine.

The girl, a pretty thing named Emma Bailey, been no match for him, even though she'd fought like a little tiger. He'd had to be careful, to make sure he didn't really hurt her, what with his excitement and her being all scared and freaking out.

He'd seen the terror and even anger in her face in the ten seconds it took to get her under control, then quickly zapped into submission by thousands of volts from his Vipertek mini stun gun. Pretty good kick from something not much bigger than a deck of cards.

Then quickly into the rear of the van. She'd gotten shaken up a little, no doubt. But she'd be okay. Like his buddy sometimes said, a little pain never hurt nobody...

He looked at his Timex digital watch. It was now 9:16. He'd climbed out of the van to grab Emma Bailey at 8:44, which wasn't his favorite time. He took a little comfort in the $8 = 4 + 4$. He could live with it, but didn't feel great about it.

Almost half an hour had passed...

When he was experiencing this kind of damn rush, he liked to think about times. He preferred hours and minutes which lined up in a pattern for him. They seemed like a message from on high that all was right with the world. Like the neat order of 11:11, or the wackiness of a time like 3:21...

But he'd been at Emma Bailey's mercy, right? He'd been waiting in his van in front of her house for almost an hour... waiting for her to get home from wherever the hell she'd been.

He'd gotten all warm and happy when a Jetta pulled up across the street, driven by some other girl, and Emma Bailey had climbed out. The other girl had quickly driven away, which showed the time was lucky. One less complication.

And that's what he was thinking about—numbers—as he drove slowly and steadily toward the safe place, when he suddenly remembered something: Emma Bailey's stupid cell phone.

Panic flooded him. He smacked the steering wheel. *Shit!*

He'd forgotten to deal with the girl's cell phone, even though it had been part of the detailed game plan. Every seventeen-year-old girl had a cell phone somewhere on her. It was medically required for teens these days, his buddy had joked one time.

But for people trying to stay clear of the cops, cell phones were the goddamn devil. Even if you didn't make a call, some government button pusher could triangulate three satellites and pin you to a GPS grid like a bug. Watch any TV show.

The only thing worse was DNA. He knew from TV it was like your molecules had fingerprints. If you left a hair, or spit, or *anything* from your body, you might as well leave your name and a mug shot. Because the cops would knock down your door quicker than pronto. Another example of how the war was over and the government had won.

He pulled into the parking lot of a muffler shop. He crawled to the back of the van. Emma Bailey was taped up and quiet. He quickly found her phone in the back right pocket of her jeans.

Well, okay now. The man considered smashing it but didn't. He took a crumpled old Taco Bell napkin from the passenger seat and carefully wiped down the phone. Freaking DNA. Then he tossed the phone out the window onto a grassy divider in the parking lot. If he was lucky, someone would take it and the cops would chase their ass instead of his.

The man had smoked a little meth earlier that night—just enough to make his mind as shiny and focused as a boning knife. He felt an impulsive surge in his cheeks as he considered smoking a bit more right now, but shook off the temptation. It wasn't party time, yet.

He got back on the road. The cell phone problem had been solved, not to be mentioned again. Plans were great, but sometimes you had to wing it. No blood, no foul.

Now the man drove toward his finish line. To the Heart. His leg was still bouncing hard from adrenaline and excitement. He wasn't safe yet. He had to get there, lie low and take care of things. But hopefully the worst was over.

He'd had one other minor screw-up on the grab, other than the cell phone brain-fart. A little boy had been in the big front window of the Bailey home and had seen the whole goddamn thing. He hadn't noticed the boy until after he dumped the girl in the back of the van, all hogtied with duct tape. But he knew the boy saw what happened.

The man had panicked and driven off immediately. Now he was second-guessing himself. Should he have done something about the boy? Bust into the house?

No, he'd been smart to drive away. Going off plan to deal with the boy would have only made things worse. Who knew which parents were home? The boy had looked like he was screaming—someone might have been calling 911 before the van door closed. It could have turned into a real shit show if he'd tried to deal with the boy.

And besides, it wasn't part of the almighty plan.

Just trust the plan.

The man turned left and a police car drove past in the opposite direction. The driver was a lady cop, and she was alone. The man kept one eye on his side-view mirror. Would the cop turn around? Should he turn into a driveway? Hide the van somewhere?

Then the police car reappeared in his side-view mirror, coming up behind him. *Shit.* It didn't have the cop lights on, but it had to be following him...

The man was shaking harder—he could barely keep the steering wheel straight. *Shit shit.* Cops had been messing with him his whole damn life. He touched the butt of his Walther P22 pistol tucked beside his seat. His crappy little weapon.

He wished he had something more powerful. The puny Walther was all he's been able to buy on the down-low, through his buddy. But it was plenty deadly. And he knew he had the balls to use it to defend himself and Emma Bailey, if it got to that.

The man reached a stop sign at a four-way intersection. He carefully came to a full stop, even paused an extra moment. His plan had been to turn left, but he didn't want to lead a cop closer to the Heart. So instead, he broke the plan again and drove straight.

The cop car did too. *Damn.* It was right behind him, close now.

And so naturally, the man panicked a bit. He saw a driveway with big stone pillars coming up on the right, and he put on his signal and turned in. Some property he'd never seen before, with high bushes framing a long driveway.

It would force the lady cop to commit—either follow him down the driveway or go on about her damn business. If this turned into a confrontation, at least they'd be hidden from passing vehicles by the bushes. The man wished he had a silencer for his pistol.

In his side mirror, the man saw the police car stop out by the street. The man kept slowly driving his white van down the driveway, like he was just some schlub delivering a package to the homeowner or whatever.

His hands were still fucking shaking. *Shit shit.*

The driveway bent enough that the police car disappeared from his side-view mirror. But at least it hadn't come screaming down the driveway after him.

The man reached the end of the long driveway and saw a huge cedar-shingled house, probably some bank weasel's summer cottage. The man pulled his van into a brightly lit turnaround area and thought hard about the damn situation.

Should he lie low here awhile? Maybe the lady cop was waiting for him up at the road? But if she'd called for backup, a string of police cars would close in any minute. She'd have him trapped.

He wished he had time for a quick hit on his crank pipe. Just enough for a turbo boost. His whole body ached for it.

Maybe he should head right back up the driveway and confront the lady cop, take her by surprise. His pistol was only a .22, but up close? It'd be plenty if he had the jump on her. Like in any fight, the aggressor usually wins. And he was totally jacked to step up, with his life and liberty on the line.

He looked back up the driveway as far as he could, his mind working in overdrive, his chest tight like it was being squeezed by some invisible strap. This was not part of the big plan.

What to do, what to do?

The man heard a hard rap on his passenger window and almost shat himself. *Jesus.* A woman was standing there looking at him. She was probably in her early fifties, kinda skinny and pale with a bald head. But full of attitude, with hands on her hips. She was wearing some kind of barn jacket with the sleeves rolled up. Glasses perched up high, where her hair should be.

He slipped his hand around the grip of his .22, down in the seat crack, and lowered the passenger window.

"Can I help you?" she asked. Her voice dripped suspicion. Or bitchiness. Something the opposite of friendly.

The man gave a weak smile and almost lifted the handgun. Instead, he started bullshitting. "Good evening, ah, ma'am! We're fixing roofs in the neighborhood and can replace yours real cheap. Can I give you a free quote?" He fought off the urge to do a quick shoulder check, to make sure the law wasn't coming down the driveway.

The bald lady crossed her arms and puckered her mouth into a little circle which looked just like a butthole. "After nine o'clock?" she asked.

Jesus. "Oh, we work long hours, but I hear ya. I'll come back tomorrow, not too early." The man gave her an apologetic wave with his left hand and started closing his window. His right hand stayed on his little pistol, down out of sight.

He needed to get out of there and didn't want the lady to remember him. His left hand was still shaking. He had to drive up to the street, and if the lady cop was waiting, he'd have to fight his way to freedom.

"What company are you from?" the woman asked, peering in and looking around the front seat. "Are you on Angie's List?"

Nosy cow! Did he have to shoot her to shut her up? This was getting too damn complicated. He took a deep breath and tried to smile.

Just trust the fucking game plan.

"Boston Roofs," he improvised. "We're on all the good lists, absolutely." He shut his window the final few inches. Then he gave her another little wave, all deferential and sucking up. Like rich folk expect.

He backed out to the spot, finding to his horror he came within a damn inch of driving on the woman's lawn. He took another deep breath, then drove slowly up the driveway. The bald lady watched him go. Again doing the butthole thing with her mouth, maybe even a little more disapproving than before. It rattled him.

The man moved his .22 to his lap, ready to go. Do or die. Sink or swim. Shoot or—

He reached the road, and no freaking cops were in sight. He sighed with relief and slowly drove back to the intersection where he'd gone off the path. Then he and young Emma Bailey were back on the practiced route.

They had only two miles left to go. To the safety of the Heart. To success.

He turned his van left onto a back road with a dead end sign. It was basically a gravel lane scattered with smaller, older houses. A pretty run-down neighborhood for the Cape.

But he knew the lane wasn't a real dead end. He'd been down it pretty regularly for years. The dirt road officially ended at a small wetland parking lot, where bird watchers and other weirdos would park and wander in the marshes and the light woods.

Off to the side was a thinner path worn in the grass by municipal workers or whoever drove back here to pick up trash. And one hundred yards down that path, it split in two. If you took the left path, as he did, you soon reached the back side of a new subdivision.

With a quick bang down off the curb, his van was back on paved roads again. In just a few more minutes, he'd be out of reach. It would be easy to carry the girl into the Heart, where she'd be safe and warm.

One damn grab down! Two more to go...

His deep excitement came rushing back. Other than one random police lady, the planned path had avoided all roadblocks and cop activity.

In just a few days, the man in the van would head over the Bourne Bridge and leave all his troubles behind. Sunshine and freedom. Sipping beer on a dock, like his buddy always described. It sounded like heaven.

The man in the van had been nowhere major. He'd never even left the damn state, but he wasn't nervous about it. No, sir. It was all in the game plan. Nothing would stop him now.

Trust the plan. Trust the man. It was all happening...

CHAPTER FOUR

When Pepper arrived for work at the New Albion police station the next morning, he could tell that the emergency situation was ongoing.

His dad had left home before Pepper woke, or maybe he'd worked all night. The first twenty-four hours were crucial when investigating a kidnapping, and his dad got more heavily involved in big investigations than typical police chiefs.

Pepper parked his old truck in a space reserved for police personnel. He saw a crowd gathered on the front lawn, so he walked around to the side door, swiping his ID card to enter.

"Hey, young Ryan!" said Officer Randy Larch, punching his shoulder as he walked past with a cup of coffee. "You see the crowd out front? It's the same at every station in the Lower Cape. Volunteers to help search for the girl."

"Cool," said Pepper, careful not to rub his shoulder.

"It'll be a miracle if they find her, but it's better than nothing."

Pepper knew what Larch was getting at. Cape Cod is over three hundred square miles in size. Law enforcement and civilians would need to search about three hundred zillion places in their hunt for Emma Bailey. And any search efforts in marshes or woods would be to locate her dead body.

"The focus is on the Lower Cape for now. You should see the map Weisner has just for New Albion. We're getting a ton of civilian tips—every time someone sees a white van, they call. It's nuts! But every time she puts a pin in the map. She's organizing teams to canvas the areas where the pushpins are in clusters. You should volunteer."

Larch explained that when a stranger abducts someone, the police need to recover the victim within three hours or else the victim is probably dead. Kidnappers who kill often dump the body and flee the area.

Pepper checked his watch. It'd been thirteen hours since the kidnapper took Emma Bailey.

"So we're flat out," Larch said. "Her info's in the NCIC database. Every town on the Lower Cape is doing searches just like us. And your dad has Sweeney working through a list of sex offenders registered in town. I cross-referenced that list to RMV records for white vans."

Kevin Sweeney was his dad's most senior detective, a transplant from Boston P.D. somewhere in his mid-thirties. He'd been with the department for five or six years. He was approximately 5'8" and built like a former weightlifter. Pepper didn't know him well, but he seemed like a nice guy and his dad had commented once that Sweeney was a real pro.

Pepper's main assignment this summer was to sit in a small, windowless room and enter case info into a new database, which was a soul-crushing way to spend his last summer before college. So of course he would volunteer to help the search effort. He headed to the front lobby, looking for his supervisor, Sergeant Roxanne Weisner.

Volunteers jammed the lobby, and Pepper knew there were plenty more outside. He saw a middle-aged couple whose lawn he used to mow. He spotted his retired dentist talking loudly to the mother of a girl he dated super briefly in high school. Pepper didn't go over to say hi to any of them.

He saw a big guy in mirrored sunglasses going from police officer to police officer, chattering excitedly. It was Fester Timmins, who had been in Jake's year at New Albion High School. A pretty good high school wrestler, in his day. Timmins was about six foot tall and fifty pounds overweight. Today he seemed excited, like this was a party.

Timmins stopped to talk to Randy Larch, who'd joined the crowd to help organize the civilians. They were laughing about something and the guy gave Larch a bearhug. Pals? Pepper cruised right past, still hunting for Sergeant Weisner.

Then Pepper saw his big brother Jake on the other side of the crowd. He was talking to Gus Bullard, their old high school hockey coach. Bullard was a big guy—slightly shorter than Pepper but heavier. He was a former athlete who had gained weight by his early fifties.

Jake appeared to be telling his old coach a detailed story, and Pepper could hear Bullard's too-loud laugh from across the crowded room.

Bullard had always loved Jake but was much less a fan of Pepper. As Pepper pushed through the throng of people, he tried to slip right past his brother and his old coach. But a strong hand grabbed his arm. Coach Bullard.

"Hey, Pylon! You helping with the big search?"

Pepper hated that old nickname his coach had given him to make fun of his relative lack of speed on the ice. He shrugged and said, "Maybe."

Coach Bullard shook his head, looking disappointed. "You missed my big party last night too! What's your excuse this time?"

The New Albion high school had thrown a retirement party for Coach Bullard after twenty-four years of coaching the varsity hockey team. To celebrate his record and to ease Bullard's forced retirement—he'd wanted to coach a twenty-fifth season, but the athletic director was bringing in new blood for a new era. Pepper had been performing with Brad and the Pitts at the Beachcomber in Wellfleet last night, but he doubted he'd have gone to Bullard's extravaganza even if he'd been free. He wasn't a fan.

Pepper made a somewhat apologetic face, then slid his arm loose and quickly moved away. Where the heck was Weisner?

Pepper found her hurriedly working in the conference room. His supervisor was consulting a list of tips received on the town's public hotline—sightings of white cargo vans, unusual activity noticed, that sort of thing—and was pin-pricking a large copy of the New Albion map.

Weisner was a short, pear-shaped woman in her forties with frizzy brown hair and a habitual frown on her face, especially when she was around Pepper.

"Morning, Sarge," he said. "Which search party do you want me to join?"

She didn't even look away from her map. "It's morning already? Sorry, I don't have time for you right now. You need to focus on the database and let me focus on this."

Ouch.

At the beginning of the summer, Weisner had sat Pepper down and warned that she didn't have much time to waste supervising him. It kept her from valuable police work. But since then she'd been riding his ass like a rent-a-donkey, like if she pushed him hard enough, possibly he'd quit.

Unfortunately for Pepper, there was a bad history between them. She'd caught him and Angel on the wrong side of the law a few times when they were in high school. Nothing too horrible, just teens being teens. But she wasn't exactly a fan of Pepper.

Unlike Jake.

Jake was the better student. The better athlete. Better behaved. Better freaking everything.

Jake had been a cadet part-time for the last two summers, and he'd spent a lot of it doing beach patrol on a bike. No cool cop gear except a radio, but at least he was out in the sun. And he'd gotten a great tan and a lot of girls' phone numbers.

"That's a hell of a map," Pepper said, not giving up yet.

Pushpins covered the New Albion map, and Sergeant Weisner had circled in red ink the six areas with the biggest clusters. Pepper noticed a smaller cluster of pushpins—a seventh hot spot he knew well. It was half-wooded, half-marshy area which teens often used to get away from the eyes of adults. Pepper had been one of those teens. Could that be where the kidnapper had taken the girl?

Pepper caught Sergeant Weisner by the sleeve. "Please, Sarge? Let me join a canvas team."

"Pepper, nothing personal, but I can't supervise these search parties and babysit you at the same time. I left fifty old case files on your desk, and I need you to get them all in the database today. You finally want to step up and prove yourself? That's what you need to focus on."

He wanted to change her mind. She needed all the help she could get, right? But her words stung, so he backed off. If they didn't want his help, fine. Their loss. He'd tried.

Besides, Pepper was nothing like his brother Jake. Quite the opposite. He wasn't cut out to be a cop. And he definitely didn't want to turn into his dad or Sergeant Weisner.

So he retreated to his assigned workspace—a converted drunk tank now used for storing records. It held a makeshift desk for him. On warm days Pepper swore he could smell the puke and sour B.O. of drunks from years past. Unbelievable.

Pepper's main assignment as a police cadet for the past couple of months had been to populate the department's new local database with metadata from police reports and cases going back for ten years.

Some data, such as for sex offenses, terrorism, traffic offenders, foreign fugitives, criminal gangs and parole matters, would feed as usual to the National Information Crime Center systems.

This new database would hold more local data, such as incident reports which didn't result in charges. But it seemed suspiciously like a useless project designed to keep him out of trouble while driving him crazy from boredom.

And today? After the horrible kidnapping it was harder than ever to focus on meaningless data entry.

After logging in and getting his pile of paper files organized, Pepper checked online to see what the media was reporting about the Emma Bailey kidnapping.

There was a lot of coverage. Every level of Massachusetts law enforcement was helping with the effort to find the Eastham teen and the man who'd snatched her. The Eastham Police Department had set up a command center and had held a press conference jointly with other agencies, mainly to ask for the public's help if they saw anything.

The online stories gave a description of the kidnapper from the eyewitness—Emma Bailey's little brother. The description wasn't very detailed: a white male wearing a green hat, possibly a baseball cap. And that the suspect had been driving a white van.

Pepper finally closed his browser and dug into his database work, hating every minute of work. Feeling frustrated and resentful.

"Hey, Pepper!" A young teenage girl stood in his doorway. It was Zula Eisenhower, the lieutenant's fourteen-year-old daughter.

She was tall for her age but skinny. She was a mix of her Malaysian mom and her African American dad. Zula had long black hair and wore too-big silver-framed glasses and a long baggy T-shirt, which made her look even younger than she was.

"What are you doing?" she asked. "Aren't you going out with the search parties?"

"No, I've got to stay here and do this. It sucks, but..."

"But what? You scared?"

Pepper laughed. "No, I'm following orders, even if they're stupid. That's what grown-ups do."

"Oh." Zula looked disappointed. Or annoyed? "Well, at least you get to complain about it. Have you seen Pop?" She explained the kidnapping had freaked out her mother, so she'd dropped off Zula here while she went to a doctor's appointment in Hyannis.

The Eisenhowers were like extended family to Pepper, his dad and his brother. Zula's mom invited the Ryans over for dinner twice a month, as if to fill in the void of women in the Ryan household. He loved Mrs. E for that. Pepper could barely remember his own mother, who'd died when he was a little boy. He pictured her being similar to Mrs. E—always happy and smiling. Welcoming.

"I haven't seen your dad," he said. "He probably drove to Eastham with my dad to the command center for the Bailey investigation."

"Okay, whatever... I'll just hang with you. What's that you're doing? It looks boring."

Pepper gave her an exaggerated eye roll. "*Boring*? This is the most important long-term project we're doing this summer. And it's super fun, watch." He showed her how he identified metadata on the old paper reports and where he inputted it to the new database. "When I'm done, our dads can search for patterns of local crimes, or clues like a tattoo or a scar from an old patrol report, to help solve a new case."

"I guess it's cool," she said. She watched him closely as he input a few more details into the table. "Not as cool as searching for the missing girl, but..."

"Maybe," said Pepper. "Too bad you're too young to help me with this database." Like a throwaway comment.

Zula scoffed. "Watch." She shoved him over and dragged another chair into place. She located metadata in the paper report and entered the right info into the database fields, moving quicker than he had.

"Hey, nice job, kid! I have to go do something...do you want to keep at it? I'll pay you ten bucks if you enter the rest of these reports."

She gave him a suspicious look through her big silver glasses. "You get that I read *Tom Sawyer*, right? Don't think you're tricking *me*, Pepper Ryan." She sighed. "But I'm bored, so whatever... I'll take your cash." She tossed her long hair and pushed her glasses up on her nose. Then got right back to work.

Good old Zula. Nice kid. She was as close as he and Jake had to a little sister, and he figured she was fair game for his exploitation. Like any good big brother would, right?

"Are you just going to watch me?" she asked without looking up.

And Pepper realized he had been.

Zula stopped and made eye contact with him. "If I was missing, would you be sitting here in this smelly room, or would you be out there trying to save me?"

Oof! Low blow.

"Tell you what," Zula added. "I'll bet you a dollar you can't find Emma Bailey before anyone else. In case you need more, you know, incentive."

Zula was a piece of work for a fourteen-year-old. Her guilt trip had actually gotten under his skin. And with her working on the database, Pepper now had a small window of freedom to go search the seventh pin cluster on the map, right?

"Okay, Little Ike. It's a bet!" he said. He liked to shorten Zula's last name to Ike, like the old U.S. president, because it seemed to bug her. He even shook her little hand.

Then he messed up her hair and retreated just outside her clumsy attempt to swat at him. "Ha!" he said.

Pepper walked to the station's small kitchen area and made three phone calls. Just this once, he'd do the Ryan cop thing. Because he had an itchy feeling about the seventh cluster—that Sergeant Weisner was making a mistake, not sending a team to search it.

In the back of his mind, he was thinking: *if Emma Bailey's in those woods, that means she's dead. Oh jeez, that's probably the only way.*

What would he do if he found the poor girl's body?

CHAPTER FIVE

Pepper's mind was still full of nightmarish images when, half an hour later, he was picked up by his buddy Angel Cavada to go search for the girl.

Angel was driving his beat-up red Toyota Camry which he had nicknamed *El Diablo*. It had faded gold trim and an ugly scrape down the side rear panel, but its engine almost always started.

El Diablo smelled like a mix of tomato sauce, cheese and hot cardboard because Angel spent most nights delivering pizzas. He was rumored to be the fastest delivery man in the Lower Cape and had three speeding tickets this summer to prove it.

Angel was the same age as Pepper—twenty. About 5'9," he was a second-generation Cuban-American. He had the thick dark hair, big smile and quick talk which made him popular with girls— just ask him. They became best friends in kindergarten after a vicious playground fight about whose dad was stronger.

Pepper had recruited Angel and the other members of Brad and the Pitts to form their own unofficial search party. Pepper was pumped up to be helping. To be one of the good guys, just like the crowd of civilian volunteers.

They drove to the area Pepper had noticed on Sergeant Weisner's map—the seventh cluster which wasn't getting one of her search parties. It covered a subdivision called The Crofts and an undeveloped area of woods and marshes behind it.

This little subdivision had been under construction for years. Pepper knew the developer had been short on cash for the life of the project and was completing houses slowly, using cash from one sale to finance the completion of the next house.

Pepper was also familiar with the scrubby woods and wetlands behind the subdivision because it was a popular hangout for local teenagers to drink a little, smoke a little, and do other things better done away from adult eyes.

They cruised past a long row of medium-sized houses and parked in a cul-de-sac at the end of the street near three unfinished houses.

"I got to give you one thing, *mano*: you're never boring!" said Angel, shaking his head. "What'll I do for excitement when you flake off to college without me?"

Pepper laughed. "Buddy, as long as there're ladies around here, you'll be fine!"

An old white van was parked on the street in front of one of the unfinished houses.

"No fuckin' way, right?" asked Angel. "That *can't* be the snatcher's van..."

They parked behind it and got out to look.

Angel had brought two cheap flashlights which gave off thin light. White cardboard covered the van's small back windows. Not unusual for tradesmen who might have expensive tools. There was a crack up one edge which let Pepper and Angel see inside.

They shined their flashlights through the crack and saw nothing except tools. So, probably not the kidnapper's van?

Brad St. John's van pulled up behind *El Diablo* and parked.

Delaney Lynn slipped out of the passenger side door with a tight smile. She looked happy to see Pepper, but also a bit tense. Probably because of why they were there. She was wearing short black boots, black jeans and a snug White Stripes T-shirt.

"Cute uniform, officer," she said to Pepper with a little laugh.

His uniform shirt was itchy and was a size too small for Pepper's athletic shoulders and arms. It made him feel constricted. But he just laughed as he put on a Red Sox baseball cap he'd lifted from Angel's back seat. "I like yours better!"

Brad St. John climbed down from his van, stumbled and almost fell. He was wearing white sunglasses, a Led Zeppelin T-shirt, cut-off black jeans and flip-flops. It had surprised Pepper how quickly Brad agreed to help when he called. Had he judged him wrong?

Pepper explained the plan. First, they'd check the three unfinished houses, since they were a perfect place to hide the kidnapped girl. If nothing came of that, they'd canvas the area behind the houses—a grassy area which turned into marshes, then into thin woods and brush.

The group started at the unfinished house to the right. It had doors and windows (mostly covered in paper), but looked half complete. They spread out and circled the house, peering in windows where they could. Looking for anything suspicious.

Brad yelled for them to come to his window. "A damn body! In the kitchen!"

They rushed over to where he stood.

Pepper looked in. It was much darker inside, all shadows due to the papered windows and no lights on inside. He saw a shape on the floor, a twisted tangle.

But not a body.

"It's just painter's sheets," said Pepper.

They were twisted together in a long S-shape, probably wound up and left there by the painting crew.

"Oh man," said Brad. "I thought it was the girl! I think I had a little heart attack..."

False alarm on both counts.

They kept looking, but all three houses appeared to be empty, as best they could see from the outside. There was nothing out of the ordinary at all. Lots of footprints in the dirt around the houses, made when the ground was mud during a past rain, probably. But nothing suspicious.

So, *strike one*.

They moved on to search the undeveloped land behind the subdivision. Pepper thought it made sense that the kidnapper might bring the girl to this area, which was mostly undeveloped except for some old collapsing sheds and a few half-assed tree forts which kids had built over the years.

Pepper told the others to walk side by side twenty feet apart, nice and slow, staying in sight of each other. A methodical combing. Anyone who saw anything unusual, like a piece of clothing, should yell to the others so they could all check it out. They could cover a sixty-foot strip of land pretty thoroughly.

"But if we find the girl, we split it four ways?" asked Brad.

"Split what?" asked Pepper.

"The reward. They had it all over the radio. The girl's family ponied up twenty-five grand! That's why we're here, right?"

Pepper hadn't known about a reward and didn't care about the money. But it wouldn't hurt to keep Brad and the others focused. "Absolutely. Equal split."

They marched through the tall grass and reached a scrubby area of marsh and woods, where they spread out in a line and began a slow search.

"Keep an eye on me," Delaney said to Pepper, her southern accent popping up with the word "eye." She smiled nervously at him.

Pepper's phone buzzed. He saw it was the police station's

main number, so he didn't answer. He stepped gingerly around a log which was half-covered and half-rotted and that for a second looked like a body. *Damn.* He was jumpy. He could picture how Emma Bailey's body would look if they found her there. Pepper felt a chill up his spine. Hopefully she wasn't here, because it would mean she was dead.

Brad yelled over, "Hey! What's this big blue box? It's humming!" He was from New Jersey and had been on the Cape for less than a year.

"It's a greenhead fly trap," Pepper said.

Angel explained about greenheads to Brad as they walked, obviously trying to freak him out. "This is prime season for those nasty buggers," he said. "They've got teeth like Edward Scissorhands and they drink blood."

"Yep," agreed Pepper. "Stay out of salt marshes this time of year." The greenheads had been extra thick this summer because May and June were hot and dry.

Then on cue, Brad yelped. Possibly a greenhead bit him or he thought one had? Brad skipped away, swatting his arms.

Pepper saw nothing. It'd probably been a mosquito.

"You better get a shot ASAP for Lyme disease," advised Angel. "Big needle to the stomach, like for rabies."

Brad moaned. Delaney chuckled.

"I'm surprised he got bit," said Angel. "Only the female greenheads bite...and I've never seen a female get so close to Brad."

"Hey guys, slow down!" yelled Pepper. Brad had thrashed ahead into the thin woods and was almost out of view. Pepper had never done a field search like this before, but he figured they should avoid gaps. They passed through a little clearing where teens sometimes built sneaky bonfires. They were getting into an area of low brush and spindly pine trees.

"Hey!" Delaney called over to Pepper. "I couldn't get your

'Try Me' song out of my head last night. It's special. If we had a real band, no covers, we could totally go for it. All original songs with heart and guts, like yours. Hit the road, get our act straight in the little places, then try the festivals..."

Off to Pepper's left, Brad let out a strangled and terrified, "Gaaaa!" He windmilled his arms and fell over backward. One flip-flop kicked up high in an arc over his head and disappeared into the brush.

Angel belly-laughed as they waded through the grasses and trees to Brad's side.

"I think I'm gonna puke," he coughed, lying on his back.

It turned out Brad had stumbled upon the decomposing body of a baby deer, then stepped back in horror and tripped on a branch.

"It's fucking *hideous*," whispered Brad, his face now gray. He was holding his ankle and rubbing it vigorously.

Raindrops began hitting the trees overhead.

Strike two.

The rain broke through as Pepper got Brad back on his feet. Angel dug around in the brush for Brad's flip-flop but didn't find it.

"Let's go to the van and wait out the rain," Pepper suggested. He wanted to finish searching the area—they couldn't give up so quickly.

They headed back to the vehicles. Brad leaned on Pepper's shoulder and hopped along, since the ground was full of sharp branches and rocks. Every time his bare right foot touched anything, he groaned loudly.

"Aw, man! I think I broke my ankle!" Brad whined.

They were all soaked by now.

"Hold on to that tree," Pepper said to Brad. Then he tucked his shoulder under Brad's midsection and lifted him into a fireman's carry. Brad was a string bean, but he was heavier than Pepper expected. Must be all the alcohol...

Angel led the way through the heavy rain with the two weak flashlights shining a little light on their path. Then came Pepper, staggering under Brad's shifting, complaining weight. Delaney brought up the rear. Pepper could hear her singing, high and sweet. He turned his head, and she waved Brad's only remaining flip-flop.

"You look good wet," Pepper said to her. Weak line, but man, it was the truth. She looked gorgeous, despite her wet clothes and hair. Pepper stumbled on a fallen branch, and he and Brad almost hit the ground. Pepper caught his balance at the last second.

He kept his eyes forward after that.

They cleared the edge of the marshy woods and were slogging through muddy ground to the vehicles when a police car came racing down the cul-de-sac with its red and blue lights flashing wildly and its siren screaming.

Strike three.

Pepper and his bandmates stood in the mud (other than Brad, who was still slung over his shoulder) as the officer jumped out of the police cruiser and drew his weapon, pointing it at them through the rain. "Put down the body and put your hands up!" hollered the officer. Pepper heaved Brad off his shoulder to splat in the mud.

"Hey, Randy!" Pepper yelled, recognizing the police officer. He pulled his baseball cap up to show his face. It was his kinda buddy, Randy Larch. Pepper waved his hand a little, friendly but cautious.

Officer Larch peered through the rain. "Pepper? What the hell are you doing with a dead body?"

"I'm still alive," protested Brad. "I just need a doctor..."

"Well, this is ridiculous," commented Delaney. Then she

laughed—a high, clear laugh which cut right through Pepper, to his spinal cord.

He burned with embarrassment because she was right. She must think he was a dumb kid, playing cop.

Larch explained to them that multiple residents of the Crofts subdivision had called in tips about the white van parked at the end of the cul-de-sac. They also reported an unidentified group of people trespassing in the construction sites and entering the woods. The desk sergeant decided the tip was hot enough to warrant a drive-by and Larch got the call.

"You know Sergeant Weisner's been trying to find out where you went?" Larch asked. "I haven't seen her this pissed off since... hey, you know what? Maybe never."

Shit.

Larch gave Pepper a wave. "You'd better ride back to the station with me," he said. "Seriously, kid, what the heck were you thinking?"

CHAPTER SIX

Pepper's office was always small and uncomfortable, but especially at that moment, because his dad and Sergeant Weisner were in it too. And they were both pissed at him.

Sergeant Weisner had laid into Pepper about abandoning his database work, but then she noticed the cheap plastic To Do tray, which was empty, and the Done tray, which was full. "You finished all fifty files?"

"Isn't that what you wanted?" he asked, trying to sound innocent. *God bless Zula!*

Pepper's dad looked exhausted, like he hadn't slept a minute since the Bailey kidnapping. "I don't have time for any shit right now, son. If you can't follow orders, you're hurting more than you're helping."

Pepper's cheeks turned red, but he didn't reply.

Barbara Buckley from Dispatch appeared at the office door, looking excited.

"Eastham's got a POI!" she said, sounding out of breath. "A level three who lives in New Albion. Detective Ingram's holding on line two." Pepper knew a level-three sex offender was the worst of the bunch, with a high risk to re-offend. A serious danger to the public.

His dad jogged to his own office, with Weisner in his wake. Pepper followed. His dad logged into his computer and pulled up the Sex Offender Registry Board website and searched for New Albion. Keeping the results on his screen, his dad made a shushing gesture to them (mostly to Pepper) and took the phone call, putting it on speakerphone.

Pepper's dad knew Detective Ingram. After quick hellos, his dad told the detective he was on speakerphone with others listening. Then Ingram explained his call was about a New Albion resident named Casper Yelle.

His dad clicked on the man's name on the SORB search result and full info popped up. White male, age thirty-nine. It showed Yelle was convicted of rape and abuse of a child, and indecent assault and battery on a child under fourteen years of age.

Yelle had registered in New Albion four months earlier. His address was in the Langham Arms, a worn-out complex of the least expensive rental apartments in New Albion. The same place where Pepper's crush Delaney Lynn lived... It was a large complex built in the 1960s—three apartment buildings, maybe twenty units in each, but still! A scary coincidence.

Detective Ingram explained that Yelle had been rubbernecking at the Bailey home about an hour ago in a tan Jeep Wrangler when a uniformed officer approached him. The officer waved him on, but the man asked whether they'd had found the girl yet. He'd acted strangely about it, like it was something funny.

The officer asked Yelle why he was on that street, and he'd said it was a free country, that kind of crap. Smirking the whole time.

So the officer pulled Yelle over and ran his ID and license plate. The search showed he was a registered sex offender.

"So we figured, he might be a sicko who gets a kick out of

seeing the scene of a crime," said Ingram. "Or maybe he's our kidnapper."

"Or both," muttered Pepper.

Ingram explained that the officer didn't believe he had cause to detain the man and so had let him go.

"Since Casper Yelle's a level three and on parole, I was hoping you guys could get to his place, ASAP?" asked Ingram. "Hold him while you search his apartment and his Jeep?"

"Sounds like a plan," said Pepper's dad.

Pepper could feel his pulse quickening.

Pepper was shocked when his dad let him stay and even explained the situation.

The good news was, since Casper Yelle was on parole, his parole officer owned his ass and could search his apartment without a warrant. The P.O. only needed reasonable suspicion, which basically meant anytime.

Sergeant Weisner disappeared, then came back in two minutes. She told them Yelle's parole officer was a guy named Charlie Brown.

"Seriously?" asked Pepper.

"Sweeney's hunting him down...he didn't answer his phone," she said.

His dad and Sergeant Weisner strategized about what to do in the meantime. Did they have probable cause to enter and search Yelle's apartment without the P.O.?

"We've got to go in," said Pepper. "How can you wait? Yelle might have hurt the girl. He might be hiding in there. He could—"

His dad interrupted. "We know that."

His dad asked Dispatch to patch him through to Randy Larch and another officer, a rookie named Klein, who were out together on patrol. He explained the situation and told them to do a door knock of Yelle's apartment at the Langham Arms.

Then the three of them waited, not talking. Just picturing what might play out across town. Everything that could go wrong, or maybe right.

Larch called Pepper's dad's cell phone, reporting that no one answered at Yelle's door. They'd seen a Jeep with Yelle's registration in the parking lot.

"What do you want us to do now, Chief?"

"They've got to kick it in," said Pepper in a low voice.

His dad gave him a look. "Stand by in the lot for Casper Yelle to get home or for his P.O. to arrive, whichever happens first. Then let Sweeney know."

Two minutes later, Detective Kevin Sweeney stuck his head in the door and gave a quick update. He was still trying to reach Charlie Brown to facilitate the search and to locate the man. As a level-three sex offender, Yelle had to wear an ankle bracelet and his parole officer could track him down with GPS coordinates.

"And another interesting fact," said Sweeney with a little smile. "Yelle has a second registered vehicle—a white Dodge cargo van."

Sweeney added that he had called Detective Ingram in Eastham and asked him to have someone show Emma Bailey's younger brother a photo array which included Casper Yelle's picture, hoping for a positive ID. Ingram would give the county sheriff and the D.A.'s office the heads-up about the move.

"Now it's a waiting game," said his dad. "Son, why don't you get back to your work?"

Pepper left them with a shake of his head. How could he do data entry while time was running out for Emma Bailey?

The answer was, he couldn't.

Half an hour later, Pepper returned to his dad's office, bringing him a steaming cup of coffee as an excuse to learn the latest developments.

His dad looked up from his computer.

"Thanks, son," he said, taking it.

His dad's cell phone rang. It was Randy Larch.

Pepper lingered in the doorway. His dad took pity on him and put Larch on speakerphone, telling Larch that Pepper was listening.

"Chief, you ain't gonna believe this," said Larch.

He and the rookie Klein had parked at the far end of the lot, waiting for Yelle to appear or for his P.O. to join them and do a warrantless entry and search under Yelle's conditions of parole.

"So we're waiting," Larch said. "A brown Lexus comes into the lot. Three white males get out and go up the stairway to Yelle's corridor. It's wide open, so we had a visual the whole time. They stopped outside Yelle's door and then I heard a bang. They were busting out the doorknob with a sledgehammer. Popped the door in two hits.

"Me and the rook hurried up the stairs and got the three guys in cuffs. Here's the weird part: it's Emma Bailey's uncle with two of his sons. They busted in to search Casper Yelle's place for Emma."

"Ah, shit," said his dad. "How the hell'd they get his name?"

"A great question, which I didn't ask them at the moment. Because of the, ah, legal sensitivities and whatnot."

In other words, Larch feared that a police officer, maybe even one from New Albion, had spilled the beans to the Bailey family. *What a mess...*

Larch continued. "So, ah, I decided to call in for instructions."

Pepper knew what he would instruct if he was in charge.

Emma Bailey might be tied up somewhere in Yelle's apartment. She might be in terrible shape.

His dad gave Pepper a long look.

"You and Klein need to search the apartment very carefully to make sure you're not in any physical danger," his dad told Larch. "You know what I mean? Search good and careful."

Behind his back, so his dad wouldn't see, Pepper crossed his fingers for luck.

CHAPTER SEVEN

Larch reported back five minutes later with nothing but bad news.

"All's clear, but there's no sign of Emma Bailey or Casper Yelle," said Larch. "We found one weird thing—a circular enclosure made from chicken wire. Kind of flimsy if it's for caging someone. Just kinda weird."

"Maybe if he'd already tied up his victim?" Pepper speculated.

Larch continued in his official monotone. "And we found a cardboard box in his bedroom closet with a couple dozen pairs of women's underwear. The sexy kind—thongs, boy shorts, that sort of thing."

"Good job, Randy. Call dispatch for a unit to transport the Baileys back here for booking. You and the rook stay put. See if you can get Yelle's door to close properly. We don't want him to see a problem and take off."

Pepper's dad hung up.

"I don't blame the Baileys," said Pepper.

"That's not how a good cop thinks," said his dad. "We can't have vigilantes running wild."

"Good thing I'm not a cop." Pepper could totally understand why Emma's relatives did what they did. They must be out of their minds with worry about her. He hated to imagine the pain they must be feeling, knowing a monster like Casper Yelle might be holding their daughter.

His dad began explaining the legal ramifications for the Bailey relatives. One offense for breaking and entering. Another offense if they got Yelle's address from the Sex Offender Registry Board website. They could be looking at prison time and fines. What a bunch of dumbasses, etc...

But Pepper wasn't listening. He was thinking about Emma Bailey. She might need food and water. She might need oxygen.

What would his dad do if he or Jake were missing? Hopefully, he'd tear the world apart.

Pepper could only begin to guess how the poor girl was suffering—if she was still alive.

———

Emma Bailey sat against a cold, hard wall in the dark, scared. Freaked out, actually. And totally, totally pissed off.

She didn't know what the hell had happened to her.

I mean, she knew some douchebag had grabbed her right off the sidewalk in front of her house. She'd like, frozen up, then she'd fought back, but there was nothing she could do. The asshole had even tased her.

Now she'd woken up here, wherever here was. She looked around and tried to figure it out. It was mostly dark, except for one light. She was leaning against a hard, cold wall which felt kind of sloped. Her hands were tied up with something that dug into her wrists—plastic? So were her feet. She was pretty sure she still wore the clothes she'd had on when she was grabbed—skinny jeans and a T-shirt.

She squirmed forward and tried to roll over, but something

else was tying her to the wall. She could only move a few inches. *Fuck!*

She saw a shadow move, and then a man came into the faint light. A large man. He squatted down. The douchebag was wearing a mask of the green ogre dude from the kids' movies. *Shrek.* She could see the weirdly long, thin green ears with bulbs at the ends. The flat nose, the stupid smile. The only holes in the mask were for the eyes.

Emma spat at him, aiming for those little eyeholes. She missed, but was happy he jumped back. *What a dick!*

"Hello, Emma," the man said, his voice muffled by the stupid mask.

"Hello, Needle-dick," she answered. "You need to let me go. Right fucking now." Then she screamed as loud and long as she could. And that was pretty damn loud and long. Bloodcurdling. She had the best scream of all her friends.

Her scream echoed around them.

The green mask studied her. "I think we're getting off on the wrong foot," the man said. "You should be nicer to me. I'm your only source of food and water. I'm your everything now."

He sounded like he actually believed his own bullshit. "That's the ugliest fucking mask I've ever seen," she said. "But I'm guessing you're, like, more butt ugly than Shrek? So you think it's an improvement?"

The man smacked her knee, causing a sharp sting of pain. "You've got a mouth on you. We'll have to do something about that."

She flung her knees to the side. "You better not touch me again. My dad's a Marine. He'll rip off your—"

"Your dad's not relevant anymore. I'll be looking after you from now on. You be nice and I'll be nice. Are you thirsty?"

Emma was. But she wasn't going to tell him that. "It stinks in here," she said. "You ever hear of deodorant?"

Shrek studied her again, but she couldn't tell his reaction. "Open your mouth and I'll pour in a little water," the man said. "It'll make you less cranky."

Emma wanted to defy him. She wanted to tell him to pound sand. But she was super thirsty. Why punish herself?

So she opened her mouth and Shrek slowly trickled water in. It wasn't very good water. It was kind of chalky. But she gulped it down as long as he poured it.

"Ugh. It tastes as bad as you smell," she said, coughing.

The man smacked her cheek. "I put a little something in the water to help you sleep, since you must be uncomfortable. See? I'm taking care of you already."

Emma tried to spit out the chalky residue in her mouth. She was shaking from anger and fear. "Could you do one other thing for me?" she asked.

"What?"

"Could you please take your roofie water and your little Taser and shove them up your ass? Then pull the damned trigger. Thanks so much."

The man didn't respond this time. A moment later, he pulled a mask over her eyes and everything went black.

She heard his footsteps, clattering on what sounded like metal stairs, and then a heavy door shutting with an echoing thud.

Alone, Emma began crying in the dark.

Please, could someone save her? Find her quick and catch the sick bastard in the Shrek mask. Get her the hell out of there.

She could feel the chalky drug affecting her...feel her thoughts slowing, her body sagging harder against the cold wall.

Be strong, she said to herself. Someone would come soon to help her.

And her dad was going to kick Shrek's ass. That was her last thought as she slipped away into a drugged, feverish sleep.

CHAPTER EIGHT

This might be it, thought Chief of Police Gerald Ryan, when Detective Sweeney brought in Casper Yelle to the station forty-five minutes later.

They were accompanied by Yelle's parole officer, Charlie Brown, a thin, unhappy-looking white guy in his late twenties. Brown's monitoring center had pinpointed Yelle's ankle bracelet coordinates, and they'd picked him up on foot, two blocks from his apartment.

As a level-three sex offender, Yelle was wearing a GPS monitor, which looked like an old-school pager attached to a belt locked to his ankle. It was designed to alert the parole office if he tampered with it.

Yelle's conditions of parole required him to let his parole officer search him and his property at any time, for pretty much any reason. Parolees effectively forfeited most of their Fourth Amendment rights.

Yelle was also required to answer any questions his P.O. asked him. That's why Gerald wanted Charlie Brown to take part in the interrogation—Yelle's conditions of parole didn't require him to answer police questions. He hoped the man wasn't aware of the distinction.

If Yelle didn't like Brown's questions and invoked his Fifth Amendment right to be free from self-incrimination, he'd be in violation of his parole terms and would probably land straight back in prison. Yelle would have to weigh the damage of not talking versus talking himself into trouble for the Emma Bailey kidnapping—new felonies and then even lengthier prison time.

Sweeney parked the suspect in a too-warm interview room, handcuffed to the table. They left him there to sweat. And hopefully worry.

But Gerald was preoccupied with his son Pepper as he reached the recording room to watch the Yelle interrogation.

Pepper had ambushed him in the hallway, asking if he could sit in. The kid's face had fallen hard when he'd said no. But the recording room was tiny and it would already have four people crammed in there: himself; an overweight detective from Eastham named Paul Thunberg, who was helping Detective Ingram on the Bailey case; Don Eisenhower; and a detective sergeant who would handle the audiovisual equipment.

Gerald had invited the Eastham detective because multiple jurisdictions were investigating the Bailey kidnapping at the same time and they would step on each other's dicks if they didn't coordinate.

He also included Lieutenant Eisenhower to watch the interrogation because he trusted Don's instincts. Hell, he trusted him as a cop and a man more than anyone in the world. It was unusual for a police chief and a lieutenant to watch a suspect interview, but this case was too big and too raw for Gerald. He needed to look the suspect in the eye.

So Pepper's big frame would be one body too many. Pepper had stomped away, his face a storm cloud. The young man was energetic, full of life. But with a chip on his shoulder. Insecure. Which made little sense. What was Pepper now—6'3"? Strong and a good athlete. He had a bunch of friends and girls seemed to like him. Luckily, he'd gotten enough of his mom's good looks. Maybe most twenty-year-olds were insecure, whether they showed it or not?

Gerald pushed thoughts of Pepper out of his mind when he stepped into the recording room. He needed to focus on Casper Yelle. They needed to pin Yelle to the wall and find out if he was the kidnapper, quickly. And then find the girl...

Everyone was waiting for Gerald. The recording room was not much bigger than a janitor's closet, and it was half full of video equipment: DVRs, monitors and headsets. They all had to remain standing other than the detective sergeant working the AV controls.

The room was also damn hot, and someone needed to switch to a stronger brand of deodorant. But nobody said it. Nobody was joking around, which was unusual for cops.

The video and sound equipment recorded as Yelle sat alone in the interview room. Everyone in the recording room fiddled with their headsets and watched the suspect on the monitor in silence.

Gerald studied the suspect carefully. Casper Yelle lived up to his first name—he was pale as a ghost. Eyes a bit sunken. Other than that, he was a plain-looking middle-aged white guy, balding up top and a light brown ponytail. He looked tall and heavy. He wore a plain white T-shirt and tan cargo shorts.

Charlie Brown had filled them in on Casper Yelle, saying he was a sexual deviant, a narcissist, and had a near genius IQ. But he'd kept his nose clean in New Albion as far as Brown knew. Until maybe now.

Yelle was wiggling and fidgeting in the chair, his eyes moving around the room.

Yelle sat up when Detective Sweeney and Officer Brown entered the interview room. Sweeney sat across from Yelle and Brown remained standing. Brown began pacing up and down, looking pissed, as they had choreographed in advance. They staged everything in a suspect interrogation.

The plan was to leverage Yelle's conditions of parole to find out his alibi for the time Emma Bailey was abducted to see if he was lying, and to gather any other information they could get from him.

Detective Sweeney, Gerald's most senior detective, was a transplant from Boston. He'd joined the department six years ago. He was a likable guy and had an easy style. Perpetrators seemed comfortable chatting with him. Detective Sweeney identified everyone in the room, noted that the interview was being recorded.

"This is harassment," said Yelle.

"Shut up, Casper," said Brown. "I don't get paid enough to spend my day off with you. You're going to answer our questions, and then I can get back to my barbecue." Brown asked Yelle to explain why he had been outside the Bailey house when the officer stopped him.

Yelle repeated what he'd told the Eastham officer—he was curious if the girl was home safe yet.

"Bullshit," said Brown. "One more lie and you're going to Shirley." Shirley was the Souza-Baranowski Correctional Center, the only maximum-security prison in Massachusetts.

Charlie Brown reminded Yelle he needed to fully and honestly answer questions as a condition of his parole.

"Mr. Brown, I am being honest. I didn't do anything," said Yelle. But he wasn't looking at the parole officer. He was looking at the video camera in the room's corner. Like he was talking to the people in the recording room.

"Then let's clear everything up," said Sweeney with a smile. "Where were you last night?"

"Mr. Brown knows where I was. I have this elegant ankle jewelry which tells him everywhere I go."

Sweeney was still smiling, still looking supportive and relaxed. "Absolutely. But you need to help us help you, right? So tell us all the places you were yesterday, starting at five p.m.."

"Yesterday? I got out of work at the machine shop at five o'clock sharp. I bought some Taco Bell down the road and ate it in their parking lot. Then I drove home."

"What were you driving?" asked Sweeney.

"My Jeep. I worry about it because the machine shop's next door to that contractor park, the Big Red Yard? Those cretins use our parking lot for staging. They leave trash everywhere. I've even found them sitting in my Jeep, smoking cigarettes when I had my top and doors off."

Gerald knew Yelle was employed at Johnston Precision Machining out on Richards Road. They fabricated replacement metal parts for industrial machines. It was one type of business on the Cape which routinely hired parolees.

Brown stopped pacing and put his hands on the back of the empty chair next to Sweeney. He leaned toward Yelle. "You drove straight home around five-thirty? Then you stayed there until morning?" Brown sounded very skeptical.

"Come on, Mr. Brown, you know I did! You have the GPS data to prove it!"

"Did you know someone broke into your apartment today?" asked Sweeney.

"Oh my God! What?" Yelle looked genuinely surprised.

"Do you know anyone who'd do that?" Brown asked.

Gerald watched the back and forth on the monitor. Yelle looked alarmed and confused.

It took a while for Yelle to speak. "No way. Nobody. Assuming it wasn't a rogue member of law enforcement?"

"Nah, it wasn't us," said Brown. "And we don't need to knock down your door. I can search your apartment anytime I want to. You don't have the same rights as normal humans. After I finish wasting my time here, I'm going over to your apartment to search every inch of it."

Yelle laughed, sounding only a bit nervous. "I thought you needed to get back to a barbecue. But please, feel free."

Brown glowered at him. "How about you save us both some trouble and tell me what I'll find there?"

Yelle sniffed. "Absolutely nothing that worries me."

In the recording room, Eisenhower said, "He's not looking so confident now."

"The asshole fucking did it," said the sweaty detective from Eastham.

Gerald just kept breathing through his mouth and listened, watching Yelle's face and body language.

The interview went back and forth for thirty minutes, with Brown leading the questioning, using his leverage as Yelle's P.O. to push the man. Sweeney jumped in from time to time, expanding the timeline, drawing out of Yelle where he'd been during the past two days, hour by hour. Then they circled back and verified everything, trying to trip him up.

Casper Yelle answered every question. He seemed to say as little as possible without overtly breaking his conditions of parole. But everything he said was with a condescending edge. Yelle was either a smartass or he was trying to deflect. Like he had something to hide?

"You haven't been doing any under-the-table home security alarm jobs since you got out of prison, right?" asked Brown. "You've only worked at the machine shop, like we discussed for the last three months? Since you can't be near minors, right, Casper?"

"Of course not!"

Yelle's old career, before his arrest and conviction for the sex crime, had been installing home security systems as an independent contractor.

Sweeney's cell phone rang. He checked the caller ID, then chuckled. "Oh man, are you toast," he said to Yelle. "Try to relax, we'll be back." Then he and Brown left the man alone in the small, depressing room.

———

The call had been from Detective Ingram of the Eastham Police, about how the photo array had gone with Emma Bailey's little brother Mason, the witness.

In the large conference room, Sweeney updated everyone. Ingram had shown the boy a set of six photos, including Yelle and five other men who resembled him. Mason initially chose Yelle's picture and said he was probably the guy. Then the boy started shaking and crying.

Ingram waited an hour, then asked the boy to look at the photos again. This time the boy wasn't as sure and didn't identify Yelle as the abductor. He picked a different picture.

So, not great.

They let Casper Yelle sweat for half an hour, then resumed the interview. Gerald and the others crammed back in the recording room.

"Okay, about your apartment," said Charlie Brown. "Tell me about your wire cage."

Yelle froze. "I'm planning to purchase a pair of cockatiels. To breed them and sell the chicks."

"Funny, it looked more like one of those Faraday cages," said Sweeney.

A Faraday cage is a mesh enclosure of conductive material, designed to block electromagnetic fields. If Casper Yelle was inside it, he could remove or disable his ankle monitor and the cage would block any signal from the ankle monitor to the parole office.

"Pardon me?" asked Yelle.

Brown scoffed. "You were a tech guy. You fucking know what that is."

Yelle seemed a little more pale now. "It's just a bird cage. Is there some condition of parole which prevents me from breeding birds?"

"Not if that's true," said Sweeney. "But yes if you're lying. It'd be truly life changing for you."

Sweeney waited. Gerald knew he was hoping Yelle would say more. But Yelle stayed silent, fidgeting restlessly.

So Sweeney moved on. "But you'll be happy to know—the people who broke in, they didn't steal your ladies undergarment collection."

Yelle stopped fidgeting.

"What're you doing with women's undies?" asked Brown. "I could violate you just for that."

The man's answer was cold and careful. Seemingly emotionless. "They're mine. I wear them to express my sexuality."

Brown snorted. "You expect me to believe suddenly you're a cross-dresser?"

Yelle said nothing.

Gerald wondered if Yelle bought or stole the women's underwear for kicks. Or had the man gathered them from victims like Emma Bailey—was he some kind of serial kidnapper? They would have to test the underwear for DNA.

Sweeney changed topics again, trying to keep Yelle off

balance. "By the way, where's your van parked today? It's not at your apartment."

Watching the monitor, Gerald thought Yelle looked scared for the first time. His color reddened slightly.

"My van? Someone stole it two days ago."

Brown banged on the table. "Stop jerking us around, Casper. This is your last chance. Someone stole it?"

"Yes!"

"So you filed a police report?" asked Sweeney.

"I was planning to. Honestly. Then I saw on TV about the poor kidnapped girl. And that the perpetrator was allegedly driving a white van. I thought someone might have stolen my van to abduct the girl. So I was waiting to report it in a couple days. Perhaps it would turn up first. Maybe after you catch the perpetrator behind the wheel." Yelle paused to think. "But if you don't mind, I think this might be a wise time for me to talk to a lawyer. If you have any further questions."

"Where is it, Casper?" persisted Charlie Brown. "You don't talk, you go straight to Shirley. Then you'll get a fucking lawyer, too late to do you any good."

"And maybe a new boyfriend in max security who'll appreciate your taste in underwear," added Sweeney.

But Yelle refused to say anything more. He just kept looking around the room, like he was avoid making eye contact with things no one else could see.

Gerald wanted to learn what the others thought, especially Don Eisenhower. But having watched the interrogation closely, Gerald was confident about two things: Casper Yelle was hiding something. And if he was the kidnapper, they'd nail his smug, high-IQ ass.

They left the suspect in the interrogation room. Gerald sent Charlie Brown and Kevin Sweeney to Yelle's apartment to retrieve the box of women's underwear and search the apartment again more thoroughly.

Don Eisenhower put out a BOLO for Yelle's white van.

Right about that time, the New Albion police station's phones started ringing with calls from crime reporters asking for confirmation whether the kidnapper was in custody.

Had whoever tipped the Bailey family about Casper Yelle also tipped the media? Gerald told the receptionist to refer the media to the Eastham police department.

Because he had nothing good to say, just yet...

CHAPTER NINE

Pepper received a mysterious text from Delaney inviting him to come to Sandy's Restaurant for dinner at six, don't be late.

She explained nothing, and Pepper didn't ask. It would be a great chance to keep getting to know her. And maybe finally ask her out...

He called Angel, who agreed to join him at Sandy's as his wingman. He had a rare Friday night off from delivering pizzas. Sandy's Restaurant had the best lobster rolls on the Lower Cape, possibly in the world, so he'd known Angel would say yes.

Pepper cruised down Shore Road, parked in the big lot for Sandy's Restaurant and walked inside. It smelled like freshly baked bread. His mouth ran with saliva. Sandy's really was Pepper's favorite place to eat in town—it was just a big bonus that Delaney worked there.

Pepper asked the hostess, a high schooler with a nose stud and long blonde hair in a ponytail, if he could sit in Delaney's section. The girl didn't even try to hide her smirk as she grabbed a menu and led him through the bar area toward the restaurant section.

The TV mounted high over the bar was on a Boston news station, and the screen showed a story about the Emma Bailey kidnapping. The sound was off and the banner headline read "Greenhead Snatcher Update."

Pepper paused to see the news story. "Greenhead Snatcher" was the dramatic new nickname for Emma Bailey's kidnapper, coined by some news anchor because Emma's little brother had told police the man had a green head. That meant the kidnapper was likely wearing a green hat, but the new nickname had quickly spread among the media.

And sure, greenhead flies were a plague on the Cape most summers. But to Pepper, the nickname seemed smart-alecky. Insensitive?

The TV picture cut to a man in sunglasses being interviewed, looking important and puffed up. It was Fester Timmins, Jake's old classmate who Pepper had seen in the mob scene at the police station of volunteers to help search for Emma Bailey.

How did Timmins get himself on TV—playing a concerned citizen? Pretending he was a witness? Sure, yesterday he'd joined the search, but...

Pepper wished he could hear what the guy was saying. He looked crazy excited. He was waving his arms as he talked, then took off his sunglasses to make a particularly important point. Presumably.

He didn't know what Timmins did for work. He was pretty sure it had nothing to do with law enforcement.

What's his deal? he wondered.

The hostess sighed, so Pepper gave up on the TV and followed her to a table.

After he sat, Pepper pushed the menu aside because he always ordered the same thing—lobster rolls. Sandy's lobster rolls were traditional, but somehow they were better than anywhere else. They came with the usual toasted, split-top hot dog bun. One nice long lettuce leaf. Big chunks of lobster tail and knuckle meat. A sprinkle of paprika.

Sandy's gave you two choices: drizzled with drawn butter or tossed in mayo. Pepper was religiously in the mayo camp, and Angel was a butter guy—just another example of how Angel was a heathen.

The place mats at Sandy's restaurant were a map of Cape Cod, shaped like a flexing arm stretching into the Atlantic Ocean. The map was decorated with the usual cliched items: lighthouses, whales, seagulls and major shipwrecks over the centuries.

Pepper studied the map, wondering where Emma Bailey might be. New Albion was on the Lower Cape, near the elbow of that flexing arm. He wondered whether the suspect Casper Yelle had confessed yet. If not, there were a thousand places he could have hidden the girl.

Tens of thousands, if she was dead. If Yelle had killed her and then disposed of her body, there were lots of marshes. Or if he had a boat, he could take her out to sea and toss her overboard.

But Pepper couldn't think about that possibility. She had to be alive.

If Yelle's plan was to take her away off the Cape, he could take two bridges: the Sagamore or the Bourne. Or again, he could escape by water. No one would ever know.

Angel arrived and noisily plopped down across from Pepper. Angel was wearing a pink T-shirt that said "Casanova." Some wingman.

"Hey, *mano*," said Angel. "You order for us yet?"

"Just sat down. And I couldn't order you lobster rolls with butter. It's an abomination."

"Lobster always comes with drawn butter," complained Angel. "It's a classic, just like me."

"Not on a hot dog bun," said Pepper. But he cut off the debate because Delaney appeared at their table. She didn't look very rock-and-roll today. Knee-length white skirt and a puffy white shirt. But she still looked beautiful.

She smiled at them. "Hey guys, you showed up!" She looked over her shoulder distractedly. "Sorry, I'm slammed right now. What can I get you to drink?"

He and Angel both ordered iced teas, and Delaney hurried away, all business.

Was he going to have time to ask her out?

She trotted back with their drinks and took their food orders. Then left them again quickly.

"Either she's super busy or you need a shower," said Angel.

"Thanks, buddy."

Angel was jabbering about a trip he'd made to Ocean State Job Lot, a discount store, to buy tiki torches. He had fallen in love with the checkout girl. Maybe the third time Angel had fallen in love that week and that was only the girls he'd told Pepper about.

Pepper was only half listening as Angel talked. He was watching Delaney, who was all over the place, usually with her hands full. Practically running.

Okay, possibly it wasn't his smell.

Pepper noticed Brad St. John's roommate, Dennis Cole, the biker guy who claimed to have music industry connections, enter the restaurant and saunter toward their table.

Hmm. Was this why Delaney asked him to be here at six?

Cole came over and rested his fingertips on their table, a big, friendly smile on his face. "You guys are right on time," he said. "A rare talent for musicians."

Pepper slid over and Cole sat next to him.

"Delaney and me had a nice long talk this morning. She tell you?" asked Cole. "I have lots of connections in Nashville—you guys could go a long way down there."

"You guys?" asked Angel.

"I'm not interested in anything that doesn't include Angel," said Pepper.

The man paused, grinned at them, then said, "Absolutely! The three of you. Every band needs a beat."

"What about your roommate Brad?" asked Pepper.

Cole laughed. "Brad's a good dude. Loves his music. But he's more of a cover band guy. And he either has a drinking problem or a bad case of stage fright."

Or both, thought Pepper.

"But Brad said you're working this summer as a cop?" Cole asked.

"A cadet."

"Huh. That's great. It was horrible about the teenager getting snatched last night."

"Absolutely," said Pepper.

"You guys have any good leads yet to find the bastard who did it? Any hot tips to collect the reward Brad was talking about?"

Pepper felt uncomfortable. "Dozens of tips. Possibly hundreds. Some probably motivated by the reward, sure. Some just good people trying to help."

"I'm one of those good people," said Angel. "But picking up the reward would be icing on the cake. And it's hard to become a millionaire slinging pizzas one at a time."

"I hear that!" said Cole. "And I have a damn good theory of my own about who did it. Nothing solid enough to cash in yet. But I talk to people who don't talk to cops, you know?"

Sounded to Pepper like Cole might pull a vigilante move that would land him with the Bailey relatives in their jail cell. But Pepper wasn't Cole's keeper. "You get anything solid, call it in."

"You bet," said Cole. "Somebody's got to find that little girl quick. And thanks for your service! In fact..." The biker took out his wallet, which was secured to his belt by a chain. He slapped down enough twenty-dollar bills to cover the check, plus a fat tip.

"Your dinner's on me, guys. And I meant what I said last night —I can help you take your music to the next level. Call me if you're interested. Hell, call me for whatever. Like if you learn any juicy news about the snatcher. There's plenty of cash to go around."

Cole gave them each a half hug, then left them. They watched him stop at the front door, chatting a bit with the blond-haired hostess. Cole and the girl laughed, and then Cole strutted out the door. The guy was quite a charmer.

They heard a Harley-Davidson fire up in the parking lot, its pipes snarling like a wild animal. Other diners' heads turned toward the window, annoyed. Then the sound of the motorcycle growled away into the distance.

"Heck of a nice dude," said Angel. "Our new super fan. Who do you think he has a crush on—Delaney? Or you?"

Pepper laughed, unsure about their sudden new friend. He wasn't going to call Cole and dish any inside news about the progress of the kidnapping case. But Pepper didn't want to burn the bridge with the biker either, in case he could really help them on the music side.

Pepper threw a fry at Angel. "Or maybe he likes Cuban drummers? But hey, no harm letting him do us a favor. Right?"

"Sorry, guys," said Delaney when she arrived with their plates of lobster rolls and fries. She sighed and slid into the seat across from Pepper, next to Angel.

"I had a table of twelve who wanted to pay with six separate checks. Canadians—so damn polite I had to say yes! Someday, when I'm a rock star, this'll just be a funny story."

"Rock star, huh?" asked Angel.

Delaney smiled, pushing some stray hair back from her face. "What, you don't think? I talked to Dennis Cole for an hour this morning. He got my number from Brad. Dennis has a lot of experience with the music industry... Austin... Nashville... lots of places. He got me all worked up."

Pepper's mouth was full of lobster roll, so he gave her an inquiring eyebrow.

"I want to hit the road and gig a lot of small places," she continued. "Work up a good set of original songs and see if we can catch lightning in a bottle. Get a recording deal. The whole thing. But it takes a lot of luck too. Do you think Cole can help us?"

"Maybe," said Pepper. "Though I've got to wonder how big of an industry player he is, splitting a rental house with Brad St. John."

Delaney was so animated. "Don't you want to see more of America than just Cape Cod?"

"Not me," said Angel. "I'm a home boy. But Pepper has all kinds of plans..."

Damn Angel! Was he about to spill Pepper's secret about leaving for college at the end of the summer?

But Pepper had been picking up little signs that Angel was bummed out about Pepper heading away to college, so possibly this was more of that.

"The Cape's not boring this summer," said Pepper, changing the topic. "More like a nightmare, since Emma Bailey got snatched."

"Were you helping with her case today?" Delaney asked him. "Did they catch that psycho yet?"

Pepper knew he wasn't supposed to talk about open cases. He knew it was a mistake. But Delaney was still super worried about the kidnapping. She was looking at him hopefully with her wide, beautiful eyes. One dark hazel. One blue. Amazing...

"You've got to spill the dirt," said Angel, shoving a few fries in his mouth.

What could Pepper do? He had to show off a little... Especially after how ridiculous he'd looked the last time he was with Delaney, when Randy Larch had cut short their failed search.

So he told her and Angel the basic info. A suspect was in custody. Emma Bailey was still missing. Some people broke into the suspect's apartment, looking for the girl. Pepper hinted he knew a lot more, even though he didn't.

"Oh, and you can't tell anyone," he said. "But the main suspect lives at the Langham Arms too. Next building over from yours."

The Langham Arms comprised three brick buildings in a horseshoe shape. The middle area was a big parking lot. The complex was old enough to look tired, but not old enough to be vintage. More like 1960s run-down.

Pepper described Casper Yelle, relying on the details Randy Larch had told him.

"Oh my God, Pepper!" Delaney exclaimed, her voice shaking. "But he's in jail, right?"

"He might be out by now. He's just a suspect, he might not have done it."

"If I see a guy who looks like that, I'll scream!"

Delaney's voice was so strong, Pepper would probably hear her scream from across town.

"Seriously, you shouldn't worry. But if you see something, you know...say something."

"But it's safe for me to go home?"

Probably, thought Pepper. But he said, "Oh, absolutely."

"I've got the shivers now," she said. "If you can get a picture of him, can you text it to me? Please?"

"You bet," said Pepper. How could he not? But how was he going to get a picture of Casper Yelle? He bit into his lobster roll again. It tasted perfect. Only his promise left a bad taste in his mouth.

"Delaney!" barked a tall, beefy guy with flaming red hair and a slight accent. English? He was wearing a white dress shirt with a Sandy's logo. And an ugly tie. Possibly in his early thirties. "Table six asked for you. Again!"

"Sorry, Scooter!" said Delaney, rising and hustling away.

Pepper saw Delaney collect food from the kitchen window and deliver it to a table. Then she checked on three other tables, hustling back and forth from the drinks station and the computer terminal, taking care of her tables. Finally, she worked her way back to Pepper and Angel. Her cheeks were pink from her efforts and her hair was awry, but she looked even more spectacular.

She looked around, then sat down with them again.

"My feet are *so* fried," she said, dragging out the word "fried" in her cute southern accent, while frowning.

Pepper thought he should offer her a foot rub after she got off work, but she intimidated him too much.

Angel was filling the gap, telling Delaney about being the fastest pizza deliveryman in the Lower Cape. That he was a bit of a legend. Going on and on. And Pepper just sat there, thinking about how amazing Delaney was. Like a mute idiot.

He wanted to say something else, anything else. But he said nothing. He choked.

She was older; she was beautiful; she was too fricking cool...

"Delaney!" barked Scooter, the redheaded manager. He'd somehow slipped up to their table without them spotting him. Like he had a superpower. "Are all your other customers impeding your love life?" he growled in his British accent.

Delaney hopped up and took off. Scooter stayed by their table, hands in his pockets, following her with his eyes.

Just a diligent manager, or was there something a bit creepy about him?

Or was Pepper just jealous?

CHAPTER TEN

Unfortunately, Saturday was a perfect July day on Cape Cod—temperatures in the high seventies with just a hint of a breeze. The kind of day that the Visitors Bureau would film for its TV commercials. Perfect beach weather. Pepper knew the New Albion shore would be towel to towel with sunbathers.

Unfortunate because Pepper would not be on the sand with them. He arrived at the police station around nine-thirty, depressed to be spending such a perfect weekend day at a desk in a cramped converted drunk tank.

He was also pissed that he'd had to call Brad St. John and say he couldn't make today's Brad and the Pitts band rehearsal. Brad had been obnoxious about it, questioning his commitment to rock-and-roll and his bandmates. Pepper had bitten his tongue and taken it.

Pepper ran into Officer Randy Larch in the coffee room.

"Working on a Saturday!" said Larch. "You going for employee of the month?"

"Busy times," answered Pepper, not wanting to get into it. His dad had ordered him to work today as punishment for disappearing yesterday. "You still helping Sweeney with the Snatcher case? How's it going?"

Yes, Larch was still helping, and he was more than happy to dish the latest dirt to Pepper.

The most exciting development was that the Eastham police had used the "find my phone" feature to locate Emma Bailey's cell phone. They found it on a grass island next to a muffler shop at the edge of New Albion. About fifteen minutes from Eastham.

"So the theory is, the kidnapper drove in our direction, then disposed of her phone. Of course, he could have left it there to throw us off and doubled back somewhere else."

So the kidnapper had headed this way after grabbing the girl. Was he a New Albion local, like Casper Yelle? Food for thought...

"Anything else?" asked Pepper.

Larch had nothing else to share. Basically, the case against Casper Yelle had stalled. They'd found nothing at his apartment or in his Jeep to show a connection between him and Emma Bailey. And his ankle monitor hadn't shown he was in her neighborhood when the snatching happened.

Larch explained about the Faraday cage in Yelle's apartment and how the man could sit in the cage while he tampered with or removed his ankle monitor without setting off the alert. The Faraday cage theoretically would prevent a signal from going to the parole office's monitoring service.

"So Yelle could have deactivated his ankle bracelet? Or taken it off?"

Larch nodded. "He used to be a tech guy for a home alarm company, before he went to prison. He could spoof a GPS signal to look like he was at home and everything was fine, when he could be anywhere."

"Can we prove that?" asked Pepper.

"Nope, it's all guesses so far. His P.O. couldn't tell if he tampered with it. In the meantime, we're looking for Yelle's white van. He says someone stole it. If we find it, possibly there'll be some DNA to prove Emma Bailey was in it."

Unless Yelle got rid of the van permanently...

"Are we still holding him?" Pepper asked.

"No, Sweeney cut Yelle loose last night. He hadn't technically violated his terms of parole, and we didn't have cause to hold him. But your dad still thinks he's our number one suspect."

"What do you think?" Pepper wanted to know more. He wanted to know everything about the investigation. He couldn't help it—the hunt must be zeroing in on the Snatcher. Now it was just a matter of getting a break, grabbing the guy and hopefully finding Emma Bailey alive and well.

Larch sighed. "Every shop on Cape Cod is checking out their sex offenders and plenty of other suspects too. But your dad's a smart cop with a lot more experience than I have. I wouldn't bet against him being right. If it's Yelle, we'll get him. I hope it's not too late. The search parties have been a complete bust."

That reminded Pepper about seeing Fester Timmins on the bar television at Sandy's Restaurant. "I saw your buddy Fester on TV talking about the Greenhead Snatcher. I couldn't hear what he said, but the reporter was eating it up."

Larch laughed. "My buddy? That guy's a real character. He'd give his left nut to be a cop. He's applied to every law enforcement agency on the Cape in the last couple of years. No bites yet!"

Pepper went back to his miserable little drunk tank office and tried to focus on his database work for way over thirty minutes... practically forty minutes. But it was impossibly boring and irrelevant to what really was going on this week.

Pepper opened a new case screen in the database, titled it Bailey and populated it with metadata for the Greenhead Snatcher case. All the usual fields of info, but this time for a living, breathing case.

Then he went further, inputting a chronological list of all

information he'd learned since Emma Bailey's abduction. Sticking to raw facts, like in the other case files in the database. The timeline of events, the names and the locations. It took half an hour to input everything he knew about the Emma Bailey case.

Then, just for fun, he ran some queries against all the other files in his partially filled database. Kidnapping. Van. White van. Green hat. All the metadata he'd identified to include in his own mock file for the Bailey case.

The search results included a handful of cases. None of which seemed to have anything to do with the Emma Bailey case. So, a total swing and a miss.

Strike one.

Garbage in, garbage out, right? He couldn't conduct meaningful searches because he didn't know enough about the Emma Bailey investigation.

But, Pepper realized, maybe he had a way to fix that. And he'd promised Delaney he'd get her a picture of Casper Yelle, for her own safety.

He had to try.

The door to his dad's office groaned as Pepper opened it. The light was off and no one was there.

Perfect.

Pepper closed the door and hurried to his dad's desk. His idea was to check his dad's computer for more details about the Bailey investigation, so he could get a photo of Casper Yelle for Delaney and, as a bonus, be able to flesh out his own mock case file.

What was the harm, right? And maybe there'd be some connection between the Bailey case and one of the older cases in Pepper's database...possibly a connection which wasn't in the department's active databases.

If he found a connection, he'd show it to his dad. Maybe partially redeem himself.

Pepper knew his dad required everyone in the department to change their passwords every ninety days and that his dad couldn't ever remember his own password. He kept it on a sticky note under his desk.

He retrieved the sticky note and logged in as his dad. He realized he was breathing faster. A bit nervous.

Pepper clicked through the department files. He was looking for Bailey case info and had to resist being distracted by other stuff. Such as the payroll file. No, he felt guilty enough to be sneaking into the system for the Bailey info...

But unfortunately, he found nothing. He couldn't see the detectives' active case files using his dad's access. Another whiff.

Strike two.

Pepper logged out of the computer, hoping he hadn't left an electronic trail which would get him in trouble. He didn't need to move any higher on his dad's shit list—he was already floating near the top.

He was about to leave his dad's office when he had another idea. His dad was a bit of a dinosaur and still preferred paper files over computer files. Had he assembled a paper file in connection with the task force meeting in Eastham he'd gone to yesterday evening? If yes, had his dad come back to the office and filed it away in his battered gray filing cabinet?

Pepper found the key to the metal filing cabinet where he had seen his dad keep it for over a decade—on his bookcase under the hollow base of a ceramic tiger Jake had made in elementary school.

He quickly unlocked his dad's filing cabinet and found a manila folder labeled "Bailey." It was a lot thicker than he'd expected.

He opened the folder and read the top document. His pulse began to race.

CHAPTER ELEVEN

Pepper needed to read fast, learn as much as he could, then get the hell out of his dad's office.

The top document in the manila folder was a typed two-page summary of the investigation's progress, with small notes written in the margin in his dad's sloppy half-script and half-print.

It began with a recap of the facts of seventeen-year-old Emma Bailey's abduction, as related by the only witness, Emma's seven-year-old brother, Mason.

The boy had been looking out the window, waiting for his sister to get home because his front tooth had finally fallen out and he wanted to surprise her with his new smile. It was shortly before 9:00 PM on Thursday. Mason saw a white van parked on the street between their house and the neighbor's house to the west, but couldn't identify its make or model.

Pepper wondered why the Snatcher parked the van in that spot at that specific time. Was he stalking Emma, or just looking for opportunities and saw her?

No, Pepper's guess was the guy had to have been there waiting for Emma. It just made sense to him.

The report said the boy saw Emma's friend Katelyn Jaansen's

car pull over on the far side of the street and Emma got out. She waved goodbye as Katelyn's car drove away. She crossed the street to the sidewalk in front of their residence. Pepper's dad had written JOL? In the margin. Pepper figured that meant "junior operator license" but didn't get why it would matter.

A man had approached Emma at the curb and asked her a question, which Emma seemed to answer without stopping walking. As Emma passed the man, he ran at her and tackled her from behind. They wrestled for a few seconds, then he grabbed her and she collapsed.

Pepper's dad had added the note "taser?" in the margin.

Mason had stayed at the window and saw the man pick up Emma over his shoulder and put her in the back of the white van. Then the kidnapper looked right at the boy, who became even more scared. He ran to the kitchen and called 911.

A transcript of the 911 call was attached, but it didn't contain any other helpful information. The boy was very upset and only communicated the basic info while crying.

The 911 tape showed the boy's call was at 8:46 PM.

An Eastham police detail arrived at the house at 8:58.

Eastham police issued a BOLO for the white van at 8:58 and initiated an amber alert at 9:06.

The next section of the memo was titled "Investigation Status" and listed in bare details the roadblocks which had been set up, the numbers of tips received and followed up, the number of areas searched by police and civilian volunteers, and other basic facts.

It summarized the number of registered sex offenders on Cape Cod and the number of felons with records for kidnapping or other violent crimes. Detailed lists were attached.

Pepper heard footsteps outside the office and in one lightning move swept the file closed and tucked himself under his dad's desk.

The door opened with a sharp groan from its hinges.

The entire world paused except Pepper's heartbeat, which was definitely loud enough to give him away.

After an eternity—five seconds?—the door closed. The footsteps faded away.

Pepper sighed in relief and climbed back up to the chair. He reopened the Bailey file, flipping deeper into the stack of papers to the profiles of potential suspects or persons of interest. All men. Each man's summary was only two pages long—one two-sided piece of paper. In the top right corner of each summary was a small black-and-white picture of the man.

Should Pepper feed those men's names into his database and see if anything hit? Or would that just be redundant to what the police had already done through the live computer systems?

The first record was for Luis P. Ortega, of West Barnstable. He was a level-two sex offender with convictions for indecent exposure and assault five years prior. Pepper knew level-two sex offenders were classified as moderately dangerous with a moderate risk of re-offending.

The second was Emilio "Leo" Flammia, from New Albion. He had two convictions for indecent assault and battery on a person aged 14 or older and was also registered as a level-two sex offender.

The third was Casper Yelle, also from New Albion. His dad's number one suspect! As Pepper recalled, Yelle had a felony conviction for assault with intent to commit rape and for open and gross lewdness and lascivious behavior. He was registered as a level-three sex offender.

On this sheet, his dad had written and circled: *also priors— stalking/witness intimidation.*

There were several other notes at the bottom of this sheet.

Lied in interview—why?

High I.Q.?

Ankle monitor—Faraday?

Home on Thurs. nite?

Pepper took a close-up picture of Yelle's photo for Delaney. Then he took a picture of the full page.

He would have to think more about his dad's notes later, in a less compromising position.

Pepper thumbed forward in the file, looking at other potential suspects. The stack of records had to be half an inch thick. He stopped at random on the records of a man named Kyle Lee Jeffries. The man had been convicted of a long list of felonies, including kidnapping and aggravated assault. And he lived very close too—in Orleans. How did someone commit that many felonies, then end up back on the street?

Of course, it was very possible the Snatcher wasn't even in that pile of past offenders. He could be from another area and had recently arrived on the Cape to commit this crime. Or he could have been living nearby all his life with no criminal record.

Using his cell phone, Pepper took a picture of the first page of each other person's record, like he'd done with Yelle's. He didn't have time to copy the entire pile, but he at least wanted their names and addresses. He would add them to his mock file because it seemed productive, even if, deep down, he knew it was probably a waste of time.

Pepper finished and put the file back in the filing cabinet. He was locking the drawer when his dad opened his office door.

Strike three!

"Pepper, damn it!" yelled his dad, about as loud as Pepper had ever heard him yell. A new record.

Shit ensued. And more shit.

For a few minutes Pepper thought his dad would either kill him or die of a burst blood vessel, whichever came first.

The only good thing was his dad had jumped to the

conclusion that Pepper was unlocking the filing cabinet and hadn't actually intruded on the files yet.

He didn't tell him otherwise. He couldn't get a word in anyway—his dad was ranting and yelling and swearing in an amazing stream of anger. He sat there and took it, deserving all of it, and hoping to weather it alive.

A knock at the open door cut off his dad mid-curse.

It was Detective Sweeney.

His dad gave Sweeney a glare which should have sent him running but didn't.

"Sorry, Chief. Sorry, I know you're—" He paused. "I knew you'd want to know right away. Another girl was just kidnapped—this time here in New Albion!"

CHAPTER TWELVE

One hour earlier, the man in the white van parked on the side of Red Cedar Road to change the life of another girl named Emma.

This girl was much like his Emma Bailey, but a year younger at sixteen and a half. And maybe not quite as beautiful in the same way? But still more than pretty enough. This new Emma's last name was Addison, for now.

He knew his target was scheduled to work as a hostess at Sandy's Seafood Restaurant this afternoon. He knew her silver Volkswagen Beetle was having engine troubles and so she had walked to work the last two days. Barely half a mile, with sidewalks the whole way. So she should walk, unless the media shitshow about the Emma Bailey kidnapping had freaked out her parents and they would drive her to work today?

He hoped not.

And he hoped he'd get lucky with traffic. Saturdays on Cape Cod could be a real clusterfuck. Sunburned, exhausted families vacating rental homes and heading home. Stressed-out, hyperactive families arriving for their week in paradise, if they could find the street of their rental house. Traffic was heavier than usual even on back streets. Yep, he'd have to get lucky...

The man in the van hadn't slept for two days. So he didn't feel so great today. Kinda sluggish and confused. He was sitting in the back of the van, peeping through a small slit in the paper which covered the rear windows, when all of that changed. When he saw her!

His blood quickening, he watched her approach. She was small for sixteen years old. Long blonde hair. And a nose stud which would definitely have to go. She looked dark and childlike, walking closer and closer. But her skin color was tanned a light caramel. He couldn't see her big eyes—she had sunglasses on. But he knew it was her.

He checked his digital watch. 3:33 PM. What a sweet coincidence! Like time was a cosmic slot machine, and he'd just hit the freaking jackpot: 3-3-3. It gave him an extra burst of confidence.

He was *so* excited now. His body tensed, poised for action. He could *hear* the blood flooding his ears, making them ring and tingle.

Two cars with bicycles hanging from their trunks drove past in the other direction and quickly were gone. No other vehicles were in sight at the moment...

When the teen reached the van, the man burst out the back. And Emma Addison froze right there, her eyes like saucers, like it was damn fate.

He grabbed her golden hair and gave her a love zap with his stun gun—just enough to lock up her muscles and knock her down. He carefully lifted her into the back of the van. Climbed in and closed the doors.

Good, good, good!

Some quick loops of duct tape to bind her arms and legs and an extra strip across her pretty mouth. Then he searched her pockets and took out her phone. Live and learn!

He tucked her in with a pile of blankets so she wouldn't be

hurt as he drove. She'd be fine until he transferred her to the Heart.

Then he quickly checked outside through the slit in the paper covering the rear windows. Nobody in sight. No alarm.

He crawled forward to the front seat. Looked all around for any vehicles or pedestrians. Again, nobody!

He was getting better at this. Or was having a very lucky day, which was a damn rare thing for him. He usually got the other kind, lately.

Just in case his luck went sideways again, he took the Walther P22 pistol from his pocket and slipped it into the crack beside his seat. Rolled down his window and chucked the girl's phone across the road, into the tall grass.

All set?

He checked in all directions again. A Toyota Corolla drove toward him, face on. He saw the driver was an impossibly old man in a gray fedora hat, barely tall enough to see over his dashboard.

The little old man cruised slowly past, never slowing, never turning to look at the van or the man behind the wheel. No problem.

So it was the little old man's lucky day, too.

Moments later, the man in the white van was driving his precious cargo toward safety. Would his luck hold too?

He still felt tired. He also felt like he was speeding, which he knew would be a boneheaded screwup, what with all the cops out to get him. He looked at his speedometer and he was only going twenty in a what—thirty or thirty-five zone? But it definitely seemed like his van was moving faster than it really was.

In his side-view mirror, it looked like the car behind him, a little blue thing, was right on his ass. But when he stopped at a red light, the blue car kept driving...it was farther behind than he'd thought. And his hand was trembling something fierce. Well, okay...

Did he have time to fire up some crank? Clear his head? No, he'd have to wait. There wasn't a second to lose.

The man drove carefully, his mind bouncing.

Both of the girls he'd gathered were named Emma, which would be a minor pain in the ass. Too confusing.

Emma One and Emma Two? No, that was stupid. Sounded like freaking Dr. Seuss.

They'd work it out.

And the two Emmas would probably fight over him a bit. A struggle to be his favorite. Typical. It made him wonder which actually would be his favorite. He smiled.

He was already developing a thing with Emma Bailey. The way she sassed him back, like a love-hate, opposites-attract thing. He liked her fire.

As the man approached the last turn before he'd be home free, he saw a police car pulled over at the side of the road.

Here we go, he thought. The big test. This was it. He'd either sail by like no big deal, or this was the real beginning of the end. He touched his Walther P22 for luck. He hated the idea he'd be outgunned by a cop's bigger handgun but too late to whine now, huh?

He hated cops, just like every other part of the authoritarian bureaucracy which had collectively ruined this great country and his damn life. He'd shoot first if necessary. The Walther would be more than fine from close up. And he totally knew he would pull the trigger like...well, just watch him. Cool as a cat.

He'd done three years the hard way after getting caught for that other felony thing last time. Shorter than his public defender had predicted, but every minute had been miserable and suffocating. Humiliating. Having to deal with all those idiots and animals. Going back to prison for any amount of time was definitely *not* in the plan.

Emma Addison would be overdue at work by now. The restaurant manager on duty might have already called her cell phone, which was lying on the grass where he'd grabbed her. The manager would get no freaking answer.

Then the manager would call Emma's home because some teens were unreliable. He'd ask her family: was Emma coming to work today? Everyone would realize faster than a lightning bug farts that something was wrong. They'd get hit by the quick, hard panic that comes when something important gets taken from you. The man knew that emotion and planned to never feel it again.

So, maybe forty-five minutes total until her parents would call 911? Give or take? Possibly the cop wouldn't have even heard yet that Emma Addison was gone.

Trust the plan... Trust the man...

The man drove his van past the cop, slow and steady. Other than his right hand, which started shaking like a motherfucker. Which would be a hell of a problem if he needed to use his pistol.

But the man saw in his rearview mirror that the cop car stayed put on the side of the road.

With relief flooding through him like hot water, the man rounded a curve in the road and he lost the cop from view. He made his next right, and for the rest of the drive to safety he followed the same path he'd taken with Emma Bailey.

Two down...one to go...

Some people thought he wasn't too bright because he didn't have a college degree. How could a piece of paper make you smart? The internet had everything you wanted to know, if you looked in the right places.

So he was an expert about the New World Order. Knew about their plans to depopulate from seven billion down to five hundred million. Probably by releasing a virus. Who could say for sure? Yep, changes were coming, and his nuts would not get caught in the middle of it. Not him or the girls.

He was a bit worried about Emma Addison because her family was rich—was she going to act all spoiled? There wasn't room for any princesses in the new family.

He had another epic sudden surge of emotion and conviction that it would all work out. They'd be happy together. Like the fires of heaven, filling his heart. All of them would be happy. He suddenly *knew* it, deep in his gut. Which they had to be... It was the key to the whole thing.

Because what's more important than family?

CHAPTER THIRTEEN

Maybe it was the next day.

Emma Bailey had no way of knowing. Between the drugs and the darkness of her eye mask, she didn't have a clue. All she knew was it wasn't a bad dream. Someone had snatched her. She was in some dark place that her kidnapper put her.

Emma had spent a long time banging her feet against the metal floor, trying to make as much noise as she could to attract someone's attention. It'd sounded loud to her. But she didn't know whether any noise made it through the walls.

No one had come. Probably no one had heard her. She would try again later...

Now she focused on the miserable fact that she really, really needed to pee again. She'd wet her jeans a long while ago—during the night? It was wicked uncomfortable sitting there in wet pants like a stupid toddler.

She heard a metal noise, like a metallic groan, and then the clatter of feet on metal again.

Had someone found her? Was she saved?

As her eye mask came off, she realized no. Shrek was back.

She recognized his shape from the light of his lantern even before she saw the stupid green rubber face.

Shrek kneeled at her side. She could see the mask and smell him—a mix of sweat and dirt and something else. He removed the gag from her mouth.

"Good afternoon, Emma," the man said, his voice muffled through his lame mask. "Did you sleep okay?"

She didn't answer him. She was still super scared. And super furious. But she was also thinking now, something she hadn't been doing before. *Let's see how he likes the silent treatment*, she thought.

"Less of a potty mouth now you need to use the potty, hey?" Shrek laughed.

Again, Emma kept her silence.

"Well, I've got a nice surprise for you. Hang on and we'll get you a bathroom break." Shrek bent over her, holding the light near her feet, her wrists, and then her waist. Checking she was still completely and hopelessly bound. Which she was.

"Back in the jiffy," Shrek said.

He left the lantern on the floor out of reach. Then he shuffled away. She saw him go up a metal ladder and disappear.

Where was she? In some secret bunker under a house? God, no wonder he didn't mind when she screamed.

A few minutes later, she heard a soft thump and then feet down the metal ladder again. Shrek dragged something large across the floor, and as he reached the lantern, she could see it was another girl.

Oh my God.

He pulled the new girl to the wall across from Emma. She looked about Emma's age, probably a little younger. Long blonde hair. She had a cute little diamond stud through her nostril.

Emma watched Shrek use some kind of plastic strap to bind her ankles and her hands in front of her. Then he took something else which looked like a bicycle chain. He circled it around her waist, twisted it, and then secured it to the wall. Like Emma, the girl wouldn't be able to move more than a few inches.

"I'll introduce you two later when she feels better," said Shrek. "But now it's your turn." He wrapped a longer chain around Emma's waist and snapped on a lock.

"Okay, I'm cutting you loose except for this longer chain. You'll be able to get to that chair to go to the bathroom. This isn't a chance to do something stupid, unless you want to pee your pants from now on." Then he cut her ankles and hands free.

Shit. Emma had a little more room to move, but was otherwise powerless. Shrek had shuffled away toward the ladder, taking the lantern with him. Emma had just enough light to see a metal chair about five feet in the other direction. Her hands and her feet were all pins and needles as blood flowed back into them. She got to her feet despite the sloped metal floor.

Was she maybe in a buried school bus? She'd read about some crazy person who did that to a bunch of kids years ago. Some other crazy person even built an underground bunker out of a bunch of school buses.

Was Shrek some kind of end-of-the-world survivalist nutball? Was he planning to repopulate the earth, starting with her and the new girl? Emma shuddered. Not a chance she was going along with *that* plan!

Emma carefully shuffled toward the chair and inspected it. It was a metal frame chair with a rough hole cut in the wooden seat and some kind of bucket beneath it. Like redneck camping gear, she thought. But she pulled down her jeans and did what she had to do. It was such a relief!

As she peed, she ran her hands around the arms and legs of the chair, feeling for anything loose which she could quietly take as a weapon. But she found nothing.

"Where's the toilet paper?" she asked when she finally

finished.

Shrek didn't answer.

"Seriously? You mastermind these kidnappings but you don't think to, like, get toilet paper? So you're a big creep *and* a big idiot? Congratulations! You obviously thought this thing through as best you could."

"Our mistake," Shrek said. "I'll get some for later. Now you need to go back to your spot and sit down against the wall again."

Emma thought about ways she could resist. She could stay at the toilet chair, refusing to do what he said. Or she could go back to her spot, wait until he got close to bind her up again, and then fucking attack him. Maybe kick him, or punch him in the dumb mask.

But Shrek was a crapload bigger than her. And she was chained at the waist. It wasn't like she could surprise him and then make a run for it. *Damn!*

She didn't know what else to do, so she shuffled back to her spot and sat down like he said. She was straight across from the new girl with a foot or two of space between their feet. The girl was slumped against the wall, head to one side, unconscious.

Shrek kneeled beside her and reattached the shorter bike chain around her waist. Then he zipped together her feet with plastic straps, like cops use when they don't have handcuffs.

The man gave her two sandwich rolls with what tasted like turkey and cheese inside. She'd been gluten free since June because of beach season, but she didn't care about that now. She wolfed down the food. She'd needed to go to the bathroom so bad she hadn't even realized how hungry she was.

"If you want something to drink, you need to ask me for it," said Shrek.

Asswipe. What was this, some kind of lame psychology trick? "Fine," she said. "I want something to drink."

"Politely."

"Please give me some crappy water!"

He paused, as if he would jerk her around some more, but then handed her a water bottle.

The water had the same chalky taste as last time. But she kept drinking. What choice did she have?

"Can I take a little walk? Please?" she asked, wiping her mouth. She needed to figure out where she was and whether there was a way to escape.

Shrek laughed. "Sorry."

But she didn't give up. "My legs are cramped up," she lied. "You need to keep me healthy. My parents'll pay good money to get me back. We aren't rich, but they'll try. You need to call them. And for now I need a little exercise. Even murderers on death row get exercise."

He didn't answer. He just kneeled beside her again and zipped a plastic binding on her wrists. She tried to keep her wrists apart a bit, and the binding ended up slightly looser this time. Score one for Emma.

She could already feel whatever shit he'd put in her water starting to work.

"Sit tight," said Shrek. "I'll introduce you to the new girl when I get back. She's younger than you, so try to set a good example." Then he squeezed the corners of her jaw to force her mouth open and fastened her gag back in place. It was cold and plastic and she thought she was going to throw up from the taste.

She'd been about to tell him to take a walk for her—right in front of a speeding truck. But he left her leaning there against the cold wall, unable to speak or even move much. The eye mask slipped over her eyes and she fell into darkness as Shrek's feet clattered away.

Her last drowsy thoughts were: Who was the new girl? Where was this psycho holding them? And please oh please...was *anyone* coming to save them?

CHAPTER FOURTEEN

On Sunday morning, Pepper woke up like he'd been slapped by a cold hand.

A second kidnapping. This time in his own town.

Pepper was humiliated about getting caught snooping around yesterday by his dad, but he still wanted to help. How could he not? He couldn't just watch the nightmare unfolding around him and ignore it. He couldn't sit at home. He had to find out how things were going.

He didn't put on his cadet uniform. However, he dressed a little better than if he was just going to bum around town for the day. Then he drove to the police station.

Three TV trucks were out front with a small crowd of civilians. Pepper used his ID to swipe himself in the side door.

He was walking past the conference room when the door opened and Detective Kevin Sweeney came out. Pepper glanced in and saw his dad and two men in suits that he didn't recognize.

His dad glanced out at Pepper, then shut the door without stopping talking.

Sweeney walked toward the coffee room so Pepper followed

him. He found Sweeney sniffing the coffee pot and making a face before pouring himself a cup.

"Hey, kid," said Sweeney. The detective was usually friendly to Pepper—he seemed to get a kick out of him.

"Don't drink that crap. I'll make you a fresh pot," offered Pepper. "You must have had a long night."

"A hell of a night," said Sweeney, sitting at a table, waiting for the coffee to brew. He looked pale and exhausted. "Do you know the new missing girl, Emma Addison?"

"No." Pepper had already heard the girl's name—it was all over the news and the online version of the *Boston Herald*.

"She was walking to work. She hostesses at Sandy's."

"Seriously?" asked Pepper. "I ate there two nights ago!" And he faintly remembered a teenage girl at the hostess stand. Blonde hair? Kinda pretty? Maybe with a nose stud?

"We've been going at it all night and we've got zip. Thank God the FBI's down from Boston."

That must have been the two men in the conference room. FBI agents. Just seeing them gave Pepper more hope for Emma Bailey and Emma Addison.

Sweeney sighed. "They've got people who can build a profile of the Snatcher. Try to figure out what makes him tick. What mistakes he might have made...where he'd likely take the girls."

"He must know the Lower Cape pretty well to get away clean both times," offered Pepper.

"Absolutely. We had everyone out all night, same as the other shops up and down the Cape. Roadblocks everywhere, but nothing. It's like he just disappears."

Sweeney got up and poured the stale coffee down the sink and held out his mug. Pepper carefully poured fresh coffee for him.

Sergeant Weisner appeared in the doorway. She made a face. "Pepper, what're you doing here on a Sunday?"

"Just trying to be helpful."

Weisner gave him a look which said *good luck with that.* "Sweeney, we got another batch of tips for you to look at. All kinds of random crap. The Greenhead Snatcher is planning to escape by boat. The Greenhead Snatcher has a plane. It's like the public's gone nuts."

"Or they're all fishing for the reward," said Sweeney.

Weisner turned to go, then looked back to Pepper. "You don't have to go home...but you can't stay here. Go! I don't want to see you in this station until Monday morning." With a final glare, she left them.

"Thanks for the coffee, kid. And don't worry about Weisner," said Sweeney. "The second Emma lives on her street and she's beyond pissed off. Totally gone. Just stay out of her way and watch us find this bastard. And if Weisner gets to him first? He'll be begging for a nice safe prison cell."

As Pepper climbed into his truck, his phone rang. It was Delaney Lynn and she was upset.

She was at Sandy's Seafood Restaurant. The manager had called in the whole staff for a morning meeting. But the police were there, and they'd interviewed them each individually. Had anyone suspicious come to the restaurant recently? Did Emma have any stalkers she knew of? Questions like that.

"What'd you tell them?" he asked.

"The truth! I didn't see anything strange. Pepper, I'm freaking out, that poor girl! Her family!"

"The police are doing everything possible," he said lamely.

"I've got to go over there," she said.

"Where?"

"To Emma's house. They must be shattered!"

"I'm sure they are. But you can't just show up. The police'll be interviewing them. You really don't want to—"

"Pepper, I wasn't asking for permission! If the family sends me away, fine. But I knew her! I've talked to her parents a ton of times at Sandy's. I just want to hug them. And cry with them. It's the least I can do."

Pepper knew how she felt. He wanted to help too. He wanted to be all in.

"Let's go together," he said.

CHAPTER FIFTEEN

Pepper didn't know much about real estate, but he knew a multi-million dollar view when he saw it.

The Addison family's house was bigger than average for New Albion. It was near the crest of a hill on Dill Beach Way, about a block inland from the ocean, but the elevation gave them a broad view of the Atlantic Ocean below.

A New Albion police cruiser was parked in front of the Addisons' house. The vehicle was empty.

Pepper parked behind it, and they walked to the front door. Delaney rang the bell.

Officer Dooley, the redhead, answered the door. "Pepper Ryan! What's up?"

"Hey, ah, Dooley." Pepper couldn't remember his first name. "This is Delaney Lynn. She's a friend of the Addisons. She wanted to see how they're doing, if that's cool?"

And Dooley stepped aside to let them in. Just like that.

The Addisons were together in their big kitchen with a handful of friends. Mrs. Addison, an attractive middle-aged woman with frosted blonde hair, gave Delaney a big hug, and they both began to cry.

Mrs. Addison introduced them to three teenage girls. Emma's best friends.

Delaney also hugged a younger blonde-haired girl—Emma Addison's only sister, Shauna. She was about fourteen years old. Shauna looked scared, upset and vulnerable, like she would collapse any second.

Pepper shook Mr. Addison's hand and said he was sorry about everything. It sounded lame, but Mr. Addison just nodded and said nothing.

"Pepper's dad is Police Chief Ryan," said Delaney, wiping her eyes. "And he works for the police too."

Pepper needed to explain. "I'm not—"

"Is there any news?" interrupted Mrs. Addison.

"I, ah, haven't heard any developments, but everyone's doing their best. And the FBI's arrived and they're helping too."

"The FBI?" Mrs. Addison looked encouraged.

Pepper took the opening to ask what he'd been wondering about the most. "Do you know if your Emma has any connection to the other girl, Emma Bailey? Did they know each other?"

Mrs. Addison shook her head. "No. We told the detectives that already. Why? Do the police think there's a connection?"

"Not that I can say. I was curious, though, since they're close to the same age and live in nearby towns."

"Our Emma plays for her high school soccer team," said Mrs. Addison. "So she's played against Eastham High. Does the other girl play soccer?"

Pepper felt stupid, asking questions with no basic knowledge. "The detectives will check any sports connections or anything else," he said.

"Well, if you're talking to them too, the Baileys? Please tell them we're so, so sorry for..." And Mrs. Addison began sobbing heavily.

Mr. Addison enveloped his wife in a hug. "Why're you here again?" he asked Pepper.

Uh-oh. "Ah, Delaney wanted to tell you how sad she was about everything and make sure—"

Mr. Addison cut him off with an upraised hand. "This is a horrible time. It's like we're stuck in some nightmare. I think you'll understand we'd like to have some privacy. Now."

Pepper felt terrible.

Officer Dooley was in the kitchen doorway, and he raised his red eyebrows and jerked his thumb over his shoulder toward the door.

Delaney gave Mrs. Addison another hug, and then Pepper accompanied her out of the house.

That hadn't gone well.

But one of Emma's friends named Juliet followed them outside. "Hey wait!" said the girl. Juliet was a skinny redhead with milky pale skin. When they'd met her inside, she hadn't said a word. Just repeatedly blew her nose. She still had a wad of Kleenex in her hand.

"That sucked," the girl said. "You were just being nice."

Delaney gave the girl a long hug.

The girl blew her nose again, then said, "I just wanted to tell you guys, because I wasn't here when the cops interviewed everyone—I don't think Emma knew the other girl. The other Emma. We were super close, and Emma would have said something after, you know... When that Emma got snatched."

"Thank you," said Pepper.

The girl sniffled. "It had to be the sketchy guy at the restaurant. That's who the cops need to look at."

"Which guy?"

"The manager guy, Scooter something. Emma called him Scooter the Stalker, he hung around the hostess desk so much."

"Scooter McCord, the assistant manager?" asked Delaney, sounding skeptical.

"He asked her to go to a movie with him. He said it was as friends, but Emma knew he wanted more. And he's like, ancient! She laughed at him. Really shot him down."

Scooter had looked to Pepper like he was in his early thirties. Was that ancient to a teen?

"Did you tell the detectives about Scooter asking Emma out and her saying no?" asked Pepper.

"I haven't talked to them yet."

Pepper recited for Juliet the main number to the station, which Juliet quickly saved in her phone. "Ask for Detective Kevin Sweeney," he said. "Tell him what you told me. It'll help."

"Pepper Ryan?"

Pepper turned and Sergeant Weisner was standing on the flagstone walkway, looking as pissed off as ever, her hands on her hips. Her mouth was open—with shock? Or anger? "I can't believe I'm seeing your face again today." Weisner never looked too healthy, but she definitely looked redder than usual.

"You said I didn't have to go home..." he tried. But he gave her a wave of surrender as he spoke, hustling away to his truck with Delaney.

———

"Scooter McCord? No way!" said Delaney. "Sure, he flirts with everyone at work, but not very well. You saw him a couple days ago, the redheaded guy on my ass when you were in for dinner? He's a pest, but I can't see him kidnapping anyone."

"Do you know if he was working Saturday afternoon? And last Thursday night?"

"I'm not sure. I can check."

Pepper thought for a bit. "Have you ever seen him driving a white van?"

"Just the restaurant's catering van. It's white."

"But it has the restaurant's name on its side, right?"

"Yes, but the sign just clips on. It's kind of cheap. He could have taken it off, no problem."

Pepper was about to ask more questions when he noticed another vehicle parked inches from his rear bumper. It was an old gray minivan with a dent in the driver's side door. And a man was leaning against Pepper's truck. A further bad development to Pepper's day. It was Fester Timmins, the town cop wannabe. The man had his thick arms folded, which pushed out his man-boobs. Not a great look.

"Pepper Ryan! Pepper. Ryan..." Timmins said it just like that. As if his emphasis carried some special weight.

"Hey, Fester," he said. He would have climbed in his truck, but Timmins was leaning against the driver's door. So Pepper waited.

"I go by Francis now. My legal name. Nobody calls me Fester anymore. What're you doing here at the victim's house? Police cadet special assignment?"

So Timmins knew he was a police cadet? "Just visiting the family," Pepper said. "Passing along our condolences. Why?"

"Just seemed funny, you here at the victim's house."

I could say the same about you, thought Pepper.

The man gave him a big smile. "But since we're both here, let's touch base. Any good leads?"

Was this guy serious? "I'm not involved in the Greenhead Snatcher investigation," Pepper said. "I'm doing old case stuff in a computer database. Totally out of the loop."

Timmins looked skeptical. "Really? You gotta be curious, Ryan. It's what separates us from the monkeys."

"Yeah?" asked Pepper. "I thought monkeys are curious."

"Like Curious George," offered Delaney from the other side of his truck. "He's definitely a monkey."

"Yeah, in a picture book," scoffed Timmins. "I'm serious. I've gotta do what I can, find out what's up with this Snatcher dude."

"You after the reward?" asked Pepper.

"Reward?" Timmins laughed. "I'm planning to hang out my shingle as a private investigator any week now. It'll sure help business if I bring down the Greenhead Snatcher."

A private eye? Usually people in that line of work were ex-law enforcement. But whatever.

"Well, I saw you on TV. You know what they say—there's no bad publicity!" Pepper eased Fester Timmins to the side and climbed into his truck to drive Delaney home.

Delaney was shaking, so Pepper pulled over at the end of the Addisons' block.

A tear ran down her pale face. He reached over to hold her, and she fit in his arms like the most natural thing in the world.

"That Fester guy made this seem like a big game. But it's horrible," Delaney said, her voice trembling. "It must be like a bad dream for her parents. And I can't imagine what Emma is going through. Both Emmas..."

Pepper suddenly felt guilty about his own unofficial dalliances with the Bailey case. Was he treating it like a game too? No, he was just trying to help in his own small way. Not for the big reward, or to win a job in law enforcement.

He gave Delaney a hug and then kissed her wet cheek. To comfort her, but it still sent electricity through him. Her wet strands of hair stuck to her face, and she looked young and vulnerable.

"I'm not sticking around the Cape much longer," she said.

"These snatchings have me pretty freaked out. And I'm going nowhere musically on the Cape. Something tells me we won't get famous with Brad and the Pitts." She laughed with a shake in her voice. "I'm going to talk to Dennis Cole some more and see how he can help. Maybe I'll give Nashville a shot."

"Nashville? You seem more like a rocker to me."

"Hey, I grew up on an onion farm in Georgia! But I'm nervous about doing it alone. I probably need a partner."

It shocked Pepper, what she might be saying.

Tell her about Harvard, dumbass, he thought. *And tell her you'll think about Nashville too!* But he didn't.

Maybe deep down he didn't want to make any more promises he would later regret. Or he knew he wasn't free to just pick up and take off with Delaney—too many other people were counting on him to keep his commitments.

As his mind raced, trying to decide, Pepper remembered the sharp advice Gus Bullard, his mean old hockey coach, seemed to always come back to: *Pylon, you ever notice how it's always someone else's fault, not yours?*

But Coach Bullard was a jerk and a bully. Pepper would not let that guy's old rantings mess up his decisions now.

After too long of a pause, Pepper said, "Seriously, you'll be great." He looked down at her in his arms, and she gave him a thin smile that he couldn't quite read.

CHAPTER SIXTEEN

When Pepper reached the Langham Arms to drop off Delaney, he texted her the black-and-white photo of Casper Yelle, the man who might be the Greenhead Snatcher.

"He looks kind of familiar," Delaney said, frowning.

"You've probably seen him around the parking lot. Or at work? It's a small town... But tell me if you see him again."

After a final long hug, Delaney left him.

Then Pepper did something he hadn't mentioned to her—he drove to Eastham to talk to the Baileys.

Traffic was typical for a Sunday on the Cape. Slower than reasonable and most people didn't know where they were going. Or they weren't going anywhere in a hurry... So, tourists. Pepper tried to relax and go with the flow but completely failed. He was too impatient to talk to Emma Bailey's family.

He arrived at their home about twenty minutes later. It was a quiet, modest street. The Baileys lived in a snug Cape-style house with faded cedar shingles. Their home was less than half as large as the Addisons'. And further inland from the water. So, a very different price range. But overall, it was very similar in size and style to Pepper's own family home. A classic Cape house.

Pepper wanted to find an answer to the big question eating at him—why Emma Bailey? And why Emma Addison? Were they both just horribly unlucky? Or was there some connection between them? A connection that might be a triangle, with the third point being the Greenhead Snatcher?

There was only one way to find out.

He saw a Barnstable Sheriff's Department vehicle parked at the curb, so he continued past and parked half a block down from the Baileys.

The deputy was probably there to protect the family from news reporters and random voyeurs seeking a glimpse of the victim's home and family. Pepper had gotten a good look at the deputy as he drove past—a huge guy who looked like he was texting on his phone, head down.

Pepper walked rapidly back to the Baileys' house, cutting across their lawn to the front door.

He didn't know the Baileys and wondered if they would talk to a random stranger who showed up at their door while they were in shock and grieving. It had only been three days since the Greenhead Snatcher abducted their daughter. Two days since New Albion police arrested several Bailey relatives at Yelle's apartment.

But Pepper had to try.

He reached the Baileys' front door and rang the bell.

"Hey!" came a bellow from the direction of the street. The deputy must have finished texting and noticed the person at the Baileys' door. Pepper didn't turn to look. Innocent and confident, right?

A balding middle-aged white man wearing an untucked golf shirt opened the front door. He had a swarm of blue tattoos on both forearms. Mr. Bailey?

"Desmond? Who is it?" a woman's voice asked from somewhere in the house. The voice sounded tired, scared and hopeful. Every time the doorbell rang, it could be news about Emma, good or bad. Every ring must almost give them a heart attack.

"I'm Pepper Ryan," he said to the man. "Can I talk to your family for just a minute? I have a message for you from the Addison family. Emma Addison's parents?"

In his peripheral vision, Pepper saw two distractions. One was the massive deputy trotting up the front walk. Shaking the Cape.

The second was—God's truth—a tan Jeep Wrangler that cruised past with Casper Yelle's pale face in the driver's seat. Pepper was 99% certain.

Back for another look? The creep didn't learn his lesson last time?

"Sorry, Mr. Bailey," said the deputy as he arrived on the porch. He was a white guy, probably in his late thirties. Plenty of muscle but also plenty of fat. An ex-college athlete who saw more food than exercise these days? The deputy was sweating heavily.

"Just for a minute? It might help," Pepper pleaded to Mr. Bailey.

A woman appeared behind Mr. Bailey. "You have a message from the Addisons?"

"Absolutely."

Mr. Bailey sighed and said to the deputy, "It's okay, Len. This is a personal visit. But probably a very short one."

Pepper didn't tell the deputy he'd seen Casper Yelle, since by now the man and his Jeep were long gone.

With Deputy Len crammed back in his patrol car, Pepper sat with Mr. and Mrs. Bailey in the living room. The Baileys sat on a sofa and he sat in a wing chair.

Pepper could see a dozen pictures of their daughter Emma on

the mantel above the fireplace. One in a ballet costume. Another in a fancy dress—a junior prom? She had shoulder-length dark brown hair and was very pretty. In each picture Emma had a mischievous smile.

There were also four pictures of a younger boy, also with brown hair. Obviously the brother who'd seen the snatching.

"I visited Emma Addison's family earlier today," said Pepper. "They said if I saw you, to let you know how sorry they are for what you're going through too."

"I'd love to talk to the Addisons," said Mrs. Bailey. "They're the only ones who really know how we feel right now. The—" Her voice choked off, and she began sobbing quietly. Like she didn't have the strength anymore to cry louder. Her husband hugged her and rubbed her back.

"Why would they expect you to see us too?" asked Mr. Bailey, sounding annoyed.

Pepper regretted coming here and felt like a complete asshole. What the hell was he doing?

"I work for the New Albion police," he said. *Not a lie. Not the whole truth either...* "I was following up with them to see if they had remembered any connection between their daughter and yours."

"You look young for a cop," said Mr. Bailey.

Pepper had to keep pushing. "Do you know if your Emma knows Emma Addison?"

Mrs. Bailey was looking at him funny now too. "The other police asked us about this over and over. We told them we don't know any connection."

Pepper nodded, trying to look soothing. And professional. "Absolutely. I wanted to make sure you haven't remembered anything since you talked to the detectives. Any little connection."

A boy walked into the room and stopped. He was around seven years old. Had to be Emma's little brother, Mason.

"What's going on?" the boy asked. He sounded even younger than he looked.

"This man's from the police. He's checking to make sure we didn't remember anything that'd help bring Emma home."

"Call me Pepper," he said to the boy, smiling. Fake Officer Friendly. Pepper could remember being his age. He'd avoided adults like they were aliens.

"I remembered something," said Mason.

"Something you didn't tell before?" asked Mr. Bailey. The boy's father suddenly sounded anxious. Excited.

The boy nodded. "I remembered I saw the Greenhead guy somewhere before."

Pepper got excited too but tried not to show it. "Do you remember where you saw him?"

"I'm not sure. I think on TV."

"TV? What show did you see him on? The news?"

"I forget. But it was on TV."

Pepper thought for a bit, then asked, "What made you remember that?"

"I saw the news about Emma and they were talking about him. And I pictured what he looked like when it happened. I never saw his face too good. Just his green head."

"What did he look like?"

"He looked like you, but older. And with a fatter face. And a lot meaner."

"That's great, Mason," he said. He would have to pass along this tip to Detective Sweeney. Someone would follow up, interview the boy more thoroughly and show him a photo six-pack again. "Can you think about that some more? Maybe you'll remember something else. It'd be a big help."

The boy looked happier. The parents looked more optimistic too. Pepper was glad his visit had helped raise their spirits a bit.

"I won't take any more of your time," he said. "But please

know everyone's working hard to bring Emma home. Both Emmas."

"You promise?" asked Mason, brightening even more.

"I promise. I'll bring Emma home... Or I'll die trying." As soon as the words came out of Pepper's mouth, he realized how stupidly mistaken they were. Crazy promises that could only give false hope. *Writing checks his dumb butt can't cash...*

Pepper's cheeks reddened and he made a hasty goodbye. Hoping the Baileys wouldn't take his promise to heart. Hoping they'd forget. Because Pepper knew he never would.

Idiot.

———

Pepper was driving back to New Albion when his cell phone buzzed with a text from Delaney. *Freaking out! U there?* it said.

What's wrong? he texted back.

After a pause she replied: *Someone outside!!!*

Then his phone rang. "I need you to come over!" said Delaney, her voice high and panicked.

"Tell me what happened."

Delaney started sobbing. "Someone was at my door. I heard footsteps and somebody knocked. I'd just showered, so I didn't open it. I just looked through the peekhole."

"Was it Casper Yelle? The guy in the picture?"

"I couldn't see anyone. But then the person shook the doorknob real hard, so I backed away, you know? And then the person kicked my door three times, really hard. So I ran into the bathroom and called you. I'm kinda freaking out here... I think it was the Greenhead Snatcher!"

CHAPTER SEVENTEEN

Pepper was a ten minute drive from Delaney's apartment. He made it in five.

He'd told her to hang up, call 911, but she didn't want to overreact. So he stayed on the phone with her. At his suggestion, she checked the lock on her door and closed her blinds.

At one point she said she heard footsteps near her door again. When she looked through the peephole, the fishbowl view was empty.

Pepper hastily parked in the Langham Arms apartment complex's large lot and jogged toward Delaney's building, which was the left side of the U shape of three buildings. Each building had exterior walkways, like at a cheap motor inn.

Delaney was on the second floor, but Pepper didn't know which apartment exactly. He'd never gotten closer to her place than the parking lot.

He took the shaky metal stairs two at a time up to the green fake-turf carpeting of the second floor. "Hey, I'm here, which apartment?" he asked into his phone.

Pepper saw a door open halfway down the hall. Delaney's face peered out. Then she stepped into the hallway in a

Ramones half-shirt and faded cutoff jeans and gave him a thin smile.

"Thank God! Pepper, I'm *so* sorry! It seems silly now, but I was totally freaking out!"

The door next to her apartment opened, and a tiny elderly woman in a pink bathrobe stepped out.

"Oh, it's you making all the fuss!" the lady said to Delaney. "Who's this?"

"Hello," said Pepper, smiling.

"You got a lot of male visitors today. Lots of fuss." The lady sniffed—clearly she wasn't a big fan of male visitors or fuss.

"Did you see the person outside her door a little while ago?" asked Pepper.

"The last fellow sniffing around? I saw him through my blinds. He came and left, then came back. I don't like it, we got enough noise here."

"What did the guy look like?"

"Tall like you. He was wearing a hoodie and sunglasses...he looked like a drug sniffer! I almost called building management, but then the guy took off around the corner."

Pepper had seen no video surveillance cameras for the parking lot, the stairs or the hallway. He showed the neighbor the grainy picture of Casper Yelle, but she couldn't say if he was the man in the hallway.

"This used to be a nice place," she sniffed, then shuffled back into her apartment, slamming her door.

"You must feel pretty protected with a neighbor like her," Pepper joked.

"We'd better go inside before she calls 911," laughed Delaney. She looked like she was feeling better already.

Pepper followed her in. Her half-shirt revealed the first verse of the pretty script tattoo down her back, which he now recognized as the opening lines to "American Girl" by Tom Petty and the Heartbreakers. The rest of the song disappeared into the back of her cutoff jeans, but he could imagine the lines...

Delaney closed the door and gave Pepper a huge hug. "I'm still a little freaked out," she admitted. "Can you just stay a while, take my mind off it? The two missing Emmas...and to think the guy who snatched them might live in the next building over!"

Casper Yelle? "He's not the only suspect," cautioned Pepper. "Maybe he did it, maybe not. I'd like to see some real evidence which puts him at one of the kidnappings when it happened."

"Could he have had a partner?"

"Possibly. Kidnappers usually act alone, though." Pepper had learned at the police station that the FBI had confirmed this for the kidnapping task force.

Delaney shivered. "Let's talk about something else," she said. She pushed up against him, and without thinking he put his arm around her. Gave her shoulder a squeeze.

"I was alone in the bathroom, totally losing it," she said in a quiet voice. "I just wanted to be someplace as far away from here as possible."

Pepper hugged her again. Then he smiled down at her. "I know the perfect place."

CHAPTER EIGHTEEN

"I love this guy!" said Delaney.

Unfortunately for Pepper, she was talking about Zac Brown and his song that filled the truck cab. She had taken charge of the radio as he drove to their surprise destination.

"Aha!" laughed Pepper. "So you're a little bit country!"

She punched his shoulder. "More than a little!" She explained she'd grown up on a small farm in Vidalia, Georgia.

"You're ridin' with a former Teen Miss Vidalia Onion, thank you very much!" she said, putting on a thicker southern accent.

He laughed.

She shared that besides growing a lot of onions, they'd raised cows, chickens and geese. Killed their own farm animals for food. "You should see me with an axe!" she laughed.

"Hey, fair warning. I get it, you're a badass."

She pinched Pepper's side. "No, I'm a farm girl. You've got to be tough to survive."

She turned up the radio, and they sang along with Zac. Fucking great vocalist—you could tell Zac Brown meant what he sang. That's what Pepper was always trying to do, but he wasn't sure how successful he was yet.

Delaney started laughing when he pulled into the parking lot of Pirate's Cove Mini Golf in South Yarmouth.

"Oh my God, Pepper!" she laughed. "I haven't done mini golf in *so* long! Like, since I was a teenager!"

Pepper had been a teenager last year. He just said, "You'll probably be real rusty."

She punched his shoulder. "And this place looks *amazing!*"

It actually was amazing. Pirate's Cove was the Mount Everest of mini golf. Its holes were steep, twisty and tricky, weaving up and down a hill around a gigantic pirate's ship resting in a fake lagoon. It could be an intimidating test for rookies or the uncoordinated.

Pepper had been on dates at Pirate's Cove starting in middle school—it was always a great way to have fun and flirt and chill out on a warm summer afternoon.

He decided he'd take it easy on her so she wouldn't feel bad. He wanted her to have an escape from the recent bad events back in New Albion.

After Pepper paid, they picked a colored ball and putter, then headed to the Blackbeard Course. Delaney stepped up and put her green ball on the rubber mat. "Okay, honey," she said, her hands now on her little hips. "What's the bet?"

Bet? "Ah, loser buys ice cream?"

She laughed. "What're you, twelve? How about winner gets to decide where we go and what we do next? Anything goes. You up for it?"

Pepper's mind began racing with all kinds of dirty possibilities which probably had nothing to do with what she had in mind.

But he said fine, whatever. Tried to sound casual and not too horny at all.

Besides, maybe a little bet would help her focus on the mini golf and forget the Greenhead Snatcher situation for a minute.

There's nothing less stressful than playing mini golf on Cape Cod on a warm summer afternoon.

Or so he thought.

It turned out to be pretty stressful for Pepper.

First, Delaney was excellent at it. And she trash-talked him every time he got over a putt. His little purple ball seemed to have something wrong with it—it wobbled away from the hole if he hit it too softly. Which made Delaney snicker. And if Pepper hit his putt too hard, his ball popped over the tin hole and took off in the wrong direction.

Which made Delaney crack up every time. She was laughing at him and wiggling her butt when she putted and just having a hoot of a time. Mostly at his expense.

Delaney had taken control of the scorecard and mini pencil, and she announced to him after each hole just how far ahead she was.

After nine holes, she was five strokes up. But she hadn't mentioned the kidnappings. She was laughing and goofing around and having a blast. He was too.

But he was super competitive at heart. And he was a damned athlete. He tried to focus and catch up.

Pepper picked up a stroke on each of the following two holes, and that's when she started cheating. She came up behind him when he was putting on the twelfth hole and put her arms around his waist. "Y'all need a lesson?" she asked, squeezing against him and rocking back and forth. "It's all in the hips, see?"

Pepper putted and his ball hit the brick at the edge of the course and hopped over, rolling through the short grass and slipping into a little fake river.

"Oh, that's gonna cost ya!" Delaney laughed.

No girl, of all the girls he'd brought to Pirate's Cove in his many years of dating, had ever been so vicious.

On the eighteenth tee, one stroke ahead, Delaney sent her ball up and into the hole in one shot.

A bullet through Pepper's heart. He'd lost.

Before they left Pirate's Cove, he bought Delaney a mint chocolate chip ice cream cone at the little store next door and tried to win a couple of arcade games. To get back a little pride. He failed.

Then Delaney tried a game which required you to time the spinning lights to stop on the right bulb. Of course she won first try, getting the prize of a key chain with a little penknife dangling from it. A cheap piece of crap, which she awarded to Pepper as a consolation prize.

"I'll treasure it," he said. She seemed much happier and relaxed. He felt that way too.

"One of my favorite bars is on the way home," she said with a mischievous smile. "Jack's 28 Club. Even though I won, I'll let you choose your punishment. Would you rather buy me a few drinks at Jack's, or take me straight back to my place?"

Pepper could just picture getting carded and thrown out of the bar in front of Delaney... But even if he had been legal, Pepper would have picked the other choice. He was impatient back then, when he was twenty.

"You have anything to drink at your place?" he asked, going for casual to hide his growing excitement.

"Good choice," she said. And she took his hand as they walked to his truck, like it was the most natural thing in the world.

"Play me your song again," said Delaney. "The one from our gig."

They were in her apartment now with an unspoken energy flowing between them. Like they both knew something was about to happen...neither of them rushing it.

He'd mixed them drinks. Pepper was trying to keep it together, taking his cues from Delaney. Not wanting to screw this up, because it was perfect.

Delaney grabbed a guitar from the corner of her messy little apartment, and she looked so adorable, what could he do?

He quickly tuned the guitar and sat on her saggy blue sofa. Then he sang his song, "Try Me."

Delaney sat beside him, watching his face intently all the way through. When Pepper looked up, he saw she had tears running down her face.

"Oh my God, Pepper. That's so romantic and sweet and just *cool*. Whoever inspired your song's a damn lucky girl."

He didn't answer. He looked away.

Delaney squeezed his knee. "Pepper you didn't...you didn't write it for *me*, did ya?"

His mind was spinning—he was scared, embarrassed and excited, all at the same time. Of course he had. "What if I did?" he asked, finally looking right at her.

Delaney gave him her foxy little smile. She leaned over and lightly put her hands on both sides of his face. They felt small and hot.

Then she leaned in and kissed him.

Delaney's hands were so light on the sides of Pepper's face that her fingertips tickled.

One of his hands was tangled in her hair. The other was on the back of her warm neck. Crazy warm.

He was almost right up against her, close enough to feel heat radiating from her body. Close enough that when she inhaled deeply, their chests touched.

Then he leaned back to look her in her beautiful mismatched eyes—one blue, one dark hazel. Their twinkle matched the smile on her lips. Then she slowly peeled her shirt over her head. In slow motion, Pepper saw her flat belly first, with a cute little silver belly ring. Then her ribcage, coming and going with her labored breath. Then her bra. Black, lacy and skimpy. Then her pale, smooth neck. And then her smile again.

She stood and, without breaking eye contact with Pepper, hooked her fingers in the top of her shorts.

And at that moment, the apartment's fire alarm split Pepper's eardrums.

———

"This might be funny eventually," Pepper said to Delaney, standing in the parking lot with a hundred other residents of the apartment complex. She had her shirt back on again, tragically.

"That's the story of my life," she sighed. "Bad timing!"

There were two fire engines, two police cars and an ambulance on the scene already.

No smoke that he could see. So, what—a false alarm? Perfect. Somebody probably burned their dinner...

Dinner! Pepper had completely forgotten that Jake was cooking a family Sunday dinner. A rare event for the three Ryan men this summer. Both Pepper and their dad had sworn they'd be home tonight by six.

It was almost that time now.

"Crap! I've got to go anyway," he said, taking her hand. "I'm late for a family dinner!"

"That's cool—I'm officially giving you a rain check. And I'd like to meet your brother and your dad some time."

"You bet!" he said, and gave her a quick, awesome kiss.

Pepper jogged to his truck to head home.

When he reached his truck, he saw it was completely blocked in its space by the ambulance. But no one was behind the ambulance's steering wheel.

And could he really hunt down the EMT to move the ambulance in the middle of an emergency response situation?

Crap.

He jogged back to the crowd to find Delaney. Maybe she could give him a lift home. But he couldn't find her in the crowd.

Double crap!

He checked his watch again: 5:50. He had to be home in ten minutes! It was only a mile to the Ryan home and Pepper did the only thing he could think of.

He started running.

CHAPTER NINETEEN

Emma Bailey was blind in the darkness.

She could hear the new girl's muffled sobbing across from her. Neither of them could speak due to the stupid gags in their mouths.

Emma was hungry and needed to pee, but there was nothing to do about that. She wasn't ready to wet herself again. She passed the time trying to think of ways to escape. She either needed to get loose while Shrek was away. Or else she'd have to somehow get him to take off the plastic zip ties and the bike chain, then either overpower him or just outrun him. Escape up the metal ladder.

She stretched and twisted her wrists back and forth in their plastic constraints, trying to break free. She had a tiny bit of room to move her wrists, which helped the circulation in her hands, although when she twisted and pulled at the binding as hard as she possibly could, the plastic dug sharply into her wrists. But she made sure not to cry out. Like Shrek had said, she needed to set a good example for the new girl.

She'd heard a classmate talk once about how to break out of plastic tie wraps like these—some dork showing off in homeroom what a tough guy he was, and she wished she'd listened more carefully.

The tie wrap around her wrists looped through the bike chain at her waist, so she couldn't get her wrists up to her mouth to bite through the plastic restraints.

Nothing happened for a long time other than the new girl's crying, which came and went. Emma knew exactly how the girl felt. But Emma wished she'd just freaking stop. The more the girl cried, the sadder Emma got too.

Emma heard the metal noises again and then the sound of feet on the metal ladder. Same as before—her eye mask came off and in the wobbly lantern light she saw their damned kidnapper in his ridiculous Shrek mask. Why did the man care if they saw his face? Maybe it meant he would let them go, eventually?

The man took off Emma's gag and then bent next to the other girl. He took off that girl's eye mask and gag too. The girl was awake—her face streaked with tears and her eyes were super wide.

"Emma, meet Emma," said Shrek.

They both had the same name? She didn't know if she'd misunderstood the man's mumbling through his lame mask.

"We'll have to figure out some way to keep down the confusion," Shrek said, pointing at Emma Bailey. "Maybe I'll call you Mad Emma. And I'll call you Sad Emma," he said, pointing at New Emma. "It would have been easier to use your last names, but those don't matter anymore, as you'll find out."

Emma didn't know what the hell he was talking about.

"Since we're all getting friendly, what's your name?" she asked him. Her instinct was to gather information about her kidnapper. Who knows what it might lead to. Some other way out of this hellhole, like if she talked him into letting them go.

The man laughed behind his mask. "My name'll have to wait."

Emma was getting pissed off again. "I call him Shrek,

obviously," she said to New Emma. "I'm sure he's even uglier without the mask. So hopefully he'll keep it on."

The new Emma didn't answer.

"Mad Emma, you just put yourself at the back of the potty line," said Shrek. He went through the ritual of switching New Emma to a long bike chain and pushed her away from the light toward the portable toilet chair. Emma watched the girl in the shadows tentatively take care of her business, holding her chain out of the way.

Shrek told New Emma that a roll of toilet paper was on the floor next to the chair, saying it casual as if it was something he'd thought of himself, the dumbass.

When New Emma finished, the man secured her again in her spot, and then he repeated the whole process with Emma.

She took her time going to the bathroom, trying to think of any way to escape. Could she rush at Shrek and wrap her bike chain around his neck? Choke him like in a movie?

But he was twice her size. She didn't think there was any way she could beat him physically. And she didn't know yet if he planned to kill them, or rape them, or whatever the hell his plan was.

So she did nothing too risky. She just finished up and unraveled two handfuls of toilet paper from the roll. She wiped herself with one wad, dropping it into the hole in the seat, and then palmed the other wad as she shuffled back to her spot.

"Did either of you have a boyfriend?" the man asked out of the blue.

Did? The word gave Emma chills.

"You bet. I'm like, super in love with him," Emma lied. "He's in the Army and he has a knife bigger than your you-know-what."

Shrek just laughed. "How about you?" he asked New Emma.

"No," the girl answered quietly, her voice shaking.

"I'm doing you girls a favor. Something's been missing in your life. Whether or not you know it."

"Whatever," said Emma. "If you want to do us a favor, can you tell us if we're still on the Cape?"

A pause. "Yes, we are," he said. "That make you happy?"

Okay, progress. "You bet," she answered. "While you're so chatty, mind telling us what you want, kidnapping us? Like, what's this about?"

A longer pause this time. "A new life," Shrek finally said. "We'll talk about it more at the right time. But for now, you need to learn how to help each other. You're family now."

God, she hated his tone. Smug and matter of fact. All powerful, or so he probably thought. What a loser!

"Sounds amazing," she said. "And you need to learn something too—how to go fuck yourself. But with a micro dick like yours, that must be wicked hard?"

Emma heard New Emma gasp.

Shrek forced a new plastic binding around Emma's wrists and zipped it hard and tight. Way tighter than last time.

Emma had been planning to slip her stolen wad of toilet paper down to her wrist, to possibly pad the wrist cuffs and give her some extra room to slip them off when he left. But it happened too fast, and she failed. She kept her fist closed around the toilet paper. Maybe it'd be useful later.

"Act like a little bitch, you get nothing but pain," he said.

Damn. She'd let her temper get the better of her, as usual, and was now worse off.

"You give creeps a bad name," she lamely yelled, as the ball gag came back up around her mouth and he forced it in.

She had to sit and watch him give New Emma food and something to drink. Probably drugged. The creep.

And she watched helplessly as Shrek gathered up his things.

He made no move to feed her next. She'd obviously pissed him off and wouldn't get any food or water this visit.

Maybe that was a win? Without drugs to fog up her head, could she come up with a better idea to get them out of here?

Without further words, Shrek picked up the lantern and moved away to the ladder, leaving Emma hungry and thirsty. But a little less hopeless.

Emma scootched as low as she could and stretched out. At full extension, her sneaker could just touch New Emma's sneaker. She pressed her foot against the other girl's foot. A moment later, she felt New Emma tentatively press back.

Emma cried as silently as she could, hoping the other girl couldn't hear her.

She had to set a good example.

CHAPTER TWENTY

Pepper had only run a block toward home before he heard the honk of a car horn.

It was Gus Bullard again, his old high school hockey coach. Same old butterscotch-colored Jaguar Xj8. Same cigarette smoke coming out the window.

Crap. Absolutely the last person he wanted to deal with right then.

But a ride's a ride.

Pepper climbed into the car, smiling warily. Coach Bullard was somewhere in his early fifties. A big man who'd been an athlete in his youth but had added sixty pounds in middle age.

"Same old Pylon!" the man laughed. "You jog as slow as you skate!"

Pylon. Coach Bullard had always thought Pepper was way too slow a skater, which he'd never missed a chance to mention. Coach knew how to push everyone's buttons, especially Pepper's.

Two years before Pepper joined the varsity team, Bullard had coached Jake. His older brother had been the complete package— a quick-as-lightning center, great hockey sense, heavy shot. Bullard had been disappointed when Jake pursued baseball in college instead of hockey. Maybe he'd decided to take out his disappointment on Pepper, the less talented Ryan?

Bullard blew smoke in Pepper's direction. "You never said why you missed my big party on Thursday! Got there too late?" The big man cracked up.

Pepper grinned weakly and didn't answer.

Jake had gone to the stupid retirement party, of course. Jake told him that the Emma Bailey amber alert had hit Jake's phone right in the middle of Coach Bullard's thank-you speech. Probably when the coach was blathering on and on about his own state championship as a student at New Albion High. And three more state titles as a coach. One with Jake...zero with Pepper.

"Run out of excuses? Or you think you're too good for us now, Mr. Hah-Vard?" Bullard laughed. "How you'll keep up with all those speedsters in Division One... It's a horse race, nothing like my days at Minnesota. When I heard you got a free ticket to Harvard, I figured you'd be driving the Zamboni!" More laughter.

But Pepper didn't take the bait. What would he do—call the old man an idiot? Or say that possibly he wasn't going to bother with college, anyway? Right...

Coach Bullard had gone pretty far as a player himself, back in the day. College out in the Midwest, then the semi-pro East Coast League. He'd been a heck of a brawler and an all-around big dog— just ask him. He'd always said he could have made it to the NHL if he hadn't gotten so many damned concussions.

Coach was blathering on. "But good for you, son. The fucking Ivy League. You just won life's lottery." Coach laughed and lit another cigarette from the car's automatic lighter. Like all those years of lung cancer medical studies had never happened.

Pepper rolled down his window and glumly thought about the tragic interruption to his date with Delaney. He hadn't had the right moment to tell her about Harvard. He hadn't told Brad St. John either, when he'd joined Brad and the Pitts. Which Pepper justified wasn't a big deal back then. People jumped in and out of bands all the time, right?

But what Delaney had said about going on the road to give music a shot together—that was an invitation which carried over way past summer. And once again he'd chickened out from coming clean with her.

Coach Bullard turned left on Shore Drive and cruised past oversized Cape-style homes with the lazy shine of the Atlantic Ocean peeking between them. They passed Rogers Lighthouse, and the houses were larger now. Mansions.

Bullard didn't seem to notice Pepper wasn't replying. Coach just kept running his mouth.

"No, I'm glad I'm retiring. High school hockey's not what it used to be. Neither's the Cape, with all the druggies and crime. No sir, I'm retiring to Florida, where the only ice'll be in my Jack and Coke. Buy a share in a nice bar by the beach, spend the rest of my day in damned paradise."

Pepper grunted. Keeping his mouth shut against the smoke.

"But I'll check the internet," said Bullard. "See if you get on the score sheet. Other than penalties."

Asshole.

The Jaguar stopped at the end of the Ryans' driveway. "Tell your dad, I hope when he corners the Greenhead psycho, he puts a bullet in the guy's head. Shoot first and think second. You should try that too up in Division One hockey! If you choke this time, you won't have anyone else to blame..."

———

Gerald Ryan was sitting at the kitchen table, more than a little annoyed, when Pepper finally walked in. Late and oblivious, as usual.

"Hey, Pep!" said Jake, over by the stove. "Food's on in one minute! Wash up!"

Gerald almost ripped into Pepper for being late, but let it slide. He couldn't remember the last time the three of them had sat down for a home-cooked dinner together. In June? When would it happen again—the night before Pepper left for Harvard or Jake headed back to Boston College, whoever left first?

As they ate the chicken, rice and salad, both sons tried to get Gerald to fill them in on the latest development in the Greenhead Snatcher case. He resisted, but they wore him down.

So Gerald gave them a basic update. Casper Yelle was still a suspect, but there wasn't any hard evidence he was their guy. They had a big handful of other suspects, including the assistant manager at Sandy's, where the second victim worked. But the case against him was thin too.

"Scooter McCord?" asked Pepper.

"Ha, no names!" said Gerald. He wasn't a gossip by nature and believed in the old "loose lips sink ships" philosophy. "But there was one big development today—the Addisons got a ransom note from the Snatcher."

Both of his sons' forks stopped in midair, as he knew they would.

"What!" exclaimed Pepper.

"Yep. Two million dollars."

"Whoa!" said Jake. "Did the Baileys get a note too?"

"Not yet. But the Addisons' letter mentioned both Emmas." Gerald explained the note received by the Addisons was otherwise very brief, stating the dollar amount and for them to have it ready on Monday. "Hopefully, it'll never come to that," he added. "Hopefully, we'll arrest the dirtbag first."

"Do you think the ransom note's from the Snatcher, or could someone else be trying to cash in on the situation?" asked Pepper.

Smart question, thought Gerald with pride. The FBI had

pointed out the same possibility. "Possibly. We're treating it as the real deal, for now."

They finished eating, each lost in their own thoughts. Until Jake cleared his throat.

"Not to brag, but either of you hear about my game today?"

They hadn't.

"I pitched a shutout. A one-hitter. That's why I cooked—to celebrate. Just the three of us. But also because I had some other big news." Jake took a long drink of milk. Wiped his mouth again.

Gerald was suddenly uneasy, sensing that Jake was nervous.

"I was in the zone today," said Jake. "Great heat, painting corners. One step ahead, every inning. But my head was extra clear because I made a big decision right before the game. I hope you'll both understand."

Gerald froze. "Whoa, whoa...don't tell me you're dropping out of B.C. to join the Mariners' system?" he asked. Instantly realizing his tone made clear how he felt about *that* idea.

"Nope," said Jake. "The opposite. I'm going back to B.C. Then I'll graduate and I'm done with baseball. I'll be going straight into the police academy."

"Seriously?" exclaimed Pepper. "You've been running your mouth about going pro since T-ball!"

Jake smiled. "I did, yeah. But this last week with the kidnappings—I've felt like a complete idiot, out there playing a kid's game while a damn predator's on the loose. I want to make a difference, like you do, Dad. I want to do something important with my life."

Gerald stared at Jake, completely surprised. "Have you really thought this through?"

"Absolutely." Jake sat up straight, looking calm and comfortable. Like a man who had chosen his path and was sure of it.

Gerald got up, walked over to Jake and gave him a long hug.

Then looked Jake right in the eye. "I've never been so proud of you, son."

When Jake looked up at him, Gerald saw a hint of a tear in Jake's eye.

"You're both crazy," said Pepper.

And Pepper left them, storming out the door to the deck. Leaving them to clean everything up—classic Pepper. But Gerald somehow bit his tongue and let him go.

Pepper crossed the lawn to the higher seagrass which separated their little back lawn from the beach. He stood looking out at the sand and the ocean that stretched away into infinity.

Jake had a ticket to live pretty much every boy's dream—to be a professional athlete. A one-in-a-million shot for most players, but the Seattle Mariners had actually drafted him. He had a solid chance of making the big leagues. Was Jake just scared he couldn't hack it? That he'd flame out in the minors? Or was he deluded to believe he could make the world a safer place, him being a cop?

End up like Dad? What was Jake thinking?

Pepper knew he wasn't a good enough hockey player to do anything past college. He was low-end Division 1 material. Too slow for today's pro game. A throwback to a more physical era. Harvard was probably already regretting having recruited him.

But to become a cop? Cops are a dime a dozen. And if you rise through the ranks and become a chief of police, that was almost a curse. For his dad, every crime in or near New Albion seemed to affect him personally. And the crimes which went unsolved were even worse—Pepper knew those cases ate up his father. Pepper always felt like his dad was thinking about work when he was with him. Like being a father would always be his second priority.

And now Jake was going down the same hole? It seemed like

the Greenhead Snatcher had snatched away Jake's bright future too. Pepper filled with hot anger at the kidnapper he'd never even met. The monster who was ruining lives all around Pepper.

Coach Bullard was an ass, but he'd said one smart thing earlier —the Greenhead Snatcher deserved the quick justice of a bullet to the head, before his chaos caused any more damage.

CHAPTER TWENTY-ONE

Pepper had a strange encounter on Monday morning when he arrived at the police station to start his workday.

A middle-aged woman was trudging down the steps of the front entrance as Pepper walked up. She looked up like she was thinking hard about something or was confused. She paused, then started walking down the steps again.

She was carrying a large manila envelope. As Pepper passed her, she tugged his sleeve, and he stopped.

"Can you help me?" she asked.

The woman was middle-aged—in her fifties? Thin. She had reading glasses perched on the top of a hairless head. Maybe a fashion choice, but not likely. *Cancer*, he decided. Or some other medical condition.

Pepper was wearing his itchy police cadet uniform, which to a civilian looked much like a police officer's uniform.

"What can I do for you?" he asked.

She introduced herself as Maureen Cleary. She lived over on Thurston Road. She told Pepper that last Thursday, the evening of the first Greenhead Snatcher kidnapping, she'd found a white van in her driveway. It was driven by a white male claiming to be from a roofing company, giving free quotes.

"But he gave off all kinds of red flags," she said. "The way he acted... He was bullshitting me, but not really trying to sell me on getting my roof replaced, you know?"

Pepper knew that plenty of scam artists operated at the edge of the roofing business. He'd heard his dad talk about them. They were bottom-feeder grifters who roamed the U.S. preying on senior citizens—giving lowball quotes, taking deposit checks and then never returning to do any work. By the time the homeowner called the police, the scammers were hundreds of miles away.

"I tried to give this to the officer at the desk. He told me to keep it. That a detective would be in touch if they wanted more information from me." She tapped her large envelope.

"You tried to give him what?" asked Pepper, a bit confused.

The woman opened the envelope and slid out a large watercolor painting of a man.

It was better than amateur. But since it was a watercolor, the image had a strange, fluid quality. Except the man's eyes. The eyes were very specific—brown, intense and a bit crazy. Pepper got the sense that if he ever saw eyes like those again, he'd be able to recognize them. The man had mussed brown hair and didn't have on a green hat like the Bailey boy witnessed.

"This is the man you saw...in the roofing van?"

"Absolutely. Took me three tries to get him right. I'm so worried you won't catch him. If this could help..."

Pepper didn't know what Detective Sweeney would say if Pepper delivered a watercolor painting from one of the hundreds of citizens who meant well, but probably had no useful info to solve the case. Just well-intended false leads.

"I called the police hotline that Thursday night," the woman said. "Who ever heard of a roofing van that didn't have a pile of ladders on top? But no one has even contacted me yet..."

Pepper felt bad for the woman. She was just trying to help, like him. It didn't matter that the New Albion police were working through hundreds of civilian tips and it all took time. Every lead mattered until they proved it was a dead end, right?

"I'll give it to Detective Kevin Sweeney," he promised her. "He's our lead detective on the case. Why don't you write your name, address and phone number on the envelope?"

The woman exhaled, closed her eyes and put her hand to her nose. "Finally," she said in a quiet voice.

Pepper saw tears welling up in her eyes.

Detective Kevin Sweeney wasn't around, so Pepper leaned into his database work. He finished inputting eighteen old cases, about as much as he could do in one burst without dying of boredom, then tried to find the detective again. He wanted to deliver the painting and hopefully learn any breaking news in the investigation.

Pepper found Sweeney in the officers' bullpen, sitting in a cubicle, typing into a computer. His suit was wrinkled and his hair was standing up in the back.

"You look like you could use some coffee," Pepper said.

Sweeney gave him a weary smile. "Hey, young Ryan! That sounds great—unless you've got something stronger?"

Pepper returned in two minutes with a mug of hot, freshly brewed coffee.

The detective took it gratefully.

"This is for you too," Pepper said, handing over the woman's watercolor painting. He explained how he'd gotten it.

Pepper wondered if Sweeney would just throw it in the garbage. He didn't. He took it out, studied it and said "Huh."

Then he leaned it against the back wall of the cubicle desk, like a parent might display their kid's art.

Emboldened, Pepper shared further with Sweeney.

"I was talking to one of Emma Addison's friends yesterday," he said. "She told me she thinks Scooter McCord is the Snatcher. One of the managers at Sandy's Restaurant? You must be looking at him already."

"Kid, I shouldn't talk much about our suspects. Nothing personal." Sweeney sighed. "But yeah, we're looking at McCord. He was off work Saturday afternoon and doesn't have much of an alibi. Same for Thursday night when Emma Bailey was snatched. He called in sick.

"If you're a detective someday, you'll see how this really works. The public jumps to tell us who did it, like your artist..." He waved at the watercolor painting. "Or Emma Addison's friend. Everybody has a theory—what we need is evidence. And so far we have diddly squat."

That news was like a stomach punch to Pepper. Emma Bailey had been missing for four days. Emma Addison for two days. The clock was ticking badly...

The detective took another sip of his coffee and stretched. "Besides, McCord doesn't have any history of trouble. We ran him through every database and we got zip. No arrests. Not even a speeding ticket. So as far as we can *prove*, Mr. McCord is an upstanding citizen."

More discouraged than before, Pepper headed back to his drunk tank office. Too many suspects, not enough resources. Sweeney would need some luck.

Pepper worked for another hour, his mind half on the database and half on Scooter McCord.

At lunchtime, Pepper decided to try to scare up a little good luck for Detective Sweeney. He drove to McCord's home address, to see what he could see.

Detective Sweeney and the other officers working the case couldn't be everywhere. What's the worst that could happen? If Pepper saw anything suspicious, he could anonymously call in a tip. Maybe from one of the few remaining pay phones in town. He knew there was one in the Star Market and one on the corner by the Gulf station up on Route 28.

McCord lived in a small Cape-style house on Clapper Street. He rented, according to the records Pepper had accessed.

A dirty yellow Jeep YJ was in the driveway, so McCord was probably home.

Pepper sat in his truck about half a block down the street, eating a roast beef sandwich he'd grabbed on the way to his stakeout, trying to decide how long he could wait and what else he could do.

He considered calling Delaney. He wanted to pick right back up where they'd left off yesterday afternoon. Which just brought up the bigger question—stick to his old college plans and walk away from her in August, or was he actually considering throwing his old plans out the window?

He tried to think about it objectively. If he stuck with his original plan to head off to Harvard, he'd hopefully play hockey and scrape through his classes and graduate. Then what, fall into the police officer rut like everyone else in his family? No, Pepper's crime-fighting efforts would be limited to this one situation, for the two Emmas' sake. Then never again...

Pepper hoped someone caught the Greenhead Snatcher ASAP and that the Emmas were miraculously unharmed. He knew it wasn't likely after this many days. Hopefully, the ransom note was a sign they would make it home alive.

He wondered if the families or the police received a follow-up to the ransom note. He'd try to find out when he got back to the station.

After fifteen minutes, Scooter McCord walked out his front

door, a baseball cap covering his bright red hair. He climbed in his Jeep and fired it up, its engine rumbling loudly. He backed out and drove away past Pepper's truck—Pepper had scooched down again to avoid being seen.

Should he follow him? Or should he take this chance to snoop around McCord's property?

Pepper mentally flipped a coin and decided to check out the property. He didn't know how long he would have, but it was too good of an opportunity to pass up.

Sadly leaving the second half of his sandwich in his truck, he walked up to McCord's front door and rang the bell. Just in case someone else was home.

No one answered.

Pepper peered in the front window. Nothing.

A high chain-link fence protected the backyard and its gate was closed but not locked. He slipped it open and walked in, closing it quietly behind him.

It was a fairly big, messy yard. It had a brick patio with weeds growing through the cracks. Three plastic Adirondack chairs were arranged in a rough triangle around a small, cheap-looking wooden table.

Across the lawn was a small shed. The kind big enough for a lawnmower and other yard equipment.

There was also a dog house. It was half the size of the shed.

But the dog house got Pepper's attention because he saw a long, black nose sticking out of its open doorway. The snout was flat on the ground, like the dog was sleeping. Or dead?

It looked like the thick, wet black nose of a Doberman pinscher.

Perfect.

Pepper tiptoed to the house's sliding door and peeped in. He saw a basic, out-of-date kitchen.

He tugged at the door. Miraculously, it scratched open. He swallowed and tiptoed in.

Think about the Emmas. Do this for the Emmas.

Pepper entered, trying not to think about the laws he was breaking.

CHAPTER TWENTY-TWO

Get in, get out, thought Pepper. *While you can...*

He saw nothing of interest in the kitchen or the living room. The living room was almost bare. It only held a television perched on a cardboard box and another plastic Adirondack chair, which matched the three outside on the back patio.

In the bedroom, Pepper saw an enormous Scottish flag, a thick white X across a blue background, hung over the bed. And a pair of silver handcuffs hung from one bedpost.

But he saw no sign of the missing Emmas or anything that even hinted Scooter McCord was the Greenhead Snatcher. Other than possibly the handcuffs? But Scooter might be into kinky stuff, nothing to do with kidnappings...

He tentatively opened the dresser drawers, looking for...what? A taser? Pictures of the two Emmas? He felt ridiculous.

But in the second drawer, Pepper found something odd. It was a UK passport with Scooter's picture, but the name was wrong—it said Harris Ross. Under the passport was a printout of a British Airways flight itinerary for Harris Ross to fly to Edinburgh Airport on Monday next week. *Bizarre.*

Had Scooter legally changed his name? Or was the passport a fake? Was the flight an innocent trip or an escape plan?

A loud rumbling sound outside interrupted Pepper's thoughts. The noise stopped.

Shit! Scooter must be home!

Pepper shoved the itinerary and passport back into the drawer and shut it. Then he raced for the kitchen sliding door.

He pulled it closed behind him, maybe a little too loud. Because Pepper saw the big, wet nose in the doghouse lift from the ground and two big dark eyes opened and saw him. Yep, it was a fully-grown Doberman pinscher.

The dog stepped from its doghouse. It wasn't on a chain. It shook furiously. To Pepper, the dog looked pissed to be woken up. And it looked even more pissed that Pepper was standing in its yard.

He gingerly picked up one of the plastic Adirondack chairs, the hair rising on the back of his neck. "Good boy," he whispered. He looked back over his shoulder to see if McCord had come into the kitchen yet. He would instantly see Pepper when he arrived.

The dog gave a long, spine-chilling growl, which changed to a fierce barking. Then the dog bounded toward Pepper, its eyes like black pools. Its yellow teeth bared. It was a freaking monster.

Pepper sprang into motion a moment after the dog. He didn't run for the gate leading to the driveway, because that's where McCord might be standing. He ran toward the back of the fence, reaching it in four strides. If Coach Bullard could see him now, he'd never call him "Pylon" again. Pepper flew, tossing the chair back over his shoulder at the oncoming dog.

But the big Doberman flew faster. It had twice the distance to cover, but it easily knocked the plastic lawn chair from its path and reached Pepper as he was midair, halfway up the six-foot chain-link fence. The dog grabbed the back of his left shoe—his black work shoe—and sank in his monster teeth as Pepper pulled himself up. Pepper desperately wiggled free of the shoe and the dog, tumbling over the top of the fence and landing in a heap of weeds and old plastic flower pots. The pots shattered under him, stabbing into his back.

The dog wasn't done. It wanted to kill him.

It took running leaps at the fence and its feet reached the top, scrambling wildly, but the beast didn't have leverage to get over. It tried twice more, then gave up, sitting down and grabbing Pepper's lost shoe in its big mouth. It started tearing the shoe to pieces.

Pepper didn't stay to watch. He rolled to his feet, rubbing his lower back to see if any pieces of plastic pot were protruding from it. Despite the pain, he found nothing.

He limped away through McCord's neighbor's backyard, around the side of the house (no fence, no damned dog!) and to the street. An older man with white hair and an impressive beer belly stood in his driveway across the street, watching Pepper limp past.

Pepper waved to him. *Nothing to see here.*

The man stared until Pepper finally turned the corner, apparently having a low opinion of strangers limping around his neighborhood with only one shoe.

Snob...

Back at his desk, Pepper rubbed his chewed-up ankle while keeping his sneakers hidden from view (he didn't own a second pair of shoes). He was trying to make sense of the little he'd learned.

What was up with McCord having a UK passport under the name Harris Ross? Pepper entered that info into his Bailey file in the database. Then he reviewed everything in the file.

He still believed Casper Yelle was the more likely suspect. He knew Detective Sweeney was still trying to unravel Yelle's alibis for the times of the kidnappings. For example, he'd applied for a search warrant to check the surveillance tapes to confirm Yelle had left work at Johnson Precision Machining when he'd claimed on the evening Emma Bailey was snatched.

Pepper knew one of the big frustrations for detectives was the time needed to do things by the book. To make sure they not only solved crimes, but built cases which would hold up in court.

It seemed unfair to Pepper that the legal steps took so long when time was short. He wished he could do something to either break or confirm Yelle's alibi from Thursday. Anything to help Detective Sweeney.

Pepper's phone buzzed with a text from Dennis Cole.

Ryan! Meet me Big Red Yard, 4pm. Got news about u no what

Huh. Either Brad St. John's biker roommate had something exciting to tell him about a music opportunity, or else he was still digging around like a vigilante on the Snatcher case. Which Pepper still didn't approve of, even though he'd been doing the same thing.

Pepper knew where the Big Red Yard was. It was the sort of industrial monstrosity which becomes a landmark for locals. Landscapers and other contractors with trucks and equipment rented space in its three-acre lot. He had even been in there once or twice, years ago.

Then he recalled that the Big Red Yard was next door to Johnston Precision Machining, the place where Casper Yelle worked. And Pepper got a big idea. He would meet up with Dennis Cole at four o'clock, but he had to investigate something else first...

CHAPTER TWENTY-THREE

Were the answers here? Or just more trouble?

Pepper balanced those thoughts as he parked at Johnston Precision Machining on Richards Road, an industrial street at the far edge of New Albion, around 3:30.

From the report he'd copied out of his dad's file, Pepper knew Casper Yelle's alibi for the Thursday night Emma Bailey was snatched. Yelle said he'd left work at the machine shop at exactly five, gone to Taco Bell and eaten there, then driven straight home to his apartment, where he stayed all night.

Pepper had figured out a simple way to prove whether the first part of Yelle's alibi was true or a lie. Now he just had to have the guts to follow through.

The entrance had a big sign which said *"Johnston Precision Machining—full service machining, welding and fabrication since 1978."* And below, in smaller letters, it said, *"Our work is sometimes boring."*

"Ha!" laughed Pepper, entering.

In a small lobby with gray carpet and gray walls, Pepper found a very thin young woman with curly hair, possibly late twenties, sitting at the front desk. His first thought was she looked like a bird. The woman was typing on her computer and didn't acknowledge him at first. After a long minute or two, she looked up.

Pepper gave her what he hoped was a winning smile and tried his line of bull crap. He said he'd been driving on Richards Road on Thursday afternoon when a truck pulled out of the Big Red Yard next door and clipped his vehicle. It'd driven off before he could get its license plate.

So he was hoping, he said, that Johnston Precision Machining's security cameras had caught the accident. Would she mind if he looked for just a minute? Pepper wasn't a great flirt, but he did his best, making strong eye contact and smiling again, while trying to look sad.

The bird lady didn't fall for any of it. *Ouch.*

She said she wasn't authorized to let anyone look at their security footage. She said she wished she could help him, but couldn't. And that their camera didn't cover much of the street, anyway.

She was already looking back at her computer, dismissing him. Pepper saw a reflection of her monitor in a framed picture behind her and saw she was losing at a game of solitaire.

Pepper sighed as heavily as he thought might be believable. "I have a thousand-dollar deductible for hit and runs," he said, trying to sound pathetic. "I know you're busy—could I pay you for your valuable time?" He held up two twenty-dollar bills and a ten. All the cash he had on him.

The bird woman studied him, then looked over her shoulder at a door with a small window. Pepper guessed the door led to the shop area where Casper Yelle and others did the machining work. But she plucked the money from his hand, and they were in business.

The woman pulled up the security footage on her computer,

minimizing her game of solitaire as Pepper stepped around the counter to look over her shoulder at the monitor.

"Five o'clock Thursday on the button?" she confirmed with Pepper. He nodded to her, with one eye on the door with the little window.

She opened a file, fast-forwarded the video to 4:58, then hit "play."

The image was of a wide-angle camera at the front of the business. It covered most of the parking lot and a sliver of Richards Road. Traffic flashed past, too fast to make out the cars' details. Which made sense. The camera was there for the parking lot.

Pepper noticed the camera cut off the far back corner of the parking lot. Possibly a compromise because their camera didn't have a wide enough angle lens to cover the entire lot. Or a second camera would have cost too much for the owner to bother. Either way, it was a blind spot. But Pepper was there for evidence of Casper Yelle and his tan Jeep Wrangler.

The woman let him watch until the video time stamp said 5:05 PM. "Like I told you," she said. "Our camera can't see much of the street."

But Pepper hadn't been watching the blur of traffic. He was watching the parking lot and who exited the workspace.

There were many vehicles in the parking lot, but none of them were the Jeep Wrangler that Yelle said in his interview he'd driven on Thursday. But there was a white van. Pepper couldn't make out the license plate.

Pepper watched video of three men leaving the machine shop, getting into vehicles and driving away. None of the men looked like Yelle. The white van remained. Pepper also watched for vehicles departing from the blind spot area at the very rear corner of the lot. He didn't see any.

The door behind them groaned open and the bird woman quickly minimized the screen with the video footage.

Two men entered the lobby. One was a short, thin guy in his sixties. But he had the expansive posture of a man in charge. With him was Casper Yelle. Pepper immediately recognized him from his photo, but he hoped the man had no reason to recognize him.

"Judy, what's going on? Is everything okay?"

Pepper began taking tiny steps away from the computer, back toward the other side of the counter.

"Yeah, no problem," said Judy, making nervous, flitting gestures with her hands.

"Who are you?" the short man demanded.

"I was just, ah, looking for directions."

Casper Yelle stood behind the short man, saying nothing while watching everything.

"He was just leaving," said Judy, taking a sip from her water bottle. Her face had gone pale.

"Thanks for the directions," Pepper said to her. "And hey, funny sign out front! Good one!" He left quickly.

The men didn't come after him.

Pepper hoped Judy wouldn't get in trouble. But he guessed she would, and he felt terrible about it.

His blood was pumping as he jogged to his truck, looking back over his shoulder. He saw the two men in the doorway, watching him go. But Pepper was too deep in thought to care.

Casper Yelle had almost certainly lied during his interview about leaving in his Jeep at five o'clock on Thursday. *Why?*

It was time to meet Dennis Cole—if Pepper could get through the closed gate.

He drove his truck out of Johnston's parking lot onto Richards

Road and quickly pulled into the driveway to Big Red Yard next door. A faded sign said Lower Cape Contractor Park, but no one called it that.

The Big Red Yard was a three-acre madhouse of trucks, containers and heaps of wheelbarrows, tires and other equipment. If you were a landscaper or tree topper or whatever and needed a place to store your work vehicles overnight and have a base of operations, this was the place on the Lower Cape. Other options existed, but this was the cheapest.

The property was surrounded by an eight-foot brick wall painted bright red, topped by rusty loops of barbed wire. And the entrance was controlled by a rolling gate, also with barbed wire.

By good luck, Pepper was right behind a pickup truck towing a landscaping trailer. It stopped just short of the gate. The driver waved a small gray card at a reader and the gate rattled open with a long, grinding squeak.

Pepper pulled up behind the truck and followed it through just before the gate slid closed.

He was glad he had a truck too as he drove along the rough dirt lane into the lot. The potholed lane split into four lanes which each zigzagged away into the tangle of containers, trucks with trailers, and piles of discarded equipment. There were small dump trucks, bucket trucks, and vans. Especially white vans.

There were also shipping containers like the ones hauled around by eighteen-wheelers. The containers had big ads on their sides for companies like Budweiser and Evergreen. Some containers were so rusty the ads were illegible. Pepper knew that contractors used the containers to store equipment. All in all, the place was quite a maze.

And crowded. Pepper figured contractors paid by the square foot and only rented enough real estate for their needs. Not one inch more.

Luckily, he found Cole quickly. The man was welding a

trailer close to the front of the property. He was near a small brick building with a neon sign which said Office. Half of its letters were burned out, so the sign just said Off.

Pepper parked his truck and was about to climb out when he almost had a heart attack. He saw an enormous dog—so big it made the Doberman pinscher from Pepper's earlier misadventure at Scooter McCord's house look like a puppy. It was the biggest dog he had ever seen.

This dog looked like it was mostly English mastiff, with possibly some wolf blood mixed in. It was the size of a small pony and had to weigh well over 200 pounds. Probably weighed more than Pepper.

It had a wide metal collar and was tethered by a thick chain. The dog was ripping at the ground with its enormous paws. It wasn't growling. It was watching him and Cole, as if deciding which of them would be today's appetizer and which would be the main course. The beast would be intimidating on any day to anyone who wasn't carrying a rocket launcher. But today? After that Doberman had already almost ripped apart Pepper? No, this was too much.

Cole was working about five feet beyond the full length of the dog's chain. Pepper watched the dog gallop at the man and flip backward when he reached his chain's maximum. After only a few seconds, the dog repeated his effort. It looked like the dog was intent on either breaking his chain or his neck.

Cole picked up a rock the size of a softball and threw it hard at the dog. The rock hit the dog's side with a thump, but the dog didn't flinch or bark. It just stared at the man, as if it was taking his number. Adding Cole to his shit list. The dog was actually scarier than if it had barked.

Pepper climbed down from his truck, carrying the second half of the sandwich he'd abandoned at lunchtime during the McCord house debacle.

"Here you go, boy," he said, lobbing the sandwich near the beast. Pepper pitied the dog, but he wasn't stupid enough to hand-feed it. He wanted to keep his hand.

The dog snatched the food up out of the mud and swallowed it whole. Then he stood still, looking at Pepper expectantly.

"Sorry, boy, that's all."

The dog started whining, in a low voice which sounded like a dump truck with a bad transmission.

"Hey, Ryan!" said Cole, setting aside his welding mask. "Meet Stinky, the Big Red Yard's guard dog. That fucking dog's been coming at me for the last hour. He's lucky I haven't beaten him silly yet."

You throw one more rock at Stinky and I'll toss you to him like that sandwich, thought Pepper. But out loud he said, "I got your text. What's up?"

Cole shut down his welding equipment, then gestured for Pepper to follow him. They walked to Cole's truck and climbed in. The truck was full of fast food wrappers and empty coffee cups.

"Thanks for coming, man," said Cole. "This place is a goldmine for me. Just last week, I welded a temporary manhole on a delivery truck. Five hundred bucks—*cha-ching!* And someone's trailer hitch or whatever's always breaking in here. Speaking of money..."

"You've figured out how I can make millions off my songs?"

Cole laughed. "Maybe. But something else first. I heard on the radio the reward for the two kidnapped girls is up to a hundred thousand dollars. Crazy, right? And I think I figured out who's the Snatcher."

CHAPTER TWENTY-FOUR

Dennis Cole's statement surprised Pepper. *He knew who the Greenhead Snatcher was?*

"Yeah? Who is he?" Pepper asked.

Cole grinned at him. "No, no. Not yet. But since you work at the cop shop, I need you to do me a solid and fill me in on how the reward thing works. If someone's already a suspect, but I give the cops info that helps convict the bastard, do I still get the money?"

Pepper thought about it. "Sure, why not? If you tell them something that's key to catching and convicting the guy, I bet you'll get the money."

Cole chuckled. "I better. But about the case...how's it going? You know, give me an idea if I'm chasing a dead end or if I've got a fucking good idea."

Pepper knew it was a bad idea to share inside info about the investigation with Dennis Cole or anyone else outside of the police. Especially after the trouble that the Bailey family got into with vigilante activity.

But he was still annoyed at his dad and law enforcement in general. So he did what he knew he shouldn't. He gave Cole a full recap of the case's progress. Casper Yelle. Scooter McCord. The ransom note. All the details and other big events which Pepper had either seen or learned over the past four days.

Cole had a pencil and a battered notebook, and he wrote notes as Pepper talked. "How many other suspects are the cops looking at?" Cole asked.

Pepper didn't remember them all, so he pulled out his phone and flipped through the pictures of suspect reports in his dad's file. He read out each suspect's name and address, about twenty of them, and Cole carefully wrote it all down.

When Pepper finished, the biker offered him a fist bump.

"You da man, Ryan. I need you to do two other things. Find out if the detectives have a list yet of all the girls named Emma in the Lower Cape. They must have thought of it already, right? The Greenhead fucker must be targeting girls with that name for some sick reason, don't you think? So first thing, get me their Emma list."

"Ah, I'll see what I can do," said Pepper, with a sinking feeling in his stomach. That was probably something the detectives had already focused on, but he didn't know how he would get a copy of their list.

"And let me know how the case's going from now on, okay? Like you and me are a team. You fill me in if the case goes in some new direction, or they get any big breaks. Maybe we can find those girls faster than anyone else. We'll chop the reward fifty-fifty. Next stop, Nashville!"

Pepper was only twenty years old, back then. He had only heard a little about ideas like ethics and conflicts of interest. But he knew he felt like crap, deep in his gut, when he answered, "Okay."

Another fist bump.

Pepper walked back to his truck. Stinky the monster dog, was lying flat in the mud at the end of his chain, his huge face pressed to the ground and his bloodshot brown eyes fixed on him. As if he'd heard the whole conversation. As if he was glad he was only a dog on a chain in the mud and wasn't Pepper.

Pepper didn't blame him.

The man who'd snatched the two Emmas was nervous as he methodically climbed down the metal ladder to check on the girls.

This part of the job hadn't gone too well. He felt as if he was the one tied up—he was too freaking handcuffed by limits on what he could do to get the girls to get with the program, ASAP.

The plan said, be nice to them, for good reason. No beating them up, no grabbing teenage titties, nothing like that—not yet.

He knew the teens were scared, which made total sense. The older one, Emma Bailey, had a hell of a temper and was setting a bad example. She was fighting back, even though she was helpless. It worried him. It wasn't part of the plan. He hoped Emma Bailey had settled down and would behave today. She hadn't eaten or drunk since yesterday, which hopefully would help.

Trust the plan. Trust the man.

He pulled down the Shrek mask over his face, which he hated, because it only let him breathe hot, stale air.

He began by taking off the eye masks and ball gags off from both girls.

"Hey, smelly Shrek's back! Too bad we can't hold our noses!" said Emma Bailey.

Damn! He'd had a lot going on this week and hadn't had extra time for showering or doing laundry. He'd kidnapped a freaking Mean Girl...

"We're going to try something new," he said, fighting to keep his voice calm. He didn't want Emma Bailey to think she was scoring any points. "I'm going to free you both up and you can use the toilet and then eat and drink together. You two have to start acting like a team. Like sisters."

"I haven't got a sister," said Emma Bailey.

"I do," said Emma Addison quietly. Then a little louder: "But she's a pest!" The girl half laughed, half sobbed.

The man in the mask attached the longer bike-chain tethers and removed their short chain tethers. Then he used his knife to cut the plastic tie wraps at their hands and feet.

"Can you give us some privacy to take a leak, you perv?" asked Emma Bailey.

"You need to learn to talk nice," he snapped back.

"Do any women talk to you if you don't kidnap them?"

"Don't get him mad," said Emma Addison, in a scared little voice.

"Hush up, I know his game," said Emma Bailey. "He doesn't know what the fuck he's doing. He's too stupid." And she laughed!

The man had to resist the impulse to freaking knock her down. He could feel blood rising in his ears, behind the hot Shrek mask.

Who the hell did she think she was? He barely controlled himself, stepping back toward the ladder, crossing his arms and watching them as they moved to the toilet chair.

He saw them whispering a bit, but didn't intervene.

When the girls finished, they shuffled back to where he'd laid out food and water (with the usual sleeping pills ground up in it). Only the younger girl, Emma Addison, began eating and drinking.

"You only get a few minutes," he warned Emma Bailey.

"I'm all set," she said, calm and cool.

The man groaned. Now what the fuck—she's doing a hunger strike? Did she think she could throw him off, make him change the whole plan? What the hell was the point of her defiance?

This wouldn't last. Who was the old Indian guy who did a hunger strike, became a big hero with a movie, but he died...

Gandhi something? Was that the hippie protest bullshit they taught in school these days?

But this girl was no freaking hero. She'd be begging for food and even sooner she'd be begging for water. The man knew a person would die of thirst in a few days. She could starve herself for longer if she drank something. Weeks?

The man didn't know the science, he'd have to look it up. But he believed in his gut the brat would give up and get with the program.

Wouldn't she?

CHAPTER TWENTY-FIVE

Pepper was back to work in his converted drunk tank by four-thirty, punching info about old cases into the database with one eye on the door. He expected Sergeant Weisner would pounce at any time to give him hell about disappearing.

He had promised to get Dennis Cole the list of Emmas in the area, but now he felt sleazy about following through with it. The biker didn't have any business getting involved—the reward wasn't a legit reason for Cole to carry out a personal hunt for the Greenhead Snatcher. And giving him a copy of something that was part of the official investigation...it just seemed wrong.

Pepper cruised past his dad's office. His door was closed and faint voices drifted through. Better not to interrupt. Luckily, he cornered Detective Sweeney in the officers' bullpen.

"Young Ryan, what do you know?" asked Sweeney with a smile.

Maybe Sweeney would be open to a little old-fashioned horse trading of info. Only one way to find out.

"I heard some crazy info about Scooter McCord. He has a passport from the United Kingdom with his photo, but a different name."

"Oh yeah? Who told you?"

"Just someone who wants to stay out of trouble. Have you gotten a warrant to search his house yet?"

Sweeney studied him with a hint of a smile on his face.

"We're working on probable cause to get one and aren't even close yet. Think I can talk to your friend?"

Shit. "I'll ask the person. They didn't want to get involved, so..."

"You do that. I can talk to him on the down low. Or is it a her?"

"I'll, ah, check with them."

The detective laughed and slapped his back.

"By the way," tried Pepper. "Have you put together a list of teenagers named Emma who live in the area?"

"You bet. Why?"

"Well, I could look it over if you like. See if you've missed anyone I know."

The detective sighed. "I appreciate it, kid. That list's too hot to show anyone. Completely need-to-know. Can you imagine if someone leaked it to the media? They'd have a field day with it. And someone's ass would get canned."

So, a total fail.

Pepper headed back to his drunk tank office. He'd have to create his own list of all the Emmas who lived on the Lower Cape.

He sat in front of his computer, chewing a pencil eraser. He had to start with some assumptions. Since the two missing girls were both Cape locals, not tourists, he had to assume if there was something to the "Emma" theory, that he could exclude any tourists. They probably weren't a target.

He started by searching an online White Pages site. He typed "Emma" in the first-name box, leaving the last-name box empty. For town, he typed "New Albion, MA." He would have to repeat the search for each town on the Lower Cape.

Thirty-two Emmas appeared in his search result. None of them were teens. The site offered the Emmas' ages by decade, but all were twenties or older.

Pepper sighed. This was useless. There had to be an easier way.

"What's that?"

Pepper jumped at the voice, but mid-jump realized it was not the soul-crushing voice of Sergeant Weisner. It was the high-pitched teenage voice of Zula Eisenhower.

The girl had crept to his shoulder and was looking at his list.

"Damn, Zula. What the hell?"

"Language, language."

Was the kid fourteen or forty? "I'm working, go away," he grumbled.

She peered at him through her big glasses. "Not doing very well, huh? Looks like you're not winning our big bet."

She meant her wager that he couldn't find Emma Bailey before anyone else. Which had been for what, a dollar? He'd thought she was joking, just busting his chops—he wasn't going to catch the Greenhead Snatcher before the real cops.

"Go away," he said, rubbing his temples.

She didn't. "You think the Snatcher'll strike again? Grab another Emma?" she asked.

Quick kid. Annoying, but quick.

"Probably," he said. And he meant it—another girl would probably be snatched if they didn't catch the psycho first.

Zula hugged herself. "You're probably right. Why would he stop? You know what a kill tide is, right?"

"What?"

"A kill tide. It's a super high tide which happens sometimes on the Cape in August. The currents change and there's a big flood which kills all the greenhead larvae. It stops greenhead flies from being a nuisance the rest of the summer."

Pepper had noticed there were fewer greenheads at the end of some summers, but never knew why. "So?"

"So I'm saying, I think you're right. Predators don't just stop. Little ones or big ones. Something more powerful has to stop them. That's how nature works."

Interesting, but so what? Aloud he said, "You'll get an A on your ninth-grade science report, Little Ike. Right now I need to concentrate—I have to finish this list and I'm getting all the wrong results so far."

She sighed. "Pepper, you're *hopeless*. You're trying to get a list of all teenage girls named Emma who live in the area, right? Why would they be on a white pages website? Go get some fresh air, let me do this the easy way."

"What?"

"Saying 'what' over and over doesn't make you look any smarter, Mr. Harvard. Take a walk, let me do my thing."

"Does your dad know where you are?"

"Shoo."

Over the years, Pepper hadn't yet won a battle of wills with Zula. So he grabbed his gym bag from under the desk and shooed.

Pepper pushed himself with a hard workout at the Globe Gym location around the corner.

An old high school buddy at the front desk was giving him a special discount rate for the summer. As a tit-for-tat, Pepper had promised to help the guy with any speeding tickets he might get. Somehow.

Pepper had promised himself he'd work out more frequently. He needed to arrive at Harvard in top shape because captain practices for the hockey team would begin not too far into the school year. He knew the other guys would arrive in mid-season fitness, ready to fight for their spots on the team.

Pepper called to mind his asshole high school coach, Gus Bullard, and every insult he'd ever thrown at Pepper. That he was too slow. That he blamed everyone but himself. That he was a loser. All the psychological bullying bullshit the coach had used to motivate him. What a psycho. Well, Pepper channeled his old abuse now and let it energize him.

Pepper pushed himself like a wild man for forty-five minutes —he kicked his cardio butt using an elliptical machine, then worked through a heavy rotation of free-weight exercises, taking only short rests. He finished with a one-minute shower.

Returning to the locker area, he saw his new nemesis Fester Timmins naked. From behind. Bending over.

A sight Pepper could never unsee.

Pepper was rubbing his eyes as the man straightened up and saw him.

"Pepper Ryan! You following me?"

"Hey, Fester..." Pepper trod barefoot to his locker, his towel wrapped tightly around his waist.

"I saw you working out, but I didn't want to talk shop until we were, you know, alone."

Okay...? "I've got to get back to the station," said Pepper.

"Roger that. Well, I just wanted to let you know, I'm officially working the Greenhead Snatcher case."

"What?"

"Yep. I've got my first client as a private eye—unofficial until I get all the paperwork done and whatnot." Then Fester Timmins, 100% naked in all his pink, beefy glory, came over to Pepper and lowered his voice to a whisper. "My client's been unfairly accused in the kidnappings. My job's proving his innocence."

Pepper fought to maintain strict eye contact. "Who's your client?"

"No, no, I'm sworn to confidentiality. But we're both looking for the truth, right? We find the real Snatcher and I'll have a very happy client. Imagine the references!"

A silver-haired man entered the locker room, causing Timmins to jump away from Pepper's side. The man gave them a long look and headed into the toilet area.

Pepper dropped his towel, pulled on underwear as fast as he ever had. "You think that's a smart idea? Taking on clients before you get a private investigator license?"

"No worries... I took it pro bono, for now! That means—"

"I know that one, Fester. Well, good luck. If you get any serious leads, call Detective Sweeney."

"Sweeney?" scoffed Timmins. "That guy's got an attitude problem. He won't even meet with me. But I'm happy to share info with you. You scratch my back—"

"I'll think about it," said Pepper, grabbing his gym bag and hustling to the exit. Not looking back at Timmins, still naked. Trying not to think about scratching his hairy pink back...

As a reward for his workout and for having escaped Fester Timmins, Pepper stopped by the Fudge Hut, the town's best place for candy and ice cream. He'd been going there since he was little. He demolished a large ice cream sundae with extra fudge and two cherries. Because he was worth it.

Pepper headed back to the police station after about an hour and a quarter's absence, carrying a cup of chocolate ice cream covered with rainbow sprinkles as a thank-you to Zula for her help. He knew that combo was her favorite ice cream and topping, having been to Fudge Hut with her and Jake countless times over the past ten years. He didn't have confidence the kid could pull much together, but he appreciated her attempt to help.

When Pepper reached his little hellhole office, Zula blinked at him from his chair, triumphantly. She handed him a piece of paper.

It was a list of thirty-eight Emmas, with their full names and addresses. All from New Albion or other nearby towns. All were teenagers.

"Holy crap!" said Pepper. "How'd you put this together so fast?"

"Social media," she said, taking a mouthful of ice cream and sprinkles. "I checked my friend lists, and friend of friend lists, covering all the teens on this part of the Cape."

"You're a teenager? I thought you were still a tween."

"Jerk!"

He dodged her attempt to smack him with her ice cream spoon as he slipped away with her list of Emmas.

Pepper had gotten another bright idea.

Pepper brought Zula's list to his dad's office. Time to partially redeem himself.

His dad was there, but also Detective Sweeney and Sergeant Weisner. Even better.

"What now?" asked his dad. He looked exhausted and older than he was. Another perk of his career...

Pepper held up his piece of paper. "I know Sweeney has a list of Emmas in the area. I have a list too—I thought maybe you'd want to cross-check it? See if any Emmas on my list aren't on yours?"

He handed the list to his dad and the three officers looked at it.

"You made this?" asked Weisner.

"It didn't take long," answered Pepper, dodging the question. "And I'm caught up on my database work." Why did they already have him feeling guilty?

"Thirty-eight names," Weisner said. "Sweeney's list is a tad longer."

"Mine's just the Lower Cape."

"His is too. And it has sixty-three Emmas." Weisner laughed. "But don't feel too bad. Thirty-eight out of sixty-three…that's just above 60%, right? That's a passing grade!"

"Damn it, that's enough," interrupted his dad. "Pepper, I'll see you at home. Goodbye." His dad's pale face had gone red, probably from embarrassment. Perfect.

Sweeney smiled, then shrugged his shoulders. "But nice try, kid."

Without another word, Pepper turned and left them there. His cheeks burned.

Fuck 'em. He'd just been trying to help.

Pepper couldn't remember being that embarrassed and pissed off at the same time. He walked right past his little hole-in-the-wall office, where out of the corner of his eye he saw Zula still waiting, eating the ice cream he'd brought her. But he didn't stop.

His phone rang and Dennis Cole's name flashed on his screen. He answered it as he walked.

"Hey, Ryan!" said Cole, his voice crackling. Not a great connection, which was a chronic problem in parts of New Albion. "We need to get together again!"

Why not? "Cool—I've got the Emmas list for you."

Cole laughed. "Good job! But I might not need it anymore. I've got a great angle on the Snatcher. I'm almost positive."

"Hey, amazing!" said Pepper. "You need to call the police right away. Ask for Detective Sweeney. He—"

"Not yet, dude. They won't pay one hundred grand for just a guess. I need a little more meat on the bone, you know? I'm so close! Meet me at my house at seven o'clock. We'll have a beer and I'll fill you in. I might even be a hundred percent sure by then. You can listen in while I call your detective."

Cole gave Pepper the address where he and Brad St. John lived, which was in a less-expensive area of New Albion out near the Big Red Yard, then hung up.

Pepper tried to decide what to do.

For a second, he considered telling his dad what Cole had said. But he couldn't take another dose of ridicule so soon.

Hell, no. He decided he would head to Dennis and Brad's place tonight and give Cole his own shorter list of Emmas. Pepper didn't feel guilty about sharing it anymore, since apparently it was worthless to real investigators. *Damn...*

Pepper headed out the side door. He couldn't stay in that police station another second.

CHAPTER TWENTY-SIX

That evening the man in the van was waiting in front of the house next door to the home of a new girl. Hopefully it would be her lucky day...

He'd had a hell of a crappy day so far—eating one big shit burger after another. Nothing was going right. He feared the cops were closing in on him. And he was even more worried about the Emmas.

He remembered the night he grabbed Emma Bailey. She was his favorite so far, even though she gave him so much crap. Someday, maybe he and Emma would look back on it and laugh.

Yes, the man was offering the girls a new life—one they hadn't even considered. A better life. Would they get it? Females were so damn complicated.

Would the girls work out? Or would they have to...

No, he told himself. Focus on the final girl. Focus on the fact that if this one goes well, everything changes.

The man's leg began bouncing with excitement at the thought.

He wasn't too worried about a nosy neighbor phoning in his van. Not anymore. With a little hard work, he was now a step ahead of the cops, a step ahead of everyone. He wasn't worried about anything. But he wished he'd had time to go smoke a little crank earlier, to get his head in the zone.

A talk radio station was yammering on and on about whether they should allow felons to vote. It was the stupidest debate he'd ever heard. He wondered whether the silky-voiced woman host or the low, mellow-voiced guest (a professor from somewhere) had ever met a hard-core felon. Let alone a felon who wanted to vote.

The man in the van wanted to call in and tell them America had gone down the freaking toilet since 9/11. Didn't anyone else see it? He wanted to call them idiots, but they'd probably bleep him out. Cowards.

The talking heads were completely missing what was going on —the ever-spreading bureaucracy, the chipping away of liberties. The slow tightening of testicle cuffs, in the name of national security. The man wondered if they'd let him say testicle on talk radio? Or he could say nuts?

As he listened to the nitwits on the radio, the man in the van wiped his driver's side window with a Taco Bell napkin. Over and over. The window kept getting cleaner and cleaner, but he thought he could do better. He kept rubbing. He tried small circles, bigger circles. The window looked better and better.

He turned on the police scanner app on his smartphone. The app broadcast dispatch calls for the Barnstable county sheriff's department. He wanted to overhear the alert that another girl was grabbed right under their stupid noses. And it might give him an edge—a heads-up when the newest manhunt for him kicked off.

He checked his cheap watch. Shit, it was almost too late!

He turned off the talk radio nonsense. It was time to focus.

His prep runs showed this third girl, a nineteen-year-old named Jessica Little, got off work at 5:30 and pretty much always arrived home in her boring little Kia Forte around 5:50. Give or take five minutes.

It was 5:48 right now. A completely boring set of numbers. Although in a minute it'd be $5 + 4 = 9$...

The other problem was the damn neighbors on the other side of the girl's house, two down from where he'd parked his van. A man and a woman were out in their front yard. Possibly around sixty years old. They were futzing around with the lawn, pointing at weeds and sometimes pulling them, sometimes not. It was a high-end lawn, green and thick. They were spraying some things and trimming other things.

He would have a hard time grabbing Jessica Little while those two gardeners were watching. He figured the woman would instantly call 911. Females always had a cell phone handy, even while gardening. Like his buddy said, it was in their DNA.

The man fingered his stupid little .22 pistol. It would do the job close up, but how would he get close to them? Pretend he'd lost his dog? Some ruse?

And while he believed he could pull the trigger, killing the couple was definitely *not* part of the plan. It would bring a whole new level of shit-storm panic on Cape Cod. No, he needed them to go inside their stupid house, pronto.

The man got an idea. He took his smartphone and punched in the nosy neighbors' address, searching to find a matching land line phone number. Success—it popped right up!

Then he took a different cell phone (a burner flip phone with no way to trace it back to him) and called the nosy neighbors' number. He watched them desperately.

The woman raised her head and cocked an ear. She put down her trowel and wiped her hands on her apron.

The man (her husband?) said something to her and she laughed. Then, *damn, damn, damn*...she picked up her tool and started digging again.

The man in the van looked both ways and saw no sign of Jessica Little's Kia yet. She should arrive any freaking second.

He dialed the neighbors' house phone for a second time.

The woman's head twitched again, and she said something to her husband. She even stood up. But she only stretched, then got down on her knees to keep working.

Damn telemarketers. They fucking ruined everything. No one answered their land lines anymore—it was always some robot voice, trying to scam you. Parasitic dumbasses. They were even worse than the goddamn government.

He saw the small blue Kia come down the street and park in the driveway. Jessica Little climbed out, looking young and happy and cute in a short skirt. She waved to her neighbors, and they said something to her. She laughed and headed toward her front door.

The man in the van sat frozen. Seething, furious. There was absolutely nothing he could do. He wanted to scream.

The front door opened just before Jessica reached it. A woman appeared in the doorway, her mother. The man had seen her before too. The mother was very pretty—an older version of Jessica. That had even been a factor in picking Jessica.

A moment later, Jessica and her mother went inside their house and the front door closed shut.

The man had freaking failed. His stomach clenched liked he'd eaten something spoiled. Rage swamped his whole body.

This was supposed to be it. Grab Jessica Little, take care of business. Then in a few days he was supposed to drive over the Bourne Bridge off Cape Cod—away and gone. Safe.

Free to start their new life.

Instead, now he had to stick around. Find another chance. Tomorrow, same time, same place? Or possibly catch Jessica in the parking lot at her work—a clothing store at the mall. No, that had even more variables and even more damn witnesses and risks.

No, trust the plan, trust the man...

He drove away, still shaking. He decided to stop by and visit his best buddy, the one guy who could always calm him down.

He'd failed and he almost couldn't take it. This whole thing had to end as soon as fucking possible. It had to. Before he freaking exploded...

But first he needed to smoke a pipe. Of course, he'd left his stuff at his place, the way his day was going. So he drove home first. He stopped a block away from his place because he didn't want anyone to remember a van at his place. Again, sticking to the plan.

That's when the man saw his bad luck wasn't over for the day. As he walked toward home, about a hundred yards away, he saw his front door open and a stranger came out! Freaking out, he scrunched down behind a car. The stranger looked both ways as he sauntered to the street and got on a Harley-Davidson bike.

Damn! Who the hell was this guy? An undercover cop? Or was it a coincidence—some lowlife biker broke into his place, coincidentally?

The man's mind raced, spiraling. Had he left his journal out? He'd been taking notes about everything he'd done and what he would do next. Which was strictly against the plan. But it was the only way to keep his head straight and keep himself *on* plan, a step ahead of the freaking cops. Had he left the damn journal on his bed?

He jogged back to his van. When the Harley roared away, he followed.

The Harley guy drove for ten minutes and parked in the driveway of a small, rundown house with an overgrown lawn. They might still be in New Albion or possibly the next town over.

The man in the van hung back two doors away, watching and trying to decide what to do. Way, way off plan...

Why the fuck was that guy in my home? And what did he find?

The man in the van checked his little Walther P22 pistol was still in his pocket. It was there, heavy and reassuring. But he didn't want to make that much noise if he could help it.

He crawled into the back of his van and took out his quieter weapon: the Vipertek mini stun gun. *Perfect.*

He didn't come up with much of a plan. He kept it simple.

He strolled to the Harley guy's door and rang it, with a big fake smile on his face. When the door swung open, the large guy in the leather vest filled the doorway, a look of annoyed arrogance on his face. "What do you—"

The man lunged forward with his stun gun and gave the asshole a chest full of thousands of volts.

The Harley guy shouted and stumbled backward, falling to the linoleum hallway floor, twisting onto his stomach.

The man saw a long knife tucked in the back of Harley guy's pants. *The snake! One more second and he'd have—!*

The man from the van saw red. He absolutely lost it. He jumped on the Harley guy's back as he tried to stand. With his empty hand he grabbed the knife from the guy's pants, then attacked with it, stabbing over and over into the guy's back.

Howling, the Harley guy heaved him off and crawled down the hallway, trailing blood.

He zapped the Harley guy with the stun gun in the ass of his black jeans. He giggled as the guy spasmed and rolled onto his back. He hopped onto the guy's big torso, straddling him. Then again stabbing with the knife, over and over. The Harley guy was barely fighting back now.

The man lost track of time. The guy under him wasn't moving anymore. He'd stabbed him, what? Fifty times?

Harley guy's head was back and his mouth was open. And his eyes. Unmoving. Blood was freaking everywhere.

Ambush me with a knife? Rage boiled inside him. *Why does everyone think they can push me around like a damn loser?*

The guy had found out differently, hadn't he? Once again, they'd underestimated what he could do when pushed.

The man took a deep breath and let it go in a long, celebratory rush. He'd won. His first win of the damn day.

So what to do now?

Think. He closed his eyes and counted to ten.

Okay. First, he closed the front door and locked it. No one was in sight.

Second, he searched the guy's pockets, looking for his journal or any other items the guy might have taken when searching his place. He found nothing.

He left the body on the floor while he searched the house. Maybe the guy took something and had hidden it away already? But he'd only had a minute before his doorbell rang and the fight started. Where could he have put anything?

The man searched and found nothing.

So, what to do with the dead guy? Leave him? The man didn't know whether anyone else lived here. And his DNA might be on the dead guy.

No, he'd have to move the body somewhere safer. Buy himself a little more time, which was hopefully all he'd need.

With a little luck, he'd grab that Jessica Little and get off the Cape before anyone found this bloody mess.

Then nothing would matter.

CHAPTER TWENTY-SEVEN

Chief of Police Gerald Ryan could feel a new headache coming on.

He was sitting in his office around 7:00 PM with Detective Kevin Sweeney, who was giving him an update about his progress, or lack thereof, on the Greenhead Snatcher investigation.

No one, not the local police departments, the Staties, or the FBI, had a strong lead suspect. So besides trying to investigate the most likely local suspects, Casper Yelle and Alastair "Scooter" McCord, Detective Sweeney was beating the bushes and hoping something flew out, the same as every other investigator on the task force.

Sweeney was working his way through the list of New Albion's registered sex offenders, trying to interview them if they cooperated. They were all potential persons of interest in the two kidnappings.

This afternoon Sweeney had interviewed a middle-aged white man named Emilio "Leo" Flammia, who was a level-two sex offender in town. He had two convictions for indecent assault and battery on a person aged fourteen or older.

Sweeney quickly recapped Flammia's background for Gerald.

The man had worked at Murphy's Hole Marina when he first came to New Albion, scraping boats, doing whatever dirty work needed doing in the marina. He'd worked as a janitor at New Albion High School for three months until they fired him when the superintendent's office discovered his criminal record—he'd lied on his application. Flammia now did lawn care jobs in this part of the Cape.

Sweeney had questioned the man about everywhere he'd been since last Thursday morning. Flammia's answers had been simple and routine.

Of course, Sweeney was most interested in Flammia's alibis for the times of the two Emma kidnappings. On Thursday night when Emma Bailey was kidnapped, Flammia said he'd been watching TV, flipping around, and drinking beer. Mostly watching baseball, but he couldn't remember the teams playing or who won. Because of the beer and because he'd fallen asleep before the game ended. On Saturday afternoon when Emma Addison was kidnapped, Flammia said he'd been taking a nap.

The man didn't have anyone to corroborate his whereabouts at those two most important times. He lived alone.

"The Sox were off Thursday night," said Sweeney. "But there's always some baseball on. And Flammia looks like a drinker, or worse. If he was hammered, or possibly high on pills or whatever, he could have been watching whatever baseball was on. The guy didn't seem very bright."

Which was probably enough to let him forget about Flammia as a suspect. The one thing the FBI profilers were certain of is the Greenhead Snatcher had above average intelligence. Both kidnappings had been brazen and were carried out quick and clean. The kidnapper had completely disappeared, other than to send the ransom request to the Addisons yesterday. He had made no mistakes they knew about yet.

Gerald's headache was building now. He took a big bottle of

Aleve from his desk drawer and popped two in his mouth, flushing them down with coffee from the mug on his desk. It was cold and bitter.

Sweeney continued. "Flammia didn't ask for a lawyer or anything. The only strange bit was when I asked if I could search the white cargo van registered to his name. Flammia didn't get uptight about it; he just said he'd sold it two months ago. Said he'd signed over the title and everything."

Gerald considered that. "What does he use for his contracting jobs?"

"He said an old pickup truck. Didn't seem too jumpy or sweaty."

Gerald took another sip of cold, stale coffee. "So, either he's a good liar, or he didn't have a van to do the kidnappings."

"He was lying about something, they always lie about something. He's probably doing something he shouldn't. But my gut? I don't think he's our guy. He wasn't nervous enough. Or smart enough. I'll have someone follow up with the registry to see if a registration transfer is in process for his van. In the meantime, I'll keep moving down the list to the next guy, put Flammia on the back burner."

Gerald knew the Addisons had raised the two million dollars in cash today that the Greenhead Snatcher had demanded by eleven o'clock tonight. The money was ready—unmarked hundred-dollar bills stuffed in a big red duffel bag. It had been a crazy effort involving an emergency scramble by multiple banks and brokerage firms. The FBI had worked with the financial institutions to help them satisfy regulatory requirements and meet the unreasonable same-day deadline.

Gerald planned to be at the Addisons' house tonight when the Snatcher had promised to contact the family again. He knew the Bailey parents would be there too. Gerald couldn't stay away.

A large box had turned up two hours ago on the porch of a

house a block down from the Addisons. It said, DO NOT OPEN. CALL THE POLICE. The people who lived there had responded to their doorbell, saw the box and quickly called 911.

The box, carefully opened by a bomb squad, held a smaller box inside that was addressed to the Addison and Bailey families. The smaller box had a warning on its top not to open the box until they received a call from the man who had their daughters. Or else the Emmas would die.

So, the box was under guard at the Addisons' house, unopened for the time being. Along with officers from various law enforcement agencies helping with the task force.

Gerald knew that ransom situations were a bitch. Some other countries, such as Mexico, had a well-practiced industry for kidnappings, ransoms and releases. But in the U.S., kidnappings by strangers which led to a ransom rarely ended well. Of course, they weren't sure yet that the Snatcher didn't have some unknown relationship to the Emmas.

It was also true that often the kidnapper didn't show up for a ransom drop. Often, the victim was already dead.

Maybe not this time? They had to be optimistic.

No, Gerald didn't need an FBI profiler to know the Greenhead Snatcher was smart and careful. And the FBI still believed the Snatcher was working alone. No evidence to the contrary. So the money handoff would be the perfect time to grab the Snatcher when he couldn't harm the girls.

In other words, tonight was the night.

"I agree about Flammia," Gerald finally said. "Add him to the back burner. Hopefully, we'll have our kidnapper in handcuffs before the night's over."

Pepper couldn't wait to learn what Dennis Cole had found out. He arrived at Cole and Brad's place, a small duplex on Cardinal Street, a few minutes before seven.

He could see Cole's red work truck with its large silver toolbox parked on the street. Cole had parked his Harley-Davidson bike in front of it. Pepper didn't see Brad St. John's old white van.

Pepper waited in his truck until seven o'clock sharp. The news on the radio focused on the Greenhead Snatcher and a great white shark sighting by three surfers at Nauset Beach in Orleans, close to his location. The announcer said the sharks were there for the seals, not the people. Pepper wondered, *Would sharks be that picky? Food was food...*

He wondered what tourists were thinking about Cape Cod since the Greenhead snatching had begun—that now it was dangerous in the water and on land?

Pepper walked to the front door and rang the bell. He had the list of Emmas in his hand, a folded piece of paper.

No answer.

He rang again with the same result.

He sat down on the front steps and waited. Maybe Cole was in the shower or something?

Waited five minutes, rang again. Nothing.

Pepper stretched and walked around the side of the building to check the backyard. He was grateful there wasn't a dog, but he didn't find Cole either. Hmm.

Pepper returned to the front door and rang again. Still nothing. Then he tried the handle. It was unlocked. He poked in his head and yelled Cole's name.

Still no answer.

Now fully annoyed, Pepper entered. But quickly stopped. A puddle of red liquid stained the hallway floor. More blood was splattered on the walls leading to the kitchen.

Oh my God. Oh my God.

It had to be blood. Was it from Dennis Cole? Or possibly... Brad St. John?

Pepper knew enough about crime scenes to quickly and gingerly back out the front door. He pulled out his cell phone and called his dad. When his call dumped to voice mail, Pepper called again.

Eventually, his dad picked up.

Pepper told his dad the basics of what he'd found and his dad told him to wait outside. He did. He was sitting on the front steps when Fester Timmins jogged up the walkway a minute later.

Damn. At least he was wearing black sweatpants and a polo shirt.

The man froze when he saw Pepper. "Pepper Ryan, like a bad penny! What're *you* doing here?"

"I could ask you the same thing. You should take off if you don't want to get caught up in a crime scene."

Timmins put on sunglasses he'd been carrying. "I was nearby and had my police scanner on when Dispatch put out this address. Lots of first responders inbound. I thought it might be part of the Snatcher crimes they're trying to pin on my client."

Police sirens grew in the distance, and a minute later a marked patrol car slid to a stop at the curb. Officer Dooley hopped out, his red hair shining in the sunlight.

Pepper wished he was anywhere else. Absolutely anywhere without a crime scene, police sirens and Fester Timmins.

It didn't help that his dad was on his way here too. What was he going to tell him? Did he have to mention all the information from the Greenhead Snatcher investigation he'd shared with Dennis Cole?

Anywhere else...

CHAPTER TWENTY-EIGHT

Chief of Police Gerald Ryan arrived at the crime scene on Cardinal Street with Detective Kevin Sweeney, a junior detective named Enid Musto, and two patrol officers.

Pepper was waiting by the street, leaning against his truck. A man was with him.

Officer Dooley was doing crowd control, keeping everyone back from the small duplex with its door standing wide open, but a small crowd had gathered to see what was going on and it kept inching forward.

Fucking people. They swarm at any hint of blood, like blowflies.

The patrol officers joined Dooley on crowd control and pushed everyone back, then began taping out a perimeter. The detectives went to the body and began their process. Enid Musto would be the lead detective on this crime scene, since Sweeney was flat out on the Greenhead Snatcher investigation. Musto would take charge, begin documenting the scene, and coordinate with the medical examiner.

Gerald walked to his son. "Are you okay?"

Pepper looked back at him blankly. He looked like he might be in shock.

"It's okay. Come over here, sit down." Gerald gestured to the curb.

His son sat, and Gerald sat beside him.

"Tell me what happened."

Pepper explained he was meeting a guy named Dennis Cole here at his place. Cole roomed with the leader of Pepper's band, Brad St. John.

But Cole didn't answer the door. The door was unlocked, so Pepper went inside. He saw a ton of blood in the hallway and immediately stepped outside and called him.

It amazed Gerald how calm his son sounded, telling the story.

"Was anyone nearby who seemed suspicious?"

"The house was empty and no one was outside. I didn't see Brad's van, but I texted him after I called you. He's at his day job at the Taco Bell over in Hyannis. He sounded normal, and I didn't tell him anything."

Good move, thought Gerald.

"And when I came out, Fester Timmins showed up again." Pepper pointed toward the guy who was still leaning against Pepper's truck. "You may want to talk to him, find out why he's always in the wrong place at the right time..."

Gerald knew he shouldn't be questioning his own son. He should have Pepper wait to talk to Musto—she was a solid, objective detective. Or at least have Eisenhower do it. Gerald couldn't do the job properly, not with his own boy.

"Pepper, what was really going on?" he asked.

"What?"

"Why were you meeting up with Dennis Cole? Where do you know him from?"

"Like I said, he's Brad's roommate. I met him at our gig at the Beachcomber on Thursday night. Dennis offered to help take our music to the next level. Do more original songs, get more exposure."

"Was he in the music business?"

"Not really, but he claims to have lots of contacts."

"So that's why you came over here? To talk about music?"

"Mostly, yeah."

Gerald had interviewed many people in his long career in law enforcement, so he knew Pepper was partially lying. Probably skipping some important details.

Gerald started getting mad. He didn't want to say the wrong thing to Pepper and unintentionally make things worse. Gerald knew he wasn't good separating his cop and dad roles. But he was trying.

I wish my kids were kids again, he thought, looking at Pepper's pale face. An age with less real-world tragedy, less risk.

Gerald was too good of a cop to dwell on that right now. "I need you to go down to the station," he said. "I'll call Eisenhower, ask him to take your formal statement."

"Okay, Dad. Thanks."

Gerald patted his son's shoulder and got up to go inside to talk to Sweeney and Musto. "Oh, and Pepper? Don't lie to Eisenhower like you just did to me, okay?"

———

Pepper's mind was spinning as he drove to the police station. All that blood. Dennis Cole had to be dead, right?

Shit, shit, shit.

The truth was, Cole probably got killed because of tips Pepper fed to him. Cole must have been acting on his info, trying to nail the Greenhead Snatcher and get the big reward. What did he learn? What did he see? Did he actually figure out who was the Snatcher?

And where the hell was Cole, dead or alive?

So what could Pepper tell Lieutenant Eisenhower when giving his witness statement? Should he admit he gave Cole confidential information—info Pepper shouldn't have had access to? That Cole was investigating the snatchings himself to earn the reward?

Would Pepper be in even more trouble for not telling his dad earlier? His dad had seemed pissed off and looked like he hadn't slept in days. Pepper hadn't seen him at home much since the Emma Bailey snatching. He probably had only been catching quick naps, just enough to keep him on his feet. He was taking the case very personally, very hard. And now this new murder on top of it all.

Pepper had to lie, right? If he got caught, would his own dad have him arrested for obstruction of justice? For giving a false statement?

What was the alternative? Admit he'd been nosing around the investigation and spilling confidential info?

Then he probably wouldn't get arrested—his dad would just kill him.

For better or worse, Pepper lied in his official statement.

Not entirely. He told Eisenhower more than he'd told his dad. He told about meeting Dennis Cole at the Beachcomber on Thursday night. How he'd offered to help Pepper and the others get to the next level with their music. That he'd said he had industry contacts.

He admitted talking with Cole about the Greenhead Snatcher investigation, at a high level. That Cole was intent on the need for someone to catch the kidnapper soon. And that he had his own theories about the case.

Pepper didn't admit he'd looked at Dad's files and told Cole the names and addresses of current suspects in New Albion. He didn't mention the list of local Emmas he'd been planning to hand over to Cole. And he left out that Cole thought he knew who the Snatcher was.

Yep, he skipped all the terrible stuff.

Eisenhower didn't ask too many questions. He just recorded Pepper's statement and said they would transcribe it. Later, Pepper would need to make any corrections, then sign it.

Pepper left the police station. Once he reached his truck, he began shaking.

He had just screwed himself, but what else could he have done?

Pepper wondered what the hell he had been thinking. The girls getting snatched, the hunt for the Greenhead Killer, this was not a game. He had been messing with life and death.

And Pepper believed, even if the police didn't yet, that the Greenhead Snatcher wasn't just a kidnapper. He was probably a killer now too. Dennis Cole's killer. Pepper felt a cold grip on his spine.

Whoever the Snatcher was, he must have believed Cole was closing in on him, or already had him cornered, so he'd attacked Cole at his home. It was the only thing which made sense. No way it was a coincidence.

Thank God that Cole hadn't sent Pepper too many detailed texts. Would Eisenhower or Detective Musto demand Pepper's texts? He pulled out his phone and reviewed his texts back and forth with Cole. They were pretty mild. Nothing that said aha, Pepper was a liar.

Nothing that was evidence of how he felt deep down—that Dennis Cole's disappearance and probable death was his fault.

Absolutely his fucking fault.

CHAPTER TWENTY-NINE

Emma Bailey's mouth was *so* dry.

Her empty stomach was clenched up like a fist. Time was drifting, like in a dark, bad dream.

Because of the ball gag in her mouth, she had to breathe through her nose. She focused on her breathing, in and out, trying not to cry. Trying to think of what she could do to help her situation.

It was probably the next evening when Shrek came back. He took off their eye and mouth coverings and switched them from the short bike chains to the long bike chains. The man was still wearing his stupid mask, and in the light of his lantern he looked somewhere between ridiculous and terrifying.

Emma said nothing to the man. It was one of the other few things she could control. Screw him.

After a bathroom break, Shrek came back to where they stood by their spots and said to Emma, "Are you done being silly? You ready to eat and drink?"

She was fairly low energy at that point. She tried to spit at him, but her mouth was too dry. "You suck!" she croaked at him.

New Emma began eating and drinking, her head down low. Trying to stay out of it.

Whatever. "Maybe we haven't been fair," Emma said to New Emma. "So what if Shrek seems like a smelly, socially backward, capital L loser? Maybe he's so much more than that."

New Emma didn't even slow her eating to answer.

"Hey, you think his circus left town and he got left behind?" asked Emma.

Neither of them responded.

Emma's stomach cramped at the sight of the food. She clenched her teeth. Was she being stupid, holding out? Was she doing anything other than weakening and hurting herself? Her original idea, that she was taking back power by not eating and drinking, now seemed dumb.

"I have a little job for you both today," Shrek said. "Behave yourselves and I'll show you my appreciation."

Emma didn't want him showing her anything, the perv. "I'm not helping you with jack!"

Shrek gave her leash a hard shake. "Aren't you worried about your families, how sad they are? That they're wondering if you're even alive? Well, good news—I'm letting you write notes to your families."

Emma was suddenly excited. She knew her parents would be beyond desperate, and a note from her would be pure gold.

He gave them each a stubby little pencil and a piece of paper with a chunk of cardboard to use as a desk.

"Start your note by saying, 'I love you, Mom! I love you, Dad!' Then you need to add something which makes it clear the note is from you. Something only you and your family would know."

"You should just let us text them," Emma suggested. "That's, like, how I always talk to them. You still have my phone?"

Shrek laughed through his mask. "No phones."

So Emma did what he said. She put the first stuff like he said, which she would have wanted to say, anyway. Then she wrote: "I miss Mason. I miss Sunshine and if she could climb down in my arms, I would wrap her in such an iron hug. I am okay but am super PMS, so watch out, haha. Love, Emma"

Emma handed the note to Shrek, and he read it slowly.

"You have a dog named Sunshine?"

Emma was trying to send a clue to her parents in the cops or whatever that she was somewhere with no sunlight. She had actually decided to pretend "Sunshine" was a dog, but in that split second she wondered if Shrek had been watching her house for a bunch of days before he grabbed her. If yes, he'd know they didn't have a dog.

"Sunshine's my stuffed bear. I've had her since I was two." Would Shrek fall for it?

The man grunted and took New Emma's note from her hand. He read hers too, but asked no questions.

Emma tucked the stub of pencil into the waistband of her skinny jeans. Could she use it as a weapon? It was better than nothing. If he didn't remember to take it back... "So what's our reward?" Emma asked Shrek.

He took something out of a bag. It was a small chocolate cake. New Emma squealed.

Oh my God. Emma's stomach lurched and a little saliva flooded her mouth.

"See?" asked Shrek. "You cooperate and good things happen for you."

"Thanks, I'm all set." Emma barely got the words out.

Shrek didn't fight her on it. He just watched as New Emma ate and drank. He calmly returned them to their short bike chains and zip-tied their hands and feet again.

Then Shrek squeezed the corners of Emma's jaw, forcing her mouth open a bit, and slowly poured the chalky water into her mouth. He held her head in place so she couldn't avoid it. She wanted to spit it out but found herself swallowing. Cold, delicious chalky water. It tasted amazing.

Shrek patted her cheek. "This may sound sudden, since we only just met," he said. "But I'm kind of already in love with both of you."

Oh my God. "Seriously?" answered Emma, not thinking. "I think I love you too! Crazy, right? I love bad breath and creepy old guys with b.o. We're, like, perfect together!" And she laughed as cruel and harsh as she could.

Shrek pointed his finger at her face, up close. "I hope your bitchiness is a PMS thing, because we won't put up with that attitude much longer."

She looked her captor in the eye. "Put your finger near my face again—you won't be able to count to ten anymore."

The man shoved into place Emma's eye covering and her mouth gag. "Your daddies better love you," he said, his voice a pissed-off growl, close above her. "They're getting a chance to pay a ransom tonight, and they better hand over the cash with no trouble. Or this Shrek mask'll be the last thing you ever see."

CHAPTER THIRTY

Later that night, Pepper sat at home in his bedroom, badly noodling on his guitar. His fingers felt like sausages.

He'd lied to his dad. He'd lied in an official police statement.

He'd broken the law.

And he'd helped get Dennis Cole killed. Assuming he was dead. Which was a pretty damn safe assumption, he thought, based on all the blood he'd seen...

Brad St. John had called Pepper earlier, completely freaking out. He'd said he didn't know if it was Cole's blood or if Cole had killed someone, but either way Brad was heading home to New Jersey to visit his folks. Maybe permanently. Brad and the Pitts was officially going on hiatus, Brad had announced somberly. Pepper had listened and mostly commiserated, playing dumb. And feeling horrible.

By 9:30, Pepper couldn't take it anymore. He needed to tell his dad the truth. How Cole was trying to get info from Pepper—but he hadn't given too much yet... And how Cole had been investigating the Greenhead Snatcher and might have gotten close enough that the criminal killed him. Pepper needed to come clean because the guilt of lying to his dad was eating him up.

He checked downstairs. As he expected, his dad wasn't home. Neither was Jake.

He called his dad's cell phone. No answer.

He called the police station. The night desk sergeant said his dad was at the Addisons' house.

Pepper couldn't wait. He had to talk to him now, spill his guts completely. He couldn't take it anymore.

On the way, he stopped at Daggs Deli and picked up two turkey subs. As if he was just a good son trying to make sure his father was getting enough food. Completely innocent. Pepper could pull his dad aside for fifteen minutes while he ate and tell him everything. Ask for forgiveness. Get his ass kicked. Whatever. This had to end tonight.

He arrived at the Addisons' house a little after 10:30. As luck would have it, Officer Randy Larch was stationed at the front door.

Larch greeted Pepper, but said, "Kid, you don't want to bug your old man right now, no way. It's ground zero in there."

"What's up?"

Larch looked over his shoulder at the closed door. "The Snatcher's going to call any minute to set up the ransom drop. It's a full house—both Emma families, local, state and federal officers, the whole nine yards. A real shitshow."

Pepper gave his most disappointed face and showed his turkey subs. "I just brought these for Dad. He didn't get dinner. Probably missed lunch too."

"From Daggs? I haven't had dinner yet either," said Larch, swallowing.

Hmm... "I bet my dad doesn't really need both subs. One for him and how about you take this one? You mind extra mayo?"

Larch's hand was shaking as he snatched the turkey sub from Pepper's hand, and without another word Pepper was quickly through the front door.

Okay. Now he had to find his dad quickly. He just needed a few minutes to get everything off his chest. Was that too much to ask?

The living room was full of Bailey and Addison family members and some law enforcement officers. Pepper's dad wasn't there, so Pepper kept moving, acting confident, like he belonged.

He found his dad in the kitchen, talking with a pair of men in suits that screamed FBI. The first agent was taller and dark-haired. The second was shorter with blond hair. They were both thick with muscles, and their square jaws were blue with five o'clock shadows. Together they looked like those old cartoon characters, Fred Flintstone and Barney Rubble, but Pepper didn't share that sharp observation out loud. Not situationally appropriate.

"No, no..." his dad said when he noticed Pepper. He looked exhausted from the long hours and the stress. The FBI agents ignored Pepper and his dad didn't introduce him.

"I heard you missed lunch and dinner," said Pepper, trying to sound innocent. Holding up the turkey sub.

His dad gave him a heavy glare. "You came here to feed me? You expect me to believe that?"

"It's turkey, extra mayo, just like you like it."

His dad took the sub. "Okay, thanks. Now you need to go."

"No problem. I was hoping to talk to you first. Real quick?"

"Not now," said his dad through clenched teeth. "Pepper, I swear to God, I'll—"

So, this was not the time for a full confession. *Damn.* He thought his dad might pull out his handcuffs any second.

Pepper backed out of the kitchen. He was walking back toward the front door when voices in the living room got louder. Curiosity won out, and he poked his head in.

He saw the Bailey parents sitting with their boy, Mason, who had crayons spread out on the coffee table and was drawing something while ignoring all the adults. The Addison parents were sitting nearby. Pepper recognized a deputy sheriff and possibly a state policeman.

"Pepper Ryan?" asked Mrs. Addison, sounding like a hostess at a party that'd gotten out of her control.

He said hello to her with a little wave, also making eye contact with the other Emma parents. He really felt like he was intruding now.

"I'm sorry, you should probably go," whispered Mrs. Addison. "We're waiting for—"

"Nancy!" interrupted Mr. Addison as the two FBI officers came into the living room.

"We need to open the box early," said the taller agent. The one Pepper thought of as Agent Flintstone. "It'll give us a tactical advantage. There's no way the kidnapper will know."

Pepper processed all of this, standing silent. The Snatcher must have sent a box to the families, something related to the ransom drop.

Questions and comments broke out among the Emma parents, but shortly they all agreed.

"We've already scanned the box for explosives," said Agent Rubble, the shorter guy. "But as an extra precaution..." The two agents moved past Pepper into the front hall, and he slid into the living room to get out of their way. He watched the agents carry the box into the dining room and set it on the floor. Agent Flintstone took out a small knife, not much bigger than the silly little knife Delaney won for Pepper on their mini-golf date. Had that only been yesterday? Unreal.

The agents delicately opened the box, then brought it back into the living room and took out the contents.

A red duffel bag first. Then a cheap burner cellphone.

"Do your thing," Agent Rubble instructed a technician. "Location tracking and call tracing."

Agent Flintstone also pulled out two pieces of paper from the box. "Notes," he said. "Maybe from the girls."

"Oh my God!" said Mrs. Bailey, reaching for them.

"Hold on, hold on," said Agent Flintstone. He took a pair of tweezers and held up one note. "Don't touch them, we have to scan for fingerprints and DNA. Do you recognize the writing?"

The two notes were written in pencil on small pieces of paper. "This is from our Emma," said Mrs. Addison.

Flintstone laid the letter on the table and everyone gathered around. Pepper saw his dad on the other side of the group—he didn't seem to notice his son was still there.

The printed note from Emma Addison said she loved her parents and sister and she just wanted to be home. That she even missed her work at Sandy's.

"You're sure it's her writing and sounds like her?" asked Agent Flintstone.

The Addisons were sure.

The Baileys were studying the second note and Pepper saw they both began crying. The little boy, Mason, didn't cry—he just kept coloring.

"It's definitely from our Emma, but she sounds kind of weird," said Mr. Bailey.

"Weird how?" asked Rubble.

"This bit about Sunshine. Like it's a pet, but we don't have one."

"A friend's nickname? A stuffed animal?"

Both of Emma Bailey's parents shook their heads.

"And the PMS thing?" added Mrs. Bailey. "It's strange she'd mention that. She's never complained about PMS to me."

Another of the FBI technicians took the red duffel bag and began sewing a micro tracking device in the bag's seam.

Pepper's pulse raced. The FBI would grab the bastard at the

money drop and they'd recover the Emmas soon after. He felt it in his gut.

"Maybe your daughter's trying to send us clues about where she's being held. We'll get our analysts on it."

Pepper was leaning against a wall, trying to stay invisible, when Mason Bailey came over to him. "Hey, I did what you said. I told the detectives everything I remembered later about the greenhead guy."

"Good job!" said Pepper, and he meant it. Hopefully it would make the boy feel a little better that he'd helped.

"This is the best I could do," said Mason. He handed Pepper a piece of paper. It was a drawing of what had to be the moment the Greenhead Snatcher kidnapped his sister Emma. A basic van. A smaller person on the ground, Emma. A creature with a green head looming over her.

It was not much more detailed than a stick figure drawing, but it somehow captured the energy of the moment. The violence and panic.

"That's great," Pepper told the boy.

"You keep it," Mason said. "And don't forget what you promised!"

Shit. Obviously the boy remembered.

"Promised what?" asked Mr. Addison, who was leaning against the wall nearby.

Pepper gave the boy a hug and whispered, "Let's keep that promise a secret, okay?"

At that moment the burner phone rang on the living room table where the technician was working on it.

Agent Flintstone told Mr. Addison to wait until the fifth ring, to help sell the fiction they hadn't opened the box until it rang.

Mr. Addison finally answered the call, putting it on speakerphone.

"Who is this?" asked a deep voice which sounded robotic.

Like Darth Vader. The Snatcher must be using some device to distort his voice.

"Bill... Bill Addison," Emma's father answered.

"Okay, Bill-Bill Addison. I'll do the talking—you do the listening. If you interrupt me, the girls die. Understand?"

"Yes," gasped Mr. Addison, looking like he might faint. "We'll do what you say, just don't hurt—"

"You're not listening, Bill-Bill. You make that mistake again, I hang up and the girls are dead. You understand? Just say yes."

"Yes."

The blond-haired FBI agent had his hand on the shoulder of a technician who was frantically trying to trace the caller.

"I want the money delivered by one driver. Not a cop. Not FBI. Has to be a civilian. I want the person who owns the blue pickup truck sitting outside the Addison house right now to drive that truck with the money and the cell phone you're holding. And I saw the guy driving it when he arrived, so don't make a switch. If a cop shows up, I'll know and the girls are dead. If I notice any drones or helicopters, same thing. You'll never see me and the girls are dead."

A chill slid down Pepper's spine. It was his blue pickup truck parked outside. The Snatcher wanted him to drive the two million dollars to the drop-off? What the hell?

"No way," hissed his dad, but low enough that the kidnapper couldn't hear.

The FBI agent gave Pepper's dad a *shush* motion.

"And to make sure you don't try anything stupid, the driver will bring your other daughter. What's her name, the little blonde? Just the civilian driver and her. And no bullshit. Oh, and they both need to wear bathing suits under their clothes.

"Put the two million in the red duffel bag in the box. Not some other fancy FBI bag. They need to drive to the Lower Cape

Shopping Plaza parking lot and arrive no later than ten minutes from right now. No tricks or the girls die. Go!"

The call disconnected.

"No way," repeated his dad. "Pepper's not driving the money. You guys have to swap someone in."

The FBI agent who looked like Barney Rubble started a stopwatch countdown on his digital watch. "Which of us look like him?" he asked. "The kid's bigger than any of us and fifteen years younger. Maybe with more time, with a wig and makeup... But he has to get on the road in what, two minutes? Or he'll be late. I just pulled up the directions. We don't have a lot of options."

Pepper took a deep breath. "I can do it," he said. "I'd just be dropping off a bag." His voice sounded like it came from a stranger.

"I'm not sending Shauna with him," said Mr. Addison. "I can't risk her life too. I don't think I can take this..."

"Mr. Addison, we don't have another blonde fourteen-year-old," said the taller agent. "The kidnapper holds the cards for now, but that'll change real fast. We have to play along. We'll put her in a bulletproof vest. She'll be fine."

"Sixty seconds," said Barney Rubble, watching his watch. "We don't want our driver to be late."

"I'll do it," said Pepper. "And I'll take care of Shauna. We'll drop the money and get out of there. The FBI and the rest of you guys won't do anything until we're clear, right?"

Mr. Addison buried his head in his hands. "I don't like it. I just don't like it."

"None of us do. But it's our best chance to get the Emmas back. Maybe our only chance."

CHAPTER THIRTY-ONE

It was all going down right now.

The FBI had rigged Pepper up with a tiny earpiece and a nearly invisible mic. And he and Shauna, the younger Addison daughter, were each wearing a bulletproof vest. Pepper took a deep breath and put his truck in drive. "You ready?" he asked the blonde girl.

Shauna nodded, sitting hunched down in a too-big bulletproof vest. The girl was sweating despite the air conditioning, and she looked pale.

"The cops'll be all around," said Pepper reassuringly. "They even have a helicopter and a boat. We'll be fine."

"Will Emma be there? Is she coming home with us?"

"I hope so," he said. "We'll see. You're a brave girl to help your sister."

"She's gonna owe me, big time," she said, as if trying to crack a joke. Then she started to cry quietly.

Pepper drove to the Lower Cape Shopping Plaza parking lot, as instructed. He arrived only two minutes late. He parked in the middle, far away from any cars. The lot was almost empty at eleven-thirty—maybe ten cars scattered around it. Was the kidnapper in one of those cars?

He parked and waited.

Pepper knew the FBI and other agencies were surveilling the situation, but they hadn't told him any other details. He wondered where they were. How were they watching? It was probably better he didn't know.

Pepper saw a man standing in the shadows by the row of storefronts, in front of a closed, dark barbershop. A vehicle drove through the parking lot, its lights highlighting the man's face as it slowed. The man turned away too late.

It was Scooter McCord! Pepper was positive—the red hair, the beefy face, everything. It was definitely him.

The vehicle parked right near where he had seen McCord lurking. It was a gray minivan with a dent in the driver's side door. Fester Timmins' ride!

What the hell were McCord and Timmins doing there at that time of the night?

The burner cell phone from the box rang. Pepper had brought it with them as instructed.

Pepper answered it. "Um, hello?"

"You need to listen and not talk, unless I ask you a question. Understand? You don't look very bright." The voice was the same as Pepper had heard at the Addisons' house. A man's voice, deep and altered electronically.

Pepper didn't answer the man, since what he'd said wasn't a question. He peered toward where McCord had been standing, but Timmins had turned off his headlights and Pepper could only see the minivan, not either of the men. Were they in on the ransom drop? What the hell other reason would they have for being at a closed shopping center close to midnight?

"Good," said the voice. "Play this straight and everyone gets home safe. Drive to the New Albion High School parking lot. Wait for another call. Don't phone or text anyone to say where you're going. If I see you on a phone or I see a cop, the girls die. Understand?"

"I understand."

The caller hung up.

Pepper wished he could communicate his destination with the police but didn't want to screw things up. So he didn't. He had to trust what the FBI told him—they'd be watching. And he'd seen them put a tracking device under the belly of his truck.

He drove to the New Albion high school parking lot. It wasn't too long ago he'd done that every day as a student. It seemed familiar but weird. The lot was empty except for one large black car parked near the entrance to the high school.

Pepper parked a fair distance from that car, nearer the middle of the empty lot.

The burner cell phone rang again.

"You and the girl get out of your car, carrying the money bag. Stay on the line."

So they did. Pepper stood there in the parking lot with the big duffel of money over his shoulder. He took Shauna's hand and squeezed it reassuringly.

The voice came over the burner phone again. "I know you're wearing a mic and an earpiece. Take them off, hold them in the air, and throw them as far as you can. Right now. Or this deal is off and the girls die."

Pepper's mind raced. Was the Greenhead Snatcher bluffing? How could he know about the mic and the earpiece? They were both too small for someone to see from a distance, even with binoculars.

No, he couldn't risk it. He took out the earpiece and the mic, held them up, then threw them across the parking lot where they slid into a puddle. Whoops—the FBI would not be using those again.

"Okay, walk toward the school with the bag of money. Now stop."

They were almost at the school building. Pepper saw the large black car was a Chrysler 300. Possibly about five years old. It was backed into a spot close to the walkway to the school's front entrance.

"Get in the Chrysler. The doors are unlocked." The call disconnected.

Pepper did as instructed and found another cheap cell phone lying on the driver's seat. And there were three cameras on the dashboard pointing at them. Covering the entire front seat.

The new phone rang and he answered it.

"Take the battery out of the old phone and throw the phone and the battery out the window. Then pop the trunk."

Pepper did as he was told, reluctantly. The Snatcher had rightly assumed the FBI was tracking the original burner phone.

"Okay, both of you go to the trunk and take out one of the black bags you'll find there. It doesn't matter which one. Stay on the phone."

Pepper and Shauna found three identical large black duffel bags in the trunk. He took out the one on the far right.

"Dump out the new bag, it's full of scrap paper. Now transfer the money to the new bag. One bundle at a time. Hold it up so I can see what you're putting in there. I don't want to see any wires or tracking tech. No bullshit. If there's a dye pack, don't transfer it."

Pepper knew there wasn't a dye pack. There was a tiny tracking device sewn in the red money bag's lining, but there was nothing Pepper could do about transferring it now.

He did what the man said. He took out each bundle of bills,

held it up, then put it in the new bag. What else could he do? Shauna stood beside him, shivering. The night wasn't cold, so she was probably shivering from fear.

"You're doing great," Pepper said to her in a low voice.

"No more talking from you," warned the man. "You're taking too long. Have the girl help."

Pepper and Shauna finished transferring the money without a word.

"Now toss the empty red bag off to the side. And put the black bag back in the trunk and shut it."

Pepper did, putting the bag in the empty space to the right of the other two bags in the trunk. He didn't want to mix them up.

"Now strip down to your bathing suits," said the voice. "Everything except your bathing suits. That includes shoes. I want to see you're not wearing a wire or a tracking device. Don't get me worried or the girls are dead. I'm watching everything you do."

"No way, I can't do this anymore," said Shauna. "Where's Emma?"

Pepper gave her a pat on the shoulder, which she shrugged off. "We have to," he said apologetically. "It'll be fine."

"I want to go home!" Shauna pleaded.

The man's voice came over the phone. "You're a few seconds away from me killing the two Emmas. Don't forget rule number one—you do what I say or the girls die."

"You need to trust me," Pepper whispered to Shauna. "We have to do this, for Emma."

Finally, she relented. Pepper took off his bulletproof vest, helped Shauna out of hers, and they both undressed.

Pepper was wearing Mr. Addison's bathing suit, which was way too big in the waist. With the drawstring pulled tight, the bathing suit's fabric bunched up ridiculously in front.

Shauna turned away to get out of her jeans. Pepper felt rotten for her, with her sister abducted and now being thrown into the middle of this ransom situation. Pepper wanted to say something to the Snatcher—to not even think about hurting the Emmas, but the man had said not to talk unless to answer a direct question. Pepper would play it straight, no matter how hard it was to keep his mouth shut.

The voice came over the cheap cell phone again. "Both of you, put your hands in the air and slowly turn around. Now leave everything on the ground and get back in the Chrysler. You and the blonde. I'm not done with her yet."

Shauna hugged herself, looking very young in her blue one-piece bathing suit. Pepper could see the goosebumps on her arms.

It took every bit of his restraint to not answer the Snatcher. He was glad the girl couldn't hear what the man was saying.

Pepper helped Shauna back into the car, closed her door, then jogged around to climb in himself.

The man on the phone grunted. "Start the car and turn on the radio, a little louder. Now you sit and wait. I'm making sure there aren't any cops around. You don't talk, you don't signal anyone. I can see everything you or the girl do. Any foolishness and you know what happens. Sit and wait."

And they did. Three minutes passed, then five. The radio was tuned to a rap music station, but he didn't try to find something better. Shauna was crying now; he could see tears running down her cheek.

Pepper turned on the heat even though it broke the Snatcher's rules. Maybe it would help Shauna stop shivering.

Was law enforcement nearby? Were they ready to spring the trap?

Pepper felt stupid and powerless, sitting there in the baggy bathing suit, waiting. It was ridiculous. He hoped he got to meet the kidnapper face-to-face at some point. He would only need a minute to give the bastard some well-deserved payback.

"I don't like it," said Gerald Ryan to the collection of law enforcement officers who had waited at the Addisons' house.

The two FBI agents and two technicians had left in a mobile tactical van to carry out drone surveillance and coordinate the deployment of various law enforcement officers as necessary.

"What part?" asked a state police investigator.

"All of it."

"A little late now," said an Eastham detective.

Gerald wished he was in the mobile van. He knew it was parked three blocks from the New Albion high school. A technician was hovering two drones high over the school's parking lot.

Two other drones would be slowly circling the area. The drones were silent above five hundred feet in the air, had night-vision cameras, a range of twenty-two miles, and had a flight time of ninety minutes. Unless the Greenhead Snatcher had extremely sophisticated equipment himself, he would have no way of detecting drones overhead.

Waiting uselessly, Gerald was mostly mad at himself for allowing Pepper to be drafted to deliver the ransom money. He should have insisted they replace him with a cop in Pepper's clothes. How could the Snatcher really know if someone else drove his son's truck? It had to be a bluff.

Unless the kidnapper was law enforcement himself? Then he might recognize the replacement driver as a cop, and the money drop would be jeopardized before it began.

But the driver shouldn't have to be Pepper. Gerald didn't question his son's bravery, although lots of things could go wrong.

It was a completely over-the-top situation for a twenty-year-old kid and a fourteen-year-old girl.

The Snatcher had sounded like he was on a hair trigger, and Gerald knew Pepper didn't have a very diplomatic attitude. One wrong move, or even one wrong word, and the girls could be killed. And maybe Pepper and the younger Addison girl too.

CHAPTER THIRTY-TWO

After an eternal ten minutes, the Greenhead Snatcher called again and spoke to Pepper. "Okay, handsome, turn left out of the lot and start driving, nice and easy. Don't speed but don't go slow. Nice and steady."

Pepper did.

After two miles, the man said. "Pull over to the side of the road."

He did.

"So you got two dummy bags and one real one. You remember which is which, smart guy?"

"Yes. I—"

"Yes is all you need to say, tough guy. Take one of the dummy bags and toss it into the marsh, as far as you can. Let's see who's watching you despite my very clear instructions."

He did what he was told.

"Okay, start driving again. I'm watching the spot you just left. If a cop shows up there, this little dance is over and the girls are dead. You keep driving. Turn right when you get to Spring Tide Lane."

Pepper drove. He knew the FBI and the police would try to

grab the Snatcher—he was glad he didn't have the details. They were the pros, not him. He shouldn't even be here. But the kidnapper was calling the shots, not him. He hoped it was all over soon...

The deep electronic voice continued. "Okay, the cops haven't blown this yet. You should reach the little bridge over Pence Creek any time, you there yet? Stop on the bridge, then get the second dummy bag and throw it over the side."

Pepper kept his mouth shut and did it.

"I gotta go to the bathroom," Shauna whispered when Pepper climbed back in.

"It's almost over," he said. He didn't care if the Snatcher heard him. The girl was scared and shaking. Fuck him.

"All right, handsome, same deal. You drive, I watch. If the cops show up at the bridge, I hang up and the girls die."

Got it, asshole, Pepper thought.

But he stayed silent and drove. Shauna was squirming on the seat beside him. She must really have to go to the bathroom bad.

"You can pee right on the seat if you have to," said Pepper, keeping his eyes forward and trying to move his lips as little as possible, because of the cameras. "It'd serve him right if you peed in his car."

He saw the girl smile slightly, but she shook her head. She must not be willing to give up, not yet.

Then the burner phone started beeping from a disconnected call.

Shit! Had the cops blown it? Did the Snatcher have a camera by the bridge? Had the police shown up where Pepper threw the second bag and been spotted? Or had the kidnapper heard him talking to Shauna?

The Snatcher had sounded completely ready to kill the Emmas. Had he hung up and headed to where the girls were being held? Ready to act?

Shit, shit, shit... Pepper kept driving, faster now, panicked and freaking out.

The burner phone rang again.

He frantically accepted the call. His chest was thumping with adrenaline. "You better not have—"

"Calm down, dummy! Must have been a bad cell signal on that road," the deep voice chuckled. "I lost you for a minute."

Pepper rubbed his forehead. "What do you want me to do?"

"I want you to listen and not talk. Rule one. Got that, dummy?"

"Yes."

"Take your next right and pull into the Dill lot."

"Got it." It was the parking lot for Dill Beach, one of the most popular beaches in New Albion.

"Park near the walkway. The girl stays in the car and you walk down to the beach with the money bag."

"No way," said Pepper, without thinking. "I'm not leaving her in a dark parking lot alone. And she needs to pee," said Pepper.

"What?"

"The girl. She needs the bathroom."

"Are you fucking with me, you piece of shit? Leave her and do what I say."

"Hey, I know you have all the cards. I'm not fucking with you. You want the money, I'll bring it. But the girl stays with me."

There was a long enough pause that Pepper wondered if the man had disconnected the call.

"You get her to pee in a bush, or right in the parking lot. This is almost over, don't fuck it up now. Grab the money bag and the two of you get down to the beach."

Pepper parked in the Dill lot, and he and Shauna got out. She was crying again. Pepper grabbed the money bag from the trunk and stood a distance away while the girl squatted next to bushes and peed for a long time.

"Clock's ticking, dummy," said the man on the phone. "Walk down the path. Since the girl's along for the ride, send her in front, carrying the bag. You second."

Pepper didn't want to push the wacko any further, so they did as he instructed. But Pepper stayed right behind her, with one hand on her shoulder. Shauna could barely carry the bag, it was so heavy.

They reached the beach and walked forward. There was a partial moon and Pepper could see the silvery sand and the dark ocean. The tide was almost all the way in.

"Dig a hole in the sand and bury the bag, right beside the biggest log in front of you. Right there."

How could the Snatcher have watched them so closely, at every stop? Did he have night-vision cameras set up and was in some kind of control center, watching from a safe distance?

Only one way to find out. Pepper walked forty feet away from the big log. "Right here?" he asked.

"Yes. Right by the log. Bury the bag, then go back to the car and drive back to town, slowly. If I see a cop near Dill Beach in the next hour—"

Pepper interrupted. "Let me guess, the girls die. I think you watch too many bad movies." He felt a bit emboldened, knowing the Snatcher wasn't watching his every move. "Now that you're getting paid, when are you letting the girls go?"

"Just do it, dummy," said the man. "I'll release the girls tomorrow, after I've checked the money's not fake or marked." The call cut off.

CHAPTER THIRTY-THREE

After driving back at the Addisons' house, Pepper followed Shauna inside, desperately trying to act calm. Like the whole crazy ransom drop had been no big deal.

His dad met him at the doorway and gave him a hug, then a slap on the shoulder. He looked visibly relieved.

Everyone gathered in the living room, including the parents of both Emmas. Shauna was sitting on her mother's lap, receiving a long hug. He didn't see the Bailey boy. Had someone found him a bed to go to sleep?

The officers filled Pepper in on the progress of the situation. They were getting regular updates from the tactical van.

An officer called the FBI agents in the van, and Pepper slowly repeated for them everything he and Shauna had done.

"We started sweating when we lost audio contact with you," said one of the FBI agents. "But our drones saw everything."

Pepper learned that high-level drones with night vision had followed him and Shauna, marking every stop. The drones had been high enough and small enough that there was very little risk the Greenhead Snatcher could have spotted them. They had watched Pepper throw the first two bags and bury the third bag.

"The snipers from the Statie SWAT team are watching each bag you dropped off," said the FBI agent over the radio. "They've got ghillie suits and are basically invisible. Nobody's getting away with any of the three bags. Which one has the two million?"

"The one we buried at Dill Beach," said Pepper. He explained the other two were just dummy bags, and an agent radioed the SWAT team surveilling Dill Beach to notify them they were guarding the key location.

Pepper reviewed everything he and Shauna had done, bit by bit. When he got to the part about them arriving at the Lower Cape Shopping Center, he told the FBI agents about seeing Scooter McCord standing near the storefronts. And Fester Timmins arriving too in his minivan.

The FBI asked Pepper's dad to send officers to McCord's and Timmins' houses to take them into custody if they were there.

Pepper finished relating the blow-by-blow of the ransom drop. Then all they had to do was wait for the Snatcher to step into their trap.

The SWAT teams waited an hour and everyone at the Addison house waited too.

Then they waited another hour. But nothing happened. The Greenhead Snatcher didn't show up to retrieve the money bag.

"It doesn't make any sense. Could the Snatcher have dug up the bag immediately? Before the SWAT team arrived?"

"The drone would have spotted him. It would have spotted anything bigger than a crab that got near that bag."

They waited one more hour. Then the FBI made a decision and radioed the beach surveillance team. "Team three—make sure the money bag's still in place."

Everyone in the house waited some more.

The word came back. One of the SWAT team members had crawled forward and confirmed. The bag was still buried in the sand beside the log where Pepper had left it. But the SWAT team member had looked inside the bag and there was a problem. It wasn't filled with money.

"Come again?" asked an FBI voice over the radio.

"It's full to the top with Cape Cod tourism pamphlets," said a SWAT team officer. "Whale watching, that kind of shit. No money."

"That can't be right!" blurted Pepper. He'd been clear about which bag held the money—the one farthest to the right in the trunk. And he'd taken out the bags, working from left to right. There was no way he'd mixed them up. It was impossible.

The FBI radioed the other two SWAT teams, at the marsh and at the bridge. Each team stealthily retrieved a black bag.

Both bags were also full of tourism pamphlets.

Everyone in the Addisons' living room sat in stunned silence. No one spoke up from the tactical mobile van either. They were all dumbfounded.

"I don't get it," said Mr. Addison finally. "Which of the three bags had the money?"

"None of them," said an FBI agent over the radio.

"What? Then where's my damned money?"

Everyone looked at Pepper, some with accusations on their faces.

"We shouldn't have let the kid do it," said Mr. Bailey.

"Check the trunk of the Chrysler," said Agent Flintstone. "We're back at the house—come on out."

They all hurried out. The tactical mobile van was parked in the driveway behind the Chrysler. Agents Flintstone and Rubble climbed out, along with two technicians.

"We already checked the trunk," said an investigator from the sheriff's office. "We searched the whole car and deactivated the Snatcher's dashboard cameras. The trunk was empty."

Agent Flintstone walked to the Chrysler's trunk and looked in. Everyone crowded around. The trunk was empty. He pulled back the black felt carpeting lining the trunk bed, and everyone saw a seam running around the floor of the trunk. At the end closest to the rear bumper were two hinges.

"Sonofabitch," said Agent Rubble. He crawled under the rear of the car, and a moment later there was a click and the bottom of the trunk dropped away.

Everyone followed the FBI agents back in the tactical mobile van, and Agent Flintstone told the tech to pull up the drone surveillance footage—from the time Pepper and Shauna left the Addisons' house. Pepper was at the rear of the group, but he was tall enough to see over everyone's heads. They watched video play back in real time...to the shopping plaza, then to the high school. There was no sound, just the video.

They watched Pepper and Shauna transfer the bundles of money to the black bag, then watched them undress. Everyone stayed quiet as they watched Pepper and Shauna get back into the Chrysler, wait for a long while, then drive away.

"Stop," said Rubble. "What's that?" He pointed at the spot where the Chrysler 300 was parked a moment before.

"A storm drain, looks like," said the technician, zooming in on the spot.

Pepper's heart sank.

"You've got to be shitting me," said someone to Pepper's left. A state police investigator? Pepper hadn't met him.

The technician replayed the footage with the Chrysler 300 in the high school parking lot.

"It has to be the storm drain," said Agent Flintstone. "Our kidnapper must have lifted the drain and accessed the trunk from below after the kid put the money inside. While they were out in front of the car, getting undressed. Or while they waited in the car after that."

Shit. The Snatcher had gotten away with the money, and the girls were still missing.

"And the footage of this parking lot ends when they drove away in the Chrysler," confirmed the technician. Both drones stayed with the car.

"Unbelievable," said Pepper's dad.

Most of them just stood silently, shocked by the mission's failure.

"Well, he said he'll let the Emmas go tomorrow," said Pepper, trying to help.

"It's never tomorrow," said Agent Rubble roughly, but his partner put his hand on his arm, stopping him from saying more.

Mr. Addison turned in the crowd and found Pepper. "Didn't you look in the bag at the beach before you buried it?" he asked.

Pepper shook his head miserably. "Why would I do that? I did what the FBI said to do. And what the Snatcher said over the phone. Straight up."

"I knew we shouldn't have sent the kid," said Mr. Addison.

The comment made Pepper's stomach tighten in a quick, hard knot. Because he knew the comment was true. The kidnapper had called him a dummy and had made him look like it. And the Emmas were still who the hell knows where...

Everyone was looking at Pepper but seemed to be trying not to look at him. Like this failure was all his fault. His cheeks flooded with shame and anger.

He'd done his damned best. He and a fourteen-year-old girl had taken a lot more personal risk than any of them had. They were being epically unfair. If Pepper's efforts hadn't been good enough, all of these law enforcement professionals should step up and catch the Snatcher themselves.

Because he wasn't volunteering to stick his neck out again.

CHAPTER THIRTY-FOUR

I won't give up, thought Emma Bailey, tied up in the darkness. She listened to New Emma sniffle and tried to believe that she wasn't bullshitting herself.

She needed to try something. Anything. When their kidnapper arrived the next time (the next day?), she was going to try to get more information out of his sorry ass. Who the hell was he? Where were they?

If she could get him talking, she might learn something to help her convince the asshole to forget this whole thing and let them go.

And having a plan would hopefully take her mind off her hunger. Emma had debated giving up on the no-food, no-water thing, but maybe she was putting a bit of time pressure on whatever the hell this guy was pulling.

When the man eventually arrived with his lantern and took the covering off Emma's eyes, it surprised her to see he wasn't wearing his Shrek mask. Their kidnapper was a white guy, his face a little too heavy like the rest of him. No beard or anything. Kind of ordinary. Not looking much like the monster he was...

"Hey, did everything go okay with the ransom payment?" she

asked super politely. She would try being nice for a while and see if he gave up any helpful info.

The man gave Emma a surprised look. Then he laughed. "For us it did."

"Great! So when'll you let us go?"

The man was freeing up New Emma and attaching her longer bicycle chain. "You ever hear of a dowry?" he asked.

"No, what's that?" asked New Emma.

Emma knew what it meant. It meant he wasn't going to let them go. *Shit*.

"Hey," said Emma. "You don't look as old as you sounded with that mask on. How old are you?"

"Old enough. A lot younger than your dads."

Whatever. "Are you from the Cape? Are we still in Eastham?"

This time the man didn't respond.

New Emma shuffled off to the toilet chair, but Emma stayed behind, still trying to get scraps of info out of the man.

"I've been calling you Shrek, because, you know, the mask. What should we call you?"

"Call me anything you want, for now. We'll get better acquainted soon."

Emma was frustrated and hungry and thirsty, and even more scared than before. She wasn't learning anything helpful. "Suit yourself. But could you please put the Shrek mask back on? So your face doesn't scare the kid?"

The man shook a finger at her. "You need to change your attitude. That's not the way a good wife acts."

"Screw you!"

The man laughed. "Not until after our wedding..."

Uh-oh.

Emma stopped talking. She did her thing with the toilet chair. She drank some chalky water but again didn't eat. She saw him notice. Good.

When the man started hog-tying New Emma with her short bike chain and the plastic tie wraps, Emma said, "How about you take us for a walk? You can keep us on the stupid chains if you're afraid we might get away. We gotta stretch our legs!"

The man shook his head. "You need to earn that kind of bonus." The man finished with New Emma, who again said nothing and didn't resist him at all. She seemed pretty much catatonic, or possibly in shock. If those were two different things?

The man crowded close to Emma to switch her to the shorter chain and tie up her hands and feet as usual. This time he paused before pulling on her eye mask and ball gag.

"I'll be happy to tell you all about me," he said in a quiet voice. "Just not yet. Trust me, darling." And the man stayed close, forcing eye contact.

A cold shiver slid down her neck. She couldn't move much, but she didn't recoil away from him. She stood her ground and tried not to throw up a little in her mouth.

The man moved his face even closer to hers until their noses were almost touching.

She didn't move.

Then he leaned forward and kissed her, roughly and firmly.

Emma froze for a second, not reacting. Then her lips opened and she bit the hell out of his lip. She felt her teeth sink in deep. Tasted blood flow. Felt the man try to tear loose. She held on with her teeth like an animal. *Fuck him!*

He slapped her across the head as he pulled back, stunning her. But she still didn't release her teeth from his lip. He basically had to tear his lip free.

She saw blood streaming down his face, his eyes wide.

He slapped her head again, harder. He pulled up his shirt and pressed it against his ripped, bleeding lip.

"Little bitch!" he yelled. "I ought to choke you out right here." His threat sounded a little ridiculous, muffled by his shirt.

He forgot to gag Emma's mouth and cover her eyes as he stormed off with the lantern, leaving the girls alone again in the dark. So, another minor victory for her.

Emma stretched out as far as she could with her legs and found the foot of New Emma across from her. And this time New Emma pressed against Emma's foot. Tentatively the first time. Then twice more, stronger. Then she kept her foot pressed there. As if New Emma was trying to communicate with Emma—the first sign of spirit from the younger girl since she had arrived in their hellhole.

"We'll be okay," she said to New Emma. "We gotta be tough and have each other's backs, okay? Just be ready if we get a chance to escape or something."

New Emma made a noise through her ball gag and pressed against Emma's foot again, harder than before.

On Tuesday morning, Pepper trudged up the police station steps, anticipating getting more flack about his failure.

He wasn't going to take the blame for the botched ransom drop. It was the FBI's show, and he'd been a reluctant volunteer. He didn't care what anyone said.

The door opened as he reached it, and the man held it open with a mock bow. "Hey, it's the two-million-dollar man!" It was Fester Timmins, and he had a shit-eating grin on his face. And some gas station aviator sunglasses.

How the hell did Fester Timmins know the details of the ransom drop screwup? If he knew, did the entire world?

Pepper groaned.

"I was just giving the detectives my statement about Dennis Cole," Timmins said. "Doing my duty. You think Cole got too close to the Greenhead Snatcher? Got too close and *pfttttt*?" He drew his finger across his throat as he made the weird noise.

Was Timmins trying to imitate the sound of a knife cutting a throat?

Pepper still hadn't learned a good reason for Timmins to have arrived at Dennis Cole's house so soon after Pepper called 911. And he thought the man's arrival at the shopping center during the ransom drop stank even more—how was the guy so wired in to everything going on?

"Hey, you're the investigator," said Pepper, and kept walking.

"Ryan! I wanted to talk to you about—"

But Pepper was through the front door and it closed on whatever Fester Timmons wanted to talk about. Because Pepper didn't.

Pepper was finished poking his nose into the Greenhead Snatcher investigation.

Well, almost finished. He walked to his desk and took thirty minutes to do a brain dump of every development in the case.

Everything he'd learned about the local lead suspects—Casper Yelle and Scooter McCord.

The notes he'd made from the Bailey family and Addison family interviews. The bloody scene at Dennis Cole's house, noting he didn't know whether it was connected to the Snatcher case. And everything that'd gone down on the ransom drop.

Pepper included everything he'd learned along the way, no matter how irrelevant. That was something his grandfather, Papa Ryan, had taught them about police work, growing up. You're just trying to figure out what happened. The more info you get, the better your chances.

He also made a long note about Fester Timmins. He got it all out of his system.

He was completing the case file because he was closing it out.

He was done. And it was just for himself, so what difference did it make?

When he finished, Pepper took a bathroom break and bumped into Officer Randy Larch, who was washing his hands.

"Hey, young Ryan! Got any money you can loan me?" The man slapped the counter, doubled over by his own lame humor.

So everyone knew about Pepper getting mowed down by the Greenhead Snatcher? He must be the laughingstock of...well, Cape Cod.

"Hey, you hear we brought in Scooter McCord and Fester Timmins for questioning about why they were at the shopping center during the ransom drop?"

"No! What'd they say?" There was no way those two guys were there by coincidence last night...

Larch chuckled. "They both had the same story. They'd gotten an anonymous call. Someone promised to meet them there at that time to tell them valuable info about the Greenhead Snatcher. McCord said he was hoping to clear his name. Timmins claimed he's investigating for a client whose name he can't disclose for ethical reasons. We sweated him and he admitted he didn't know his client's name—someone hired him anonymously over the phone."

"So that was it? Do we believe them?"

"So far we can't prove they're lying, but we'll investigate further. And we picked up one other piece of info from Timmins. The mystery caller supposedly told him the location of Casper Yelle's white van—as a show of good faith to get Timmins off his couch. And the tip was actually good. We found Yelle's van in the employee parking area behind the Stop & Shop."

Pepper got excited. "Did it have any evidence connected to the Emmas?"

"Not sure yet. Forensics is going over it right now. His parole officer, Charlie Brown, found a laptop computer with hundreds of porn pictures and videos. Some of them including underage girls. Yelle's toast—that's an automatic parole violation."

"So he's the Snatcher!"

Larch grunted. "Maybe. Sweeney and Brown went to Yelle's apartment to take him in. They found his ankle monitor there ... he'd cut it off. We've got a BOLO out for him, but he's probably long gone."

Delaney was waiting for Pepper at his favorite place, Broken Dreams Pizza and Antiques.

He had to eat, right? So what was wrong with a little lunch date? Broken Dreams had only opened last year, but it was already a local classic. Great pizza, and the entire place was full of antique furniture and other items that were all for sale.

Pepper made the mistake of driving the short distance to the pizza place and had to circle the block three times before he scored a parking spot. Cape Cod in July. People would pretty much kill for a parking spot on Main Street of New Albion. Pepper reminded himself to check his database when he got back to work to see whether anyone had literally killed someone over a parking spot in town...

Delaney looked spectacular despite being dressed to go to work at Sandy's Restaurant this afternoon. Her eyes and smile were like a one-two punch to Pepper's chest. When she laughed, he had no choice but to grin back.

Imagine being the guy who gets to make her smile for the rest of her life?

"Tell me about your family," she asked.

So Pepper told her about his mom dying when he was not much more than a toddler. How his dad had raised him and Jake.

Then he found himself talking about the Ryan tradition of

becoming a police officer. He told her about his grandfather, Papa Ryan, and some funny stories from his long career as a Boston cop. Just to entertain her.

"I'd love to meet him sometime," she said.

"He would have loved you. But he passed away three years ago."

Delaney reached across the table and squeezed his hand. "I'm sorry. About him and your mother. It must have been really tough."

After they finished and were walking to Pepper's truck, Delaney took his hand.

"Too bad about the end of Brad and the Pitts, huh?" she asked. "The shortest-lived cover band in history."

Pepper laughed. "Maybe Brad'll come back after all the craziness dies down."

"Maybe. But if I go on the road, really try to take my shot at music in Nashville, any chance you'll come with me?" she asked, then smiled. "You could even bring Angel, if you need a comfort animal."

Her question momentarily stunned Pepper. He didn't immediately say yes, but he didn't say no. "That's...wow. Are you really going to do it?"

"I want to, if I can work up the guts to take the leap."

Pepper's head was reeling with the idea. It was crazy, right? He could never...

He'd committed to Harvard and hockey. *Harvard*! Most people would give their left nut to go there. It was the best of the best. And hopefully, Pepper would show everyone—especially the jerks like Coach Gus Bullard—that he deserved his spot.

But he'd heard of lots of super successful people who dropped out of Harvard. Like the Facebook guy, Zuckerberg. They had bigger and better things to do.

What if this was his bigger and better opportunity? His own

path to success, with Delaney at his side. No fighting to survive at Harvard, maybe flaming out. No expectation that after college he'd enter the police academy, like Jake.

No, Pepper could start his own future, right now.

Nashville.

CHAPTER THIRTY-FIVE

Back at work, Pepper went hunting for Detective Sweeney.

He wanted to give him a recap of the phone conversations he'd had with the Greenhead Snatcher during the ransom drop, in case hearing it straight from Pepper helped Sweeney on his part of the overall investigation.

Sweeney wasn't in the officers' bullpen, but he seemed to be working out of the same cubicle as before. The watercolor painting given to Pepper yesterday morning by the upset woman was still leaning against the back wall of the cubicle desk where Sweeney had placed it.

Had it just been yesterday?

Between Mason Bailey's crayon drawings last night and this woman's watercolor, we could open a Greenhead Snatcher art exhibit, he thought.

Then Pepper remembered he must have left Mason's crayon drawing at the Addison house in all the chaos of the ransom drop. Which triggered another thought—had Sweeney or anyone else shown Mason the woman's watercolor painting? Maybe Pepper could confirm whether the "roofing" man who'd pulled into the woman's driveway on Thursday night was the Snatcher. If it was the same man, wouldn't that give Sweeney a new line of investigation?

And maybe the watercolor painting would trigger the boy to remember some other details about the kidnapping he'd forgotten. Some info Pepper could give to Sweeney when he told the detective he would not be getting in the way on the case anymore. A parting gift before Pepper finally stepped aside.

"What're you working on now?" asked a voice from over his shoulder.

Crap!

But it was just Zula Eisenhower. The teen had snuck up behind him and made him jump. For a split second he'd thought she was Sergeant Weisner, catching him screwing around.

"Damn, Little Ike! You can't be sneaking up on people!"

"I wasn't. I'm waiting for my dad." She studied the watercolor painting. "It's kind of ugly and beautiful at the same time," she said. "Who is it?"

"Maybe the Greenhead Snatcher. Or maybe just a roofer."

Zula sighed. "So you have no idea?"

"Pretty much. But I've got to go." Pepper stood.

"Too bad. I'm *so bored*... Do you have any more work for me?"

Pepper could set her up with another stack of cases to enter into the database, but he had an idea about something he hadn't had time yet to research. "Are you good with other computer stuff?" he asked her.

"What kind of stuff?"

"Research. It might be too complicated for you."

Zula sighed. "Skip the reverse psychology and tell me what it is."

So Pepper did. He explained he wanted her to research Alistair "Scooter" McCord and the alternative name on his UK passport: Harris Ross. To pull any public records in Massachusetts for either of those names.

"Huh," Zula said. "Is this going to help you beat me on our bet?"

She meant the dumb one dollar bet he'd find the two Emmas before the police. He'd forgotten about that.

"Maybe. Do it anyway, please?"

Zula studied Pepper for a few seconds, then smiled and pushed up her glasses on her nose. "Whatever. You obviously need all the help you can get. How do you spell the names?"

Pepper wrote them on a sticky note for her. It would probably lead to nothing, but McCord's dual name thing, and his passport and plane ticket for next week, itched at Pepper.

"I'll use your office," Zula announced, and held out a fist for a bump. So he gave her one, playing along, and she disappeared toward his office.

Then Pepper picked up the woman's watercolor painting and headed for the side door. He wanted to try a long shot...

———

A sheriff's department patrol car was parked at the curb outside the Bailey home. Pepper cursed and parked two houses short of his destination.

The officer inside the car looked a lot like Deputy Tammaro, the deputy he'd met at the roadblock when all this started. One of the few county deputies who knew him by sight. That would make it harder for Pepper to claim he was a family friend, coming over to console the family.

As Pepper walked along the sidewalk toward the Baileys' house, carrying the woman's watercolor painting of the man with brown eyes, his phone buzzed.

It was a text from Delaney: *WTF??? ASSHOLE*

What? What the hell had happened?

He texted back to her: *what? Call you soon.*

She replied immediately. *DON'T BOTHER! HARVARD DOUCHEBAG!!*

Crap!

How the hell had Delaney found out about Harvard? He was going to tell her! Now he looked like an asshole. And probably he'd been one. He was planning to fix that, and now, how the heck could he? And he hadn't lied about heading off to college. He just hadn't mentioned it...

Pepper tried calling her, but she didn't answer her phone.

Maybe he could still fix things. Go to Sandy's Restaurant and talk to her face-to-face, right after he talked to Mason Bailey. Absolutely.

As he approached the front door, he heard Deputy Tammaro's voice behind him, "Hey! Hey, Ryan? Pepper Ryan?"

But Pepper was in a grumpy mood now and he didn't turn, he just kept walking.

The Bailey house was a medium-sized ranch home. Broad and low. As Pepper walked up the front walk, he could see the big living room window the boy had looked out and witnessed his sister being abducted.

Jesus, the poor kids. Both of them.

Both of the Bailey parents answered the door.

"We're surprised to see you again so soon," said Mrs. Bailey. But not actually mentioning the botched ransom drop.

"Can I just come in for a minute?" he pleaded.

Deputy Tammaro stood outside her vehicle with her arms crossed, watching as the Baileys let Pepper into their house.

Okay, step one.

They sat with Pepper in the cozy living room and treated him like a visitor. Even offered him something to drink.

So Pepper spent a few minutes being polite too. How were they holding up? How was Mason? The family seemed to appreciate his questions.

Then Pepper got to the point. He explained he needed to show Mason a painting in case the man in it was the kidnapper. Would they mind if he talked to the boy briefly?

They said Mason was in his bedroom down the hall, doing some summer studies. Mainly to keep him busy and distract him from thinking about what he'd seen. Did Pepper really need to talk to him? Dredge it all up again? Mason had told the police everything, multiple times. And the ransom drop failure—that made things worse for all of them, including Mason.

Pepper begged for just a minute. "It might help locate Emma," he tried.

The parents relented.

The three of them walked down the hallway to Mason's room. The mother knocked gently, but the boy didn't respond. She knocked louder.

Then she opened the door and screamed.

Mason wasn't in his room.

A variety of toys, clothes and other kid stuff were on the floor beside the bed. And the window was half open.

Pepper heard banging at the front door and ran down the hall to answer it.

Deputy Tammaro stood there, handgun drawn. She pointed it at Pepper.

He slowly put his hands up. "The boy's gone! He was in his bedroom but it's empty now. He might have climbed out the window and ran away. Or maybe he's been kidnapped too."

Tammaro charged up the hall to the boy's room. Pepper followed.

The mother stood in the bedroom, crying.

The father came jogging back down the hall. "I checked the

bathroom, all the other bedrooms. I thought maybe—" He didn't finish.

The hair on Pepper's neck was prickling up. Had the kidnapper grabbed Mason to eliminate the only witness? "If it was the Snatcher, he might not have gotten very far away yet," he suggested to Tammaro.

Tammaro lifted her shoulder radio and called in the situation to the sheriff's office. All law enforcement in the Lower Cape would respond.

"Now we need to search the whole house," the deputy said, in her nearly calm voice.

They quickly checked every room on the main floor, yelling his name, their voices overlapping.

No sign of Mason.

Then they thundered down the wooden stairs into the basement.

And there, curled up on an old sofa, was Mason. He was playing video games and his eyes were glued to the TV. He had headphones on and didn't react immediately to the sudden appearance of his parents, Pepper and Deputy Tammaro.

The mother swept him into her arms, sobbing.

"You scared the *hell* out of us," the dad yelled at Mason. Then he hugged his son and his wife.

Deputy Tammaro looked somewhere between relieved and humiliated. She'd called in a major emergency and it was a false alarm.

"What're you doing here?" Mason asked Pepper. "Did you find Emma like you promised?" The boy's eyes lit up with hope.

Pepper's face was hot with shame, but he didn't answer the boy. Even the Bailey parents looked embarrassed for him.

"Pepper Ryan, you're bad news," said Tammaro, holstering her weapon. She got on her radio again, alerting Dispatch it had been a false alarm. Calling off the help. She sounded sheepish. She was relatively junior and would probably take a lot of heat for this incident.

Pepper didn't want her to get in trouble. It was absolutely his bad. He would take all the heat again. And no one would care that he'd screwed up because he was afraid for the boy's safety.

The air conditioning system kicked on in the basement with a heavy shake and groan. It sounded like the Baileys had skipped getting an annual tune-up. Blessedly, Pepper was standing directly under a vent. The cool air washed across his face, making him feel a bit better.

For a moment.

Then he remembered Mason's bedroom. The boy's window had been half open. Who did that if you had air conditioning?

The Ryans didn't have central air—his dad had always considered it a waste of money. They just opened windows and prayed for a breeze.

"Mason, did you open your bedroom window before you came down here?" he asked gently.

"I think you should leave now, Ryan," said Tammaro. "You've caused enough chaos for one week."

"No way," Mason scoffed at Pepper. "Mom says we can't cool off the whole Cape..."

Mason didn't open the window?

Pepper looked at Tammaro, then raced for the stairs.

CHAPTER THIRTY-SIX

Pepper burst into Mason's room.

The window was still halfway open, the curtains rippling in the light breeze. He looked around the bedroom. No one was there.

Pepper saw a kid-sized bed. A small desk. Posters of Harry Potter characters all over the walls. A closet with its door open an inch. Some toys, a soccer ball, and a half-completed White Mountain puzzle which appeared to be a collage of breakfast cereals. Some clothes scattered on the floor.

Deputy Tammaro reached the bedroom a second later. "Ryan! Get your ass out of this house now or I swear I'll arrest you!"

Pepper ignored her. He dropped to the floor and checked under the bed. A few socks and some comic books. And dust balls.

"Ryan!" repeated Deputy Tammaro, louder.

Pepper saw the Bailey parents had reached the bedroom, pausing in the doorway behind the deputy. The parents looked panicked.

Pepper scrambled to his feet, looked around, then headed toward the closet.

Deputy Tammaro was turning red. "Ryan, I—"

Pepper was two feet away from the closet door, his hand coming up to grab the knob, when the door whipped open. It was a solid door, and it hit Pepper hard, knocking him backward. He stepped on the White Mountain puzzle box, which crushed and slid under his foot, almost causing him to fall.

As Pepper tried to regain his balance, a large man sprang from the closet and charged at him, knocking him backward over the small bed.

Deputy Tammaro yelled and leaped forward.

As he fell, his arms windmilling, Pepper had a brief view of the intruder. The man's head was covered in a blue ski mask. Dark pants and shirt. He was big, Pepper's height or so, but heavier.

Pepper formed this quick impression—like a camera snapshot —as he fell backward, before his head cracked into the nightstand. Before he saw a painful burst of stars. Then he saw the man take three steps across the room and dive out the open window.

Pepper would swear he heard the person laughing as he disappeared.

Deputy Tammaro drew her handgun and ran to the window, shouting, "Stop!" as the man's legs disappeared over the sill. She leaned out, pointing her firearm. "Stop or I'll shoot!" she yelled.

Pepper could see her weapon track from left to right. Following the fleeing man. But she didn't fire. She was probably thinking "excessive force," and he knew she was right, unfortunately. If she shot a fleeing suspect in those circumstances, she'd be the one to go to prison.

"Bastard!" she exclaimed. Grabbing her shoulder mike, she said, "Dispatch, new emergency at 56 Yale Street," she said in a strong, steady voice. "Suspect is a large male, dark clothing, escaping north on foot. Requesting assistance."

As Pepper sat up, his vision swimming from the blow to his head, he saw Tammaro shove past the Baileys and disappear toward the front door in pursuit of the Greenhead Snatcher.

The intruder had gotten away cleanly, like a ghost.

Or like a predator with a detailed getaway plan. Multiple officers combed the neighborhood in vehicles and on foot for the next hour, with no results.

Pepper stayed and gave a statement to a pair of detectives who arrived from the sheriff's office. He knew Deputy Tammaro was in for a long day of interviews and paperwork herself. He wondered if she wished she'd fired her weapon, damn the consequences. He wished she had—the Snatcher deserved no better.

Pepper's phone rang. It was his dad. He considered letting it go to message, but sighed and answered the call.

"Pepper, why did you go to the Bailey house?" his dad asked. He sounded frantic. Worried. And he didn't wait for Pepper to answer. "When the officers on the scene release you, I want you to come straight to the station. Don't stop to eat. Don't stop to take a leak. Straight here."

Shit.

"I'm glad you're okay, son," said his dad. He sounded like his voice was choking up. "But you took a heck of a risk again. I need to hear the whole thing from you, because what I've been told so far... I just can't believe it. So get your ass back here as soon as they clear you from the scene."

CHAPTER THIRTY-SEVEN

The next morning, Wednesday, Gerald Ryan had to give Pepper a ride to work because his son's old truck refused to start. Some kind of engine problem? Pepper had probably neglected to change the oil.

Luckily, they were heading to work at the same time, which was rare. Gerald usually beat his son to work by at least an hour.

They rode mostly in silence, each deep in their own thoughts. Pepper put some country station on the radio, so the lack of conversation wasn't too awkward.

Gerald Ryan was quiet because he'd decided during the night he was going to fire Pepper today from his cadet summer job. He'd talked to the Barnstable County sheriff (a good guy, Gerald had known him for years) to make sure he had the full story about the latest incident at the Bailey home.

Gerald believed firing Pepper was the only right decision. He would persuade—or force—his son to leave the Cape. Whatever it took. He'd convince Pepper to head off early to college. He could lift weights and skate...while getting mentally ready for his school year. And get the hell away from this Greenhead Snatcher situation.

Because Pepper was sticking his neck out way too far.

Sure, his son had essentially saved the Bailey boy. But he'd had no business being there. He was practically a vigilante, like Emma Bailey's uncle and cousins who were arrested on Friday for breaking into Casper Yelle's apartment.

And to be honest, it made Chief of Police Gerald Ryan look like a damned nitwit. Like he had no control over his own son.

Most important, he needed to fire Pepper for the boy's own safety. If that perp had jumped from the closet with a knife or a gun, he could have killed Pepper. Gerald could be at the morgue right now, looking at his son's pale, lifeless body.

The same with the ransom drop fiasco. Pepper should have been nowhere near it. Gerald blamed himself for that one.

No, he had to take his son completely out of the Snatcher situation. The only thing keeping Gerald from pulling the trigger on firing Pepper was that he wanted to talk it over with Don Eisenhower. He respected his lieutenant's opinion more than anyone he'd ever met. Don would give him his honest, no B.S. opinion.

Then, at lunchtime, Gerald would ask Pepper to join him for lunch. He would order in some sandwiches, lay out all the facts for his son and give him a chance to defend himself.

Then Gerald would fire his son. Damn straight.

But it turned into a hell of a morning for Gerald.

The Greenhead Snatcher case had pushed everything else to his back burner, and some of it was now catching fire. Ongoing cases to discuss with the investigators and Don Eisenhower. Phone messages which were long overdue for him to call back. Personnel and equipment decisions to make for next year's budget. One thing on top of the next.

When he stopped by Pepper's little office to invite him for a sandwich, he wasn't at his desk.

Gerald didn't have time to play hide and seek right now. In a half hour he needed to head with Detective Sweeney to a Snatcher task force meeting at the command center over in Eastham.

Kevin Sweeney could have represented New Albion just fine, normally, but after what had happened last night with Pepper at the Bailey house? No, Gerald was going to be there and didn't care that a chief of police belonged back at his own station, sitting on his ass.

But Sweeney would be ready to give their update. The best New Albion suspect was still Casper Yelle, who'd slipped his ankle bracelet and hadn't been located yet. Sweeney was still gathering info on Scooter McCord and other locals who were persons of interest. People without alibis who had means, motive and opportunity, in varying degrees.

Gerald hoped *someone* among the other jurisdictions—five town police forces, the Barnstable sheriff's office, the state police and the FBI—had made a breakthrough. Possibly after the incident at the Bailey house?

Gerald couldn't wait all day for Pepper. He took a yellow sticky note and wrote:

Gone to Command Center. Back by 5 to give you a ride home. We need to talk. Dad.

He stuck the note on the computer screen, pressing the sticky part extra hard to make sure it would stick. Then as an afterthought, he secured the note to the screen with a piece of scotch tape.

It wouldn't fall and Pepper couldn't pretend he hadn't seen it.

Pepper sat on the front steps of the police station, pissed off at the sunny July afternoon.

He'd returned from a midday workout at Globe Gym, which hadn't given him the stress release he'd hoped for. He needed to fix things with Delaney Lynn.

And then he needed to fix his life, overall.

Pepper had tried to call Delaney this morning and talk to her about the Harvard thing, but she didn't answer her phone. An hour later, he'd called again and left a long-winded, apologetic message.

An hour after that, he'd texted her. No response.

Sitting on the police station steps, he dialed her number again. It dumped to message. He hung up, totally bummed out, and headed in to his brain-dead database work.

Pepper had almost reached his office cell when he got a call from Ron's Garage, who had towed his truck from his house that morning.

"H_2O," said Gabriel Moreno, the mechanic. Gabriel had played youth hockey with Pepper until he'd dropped the sport after their first peewee season when he'd fallen in love with pulling apart old cars and putting them back together. "Your problem's just regular old water."

"What?" asked Pepper, thinking he'd misheard. Two officers were having a loud conversation right behind him. Pepper walked into his office, closing the door to block them out.

"You got water in your gas tank and it got into the cylinders. The pistons can't rotate, so no fuel combustion, no compression, no nothing."

Perfect! Goddamn water in his gas tank? What else would go wrong this week? He didn't have money for this crap—he was close to broke already.

Gabriel went on talking. "I'll drain the fuel tank and put in new filters...hopefully I won't have to take the tank off. I should have it back on the road tomorrow morning."

Pepper swore, then asked, "Did the water get in through some kind of leak in the tank?" He was picturing a huge repair bill. "Will this keep happening?"

"No, I think we've got someone running around town with a sick sense of humor. It's rare to get so much water in a gas tank. Must have been a few gallons. The weird thing is, it's the second time this week I've seen it. Totally crazy." The mechanic paused, then added, "By the way, the other car with water in its gas tank was a Volkswagen Bug that belonged to the teen who got kidnapped—Emma Addison? You think the nut who snatched her could have messed with both your rides? If not, it's a hell of a coincidence..."

Pepper sat at his desk, grinding his teeth.

He knew there was no damn way it was a coincidence. The Greenhead Snatcher must have screwed with his truck—as payback for stopping him at the Bailey house? Or to slow him down? Both?

Little did the kidnapper know, Pepper was trying to back away from the damned case anyway. Everything he'd did on the Greenhead Snatcher case got him into trouble, and none of it got them any closer to finding the poor kidnapped girls. It was time for Pepper to leave the investigation to the so-called pros.

He noticed his dad's note taped to his monitor. He decided he'd take his dad up on the offer of a ride home. Then he'd ask to borrow his dad's SUV and drive to Delaney's apartment. He owed her a full explanation about Harvard. He hadn't lied to her, but he was ashamed that he hadn't told her about his plans. Although the way he was feeling lately, maybe he wouldn't stick to the college and hockey plan.

He sat thinking about that idea some more and felt a growing excitement in his chest. He already had a great Plan B—Nashville with Delaney. Even without the industry connections of poor Dennis Cole (wherever the hell Cole was, dead or at least brutally wounded?), going to Nashville was still a legitimate option. He and Delaney could work hard and make their own break.

Only two things had made Pepper completely happy that summer: being around Delaney and performing on stage. So maybe being a professional musician was the right future for him, after all.

Pepper took out his phone and texted Delaney: *Need 2 talk. I have big news for u. And us.*

Sending the text felt great. His new Plan B absolutely seemed right.

Then embarrassment flared up—what would he do about Harvard? He could picture breaking the news to them: *Sorry, someone else will have to be last in the class and slowest on the hockey team.*

Maybe Harvard wouldn't care a bit. They must have endless candidates for his spot. They might be relieved if their weakest link did the right thing and walked away.

The harder part for Pepper would be breaking the news to his dad: *Sorry, I quit. And I'm skipping the college thing. And I'm definitely never going to be a cop.* Pepper knew it would probably hurt his dad more than anything he'd ever said to him. Letting down a three-generation Ryan tradition...

But Jake would be a cop—he'd keep the miserable tradition alive. He'd be the good son for both of them. Pepper would try to find a gentle way to break the news to his dad.

Pepper sat, full of mixed emotions, getting absolutely no work done. He was just thinking and planning. And the more he thought, the more his trepidation turned to excitement.

Then he got a text back from Delaney around four: *U saying Scooter is wrong about harvard?*

It shocked Pepper. Scooter McCord? How the hell did he even know who Pepper was, let alone that he was heading off to Harvard this fall? Sure, Scooter had lurked around his table in Delaney's section. Had he gotten jealous? Pepper pictured Delaney talking him up in front of Scooter to get the assistant manager to leave her alone. Then Scooter digging around about him and spilling the college news to upset Delaney.

Pepper needed to talk to her face to face. Then he'd love the chance to do the same with Scooter McCord...

He texted Delaney again: *Can I see u 2 explain?*

A few minutes later, the response:

Ok come over. Better b good!

Pepper quickly responded, promising he'd be over right after work.

He absolutely couldn't wait to make things okay again with Delaney.

Pepper spent the afternoon feeding the database. A slow torture. In the back of his head, he was thinking about Delaney Lynn and what he'd tell her.

Five o'clock passed. Then 5:15. His dad was goddamn late... again! Making the score: the badge 99–the son 0. Pepper texted his dad, got no answer. Pepper completely understood how important the Snatcher case was. No debate there. But his dad couldn't take ten seconds to text back?

Pepper sent another text to his dad and again got no answer. 5:25. *Shit.* His dad had probably gone for coffee with one of his law enforcement buddies. Or dinner.

By 5:35, Pepper's nervousness about Delaney had burned off and been replaced by anger. His dad hadn't returned to the station yet and still hadn't responded to any of Pepper's texts. And Pepper's chance to make things right with Delaney was slipping away...

That's when he decided he was getting the hell out of there immediately.

Back in April when Pepper had begun his cadet job, his dad had specifically ordered him to never take home a work vehicle. It would look like shit, he had explained, like Pepper was taking advantage of the Ryan name. Abusing the public trust. All that stuff.

But Pepper was too pissed at his dad to worry about consequences.

He checked the motor pool pegboard behind the duty desk and saw the keys for two police cars. One of them was the brand-new SUV—the Ford Explorer Police Interceptor model—only one week old. Probably didn't even smell like vomit yet. So he grabbed the keys.

He didn't really give a shit how mad his dad would get. He had to get to Delaney's and was tired of wasting the little money he had on taxis when this situation was his dad's fault. Once again, Pepper was the afterthought.

What would his dad do when he found out he'd borrowed a patrol car? Fire him?

Oh, please... Pepper could only be so lucky.

CHAPTER THIRTY-EIGHT

Emma Bailey quietly conspired with New Emma as they used the pathetic toilet facilities.

Their kidnapper was fairly far away, giving them space. The man was wearing the dumb Shrek mask again, which hid his screwed-up lip. Emma hoped it hurt like hell.

She was amazed the man hadn't mentioned what she'd done to him. He was acting as if she hadn't bitten his lip off. Why?

If Shrek could hear her and New Emma whispering while Emma peed, he didn't say anything. He seemed frazzled. And jumpy. Like this whole thing was wearing on him.

Good.

The girls shuffled back from the toilet chair and New Emma picked up food, but Emma didn't. She just took a sip of the drugged water. She still wasn't giving in on the food thing. She still wanted to stay on the offensive. So she started carrying out the plan she'd whispered to New Emma.

"I'm sorry I bit your lip," Emma said. She made sure to really sound sorry. "You surprised me—it was like a reflex."

The man didn't respond, but at least he was looking at her.

"I hope you can forgive me," she continued. "And if you don't want even more blood around here, can you please get us some stuff?"

This time Shrek responded. "What?"

"My period's about to start. I get it super bad. Did you stock up any feminine hygiene supplies?"

"Ah, no." The man seemed embarrassed.

"Oh yeah, it's gonna get bad soon. It starts slow, then it'll get even worse than your lip. A few more days and then it peters out. Emma's gonna need them too, I bet. Pretty soon. We need you to buy small, medium and large maxi pads. The same for tampons—small, medium and large. And five bottles of Summer's Eve."

"Summer's Eve?"

Emma laughed. "You don't even want to know. Let's just say, I'm guessing you don't, like, want us all infected down there below the belt. Right?"

Emma's hope was that a guy with a ripped-up face who bought such a weird combination of feminine care products might attract some attention from the checkout clerk. Half of the Cape was looking for them, she had to believe that. Would the clerk think Shrek's purchases were weird? Maybe say something to the cops?

"We'd really appreciate it," said New Emma, playing along like Emma had coached her. The girl even smiled a little, for the first time Emma had seen.

"Oh," Emma added. "And get, like, half a dozen things of ladies deodorant." Ramping things up... "Sorry, I'm getting ripe already."

The man in the van drove through the Cape Cod afternoon, cursing his bad luck.

He absolutely needed to get going with part two of the plan, but he freaking couldn't. He'd failed to grab the third girl, Jessica Little, despite multiple attempts. First the nosy neighbors and now the Littles' house was completely dark. Like they'd gone away somewhere. And they hadn't collected their mail. Had they gone on a freaking vacation? Or were they overreacting to the news stories and had taken their daughter out of town for safety? It was ridiculous, but possible. What were those called— helicopter parents? Tough to say.

He needed Jessica Little. Needed to get her...down to the core of his being. Three was the number. Three was the end of the first part of the plan and the beginning of the endgame. No point arguing about it.

Fuck! He couldn't wait around for some undetermined number of days...they'd be risking too much. He thought about the two Emmas and their suffering, chained up in the Heart. No, this couldn't continue. There had to be a different way.

And now the Emmas had thrown this female hygiene curveball. Buying a ton of female products had definitely *not* been part of the plan. But what could he do? He needed to decide by himself and both options were bad.

The man drove toward the Rite Aid pharmacy. He assumed there'd be different brands of women's stuff—he didn't have a clue. So he'd clear the place out. All the female creature comforts. Buy different brands and different sizes. Let the girls sort out what they needed.

He had to look at it as an opportunity to score some big-time trust points. Show them they would be provided for. And that he'd forgiven Emma Bailey for biting his lip, the hellcat.

He would show them the strength of his commitment. Emma Bailey would come around, and Emma Addison would come around too. By the time the new family was away and together, he would be their new favorite.

And while he was at the pharmacy, he'd pick up some anti-bacterial crap for his lip. It still stung like a bitch.

For obvious reasons, he hadn't been able to go to a freaking hospital. No, he'd used ice and a needle and thread and taken care of it himself. It'd hurt like a motherfucker and he was glad he hadn't been within swatting range of Emma Bailey—he'd have done some damage to the girl. He hoped his Frankenstein mouth didn't lead to questions at the pharmacy.

The man was glad he'd taken a few minutes earlier for a quick session with his pipe. Not a biggie. Just enough crank to lift his spirit to a hundred times its usual size. He felt so *more*. So damn *alive*. It was like giving himself a superpower, along with the guts to use it. A solution would present itself. He truly believed it.

The man in the van not only saw the road and what was in front of him—he could see everything in the corner of his eye too. His head was on a swivel, taking it all in. He was on point.

It was the upside to meth no one talked about. Hell, the U.S. military gave speed to pilots to help them in battle.

As he drove to the pharmacy, the man surfed the FM radio dial from station to station, listening for news. Everyone was talking about the Red Sox, as if that was the most important thing in the world. Something about a big win last night over the Yankees.

I honestly don't give a shit about the Red Sox, thought the man. Sure, he watched it, 'cause it's what's on. What're you going to do? But when they win, he didn't win himself, right? So fuck you very little. From now on he was going to only give a shit about his own shit.

The man reached the Rite Aid, where he bought out the whole damn female hygiene section. And remembered to grab antibiotic Vaseline for his lip.

The elderly woman who rang up his purchases didn't make any comment. She probably saw weirder purchases every day.

Then the man strolled next door to the package store, where he bought some liquid courage. He grabbed the cheapest whiskey they had and a six-pack of Busch beer, then got back on the road, thinking about his bad situation.

If Jessica Little was on vacation somewhere, screw it—the bridge to freedom was still calling his name. Unfinished business was better than getting taken down like a dog. He had the Emmas...and he was going to have more money to spend than he'd ever had in his life, thanks to the Addisons paying the big fat ransom.

Everything would be just fine. He'd make a quick stop to see if his buddy was home—bum a beer, shoot the shit—then he'd head back to check on the Emmas. He'd give them all the female crap and some extra food and water—if they were nice to him. And why wouldn't they be, after how he'd bought all the embarrassing female devices?

He sipped a Busch roadie as he drove. Cold and delicious. He didn't know why anyone bought fancier beers. It wasn't meth, but what was?

As he turned onto Lower County Road, he glanced at the dashboard clock: 5:43. Like a countdown...

And when he looked forward again, on the sidewalk about a quarter of a mile along, he saw the perfect solution to his damn problem. It was a pony-tailed girl, on the shorter side (maybe a young teenager?) walking alone in the same direction he was driving.

Going his way...

The man in the van had only a moment of indecision. Of fear. This girl wasn't part of the plan. He'd done no recon at all. He didn't even know her name. It was too freaking random.

He scoured the road ahead and checked his rear mirrors. No cars or pedestrians in sight.

Just him and the girl. Fate?

The man in the van decided it was. His fate. Her fate. Their fate. A quick grab, then move to part two of the plan—getting far, far away from Cape Cod. To the place in the mountains. To their new start!

CHAPTER THIRTY-NINE

Pepper drove the police SUV through the rain, belting out a Kings of Leon song like an idiot.

He was nervous about seeing Delaney, what he would say to her. They'd go to his house long enough for him to change out of his uncomfortable cadet uniform. She'd get a kick out of it, a joy ride in a cop car. Especially when she learned that he'd made his choice, and it was her. And making music. She'd be totally excited.

Freedom. Together. He still had to tell his dad and Jake. He knew there'd be trouble, but he'd decided. He'd quit—if his dad didn't fire him first.

Fire him...

Pepper decided he would sit his dad down later that night and give him the news. Pepper wasn't going to Harvard this fall. And he wasn't ever going to become a cop. He would be a musician. He and Delaney were leaving this week. And that was that.

He knew his dad would flip his lid. Throw away an Ivy League degree for a guitar and a girl? Pepper could already hear his gravelly voice.

Maybe it had been the wrong day to swipe the police SUV. The weight of it hitting him now.

He came down the hill on Roger's Folly Road. As he approached the intersection with Lower County Road, he saw a brown cargo van pulling onto that road from a grassy strip between the road and the sidewalk. It was approaching the four-way stop to his right.

Pepper noticed a white bag in the grass. Maybe a kitchen garbage bag? No, something smaller.

The van's right-turn signal was flashing. The driver—a guy in a green trucker's cap—looked at Pepper and their eyes met. Maybe he distracted the driver because his van rolled a few feet into the intersection before he stopped.

Pepper remembered that the man spat out his window in his direction and drove straight, not turning despite his turn signal.

And at that moment Pepper got an even wilder inspiration.

He would stop blaming others for his troubles and his future, once and for all. Fuck that! He was going to take action to force his freedom in a crazy act of revolution. Pull over the brown van for running the stop sign. Call in for backup. When another officer arrived, they'd send the driver on his way and take in Pepper to be dealt with by his dad.

It'd be a serious fuck-up. What could his dad do then but fire him?

And what would everyone expect him to do then—even want him to do—except go the hell away?

Which was exactly what he wanted.

Instead of going straight toward Delaney Lynn's apartment, Pepper turned left, following the brown van. As he turned, he thought, *Pepper, you're nuts.* He was about a hundred yards behind the van, which was moving at a slowish pace, probably five miles under the thirty MPH speed limit.

Pepper caught up to the van and settled in about twenty yards back. White paper covered the inside of the van's twin small rear windows. It looked the same as thousands of other basic work vans all over the Cape. And not much like the notorious white van his dad and law enforcement had been hunting on the Cape that week in connection with the two Emma kidnappings.

Kings of Leon reached the bitter end of their song and a decent Black Keys tune started up, but Pepper killed the music. Then he turned on the police radio and lifted the mic. First time ever, but he'd seen his dad and others do it for most of his life. Still, he fumbled around. Then he hit the talk button. "Ah, Dispatch?" he asked.

Pepper's stomach was suddenly in his throat. It was one thing to get a self-destructive idea. The way people standing near a ledge getting a momentary impulse to jump, which they almost always dismiss just as fast, leaving their toes tingling while staying alive. That self-preservation instinct...

Barbara Buckley's voice crackled on the radio, acknowledging.

Shit. What was Pepper going to do? It wasn't too late yet to bail out of his idea.

And then it was. "Ah, Dispatch, this is Car Two-Two," said Pepper. "Please send units for, ah, backup. Lower County Road, east of Roger's Folly."

Long silence, then: "Is that you, Pepper? Repeat that—"

Instead, he hung up the mic. He fumbled around the dashboard and eventually found the switch to activate the roof lights and siren. His heart jumped as he flipped it. *Pepper, now you're fucked. Congratulations, you're fired for sure.* His right foot didn't belong to him—he barely felt it, heavy and strange, as it floored the gas. His siren screamed in his ears.

The brown van maintained its pace for thirty seconds, then slowed and stopped on the road's muddy edge. It was still raining lightly.

Pepper parked ten feet behind the van. He sat watching his

windshield wipers scrape back and forth, trying to decide what to do. *Nothing more, right? Just sit there...hadn't he screwed up enough already? Just wait for backup to come and talk to the van driver...send him on his way.*

Then everything went to hell. The van's brake lights lit bright red as its engine turned on again. With a roar, the van backed hard at his SUV and slammed into his front end.

Pepper launched forward into the steering wheel, hitting his chin. But his SUV's air bag didn't pop.

The brown van roared away in a cloud of mud and exhaust, headed up Lower County Road toward Route 28.

Holy shit! thought Pepper, cradling his chin in his hands. His whole body started shaking. He was freaked out. And he was damned mad too.

He had to admit he wasn't thinking clearly at that moment. He wasn't thinking at all.

Pepper put the SUV in gear and slewed wildly back on the road in pursuit of the van.

CHAPTER FORTY

Pepper wrestled with the SUV's steering wheel and floored the gas.

His battered vehicle shuddered, and steam or smoke was seeping from under the hood. The SUV's bumper crash guard had provided some protection, but something must have been shaken loose by the impact.

Most important, it still drove.

And the asshole's brown van was no match for the SUV's police interceptor engine. Even with the damage it'd sustained. Pepper was alongside the van in less than a minute, his siren wailing in his ears, and he swung his steering wheel hard to the right, sideswiping the van. Like he'd done many times before... playing Grand Theft Auto.

The van swayed away from him, then lurched back onto the road. Pepper could see the driver's face—furious and pale. He was yelling something Pepper couldn't hear through the closed windows.

Pepper pulled a few feet ahead of the van, then swung his steering wheel again, colliding with it even harder. The van launched off the road across a grass strip and crashed into a tree.

Pepper braked and pulled off the road, sliding to a stop in the wet grass fifty feet down the road. He groaned, unhooked his seatbelt and climbed out of the SUV.

The driver-side door of the van was caved in, but Pepper saw its passenger door swing open. The driver crawled out and stumbled toward the road. A green trucker's hat fell off his head into the grass.

"Stop!" yelled Pepper, running toward him.

The man reached the road twenty feet from the brown van. He slipped on the wet pavement, then recovered. He pointed a handgun at Pepper.

He skidded to a stop. He was completely unarmed. An incredible rush of energy flooded his mind with thoughts. *Run away! Fight!* Both primitive choices blasting his brain in that instant, tearing him in half.

Pepper chose to run...right at the man with the gun. Maybe instinct, maybe just more epic stupidity.

Pepper heard three shots and liquid fire erupted low on his side. He stumbled, then somehow kept running.

He tackled the man and they fell in a tangle as the man fired again. Pain stabbed into Pepper's shoulder. They began wrestling desperately on the wet asphalt. Pepper heard another shot but didn't feel an impact. He needed to rip the gun free or rip the man's arm from its shoulder socket. Either would do.

And neither of which worked. The man was strong too, and wild. They ended up tangled together, both lying on the arm holding the gun. The man grabbed Pepper's hair with his other hand and was trying to tear himself loose. The man's face was flushed crimson and his eyes were impossibly wide. The man's lip was swollen like he'd been in another fight. It was stitched up with black thread but was oozing blood.

Way in the distance of his senses, Pepper heard a faint *thump, thump, thump*. His own heartbeat?

They fought like animals on the wet road—locked together. Kicking, pulling, looking for any advantage. Pepper had been in more scraps than he could count as a hockey player. He was known to be good at it. And he'd boxed Golden Gloves in high school, with mixed success. But this was a completely different fight. One of them was about to die.

Pepper could hear sirens from back toward town. Too far and faint for help to arrive in time.

The man screamed as he ripped his gun hand free and swung the barrel toward Pepper. He shoved away the man's elbow with his right hand while desperately grabbing at the weapon with his left. His hand closed on the cold metal.

The handgun fired again. Pepper felt a shock of pain in his left thumb and the man screamed "*Aghhhhh*—!" An inhuman, broken sound. The man jerked backward and thrashed wildly on the ground under Pepper. Blood was spurting from the man's neck. The gun slid and hit the road. Pepper kicked it away.

Still no civilian or police cars. Where was everybody?

Thump, thump, thump. That sound again, echoing in his ears. Louder. His hand was bleeding and his thumb was wrong. He wrapped his index finger around the bleeding stump of his thumb and squeezed hard. Then he raised the hand above his head, hoping it might slow the bleeding.

His vision was shrinking—all black at the edges and weird. His shoulder was going numb, his side was on fire and the world was spinning under him.

The man tried to crawl free. Pepper pulled himself onto the man's chest, using his legs to pin the man's arms to his side. Using his uninjured hand, Pepper firmly pressed the bottom of his itchy police cadet shirt against the man's neck, trying to contain the bleeding. The man's blood continued to spurt against his hand.

The man began to spasm and his bloody mouth twisted in a grimace. The man said weakly, "We can't—" Then started coughing, or laughing. Pepper couldn't understand the rest of whatever he was saying. The man's brown eyes bugged out with rage. *Had Pepper seen him somewhere before?*

The man swore, then spat blood. It hit Pepper's face, stinging his eyes. He lifted his chin but kept his hand and shirt against the man's gushing neck.

"We won't—" groaned the man, or possibly the words were just a big exhale. His body gave two kicks. Then the man's brown eyes faded to the cheap, dull brown of his van. They froze and were suddenly empty.

Pepper began to cry, alone there in the street.

Time passed, Pepper couldn't say how long. Then he felt a strong hand shake his shoulder.

It was Lieutenant Donald Eisenhower. Pepper had never seen Eisenhower's African American face so pale. Or so close. It was ridiculous.

"Hey man, what's up?" asked Pepper. He didn't recognize his own voice. Thick. Slurred. He gingerly raised his hand in greeting and saw it was stained blood red.

Thump, thump, thump.

"Hey...you hear that?" asked Pepper.

Lieutenant Eisenhower was bent over at his side and answered him. But Pepper couldn't follow his words very well, because the lieutenant's head was lazily splitting into a mosaic of Eisenhowers. Like Pepper was looking through one of those kaleido-thingamabobs he'd played with as a kid... What was Eisenhower saying?

Pepper tried to wipe the blood off his hand on the wet road. But the blood only smeared. He was in a ton of pain and his hand looked wrong now. Why wasn't the rain washing it clean?

He saw a small group of fuzzy people behind Eisenhower, gawking down at him. The evening sky behind them was a broken shade of gray. Were they civilians? Like what, this was all a goddamn show?

Pepper tried to push himself to a seating position, but his hand landed on someone else. He saw it was a man who was also covered in blood. This man was dead still. A wet green baseball cap lay in the street at his side.

Eisenhower slapped his cheek, as if to make him focus. But the slaps felt way too feeble. What was wrong with the lieutenant? Was he hurt too?

"What happened, Pepper? What the holy hell did you do?" Lieutenant Eisenhower asked.

Pepper could barely hear him over the *thump, thump, thump*. He tried to clear his head and answer. *I can explain...just give me a second. Please!*

Pepper really tried. But no words came out. And now the many faces above him looked wicked scared. And way too close.

Then Pepper had a thought that gripped him like an icy hand on his neck.

If I die, I'll never get to explain...

Then his world slid to darkness.

CHAPTER FORTY-ONE

WONDERBOY.

That's what the *Boston Herald* headline called Pepper the next morning. The TV news anchors quickly picked up the story and Pepper's new nickname.

When he woke, his dad told him all about it and showed him copies of the *Herald* and the *Boston Globe*. He learned he was in a hospital bed at Cape Cod Hospital in Hyannis. His dad was in a chair by his side. Jake was in a chair by the window. Both looked exhausted and worried.

The evening before came flooding back in nightmare fashion. Stopping the van. The chase. The fight. The blood. Pepper had a sudden panic that under the influence of painkillers he might have already blurted out the truth about the brown van incident.

After a light knock at the door, Lieutenant Eisenhower stepped in, holding hands with Mrs. Eisenhower. Zula was a step behind them, looking scared and younger than her fourteen years.

Mrs. Eisenhower came over and leaned in as if to give him a hug. After seeing all of his bandages, she settled for squeezing his leg.

Zula stayed at the foot of the bed with her father, staring at

Pepper. Her eyes were almost as big as her glasses. They were red like she'd been crying.

"You look awful," she said in a hushed voice.

"Thanks, kid. So do you."

She gave a little laugh and swatted at his feet. The old Zula.

"I was just about to fill Pepper in on everything he missed," said his dad. He did so, quickly and efficiently, like he was testifying in court.

The police had cleared the cab of the brown van, then opened the back of the van to clear that too, and they had found a nine-year-old girl named Leslie Holbrook, mouth, hands and legs bound by duct tape, but awake and feisty. She was kicking the van's rear doors even as the police opened it.

"I heard thumping noises," interrupted Pepper. "But I didn't know what they were."

His dad continued. The New Albion police, the sheriff's office, the Staties and the FBI had swarmed the scene. They'd found a white bag lying in the deep grass back by the intersection —Leslie's beach bag. She'd been walking home in the warm rain with a friend which her parents had told her not to do. Once they had reached the friend's house, Leslie decided to walk the final two blocks home by herself.

Leslie's parents called 911 fifteen minutes after the van stop, not knowing where their daughter was, and a police officer had picked them up at their house and driven them to the crime scene to see that Leslie was okay.

His dad said Leslie was unharmed other than bruises received while trying to fight off her abductor, an egg on her head which might have happened when the van hit the tree, and the unbelievable trauma of the incident. The police had taken her to the hospital with her parents to be examined and treated.

"Who was the guy?" Pepper asked. *The guy he'd killed.*

"His name was Leo Flammia." His dad explained that

Flammia lived in New Albion and was one of the persons of interest they'd interviewed as part of the investigation. He'd served eighteen months in prison and was paroled five years ago. He had a small landscaping business in town.

Pepper remembered he'd been in the Big Red Yard on Monday, meeting with Dennis Cole. He wondered if Cole and Flammia had crossed paths there. And he also wondered again where Cole had disappeared to.

"We're searching his home and his space at the Big Red Yard," said Eisenhower. "And we're bringing in a K9 this afternoon."

"So no one's found the girls yet?" Pepper asked, and couldn't help looking over at Zula.

"Not yet," said Eisenhower, his face failing to hide his disappointment.

His dad continued. They'd gotten a quick search warrant and searched Flammia's home, but they found no sign of the Emmas. Nor the two million dollars in ransom money. They had discovered a yellow legal pad which had been used to write the ransom note, with indent markings on the pad to prove it.

The police also found four Rite Aid bags in the front seat of the van. The bags held all kinds and sizes of tampons, maxi pads and other feminine hygiene products.

"The Orleans police actually got a call from a Rite Aid clerk over in the Orleans Shopping Center. The clerk thought it was weird that a guy would buy so many random female items. So she reported it."

"We don't have DNA results from inside the van yet," added Lieutenant Eisenhower. "But we're confident Leo Flammia was the Greenhead Snatcher. His van was originally white—he repainted it brown within the last couple of days. Probably he hoped a cheap paint job would throw us off."

Pepper felt a little better knowing the man he killed was the

Snatcher and that the girls were likely alive. "So the other suspects —they had nothing to do with it?" he asked.

"Looks like that's true," said Eisenhower. "It's a weird coincidence Flammia lived only two blocks from Casper Yelle, our old number one suspect. We were that close to the right location..."

"Absolutely," said Pepper's dad. "Last night we showed Flammia's picture to the staff at Sandy's Seafood Restaurant. Several waitresses said he was a regular—once or twice per week that summer. Always alone. And we asked the waitresses if Flammia ever spoke to our other suspect, Scooter McCord. No one remembered seeing them talk, but no one was sure."

"The FBI's still comfortable Flammia acted alone. For now, anyway," said Eisenhower. "Even though he wasn't as intelligent as the FBI's profile had predicted."

"He might have been on something last night," said Pepper. "He seemed like he was high, unless he was just crazy."

"Either way, he's dead now," said Eisenhower. "So it's all about finding the girls now."

And there it was. Pepper knew the brutal truth, which Eisenhower wasn't saying in front of his wife and daughter. Pepper had killed the only man who knew where the girls were.

"We'll find them," said his dad. Everyone went silent for a long minute.

"So what about all these bandages?" asked Pepper, trying to change the subject. "When can I get out of here?"

"You had a .22 bullet in your shoulder," answered his dad. "You had surgery last night to remove it." He explained Pepper had also been shot in the hip, but that shot grazed him and he only had a superficial wound. "And you lost the top half inch of your left thumb. We think the same bullet hit Flammia in the throat and killed him."

"So when you get to Harvard, you'll only be able to count to nine and a half," joked Jake. Everyone tried to laugh.

"The doctors say you're still in serious condition," said his dad. "They're worried about infections. Other complications like that."

"But the database?" joked Pepper.

He was glad his dad smiled. Then his face became serious again, and he said, "You're a hero, son. But I've asked the state police to do an independent review of the incident, since you were driving a New Albion police vehicle when it happened. I've hired a great lawyer named Barnaby Stamen to sit in on the interview. It's just routine, but it's the right thing to do."

Pepper knew that when a New Albion police officer was in an officer-involved shooting, New Albion handed over the investigation to the state police to investigate. Pepper wasn't actually a police officer. And he hadn't been carrying a weapon and hadn't shot Flammia. His dad was probably taking the cautious route since he was the New Albion chief of police and didn't want any criticism about a whitewashing of the incident.

"Fine," said Pepper, but it wasn't fine. What could he do—say he'd been trying to piss off his dad, to get fired? *No way.*

He promised himself he'd keep it simple, answer the Staties' questions. He had only one goal—to not reveal the truth. Because the true story, clear and painful in his mind, was that he'd initially stopped the brown van with a stupid, selfish purpose: to force his dad to fire him. The situation had unfolded so fast and escalated so unexpectedly... He hadn't really had time to think.

Secretly, he considered himself responsible for everything which followed, including the van driver Flammia's death. It was just incredible, dumb luck the man had committed a kidnapping only minutes earlier. The entire incident appeared to be something miraculously just and wonderful. Like heroics right out of a movie. Instead of what it'd really been—selfish, immature and probably illegal. A disgraceful incident which would have sunk his family's reputation and his own future.

He didn't want to even think about it.

Lieutenant Eisenhower leaned over and hugged his daughter Zula. She hugged him back.

Pepper knew Zula was not much older than Leslie Holbrook. And that Zula was pretty much her dad's entire world. He knew with no doubt that Eisenhower would have his back, despite any open questions in the lieutenant's mind.

Pepper knew what he would do. He would keep his story simple. Get by with as few lies as possible. He could ride this thing out, right? He closed his heavy eyes.

I'll survive this week and then no one will ever know the truth.

CHAPTER FORTY-TWO

"You're a hero and a victim," said Barnaby Stamen, Pepper's new criminal defense attorney.

The man had arrived in Pepper's hospital room with his dad. Stamen was a short man—about 5'5" with a bald, shiny head and round green-framed glasses. He was wearing the most expensively tailored charcoal suit Pepper had ever seen. His shiny black shoes had little tassels.

Pepper's dad had told him Stamen was the only criminal defense attorney on Cape Cod he would hire if he was in trouble himself. Stamen owed Pepper's dad a favor and his dad had called it in and got him to the hospital on short notice.

After Stamen clucked over Pepper's injuries, he asked his dad to wait in the hall. Then he asked Pepper to tell him what happened.

By now Pepper's head was clear enough, and he'd had enough time to get his story straight. So he told his story to Stamen (the simple, bullshit hero version, leaving out that he'd been an idiot who was actually trying to get fired).

Stamen didn't interrupt. He just took notes in tiny handwriting and nodded encouragingly as Pepper spoke. When he finished, Stamen smiled. "Very good. When you tell your story to the state detectives, do it exactly like that. Focus on the facts. Oh, and don't assume they're here to help you or that they'll be fair."

"Ah, okay..." said Pepper.

"They will ask you some hard questions. The shorter your answers, the better. Don't worry, just tell the simple truth."

Easy for you to say, thought Pepper.

The two state police detectives arrived shortly after lunchtime. Neither were smiling.

They introduced themselves as Dan Miller and Wendy Chin and said they were attached to the Cape and the Islands district attorney's office.

Detective Miller was a heavy white guy with salt-and-pepper hair in his late forties—he looked like he was one fisherman's platter away from a heart attack.

Detective Chin was of Asian heritage and looked to be in her thirties. She also looked like she competed in triathlons. Ropy arms, athletic, short hair.

They both had the same severe cop eyes as his dad. Like they'd seen it all, so don't even dream about bullshitting them.

Which Pepper knew he had to do.

The detectives pulled up chairs at the foot of Pepper's bed. Barnaby Stamen had positioned his chair at Pepper's side.

Detective Chin placed a recording device on the tray table next to Pepper's half-eaten turkey sandwich. She recited the time, the location, and who was in the room.

Each detective also had a legal pad and a pen to take notes.

She stated that Massachusetts state police assigned to the district attorney's office had responded to an accident scene last night and were responsible for collecting evidence, interviewing witnesses and conducting a review of the incident, including Pepper Ryan's role in it.

"Is Pepper your legal name?" asked Chin.

"It's Peter Ryan. But you can call me Pepper."

Then Detective Chin asked him to tell what had happened last night.

And Wonderboy lied, of course.

Pepper began his narrative at the moment he first saw the brown cargo van. He stuck to what had happened, step by step, leaving out his feelings, his opinions and any side comments. Just the facts, ma'am.

Stopping the van that'd run the stop sign.

Calling dispatch for backup.

Getting rammed.

The chase and running the van off the road.

The gunshots and the fight in the street.

Pepper's first-aid attempts and the man's death.

Lieutenant Eisenhower's arrival at the scene.

Leaving out the bad stuff, like why he'd taken the police car. He left out Delaney Lynn, his plans to quit and his inspiration to get fired.

The detectives didn't interrupt. When Pepper reached the end of the story, they asked him to start again from the beginning. This time they interrupted him with questions.

"Why did you focus on the van on the first place?"

"It was driving erratically. It ran the stop sign and its right-turn indicator was signaling, but it drove straight instead. But that wasn't the important thing. I believed the van was being operated suspiciously and probably was involved in the two abductions in the Cape in the past week." Pepper said it just like Stamen had agreed was the right way to say it.

"You believed it was the van used by the Greenhead Snatcher?" asked Detective Miller, sounding incredulous.

"Yes."

"We'll circle back to that," said Detective Chin. "Where were you going? Isn't your home in the other direction?"

"I was picking up a friend on the way home."

He told them Delaney's name and address. He didn't know her phone number by heart and didn't want the Staties scrolling through his phone. Detective Miller noted Delaney's info on a little pad.

"Did you think at the time you had probable cause to stop the van?" asked Chin.

Pepper didn't like the way she hopped around with her questions. He knew it was a tactic to trip him up if he was lying...

Stamen had earlier explained to Pepper that a law enforcement officer needed to have reasonable suspicion a driver had violated a traffic law before he could pull over a vehicle. The detective's tone suggested she didn't think he'd had probable cause.

"I wasn't acting as an officer," said Pepper, as Stamen had coached him to say. "I was making a citizen's arrest." He explained he believed, based on the specific circumstances, that an abduction had just occurred.

Stamen interrupted smoothly. "And the good news is Massachusetts law is perfectly clear on this point. A private citizen can lawfully arrest someone who has in fact committed a felony."

"Can you explain again why you suspect an abduction took place before you arrived at the intersection?" asked Miller. Still sounding doubtful. Maybe even belligerent? "You couldn't have known the driver of that van had just kidnapped a girl. Not many officers could have made such a leap of intuition, let alone an inexperienced cadet."

Pepper swallowed.

Stamen fielded this question too. "The beauty of the law on this point is that it doesn't matter," the attorney said. "Mr. Flammia had in fact committed a felony—aggregated kidnapping, since he carried a firearm. There's no doubt about the evidence on that fact. It doesn't matter if Mr. Ryan had probable cause, or acted on what you would consider merely a hunch. The citizen's arrest is justified by Mr. Flammia's felony."

Detective Miller looked like he wanted to continue arguing the point, but Detective Chin took the questioning in a different direction again. She asked a series of questions about the wrestling match on the road.

"You said you saw a handgun in the man's hand. What make and caliber?"

"I couldn't tell."

"And what weapons did you have?"

"None."

Detective Miller interjected. "Then why the hell did you do it?"

Pepper paused, getting angry but trying to push down his emotions. "I was reacting to his attack. How many times should I have let him kill me before defending myself?"

Stamen held up a hand and Pepper stopped talking.

"Tell us again everything the man said to you during the struggle," requested Detective Chin.

"Not very much. No full sentences or anything. I think he said, 'We don't' and 'We can't'..." Pepper found he was sweating now as he relived the moment-by-moment details of the van incident. "At least that's what I remember."

The questioning dragged on. In total, how many shots were fired? Five, probably. Was Pepper's finger on the trigger the final time the firearm discharged? No.

Then Detective Miller swung the questioning in a different

direction. "So why were you recently involved in a ransom drop to the Greenhead Snatcher?"

"Whoa, whoa...that has nothing to do with the incident under review," objected Stamen.

"No? The kid drops off two million dollars to a kidnapper, then the next day he kills the same guy?" asked Miller, his voice making it clear he didn't believe in that kind of coincidence.

"If you want to know more about the ransom drop, talk to the FBI," said Pepper. "They'll tell you whatever you need to know about it. They were in charge, not me. And I didn't volunteer to do the ransom drop, the FBI drafted me. So I tried to deliver the money to help get the girls back alive."

"Well, that hasn't worked out very well, has it?" grumbled Miller.

Then the detectives took Pepper back to the beginning of the incident and worked him forward for a third time, branching out with their questions and asking old questions again, with new slants.

Then Miller almost got him. "Was it usual for you to drive home a police vehicle?"

Pepper's dad had specifically forbidden him to take home a police car. However, Pepper gave a less direct answer. "No, it wasn't usual. But it isn't prohibited by any written department regulations."

Detective Miller sat back, sighing loudly. "Why is it this whole incident stinks like last week's trash?" he complained. "What aren't you telling us?"

"Now, now," cautioned Stamen. "Let's keep in mind the alternative—Mr. Flammia would have gotten away with his kidnapping victim. The nine-year-old girl, Leslie Holbrook."

Miller looked angry but didn't respond.

"Man, if you'd been wrong," mused Detective Chin, shaking

her head. Studying Pepper. Finally she took out a piece of paper from the back of her legal pad and glanced at it.

"I believe you've already been notified that your police department has placed you on paid administrative leave," she said. "Don't report for work until you're otherwise notified."

Great. Minimum wage will continue to roll in.

She looked down at the piece of paper and began reading from it. "You are hereby instructed to avoid any communication with the deceased's family and any involvement in this or any related investigation. You are further instructed not to take any police action or otherwise represent yourself as a police officer while this investigation remains open."

"That sounds like a standard warning for investigations of officer-involved shootings. It doesn't actually apply to Mr. Ryan's circumstance," said Stamen.

"But he'll be smart enough to follow it, right?" asked Detective Miller. "Because if Mr. Flammia has family, their next move will probably be to file a wrongful-death suit against the New Albion police department. And Wonderboy here personally." Miller said "Wonderboy" with pained emphasis, like he probably said "hemorrhoid."

Miller turned back to Pepper. "You need to remain available to answer any further questions we may have. Especially if we determine there'll be a criminal investigation separate from this review. You understand?"

Stamen interjected. "Mr. Ryan will consider any further requests when you make them. However, he does not waive his rights either. He has been incredibly cooperative, considering his condition."

"Absolutely incredible," said Miller. "By the way, we'll get a sample of the blood drawn from you last night for toxicology tests. Are we going to find any alcohol or drug results?"

"Nope...go for it," said Pepper. He was suddenly exhausted. And depressed.

The detectives stood, putting away their notepads. Detective Chin turned off the recorder.

Finally, the detectives left.

Pepper's dad came into the room. "How'd it go?"

"He did very well," said Stamen.

His dad sighed. "I wish I'd known when they assigned Miller. I'd have asked the D.A.'s office to swap him out."

He explained Dan Miller had applied for a detective position with the New Albion police six years ago and was beaten out by Kevin Sweeney. "I've seen Miller a few times since, and he has a heck of a grudge against me. But he wouldn't take it out on Pepper. I'm pretty sure." Pepper thought his dad didn't sound so sure.

"You look exhausted," said Stamen, patting Pepper's leg. "I was about to ask for a break if they began another round of questions. But you should be proud of how you conducted yourself today and for your heroics last night. Any questions for me?"

Pepper had one question, but he couldn't ask it aloud.

How the hell do I get my self-respect back?

CHAPTER FORTY-THREE

An hour later, Chief of Police Gerald Ryan pulled up to the brutish gate of the Big Red Yard. It was a rolling steel gate, eight feet high with barbed wire across the top. Gerald beeped his horn.

Don Eisenhower was in the passenger seat. It was lightly raining. Way more rain than usual on Cape Cod in July.

The weather matched Gerald's mood because he was preoccupied about Pepper. He was scared and pissed off about what his son had gone through. He'd wanted Pepper to stay at the hospital, but he needed to be here when the K9 team conducted its search. He had to make sure they did everything possible to find Emma Bailey and Emma Addison.

Leo Flammia had had a small business as a lawn care contractor, cutting grass at various houses around the Lower Cape. From what they'd pieced together so far, he had a dwindling list of customers because he was not particularly reliable.

The man's space in the Big Red Yard held a rusty storage container, an old truck and trailer, and miscellaneous lawn care equipment. It was an easy decision to do a deeper search here for the missing girls with the help of a K-9 team.

The gate slowly rattled open.

"Pepper'll be fine," said Eisenhower.

His friend always knew what he was thinking. "Any parent can tell you their true weak spot," Gerald replied.

"Yup. Their kids."

Gerald loved Pepper, even if he didn't say it often to the boy. That is just how Gerald had always been wired. It was no different with his wife, Mary, when she was still alive. And it didn't mean he loved her any less, either—he'd never gotten over her sudden death during childbirth. He believed Mary knew he loved her by his deeds, not by words, and he hoped Pepper knew it too. That's just the way it was for Ryan men. Nothing wrong with it.

Gerald splashed his unmarked police car through one last big puddle, then parked. He climbed out, immediately soaking his left foot up to his ankle in thin brown mud water. *Shit.*

Now in an even worse mood, he leaped toward the edge of the puddle with his right foot and made it by an inch.

At least the Greenhead Snatcher was dead, he thought. And the tampons and other female items were clear proof the kidnapper had kept the Emmas alive somewhere. But did the girls have a supply of food? Water? Air?

Please, God, let the girls be okay, he thought.

Gerald saw a trailer with the sign "Office." A huge beast of a dog was chained beside the trailer's front steps. Possibly the biggest dog Gerald had ever seen. It was lying in the mud under an overhang of the office's roof, staring at him and Eisenhower like they'd do just fine as an afternoon snack.

"I hope that chain holds," said Eisenhower. Tapping his firearm absently, either as a joke or subconsciously.

Gerald chuckled. "I'm not worried—I run faster than you." He zipped up his raincoat as they walked through the mud to join

Detective Sweeney, who was standing nearby with two other officers.

"K-9 will be here any minute, Chief," said Sweeney. "We searched the area ourselves, but it's a real maze."

Maze was an understatement. Contractors rented space in the Big Red Yard by the foot, so they tried to leave no space empty. Roadways snaked through the property, but most of the place was storage containers, trucks and equipment tightly packed in each contractor's area. It was a total rat's nest of objects to climb around and over.

New Albion didn't have a K-9 unit, so the state police had assigned a team. The hope was a dog could pick up a trace of the girls that the human search had not found. The Big Red Yard was the second of ten sites the K-9 unit planned to search.

"Where's Flammia's space?" Gerald asked Sweeney.

"Fifty feet down that lane, on the left-hand side."

The K-9 vehicle rolled up two minutes later. The monster dog on the chain began barking and jumping around when it saw the K-9 German shepherd, but the police dog ignored it somehow. Damned good training.

They all plodded through the mud to Flammia's space. It was marked off with police tape.

"We just came from the suspect's house," the K-9 officer said to them. "No hits there. And this rain isn't helping Daisy. But we'll do our best..."

"That was some pretty intuitive shit by Pepper, stopping Flammia's van," said Sweeney.

Gerald grunted. "You bet. He might have the makings of a heck of a detective someday." *If he lives that long*, he thought.

The canine search took only a few minutes. The German shepherd covered every inch of Flammia's space and even climbed on the trailer and into the pickup truck. The dog had no hits.

"Broaden the search," requested Gerald.

The officer led the dog in a wider sweep, searching the area.

Gerald heard barking, and they all trotted over to where the officer and the dog waited. They were in the area neighboring Flammia's space.

The dog was tugging at a large rolled-up brown tarp. It was like an enormous cigar. A wheelbarrow and some plywood were leaning against it. The officer removed the dog, rewarding him with his voice and a treat.

Gerald's throat was tight with a lump as Sweeney and another officer unrolled the tarp, over and over. The roll thinned.

Then they stopped.

"Jesus," said Sweeney.

It was a body. But it was a man, not one of the two Emmas.

Everyone backed up. It was now an additional crime scene, and they didn't want to destroy any evidence.

"Chief, want I should check his pockets for ID?" asked Sweeney. He'd put on rubber gloves.

"No need—I recognize the body. It's Pepper's music pal, Dennis Cole."

Nothing but darkness.

Emma Bailey lay against the impossibly hard wall, the ball gag in her mouth digging into her teeth. Her eyes were blindfolded, which really didn't matter. She was still in the same dark place.

And the kidnapper asshole hadn't come back in who knows how long. Emma had wet her skinny jeans hours ago—holding off as long as she could and then finally giving in, surrendering to the warmth and relief and humiliation. Now her jeans were wet and cold down there...super uncomfortable. Her mouth was beyond dry and her stomach felt like it was full of needles. Whenever

Shrek came back, she decided, she would eat and drink. She couldn't take it anymore.

Where was he? Time flickered in and out. She probably even slept for a while. It was getting hard to tell when she was actually awake.

Something had changed, she thought. Maybe it was a little hotter in here... Had she been woken up by the sound of the door or feet on the metal ladder? She thought she heard someone shuffling nearby. Then something made a noise against a wall, toward the metal ladder.

Emma thrashed against her bindings. She tried to scream again, through her mouth gag. She tried to get whoever it was to pay attention to her. To help her.

Why would Shrek just stand there and not free them up to go to the bathroom? Give them water? Food? What the fuck was his problem now? Emma was regretting her hunger strike, big-time.

Or was it just her imagination, and he wasn't there? Was she going crazy, like in some horror movie? Or was it the damned angel of death, watching her, waiting for her last breath? Was she dying? *Oh, God...*

She even believed she felt a hand on her cheek. A light touch, then gone. She was definitely losing it.

The Baileys were good people and all, but they didn't go to church or talk about God and stuff very much. Emma started praying now, just in case. She needed help—from anywhere.

And Emma needed comfort. She pushed out her feet toward New Emma, but she couldn't locate the younger girl's feet. She swung her feet left and right as far as her bindings permitted. Nothing. Was New Emma still there? Was the girl still alive?

Emma started sobbing again. Dry-eyed, since she'd long run out of tears.

No one was ever coming again.

CHAPTER FORTY-FOUR

Pepper was now in the intensive care ward.

Unfortunately he was in a room with another patient, an elderly woman. Their beds were about four feet apart, with a too thin curtain in between. Pepper felt bad that the patient's nearness irritated him, but it did.

The decor was classic institutional. Totally, antiseptically depressing. Pepper stared up at the white drop ceiling tiles and wished he were anywhere else.

The elderly woman's monitor alarms kept going off. *Ding, ding, ding, ding*. Every time a sensor chimed, it took about fifteen minutes until a nurse or assistant came and reset the monitoring machine. It was like high-tech torture.

Since the shared room had almost no privacy, he had learned that the elderly woman broke her leg by stepping in a hole during her morning walk with her best friend.

Pepper felt terrible for her the first time he overheard the ten-minute version of her story, related in the woman's thick Boston accent. And the second time too. By now he felt terrible for himself, having listened to the whole story five or six times as her

KILL TIDE 271

kids, grandkids and other relatives and friends rotated in and out of the room over two hours.

When his neighbor's crowd finally died down, the elderly woman turned on her TV and set the sound at maximum volume. At least the TV drowned out her monitor alarms. Pepper knew from earlier conversations he'd overheard that the woman's daughter had taken her hearing aids home.

In other words, being in the hospital was mostly a miserable experience. His buddy Angel Cavada had popped in not long after the state detectives left and stayed for a good visit. He made Pepper laugh so much, the nurses finally sent him away.

Pepper dozed off and later woke to find Delaney Lynn standing by his bed. She was carrying her guitar in her hand and had flowers in the other. She had a big smile on her face, but her eyes looked worried.

"Oh my God, Pepper," she said. "You look terrible! Look at your poor hand!"

"You look amazing."

Delaney put her guitar against the wall and gave him a hug. The hug hurt Pepper in half a dozen places, but he tried not to flinch. She smelled like vanilla ice cream.

He kissed her lightly on the lips.

She kissed him back. Then giggling, she pulled away. "I don't want to start something you can't finish," she said with a foxy smile. "That's the story of my life. Bad timing!"

They both laughed.

Delaney had lots of questions about what had happened to him, and he told her the short official version.

"It must have been horrible!" she said. "What did you—" Her phone rang. "Oh, sorry, I've got to take this," she said, and slipped out into the hall.

"Was that your boyfriend, Scooter?" he joked when she came back a few minutes later.

"Ha! No, it was the other manager at Sandy's. He wants me to come in early. And he said Scooter McCord quit today. Didn't even give two weeks' notice. Said he's leaving the Cape."

"Seriously?"

"Scooter's been acting like a real asshole—for some reason he thinks I pointed the cops to him when Emma Addison was snatched. Which is total bullshit, as you know."

Pepper heard a clucking noise of disapproval from the elderly woman in the neighboring bed. She had turned off her TV and was probably doing her best to spy on them.

"And he was a perv too," said Delaney more quietly. "He got so pissed when I talked about you, his face turned almost as red as his hair! He was so excited when he threw the Harvard thing in my face. Like I was just some piece of ass for you for the summer."

"I'm sorry I didn't tell you earlier," he whispered. "I was too chickenshit."

So Pepper told her now. How he'd committed to Harvard and played last winter in the British Columbia Hockey League to get ready for Division 1 hockey. And he explained why he hadn't told her before—how he'd worried she wouldn't give him a chance if she knew he was leaving the Cape.

"I get it. And I hope you get how you hurt me," Delaney said. "Let's talk about it more when you're back on your feet." She leaned in and gave him another light kiss.

Then she retrieved her guitar and started tuning it, sitting on the edge of his bed. "Since you're a poor little invalid, I hoped some music might cheer you up."

Pepper just smiled. At that moment, he felt like the luckiest guy in the world.

She started playing the cool old song, "Me and Bobby McGee." A song made famous by Janis Joplin, but Delaney's performance sounded more like a cover of the song Miranda Lambert had done more recently. Delaney's rendition was full of passion and drama and a little bit of crazy. She sounded amazing. Mesmerizing.

She sped up for the final verse of the song, banging out the chords to the song. When she finished, Pepper clapped painfully, his intravenous wire tugging at his hand as he clapped.

"Amazing," he said. "You're absolutely amazing."

She smiled, and Pepper could think of nothing that would make him happier than spending every day going forward with her. Sharing her music, getting her to smile at him the way she was right then.

Then she surprised him by saying she'd play him a song she'd written herself. He didn't know she wrote songs too. She began playing her song on the guitar and singing along. It was tender and sweet, with a heavy edge for someone so young.

Pepper listened, hypnotized.

When Delaney finished, she leaned back over to kiss him again, this time much harder than before. A deep, passionate kiss. Almost frantic, it was so powerful.

Despite his injuries, Pepper kissed her back just as hard.

Delaney looked him in the eyes. "You never told me the big news you texted me about yesterday. Our big news?"

And now when it came time for Pepper to tell her what he'd decided—that he was all in running away to Nashville with her—he paused. Maybe because of what he'd gone through since leaving work yesterday in the borrowed cop car? Or maybe now he didn't know which decision was best? Or was he choking now... too scared to make the leap to run away with her? Some mix of all of those reasons? He couldn't get any words out.

Delaney was watching him closely and her playful smile faded.

"Seriously?" she asked.

A voice from the doorway interrupted them. "Looks like I've found the party!" It was Coach Bullard with a big grin on his face.

Coach came right in. He had a big silver helium balloon with the word *Ouch!* on it.

Pepper groaned and introduced him to Delaney Lynn.

"I made this kid the scrapper he is today," said Bullard. "But you know what we called this guy when he played hockey for me?"

"Coach, seriously!"

"It definitely wasn't 'Wonderboy'!" Bullard chuckled.

At least Coach didn't share the "Pylon" nickname. Maybe he believed he'd already succeeded by getting under Pepper's skin...

Pepper's day nurse bustled in—a large middle-aged woman with a Jamaican accent named Rebecca.

"Dr. Keith will be here in a minute," said nurse Rebecca. "So, your friends'll have to say goodbye for now." Her tone clarified this wasn't up for debate.

Coach Bullard just grinned and did something stupid with his eyebrows, leering over at the nurse. Then he gave Pepper the thumbs-up. What a character.

"You hear about the missing guy on the news? Dennis Cole?" asked Bullard.

"What about him?" asked Pepper.

"About he's dead. The police just found his body in the Big Red Yard, near where the Greenhead Snatcher kept his lawn stuff. I saw Randy Larch downstairs, and he told me."

Dead! A wave of sorrow flood Pepper's body. And probably dead because of the information he had given him. Pepper had hoped against hope Dennis Cole was alive. Just like with the missing girls.

"I bet you twenty bucks that guy was the Snatcher's partner," said Bullard. "Maybe the Snatcher killed him so he wouldn't have to split the ransom money."

Pepper wished his old coach would shut up with his half-baked gossip. What did he know? Why was everyone suddenly an expert?

Delaney gave Pepper a polite kiss on the forehead and smiled at him sadly. "Goodbye," she said, then left.

Gus Bullard began to follow her.

"Coach?"

The man turned.

"I think you're wrong about Dennis Cole being part of the kidnappings. And another thing—you were a lousy coach. I hated playing for you, just like everyone who wasn't one of your favorites. And any success I have up at Harvard? It'll be in spite of you."

Pepper heard a gasp from the elderly lady in the next bed.

Bullard's face turned red, and he was about to say something when the doctor knocked and entered. He stared at Bullard expectantly.

"His dad must be pretty disappointed by him," Bullard said to the elderly woman, shaking his head. Then he left too.

Good fucking riddance.

Pepper felt a surge of adrenaline. He knew his old coach had tried to hurt him with the last remark, but he'd failed.

Pepper was proud of himself for finally standing up to his old coach. Fuck him. He wasn't letting that guy push his buttons anymore.

The doctor poked and prodded him, then delivered some crappy news. He said Pepper absolutely couldn't get out of the hospital yet. Probably first thing in the morning, if he didn't run a temperature.

Pepper made a fist with his good hand. He was trapped in a personal hell—stuck in this damned hospital while the clock kept ticking on the two Emmas.

He had to be able to do something...

CHAPTER FORTY-FIVE

Pepper was still suffering in his hospital bed that night, a little after nine.

Not so much suffering from his gunshot wounds. The nurse had given Pepper enough of the good stuff to keep his pain in check. He was lying in bed torturing himself about everything which had gone wrong that week.

The two Emmas were still missing, time to rescue them was running out, and he had killed the only man who knew where they were.

Of course, the real cops—local, state and federal—were still frantically looking for the girls. His dad had promised him that. Pepper couldn't do much from the hospital, but he was still full-on haunted by the situation. So he lay in bed, brainstorming.

Where would Flammia have put the girls?

He made a mental list:

It had to be somewhere no one else could accidentally access.

It had to be somewhere Flammia could come and go without drawing attention.

It was probably somewhere he was very familiar with, in New Albion or a neighboring town.

Which pointed to, well...hundreds of places. Pepper didn't know enough about Leo Flammia to narrow it down further.

The unfriendly face of State Detective Dan Miller peered around the curtain, interrupting his thoughts.

"Ryan! I have a few follow-ups in our investigation of last night's incident," said Miller, skipping any pleasantries. *How are you feeling? Are you doing any better?* Nope, none of that.

"Where's Detective Chin?" Pepper asked.

"Don't worry about her. Worry about me."

Great. Without his partner, Miller was even more of a dick.

Miller turned on a handheld recorder. "I need you to tell me about Leo Flammia. How long have you known him?"

"What? I don't know him. Never saw him before yesterday."

"We got a tip from someone who saw you and Flammia together on Tuesday...the morning after the messed-up ransom drop. So now's the time to come clean. When did you first meet Leo Flammia? How did you become his partner in the kidnappings?"

What? "That's totally false. I never even saw the guy until yesterday evening when I pulled him over. That's it. Whoever's telling you otherwise is a liar. And I'm not talking to you anymore without my lawyer."

Miller clicked off the recorder. "I'm not buying the coincidence, Ryan. Maybe you weren't in the van with him, grabbing the girls. But it explains why he got away clean with the money during your ransom drop. And how he escaped at the Bailey house. Yeah, you thought I don't know about that coincidence too? You've been hanging around the edge of this situation ever since Emma Bailey was snatched. Too many coincidences to fool me."

"You're nuts."

"Yeah? I drove by to see if your lady friend Delaney Lynn backed up your story about where you were going when you ran into the brown van. She didn't answer at her apartment, so I talked to her landlord to see if he had her phone number. Do you know what he said?"

Pepper was at a loss. "No idea."

"He said she'd put a note under his door this afternoon, giving notice. It said she was moving immediately to Nashville, Tennessee. That she'd be back in two weeks for her other stuff."

What? Pepper's head was reeling. Delaney left for Nashville without him? Without even saying goodbye?

She'd been upset about the Harvard thing, absolutely. But he thought they'd gotten past that.

She had seemed pretty good when she saw him six hours ago... other than when he disappointed her by not giving her the news he'd hinted at before the brown van incident. Of course, their conversation had gotten cut short when that asshole Coach Bullard had interrupted them. She'd seemed a bit quiet when she said goodbye. However, he'd never have guessed in a million years she was about to leave town alone.

Delaney had even told him she didn't want to go to Nashville by herself. What had changed? Had the brown van incident freaked her out more than she'd said? She knew he'd killed a man last night—was that it?

Pepper closed his eyes, shocked and sad and pissed off.

At that low moment, a loud knock came from the doorway. Followed by someone who said, "Damn!"

Fester Timmons appeared around the curtain. Mirrored sunglasses and all. He looked panicked when he saw State Detective Miller. He quickly regrouped.

"Gentlemen," he nodded, massaging his hand.

"Sir, you need to wait outside," said Miller. He pointed his badge at Timmins.

"Roger that," said Timmins, and gave a little salute. As he left, he said back over his shoulder, "Pepper, we need to touch base about the, ah...case. When you're free? I'll hit the cafeteria." And Timmins left.

Unbelievable.

The detective was still looking toward the hallway. "Friend of yours?" Miller asked.

"No. More of an acquaintance."

"Not a cop, right?"

"No."

"Whatever case your acquaintance was talking about, it wasn't the Greenhead Snatcher investigation, right? Because we made it crystal clear you shouldn't have any further involvement in that case, correct?"

Fucking Fester Timmins. Every time Pepper was forced to lie, he was digging a deeper hole for himself.

"He's nobody," said Pepper.

"Again with the lies. Well, I promised you I'd nail you to the wall if you came near the Snatcher investigation again. And I meant it. So keep it up, kid. When I come back, I'll bring nails and a hammer."

Pepper waited a few minutes after Miller left, in case the detective was eavesdropping from the hallway. Unfortunately, Pepper's elderly roommate was asleep, so her TV wasn't blaring.

He picked up his cell phone and called Delaney. It rang five times, then clicked to a recording, so Pepper left a message asking her to call him.

Then he texted her a similar message.

How far had Delaney gotten on her way to Nashville? What was her plan? *Goddamn it.*

Pepper was completely frustrated now. He had to get out of this hospital. Everything in his life was slipping away while he lay in bed. And so much of what had gone wrong was pretty much all his own fault, starting with the fate of Emma Bailey and Emma Addison.

I wish I'd died instead of the Snatcher, Pepper thought. Law enforcement would have forced their location from Flammia, and they'd already be getting care.

Pepper needed to get out of the hospital. He was fed up. He had to do *something*!

He remembered his dad had a briefing sheet about Leo Flammia in the Greenhead Snatcher case file in his filing cabinet. An electric tingle shot up his neck. Was the answer to the girls' whereabouts on that sheet? Or at least a clue which would get him closer to the truth?

So he decided. Screw Detective Miller. Screw his personal consequences—loss of his hockey scholarship? Prison time? A wrongful death lawsuit?

No, he really didn't have any options. He dialed Angel's number. His best buddy, the one guy Pepper could always count on...

Time to break out of this joint.

CHAPTER FORTY-SIX

"Go, go, go," said Pepper, painfully slid into the passenger seat of Angel Cavada's old Camry.

They were quickly away, but Pepper didn't fill in Angel on his plan until they were well clear of the hospital area.

After Pepper did, Angel rubbed the back of his neck thoughtfully. "Not that I wouldn't love to get our poor hands on the hundred-thousand-dollar reward... But *mano*, you're a freaking hero. Why not leave this to the cops?"

"Hero? I killed the guy who knows where the Emmas are. I've got to do something." Pepper told him about everything that'd happened since Angel's earlier visit. The appearances by Delaney Lynn and Coach Bullard. The reappearance by Detective Miller, who basically accused Pepper of being part of the kidnappings. And the shocking news about Delaney leaving town.

Angel whistled. "Do you realize how boring it'll be around here when you head off to the damned Ivy League?"

Pepper laughed. "I just want to take a peek at my dad's file on Leo Flammia. Hopefully, that'll give us an idea where to look for the Emmas. I've got a maximum of two hours before the nurses' shift change and someone notices I'm gone. I really don't want

Detective Miller to learn I went AWOL. We need to move fast and I'll need a little luck, back at the hospital."

Pepper was wearing clothes his dad had brought to the hospital on his last visit. They were meant for Pepper's official discharge. He didn't know what they'd done with his ripped and bloody police cadet uniform. Taken it for evidence? Or had they burned it? His hand with the missing fingertip was heavily wrapped in gauze, but otherwise, he looked practically normal.

They had about a thirty-minute drive to New Albion. Pepper called Delaney's cell number again. She didn't answer—it dumped straight to voicemail. This time he didn't leave a message. Why was she ghosting him? Was she blaming him too for causing the two Emmas to die a slow, lonely, painful death by starvation or lack of water?

To take his mind off Delaney, Pepper recapped for Angel everything he knew about Leo Flammia. Which wasn't very much. Pepper's subconscious was still itching at his brain—there'd been something important about the dead van driver in the file which might lead them to the two missing Emmas. He hoped.

"I keep trying to figure out the connection between the two Emmas," said Angel. "But I don't see one. Maybe the two Emmas were a random coincidence? And the other girl he'd snatched when you stopped him, she's way younger and has even less in common with the Emmas."

Angel was talking about Leslie Holbrook, who was only nine years old. Tall for her age, but quite an age difference from the two Emmas, who were sixteen and seventeen.

"The police found a journal at Flammia's house which talked about taking the girls away to be his wives," said Pepper. "Somewhere off the grid. So why grab a nine-year-old?"

"If you try to understand sickos, you'll be confused for the rest of your life. They don't get out of bed for the same motivations as the rest of us. Their wires are crossed."

"Then what motivates you?" asked Pepper.

Angel laughed. "Me? That I'll be a rich son of a bitch. My other car will be a Ferrari, but I'll keep this Camry for driving you around."

Freaking Angel. "How'll you get rich?"

"I have some business ideas cooking," Angel assured him. "That reward for finding the Emmas would give me a great start. It's up to a hundred grand. We split it fifty-fifty and we'll be rolling in cash. You can get your shitty truck fixed. I can quit the pizza delivery, pay the whole nut for my business classes at Cape Cod Community College. Hopefully have a little left over for my first venture...maybe a Cuban restaurant. This part of the Cape would be perfect." Angel rambled on, getting more excited about his ideas for the future.

They reached the police station and parked on a dark side street. Angel stayed behind in *El Diablo*. Pepper stepped out into the hot summer night, possibly the warmest night that month. It felt good, being out in the real world again. He snuck to the station's back door and used his keycard to swipe himself in.

Pepper was about to sneak into his dad's office when he heard snoring. Long, loud and thick.

After making sure the hallway was empty, Pepper peeked into the office to confirm he was out of luck. Sergeant Weisner was asleep with her feet up on his dad's desk. Her chair was rocked back to the edge of tipping over.

And completely blocking Pepper's access to the filing cabinet. He could imagine crawling under and around her, the drawer squeaking open, and Weisner waking up to find Pepper practically in her lap. The mayhem which would follow that nightmare scenario would make all his earlier troubles—including getting shot—seem small and manageable.

Pepper retreated down the hall to his little drunk tank office. He didn't turn on the light, not even after he closed the door. How long could he wait here, hoping Sergeant Weisner would wake up and go back to wherever she needed to be, other than his dad's office?

He texted Angel: *10 min.*

While killing time before he would check on Sergeant Sleeping Beauty again, Pepper booted up his computer and the monitor lit up the room. Shit... He hoped no one would see the glow of the monitor under the closed door.

He tried to log into the department network using his dad's username and password. It didn't work; his dad must have changed his password. And now there would be a record of his failed login attempt, if anyone checked.

Beautiful.

Pepper opened his own draft database. It wasn't close to complete yet, but it had a lot of little bits of data—thousands—from over seven years of cases in New Albion.

In the search box, he typed Flammia.

Two files popped up: a report file from three years ago and Pepper's mock case file.

He opened the first file. It was a report related to Leo Flammia being fired from the New Albion School System from his position as a janitor at New Albion High School. A background check at the beginning of his second year of employment showed he had a criminal record which prevented him from being employed by the school system.

An officer was present when Leo Flammia was fired. He'd warned the man that if he returned to the school property, they would charge him with trespassing. The report said Flammia hadn't acted angry and had caused no problems when leaving the premises. There was no report of any further incident.

So, not much.

Next, he opened his own mock file in the database for the Greenhead Snatcher investigation—all the notes he'd accumulated during the past week. His interviews with the Bailey and Addison families. His conversations with Dennis Cole. His encounter with Flammia when he'd popped out of Mason Bailey's closet and run him over...

Quite a week, but the info didn't take up a lot of space. He began reading.

Footsteps echoed down the hallway and Pepper held his breath as they seemed to slow outside his door. Was the glow of his computer monitor visible under the door? Would someone think that was weird and open the door?

Would he be in a whole new level of trouble?

After an interminable pause, the feet walked away.

Pepper slowly let out his breath with relief. He needed to leave, ASAP.

He printed out the report file and his mock case file. They totaled only five pages. He grabbed a manila file folder from his desk and opened it to put in the printouts.

But two pieces of paper were already in the folder. The first was covered in small handwriting. Pepper recognized it as Zula's writing. This must be the results from her research on Scooter McCord and his alternate name. Which didn't matter now, so he didn't read it. Then he took a quick look at the second piece of paper and was shocked.

The light of his monitor showed he was holding a death certificate. The name on the certificate was Alastair McCord. It indicated that the person died twenty years ago in Brewster, not far away on the Cape. And that the person was eleven years old when he died!

What? This was totally bizarre, even though it was obviously not relevant to the Snatcher case. Another swing and a miss, but he'd have to thank Zula for her efforts when he saw her. She was a good kid... He added his printouts to the folder and took it all with him as he quietly and nervously exited the police station.

Angel was waiting in *El Diablo*. He was bummed to learn Pepper hadn't been able to access his dad's file. "Now we'll never see the Flammia info," he complained. "All this for nothing."

Pepper clicked on the overhead light and started reading through the printout of his own case file. The words were blurring together. Info about suspects who had turned out to be innocent. Info from Emma Bailey's family and Emma Addison's family...

"Am I wrong that Flammia wasn't too bright?" asked Angel. "It surprises me he didn't get caught quicker."

"He disappeared quickly after both kidnappings. Like he'd planned where to grab the girls and how to avoid the main roads, the roadblocks. Everything."

Angel frowned. "Well, I guess it helps he knew his way around the Lower Cape. He'd cut lawns all around the area for years—it said so in the newspapers."

"I guess it doesn't take a lot of smarts to be a predator," said Pepper.

"No, it just takes hard work to get away clean. But I guess on the bright side, a ton of law enforcement are working the case. They'll tear Flammia's world apart. Home, work, credit card, friends, the whole nine yards."

Something Angel said tickled Pepper's mind.

But Angel continued. "Don't worry, *mano,* the pros'll find those girls. Damn, I could have used the reward too. Count the cash, parlay it into—"

"Angel, what did you say?"

"Parlay the cash, buddy. Put it to work. I was saying I'd—"

"No, before that. About Flammia."

"Just that it's hard work to get away clean. But—"

Get away clean...

"Angel, you're a beautiful genius!" said Pepper.

"That's what I've been saying for years. Hey, what'd I say?"

Pepper was lost in thought. The only connection he had seen between the two Emmas was both of their mothers attended New Albion High School many years ago. Around the same time, but not classmates. Not friends.

And Emma Addison was currently a student at New Albion High School, although Emma Bailey wasn't.

That was a lot of New Albion High School connections, with one big kicker—Leo Flammia had worked for a year as a janitor at New Albion High School until three years ago when his criminal record was discovered and they fired him.

Pepper explained his idea to Angel.

"The school?" asked Angel. "That's a long shot. I bet someone would have noticed the guy coming and going from there... What're you thinking, the Cut Room?"

That's exactly what Pepper had been thinking. He and Angel had spent plenty of time cutting classes in their rebellious years, hiding out, screwing around. They were familiar with some parts of the high school most students didn't know existed. But a janitor probably would...

It was a long shot. But if they gave up, they'd already lost. Why not take the chance?

CHAPTER FORTY-SEVEN

At night, mostly in long shadows, New Albion High School looked more like an abandoned factory than a school.

Pepper directed Angel to pull around to the side of the school. He hadn't been inside since the day he'd graduated two years ago. But Pepper was hoping that nothing there had really changed.

"You have a flashlight?" he asked.

Angel shook his head. "Just my phone."

A door on the back side led into the science wing. Pepper felt along the top of its doorframe and found it: a long metal shim. Exactly where it had always been during his high school years. It was their unofficial access to the gym to shoot hoops at night or generally screw around.

Angel shone his phone light on the door.

The shim worked as perfectly as ever, and Pepper had the door open in ten seconds. It reminded him of their principal's speech at graduation, how things they'd learned during their time at dear old New Albion High would pay off in surprising ways over their lives.

Touché, Principal Matusicky.

Pepper and Angel headed into the main part of the school, both holding up their phones for light.

Pepper imagined what would happen if someone discovered them. A whole new level of deep shit. But he was in a bit of an emotional groove at the moment, even if he was digging a worse hole for himself. Whatever crap that followed was on his head. Fair enough. The thought was freeing.

It was dark in the school's long hallways outside the circles of their phone lights. Dark and creepy, like all the movies where the people stupidly walking through the dark halls ended up dead.

"Fingers crossed, *mano*. We chop any reward fifty-fifty, right?" asked Angel.

"You bet, pal."

They passed the teachers lounge, where Pepper had experienced his first kiss in ninth grade. The girl was Maddie Smith, his high school sweetheart. In general, those days seemed like a million years ago. But his first kiss in that forbidden room was as fresh in his mind as if it'd happened yesterday. He checked the doorknob; it was locked.

They passed long rows of dusty trophy cases. In the hockey section, Pepper saw the old picture of Coach Gus Bullard as a skinny teenager in a pile with his state championship teammates. Bullard was holding up one finger and looked exhilarated, just a normal kid. Pepper saw a similar picture from Jake's freshman year—more orderly, but just as proud of their state championship, with big grins. There wasn't a similar picture from Pepper's years, unfortunately.

In his four years of high school hockey, Pepper's team only came close to one state championship, making the semifinal round. Late in the third period of that game, Pepper had found himself in a bad situation—the only New Albion player back when two opponents broke in on him. He did what Bullard had always coached him to do when defending a two-on-one. He took responsibility for the player without the puck while trying to push the puck handler as wide as he could. Hoping to cause a panicky pass that he could pick off, or else force the puck handler to take an outside shot.

Unfortunately, the puck handler shot's from a bad angle in the high slot picked the top corner, scoring the game-winning goal. In the locker room afterward, Coach had roasted Pepper in front of all his teammates for New Albion's loss. He wouldn't even listen when Pepper tried to defend himself.

He could almost hear Coach Bullard's response echoing in his ears:

Pylon, for a kid who can't move his feet, you're damn quick to blame everyone else...

What an asshole. Pepper's cheeks burned at the memory as they went down a side staircase to the basement beneath the gymnasium. He was glad Angel didn't notice.

They finally reached a door in the back corner of the basement. The boiler room. They entered and found it unchanged, except the enormous cast iron coal furnace was cold and silent for the summer.

They walked to the far corner and moved a cart of paint cans away from the front of a door which looked like it might lead to a closet. It didn't.

It was the door to the Cut Room—a large, forgotten storage room which Pepper, Angel and their buddies had remade into an unofficial hangout when they cut class. They drank warm beer, ate crappy snacks and talked about girls. All that teenage stuff. Only the worst-behaved students knew about it...and maybe the worst janitors?

Leo Flammia had been a janitor at the high school six years ago. He'd only worked there for less than a year. But when they fired him, he could have kept copies of the building keys. Possibly with an idea to come back and get some revenge at some later date. Do some vandalism or steal things.

Flammia might have brought the girls here and locked them away in this hidden storage room.

Pepper heard a slamming noise somewhere in the building above them. A door?

"Is someone there?" asked Angel nervously.

They stood silently, listening. Who else would be in the school at that time of the night? And why?

But after waiting for a long minute, they heard no more sounds.

"Let's do this," said Pepper.

Next to the doorway to the Cut Room was an industrial rack of odds and ends. Old equipment which was outdated, dusty, forgotten.

A dented old coffee can sat on the top shelf.

Pepper pulled it down and shook it. The old key rattled inside, still in the same place it had always been.

He slipped it in the doorknob and it turned easily. Pepper flicked on the light.

They found their old room was completely different. The broken sofa was gone, as was the rickety foosball table. It was now a storage room. Full of extra sports equipment. All the indoor track gear, volleyball equipment and other out-of-use sports gear.

And they didn't see the Emmas. Pepper and Angel thoroughly searched the room. They looked behind and under everything in the room. They found no sign of the girls. *Fail!*

As they closed the Cut Room door, Pepper saw the giant coal furnace and his heart almost stopped. He had remembered something from Emma Bailey's note to her parents which arrived before the ransom drop. Something like: *she missed Sunshine and if she could climb down in her arms, she would wrap Sunshine in such an iron hug.*

There was no dog or stuffed animal named Sunshine, according to Emma's parents. But the "no sunshine" and the "iron hug" remarks, if those were clues from the girl...

No way. Could that psycho have locked the Emmas in this giant cast iron coal furnace?

Pepper walked over to it, suddenly feeling light-headed. He started sweating.

He held his fingers near the big door to confirm it was cold for the summer break. It was.

Pepper swung open the door and shone in his cell phone light. The interior was black and dirty. Impossibly dirty. Coal dust and grime coated all surfaces.

No girls were inside. Two people could have fit in there, but no one could have survived for more than a few minutes, not with all those fumes and coal dust...

Another dumb idea which turned out to be a complete bust.

"Game over," said Angel.

As they walked back to the exit, Pepper was as depressed as he could ever remember being. This search had been a waste of time. And it increased the chance he'd catch hell back at the hospital.

Worst of all, he was completely out of ideas.

Pepper's cell phone rang and he realized that actually he could feel worse. It was his dad's number flashing on the screen.

Could he let it go to message? He decided he didn't have any choice; he couldn't answer the call. He was supposed to be in his hospital bed, not trying to find the two Emmas.

Maybe his dad would think he was asleep?

Half a minute later, his phone buzzed again—his dad had left a message.

Pepper listened to it, sure he would hear the worst-case scenario—his dad upset, saying he was in Pepper's empty hospital room, wondering where he disappeared to this time.

But no. In the message his dad sounded okay...just tired and concerned. Not angry at all. He said he hoped Pepper was getting some rest and that he would stop by during the night, when he could, to check on him.

Shit. Time to give up? Get back to the hospital and hope they hadn't missed him?

Pepper couldn't think of anywhere else to look. He had to admit when he was beaten.

They climbed in *El Diablo* and headed out.

"Stop," said Pepper. "You see that minivan? Was it parked there when we arrived?" The old gray minivan sat in the shadows next to the gymnasium.

"Not that I noticed. You think we set off an alarm?"

Pepper thought the minivan looked a lot like the one Fester Timmins drove, although there were a million minivans around the Cape.

"Whatever," Pepper said. "Let's get back to the hospital."

Two minutes later, his phone buzzed again. It was a text from Delaney, finally!

It said: *The girls! Meet me @ big red yard. Now plz!!! only us*

Her text ended with an emoji heart.

What the hell? Pepper was totally confused. He texted back with just a question mark.

"You will not believe this," he said to Angel, showing him.

"That's wack," said Angel.

Pepper phoned her number, but it rang and rang and she didn't answer. He left her a worried message.

Was she messing with him? Or testing him?

Had Detective Miller lied about Delaney leaving for Nashville? Why? If the detective had been telling the truth, Delaney should be hundreds of miles from Cape Cod by now. What the hell was she doing at the Big Red Yard contractor park? And what did she mean by "the girls"? It couldn't be about Emma

Bailey and Emma Addison...she couldn't have located them herself, right?

So he sent her a second text: *What's going on u ok?*

No reply.

So, after a long couple of minutes, Pepper sent her a third and final text:

On my way.

CHAPTER FORTY-EIGHT

El Diablo crept into the parking lot of Johnston Precision Machining, next door to the Big Red Yard, just before midnight.

"Pull all the way to the back corner," Pepper instructed Angel. Pepper remembered from his visit to Johnston Precision Machining that the far corner of the parking lot was a blind spot on the machine shop's surveillance cameras. He didn't think anyone would notice an old Camry pulling into the lot during the night, but they might notice a guy standing on the Camry's hood pulling himself over the wall into the Big Red Yard.

"I'm worried that Delaney came here," said Pepper. "This is where the police found Dennis Cole's body. Maybe he was Flammia's partner, but I doubt it. I think he just saw something important enough for Flammia to kill him."

"And what—Delaney heard about Cole's body turning up here? She decided to take a look herself? Yeah, maybe... What's our plan?"

"The plan is, I climb over that thing," Pepper said, pointing to the high brick wall topped with barbed wire. "I find Delaney and get her the heck out of there. Then she tells us what's the deal with Nashville and why the heck she's inside the contractor park at midnight."

Angel nodded. "If she has some info about the two Emmas, we call your dad."

Pepper said nothing.

"And I should be the one who goes over the fence," continued Angel. "I'm not full of stitches and I have all ten fingers." He wiggled them at Pepper.

But Pepper wasn't budging. "No way, I have to go."

"At least let me go with you."

"Sorry, buddy. I need you out here on lookout. Any police or other trouble, call me."

Pepper didn't say out loud his real reason for going in alone: if the situation went sideways and he got caught, he didn't want to ruin Angel's life too. Detective Miller would do what he'd promised to do—have Pepper prosecuted to the fullest extent of the law. He couldn't let his buddy become collateral damage.

"If the shit hits the fan while I'm inside, you can't call 911 on your cell phone," Pepper warned Angel. "Do it from a pay phone. It has to be anonymous."

Angel snorted. "*Mano*, a pay phone? Where should I go, the 1980s?"

"Back on Central Street. The gas station next to the Liquor Barn has a payphone on its side wall."

So it was time.

"You still got that old blanket in your trunk?" Pepper asked.

Angel did.

"Sorry, buddy, it might get a few rips."

"Better the blanket than you," laughed Angel.

Pepper retrieved the blanket from the trunk and then climbed on the hood of *El Diablo*, which gave him enough height to get his hands to the top of the brick wall.

He doubled up the blanket and laid it over the barbed wire. It would hopefully provide a little protection.

"This is going to hurt," Pepper muttered to himself, flexing his injured hand.

Then with a heave, he gingerly climbed over the brick wall. The barbed wire poked through the blanket and scratched him as he gingerly swung over the top, swaying back and forth.

He hung from the top of the wall and dropped to the ground inside, tweaking an ankle. As he stood and shook off the pain, he remembered one of his grandfather Papa Ryan's favorite old sayings from his days as a patrol officer in Boston: *nothing good happens late on a hot summer night.*

Pepper limped quietly through the enormous maze of contractor vehicles and shipping containers that inhabited the Big Red Yard.

No lights were on in the contractor park, and it was the darkest night of the summer so far. Heavy clouds blocked the moon and stars, only occasionally letting a little moonlight peek through. Pepper pulled out his cell phone's light and set it to low. He didn't want to bump into something every few steps, but he also didn't want to announce his presence to anyone else except Delaney. And definitely not draw the attention of Stinky, the enormous guard dog he'd seen on his last time here.

Pepper assumed Stinky might roam the contractor park at night. And if he thought he already had problems, getting his nuts bitten off by that big monster would quickly go to the top of the list. If it sprang on Pepper in the dark, he'd probably die of a heart attack before Stinky's teeth sank in. Hopefully.

Pepper texted Delaney again: *Where r u?*

No reply.

"Delaney!" he hissed, breaking the silence as loudly as he dared.

So he would have to do this the hard way. Pepper meandered through the maze of shipping containers, pickup trucks, trailers and loose ends of equipment, occasionally calling Delaney's name.

He checked his phone; she hadn't responded. He texted her again: *U still at BRY?*

No answer. Maybe her battery had died? Or she didn't have good cell coverage here?

Pepper heard barking on the far side of the container park— Stinky the monster dog, agitated by something. *Perfect.* He dug around in the back of a nearby pickup truck and found a crowbar. It was heavy and cold in his hands.

Pepper wished his head was clearer. It felt thick, compressed. Fogged. From the pain meds they'd given him?

He worked his way deep into the lot. Much deeper than the other time he came here to meet with Dennis Cole about the Greenhead Snatcher case. He wondered how far he was from Leo Flammia's space. Would it still be marked with police tape?

"Delaney!" he whispered as loudly as he could, hefting his crowbar.

He was near the back corner of the Big Red Yard, or so he estimated, when he saw a light.

It was coming from the top of a home oil delivery truck. Pepper couldn't read the company name on its side.

Was someone working on their truck at this time of the night?

"Hello?" Pepper hissed. He reached its side.

The oil truck looked old—the tank had brown rust along its edges. Grass was growing high under the tank, like the truck hadn't moved recently.

The light was hanging on a hook at the top of the tank, and it highlighted an open manhole hatch cover. Pepper recalled that when he met with Dennis Cole here, he'd said he welded a manhole cover on a truck here last month. Was someone inside making repairs?

Even if emptied, the air inside an oil delivery tank would be foul and oil would coat the surfaces. Similar to the mess in the old coal furnace at the high school. No way anyone would survive for long inside unless they had an oxygen tank and mask. It would be very dirty work.

But the opening at the top of the tank was lit up. Making it exactly the kind of place Delaney would notice and explore. Had she fallen in, been overcome by fumes?

Using his cell phone light, Pepper located a ladder on the front of the oil tank, near the cab. He gingerly climbed the ladder, taking care not to drop his cell phone. It was hard to climb with his injured hand.

When he reached the top, he saw the manhole cover fully open on a hinge. He scooched over to the opening and leaned in with his phone light, bracing for a nose full of oil fumes.

He didn't smell any oil. He shone his flashlight into the dark space. Despite the tank's outward appearance, the inside appeared to have never held oil. Or the tank had gotten a hell of a cleaning. It was spotless. A metal ladder lead from the opening down into the tank.

Pepper twisted his phone to illuminate the inside of the tank. And at the far end, he saw something so surprising he almost dropped his phone.

Bodies.

Pepper climbed down the ladder to confirm the unbelievable. The metal ladder was slick, and he had to be careful not to miss a rung. His injured hand screamed from the effort.

He reached the curved floor of the tank and shuffled toward the bodies, his mind spinning.

He saw Delaney. She filled the circle of his phone's light. She was bound at her hands and feet in duct tape. More tape covered her eyes. *Oh my God, oh my God.*

Pepper shined his light farther back to where two other people lay. They looked like women and were also bound up. One had darker hair, one had blonde.

The two Emmas!

CHAPTER FORTY-NINE

Pepper dove to Delaney's side and began ripping apart the duct tape binding her hands.

He put down his phone and used both hands, despite the bandages on his injured hand. He found an edge and started making progress, unraveling the loops of tape.

How the hell had she ended up like this?

He could understand about Emma Bailey and Emma Addison. Their kidnapper Leo Flammia would have left them here totally immobilized while he was away. And the oil tank made sense. It'd be a perfect vehicle for transporting the girls off the Cape. A trojan horse kind of thing.

But Flammia had died yesterday evening, and Delaney visited Pepper at the hospital this afternoon. So who the hell had tied her up?

Obviously, someone else was working with Flammia. Had Delaney texted Pepper before she was caught? Or had her captor texted him using her phone? And why had someone grabbed her? The questions raced through Pepper's exhausted brain.

With a hard tug, he pulled the last of the duct tape off Delaney's hands, only to find two loops of tie wraps. The kind which electricians used to bind wires, or police use as cheap handcuffs.

Pepper should call for help. He needed to do it quickly, before whoever tied up Delaney returned. He would stick to the plan—tell Angel to call 911 anonymously from the gas station pay phone. Yes, that'd be smart. After he called Angel, he'd set free Delaney and the Emmas—he needed to do that himself. Then he'd slip away before the police arrived.

And he had to do it without Delaney or the two Emmas knowing he was their rescuer. No one could ever know he was there... Detective Miller would use that info to nail him to the wall as promised. Pepper's future would be toast.

Pepper picked up his phone from the tank floor and saw he had no signal. Which made sense inside these thick metal walls. He climbed the metal ladder as fast as he could, holding his phone in his teeth. When his shoulders were free of the manhole opening, he quickly dialed Angel.

Who answered after one ring. *Yes!*

"Angel, go make the call. 911. Use a fake voice, don't give your name. Just say you heard, ah, people breaking into the Big Red Yard. Say you heard gunshots so the police will respond fast. Then get back to the machine shop parking lot. I'll meet you there."

"But Delaney?" asked Angel. "Did you—"

"Dude, go! I'll tell you everything in a few minutes!"

Pepper hung up, shoved his phone in his pocket. He climbed back down, his mind still spinning.

He bumped into Delaney in the dark and kneeled beside her. He grabbed the first of the two tie wraps with both hands. Maybe if he pulled hard enough, he could break the little metal teeth which held the tie wrap in place?

He took a deep breath and pulled as hard as he could.

His injured hand was on fire.

Delaney screamed through her duct tape gag.

Shit. Brute force was definitely not going to work. Did he need to climb out of the tank and look for something sharp?

Pepper checked his pockets. He had his wallet, his house keys…and attached to his keys was the stupid little toy pen knife Delaney had won on their mini golf date. Unbelievable. Would it cut the tie wraps?

Only one way to find out. He flipped open the little knife and began trying to cut one of the tie wraps. He sawed back and forth in the darkness, using his good hand. The knife slid against the plastic, not seeming to make any impression. Pepper just kept sawing.

He stopped, took out his phone and turned on the flashlight. He shone it on the tie wrap. He could see a shiny strip where the stupid little knife had made a small impression.

Okay. That was something.

Pepper continued to cut at the tie wrap. Then he grabbed it again with both hands and yanked with all of his strength. A ragged burst of pain shot through his hands again as he pulled, but finally the tie wrap broke! One down, one to go and Delaney's hands would be free!

He began the miserable process again immediately on the remaining tie wrap. Back and forth with the little knife in the darkness, trying to keep the knife working on the same spot. But maybe slipping to one side or the other.

He checked with his cell phone light and saw he had made little progress yet. Back to sawing. He couldn't let Delaney stay tied up one minute longer. He was angry and worn out and in pain.

His mind drifted back to the big question—who the hell had done this to her? The FBI had been wrong that Leo Flammia acted alone. Perhaps they'd been right that the Greenhead Snatcher had above-average intelligence, but maybe Flammia had just been following orders and whoever had kidnapped Delaney was the true mastermind. The real Greenhead Snatcher.

Names flooded through Pepper's head as he worked on the tie wrap.

Casper Yelle. He was a sex offender and the police report said he had above-average intelligence. He had slipped his ankle monitor and disappeared. He was definitely a possibility.

So was Scooter McCord, whatever his real name was. He had a passport under a different name, he'd quit his job and had a plane ticket to flee the country...

Pepper even thought about Fester Timmins, the cop wannabe pain-in-the-ass. Why was he always on the scene so fast after trouble happened? Was he craftier then he appeared to be?

Who knows... Pepper needed to focus on freeing Delaney and the two Emmas, ASAP, and getting his own butt out of there before the police arrived.

Or even worse, before the Snatcher came back. He'd left the manhole cover open with a light on—he might return any second. Pepper would be at his mercy down here in the tank. The guy could close the manhole and Pepper would have no way to escape. The man could leave them trapped inside the tank to die, or could drive to a secluded space and shoot them later.

Pepper sawed harder, bearing down on the tie wrap.

Apparently too hard, because the knife's blade snapped in half. *Shit!* He only had left the handle and a tiny stub of blade. He almost threw it away in rage, but didn't want to hit the Emmas, so instead he thrust the stump of the knife in his pocket and grabbed the tie wrap in both hands.

This was really going to hurt...

Pepper leaned in and pulled as hard as he could, trying to break the tie wrap. Hard and relentless. Until the pain in his fingers changed to numbness. But the damned tie wrap didn't break.

He heard a clang from the direction of the oil tank's manhole cover. He let go of the tie wrap and scrambled to his feet. *Had it closed?*

Then a loud rumbling noise filled the tank. Someone had started the oil delivery truck's engine.

A moment later, the truck lurched into motion, toppling Pepper off his feet.

CHAPTER FIFTY

Pepper fell against the curved floor of the oil tank with a jarring crash. His cell phone crunched under him.

Lying on his side, he pulled it out of his pocket, touching the shattered rough screen. It didn't light up. He pushed the buttons frantically, trying to bring it to life. Nothing. It was toast.

He struggled to his feet as the oil truck bounced through the puddles and ruts of the contractor park.

What should he do?

He couldn't stay down here. He was at the mercy of whoever was driving the truck. If the person had locked the manhole cover, Pepper would be trapped with the three girls. In a minute or two, the truck could be on the road and soon be anywhere in New England.

He lunged for the metal ladder. The only sure way to save Delaney and the Emmas was to stop the truck.

Pepper realized he'd been stupid not to tell Angel about the oil truck and the tank full of victims. By the time his buddy figured out that everything had gone to crap and fessed up to the police, they wouldn't even know they were looking for a home delivery oil truck. It would be long gone.

He climbed quickly, ignoring the sharp pain of his stitches and his even more painful hand. Had the man checked the manhole cover and relocked it? If so, Pepper was screwed.

He had to prevent the truck from getting out the gate. He had to keep the girls here and the driver too. But the girls were the priority. Hopefully, Angel had called 911 by now and the police were on their way.

Pepper reached the top of the ladder and saw the manhole cover was closed.

Shit!

He shoved against it and it budged a little. The hooks which held the metal ladder in place prevented the cover from closing flush with the tank. Maybe he could force it open?

He shoved at the lid with his good shoulder. It moved a tiny bit—the latch had some wiggle room. He stepped up one farther rung on the ladder, planted his shoulder against the lid and gave an even bigger shove.

But the cover didn't open.

Pepper got a desperate idea. He took out the stubby pen knife and wiggled it in the small opening between the tank and the cover. It rubbed against something hard, so he pressed the stub of the knife blade as hard as he could, praying it wouldn't completely break off this time.

Nothing.

The truck kept bouncing through the Big Red Yard.

He tried again, just as the truck thumped through an extra deep pothole, rocking the oil tank. And he felt the stub of blade push something hard out of the way.

He put his shoulder into the lid again and pushed. The manhole cover slammed open!

Pepper scrambled up through the opening and crawled across the cold metal top of the oil tank. It was still almost completely dark because the truck's headlights were off. The night was still warm and the air felt great. He swayed with every bounce of the truck, clinging to whatever his hands found to grip. He didn't want to think what would happen if he fell from that height.

The truck was nearing the gate. He had to act.

He stood, swaying precariously, and jumped toward the roof of the truck cab. He fell for a half second—a brief moment of *fuck it*. He landed with a loud thump. The roof partially collapsed under his weight.

The truck lurched to a halt and Pepper toppled down over the windshield, slamming onto the hood and bouncing off down to the muddy lane.

Muddy, but still way too hard. He hit with a bone-jarring thud which drove the breath from his lungs. Instinctively, he rolled over and over, away from the truck, until he bumped into the side of a shipping container.

Pepper heard the splash of someone jumping down from the cab of the truck and saw a flashlight flick on. A man's voice swore (oddly familiar?) and the flashlight beam swung in the darkness toward Pepper's location.

He ignored his lack of wind and lunged forward, body-checking the man into the side of the oil truck. The man's flashlight spun away and left them in near darkness.

A punch glanced off Pepper's head as he bounced away. He retreated down the side of the oil truck away from the man. His head was ringing from the blow and from...well, probably everything over the past two days, including the drugs.

A loud, low fit of angry barking erupted somewhere not too far away. Stinky the monster dog! *Perfect*.

Pepper felt his way backward along the oil truck and circled its rear, then moved away down a narrow aisle between two containers. Trying to regroup.

What should he do? Fight? Slip away and wait for the police to respond to Angel's 911 call?

What if the man climbed back into the truck and drove away? Would the police arrive in time for Pepper to send them after the truck before it disappeared into the night?

No, he couldn't risk the man getting away with Delaney and the two Emmas. He had to do whatever it took to stop the man, whoever he was. Casper Yelle? Scooter McCord? That clown Fester Timmins? Whoever, the man was a psychopathic criminal—responsible for three kidnappings and at least one murder.

The man stomped past Pepper through the muck. So he didn't plan to drive away, at least not yet. The man was swearing and muttering things Pepper couldn't make out. Again, sounding so damned familiar. If only he wasn't so worn out and battered... If only he had a second to just think....

Pepper crouched down, and the man passed right by, close enough that he could have taken two steps and grabbed him.

But Pepper didn't. In his injured condition, he needed to improve his odds. Too much was at stake. He moved as quietly as possible away from the oil truck, ending up against a metal trailer full of lawn-cutting equipment.

Pepper's hand found the head of a rake and then its smooth wooden handle. As he pulled it upward from its holder, something hit him on the side, sharp and painful. Maybe the metal end of a shovel.

Pepper grunted and pulled back. The man's next swing hit the trailer, ringing loud, and it sounded like the shovel snapped in half.

Pepper swung his rake wildly and hit nothing.

Then something knocked over Pepper from behind. A tremendous blow, like a car had hit him.

Stinky the monster dog had found them.

Pepper smelled the bitter stench of its breath as it ripped into his shirt and tugged him upward. But it didn't bite him. It paused.

As if it remembered Pepper? Remembered him as the source of the roast beef sandwich a few days ago? No, that was ridiculous.

Then the man fighting Pepper made a stupid mistake. He swung the broken shovel handle where he thought Pepper was and he hit Stinky instead. The dog released Pepper's shirt and sprang at the man with a growl.

Pepper crawled away as the handle thumped into the dog, over and over. The dog howled furiously.

Pepper rounded the end of the lawn-cutting equipment trailer and smacked into a container. His hand touched a ladder, and he pulled himself up it, his entire body—especially his injured hand —screaming in protest.

The struggle between the man and the dog continued loudly. It sounded like Stinky was being beaten to death.

Pepper scrambled onto the top of the shipping container, huddling low to avoid creating a silhouette against the sky in case a sliver of moon broke free of the clouds. He breathed deeply, momentarily safe from both the man and the dog.

The police would be coming any minute. Pepper decided to lie low and make sure the man didn't drive away in the oil truck. He just needed to delay the man—he didn't have to beat him.

Pepper couldn't see anything of the battle below him between the man and the monster dog, but he heard the howling and growling and the sound of wood hitting the dog's body over and over.

But it was keeping the man busy... All Pepper had to do was stay on the container, out of reach.

That would have been the smart move.

But Pepper's mind focused briefly around two ideas: the man was going to beat the dog to death...and Pepper had actually figured out who the man was! He felt stupid that it took him until now.

So Pepper leaped off the container, falling, falling...goddamn, it was farther on the way down than he'd expected.

He collided with the raised handle of the shovel, then the man's shoulders, knocking him to the ground. The dog, suddenly free from the rain of blows, rolled away. It lashed out at them, missing, then retreated into the blackness with a long whine.

Pepper rolled away from the man, who fought to his feet and stumbled backward into the muddy lane, just as a wedge of yellow moon found an opening in the clouds. He saw the man's bleeding face, confirming he'd guessed right.

It was Gus Bullard. Coach Bullard.

Pepper saw Bullard's face twist into a wicked grin. "Hey, Wonderboy! Ready to die a hero?"

Then Bullard lunged for him.

CHAPTER FIFTY-ONE

Bullard was holding a broken wooden handle, which he pulled back like a baseball bat and swung at Pepper's head.

Pepper ducked, and the handle screamed past, brushing the top of his hair. He stepped back as Bullard swung it again. A more awkward swing, a backhand. This time Pepper grabbed the handle and pulled it, making the man stumble forward. Pepper lurched to the side and kept pulling, but he tripped over a bucket in the near darkness and fell to his side.

Bullard dove on Pepper, landing like a damned avalanche. Two hundred and seventy-five pounds of fury. Pepper got one knee up to catch Bullard in the stomach as he landed on him, knocking the wind from the man as he crushed Pepper.

Pepper could feel new pain in all the areas that had been sewn up after his battle with Leo Flammia. Stitches tearing, blood flowing. Except his injured hand, which felt like nothing—it had gone numb.

And even worse, he was humiliated. Bullard had played him like an idiot. He must have sent texts from Delaney's phone, luring Pepper here. And Pepper hadn't noticed anything was strange? He was as mad at himself as he was at Bullard.

"You fucked up my perfect plan, killing Leo," snarled Bullard. "Cost me my two million dollars. And life's about accountability, Pylon. I've never been able to beat that lesson into your thick head. But tonight's the night..."

Coach had always been a master manipulator and, in Pepper's opinion, a narcissistic bastard. That part made sense. He probably got Flammia to do all the snatchings, take all the real risk.

Pepper punched Bullard square on the jaw, but since he was underneath the man, his punch didn't have much power.

Bullard shook his head and grinned. He pulled his arm back and punched down at Pepper's face.

Pepper raised his head at the last second and Bullard's fist hit Pepper's forehead. The thickest part of his head—a trick Pepper had picked up scrapping in the British Columbia Hockey League last winter.

The impact of the punch threw Pepper flat backward, and he heard a cry of pain from Bullard. Fist against the front of the forehead? No contest. The man had probably busted his hand.

Pepper grabbed Bullard's shirt and rolled him to the right, but not enough for Pepper to end up on top. They were lying side by side in the mud, straining at each other and trying to get the advantage.

"It's gonna kill your old man," snarled Bullard, his sour breath in Pepper's face. "His own son, an accomplice to the snatchings. The girls would have gone free, and now you've fucked that up too. It has to look like a murder-suicide, so no one'll look for me."

Pepper's only reply was to knee the man in the gut, two times fast. He rolled free, climbing to his feet.

Somehow, Bullard found his feet almost as quickly. There was just enough moonlight for Pepper to see the man grope around in the back of a pickup truck and pull out something which looked like a piece of metal rebar.

Bullard thrust it at Pepper's face. Pepper threw himself aside, rolling away in the mud.

He regained his feet and stumbled into the shadows of a shipping container and limped around the corner, taking a hard left, which led behind a different container. All the while searching in the near darkness for something to use as a weapon. Bullard might find him any second. Pepper found nothing.

Pepper heard the sounds of someone running nearby, then nothing, then a door slam. Was Bullard changing his plan and trying to drive away? He scrambled up into the back of a pickup truck, his whole body protesting, trying to see anything in the near darkness.

The heavy footsteps came towards him again. So Bullard was staying to finish the fight. Had he retrieved something from the oil tank truck? Pepper groped around in the pickup's bed, trying to find something he could use to defend himself, and scrapped his hands on concrete blocks. He grabbed one from both ends as brutal pain exploded again in his injured hand. He ignored it, lifting the concrete block up to chest level. Pepper couldn't see enough to know exactly where Bullard was.

Mucky footsteps came along the left side of the pickup truck, and Pepper turned and heaved the concrete block like a shot put. He heard it collide with a body, heard Bullard's scream of rage and pain and the man splashing down into the mud.

Pepper vaulted over the other side of the truck and staggered farther into the maze of containers, pickup trucks and trailers. He needed something better to use as a weapon. Preferably one-handed... But it was too dark—clouds had choked out the moon again. He wove through the Big Red Yard like he was in a nightmare. And found nothing to help him in his fight.

The window of a panel van beside him exploded and Pepper flinched away. That explained what Bullard had gone to the truck for—a handgun.

Pepper bent lower and hurried forward around the front of the panel van, then down the side of a high-sided trailer parked behind it. He was losing the fight so far. However, he would stay and finish it, win or lose.

His good hand found the handle of a tool, and he grabbed it. It was only a broom. Barely better than nothing, but he kept it.

The only thing keeping Pepper going was his rage at Bullard for all the horrible things he'd done to the Emmas and Delaney. The pain and trauma they'd suffered...which they were still enduring.

He wasn't going down easy. He'd fight and cheat and do whatever it took to stop Bullard. That guy was a fucking monster and he just couldn't win. No way.

Pepper crept past the trailer and inched down the side of a container. He couldn't see two feet in front of himself. He held the broom out like a blind man's cane.

"Give it up, Pylon," yelled Bullard, somewhere to Pepper's right. Not too far away. "Quit now and I'll let the two Emmas live. They haven't seen my face... Is that a deal?"

Pepper didn't respond. He tossed his broom high in the air to his left, as far as he could. It clang against a container.

As Bullard rushed past in that direction holding his gun up in front of himself, Pepper tackled the man low and dirty.

CHAPTER FIFTY-TWO

They smashed into the side of a container, and both fell again.

Pepper got the forearm of his bad hand across Bullard's neck and wildly tried to grab the handgun with his other hand.

He couldn't let Bullard win. No way. If Pepper lost, he was dead. And so was Delaney. Probably the Emmas too. Families shattered.

And that wasn't all. Pepper's family would also be disgraced, thinking he was the monster behind all this insanity.

No damned way.

Bullard grabbed Pepper with two hands. So he must have dropped his handgun. They wrestled in the mud, like Pepper had wrestled with Flammia only one long day ago. Bullard was heavier than Flammia. Probably forty pounds heavier than Pepper too. And Pepper was wounded and exhausted.

But Pepper was younger and in better shape. And he was at least as pissed off as Bullard. They wrestled for control in the near darkness, throwing punches which mostly didn't land or do any damage.

They were both breathing heavily and Bullard was swearing, calling Pepper every name he could think of. Pepper saved the little air he had for breathing. He just wrestled and threw punches and scrapped for his life.

The stories were that Bullard had been a hell of a fighter in his East Coast Hockey League days until concussions ended his playing career. But that was a long time ago...and fighting on ice and fighting in mud were two different ways to scrap.

Bullard pulled Pepper to the right, trying to roll him over, and Pepper went with it and kept rolling. The move caught Bullard by surprise and Pepper ended up on top. He brought back his good left hand, so heavy he could barely lift it, and punched the man's face with every bit of energy he had left. He caught Bullard on the side of his jaw, heard his grunt of pain and felt him go limp under him. Probably unconscious.

A very lucky punch.

Pepper hit him one more time, just to be sure and also because he was still in a full-on rage. This punch caught Bullard square on the nose, which broke with a snap. The man didn't fight back.

Pepper sat up, still straddling Bullard. His mind was spinning.

It wasn't always about speed, Coach. Sometimes it all came down to who was willing to sacrifice more.

Pepper took a deep, ragged breath. Sure, Bullard was headed to prison. But once Detective Miller found out about Pepper's role in bringing Bullard down, he'd make sure Pepper lost everything too, like he'd promised. No Harvard and no music career either. Pepper's dad would have to resign under the scandal of all the laws Pepper had violated this week. Possibly his dad would face charges too.

All because of Bullard's savage, evil acts. Which, at the end of the day, may have just been about the old coach's anger at being tossed aside by the high school. And partially about the two million dollars of ransom money he must have felt was fair payback. What a psycho.

Then Pepper realized he had a way out, after all.

No one (other than trusty Angel) knew Pepper had been there —not if he got away before the police arrived. Justice could be quickly served, and Pepper's life wouldn't be ruined. Win-win. All he had to do was choke Bullard to death. Exactly the rough justice the man deserved for murdering Dennis Cole and kidnapping three woman.

As Pepper's hands closed around Bullard's thick neck, he realized he could see the man's bloody face. The moon had slid just enough from behind the clouds. A fresh breeze swept through the container park, followed by thin, warm rain.

Pepper squeezed, thinking about the terror Bullard and Flammia's victims must have experienced over the past week. The fear, the helplessness, being imprisoned by such evil bastards. Bullard deserved the Greenhead Snatcher nickname with Flammia. They were both just parasites. They should be wiped out. That would be Pepper's final sacrifice, no matter the consequence to him.

He could do this. He could end everything right now. His fingers tightened harder around Bullard's fat neck.

Police sirens wailed in the distance. The sound shook him like the ringing of an alarm clock trying to pull him from the deep, troubled sleep of a nightmare.

Could Pepper really kill an unconscious man?

Maybe he should just tie up Bullard and let the police take him. Pepper was light-headed, unable to decide.

If Bullard lived, everything would come out at his trial. Pepper could almost picture the manipulative bastard in court: using Pepper's involvement as a weapon, try to poison the case and twist Pepper's acts into something they weren't.

But if the alternative was for Pepper to commit murder, no. Just no.

He released the man's neck.

He would have to let the D.A.'s office try to do their job, even though the fallout for Pepper would be total. He could picture the smile on Miller's face when the state police detective kept his promise and built a case which would completely ruin Pepper's life.

Pepper climbed to his feet. *We all get what we deserve, even if the price is high. That's what justice means.* He would not kill an unconscious man in cold blood. He couldn't run away from that act if he committed it, or blame anyone else. It was the simple truth.

In that moment, for the first time in a long time, Pepper was at peace. He felt completely free, despite the consequences to himself.

He started walking, swaying from fatigue. He needed to find some rope or duct tape to tie Bullard's hands. Which should be easy, surrounded by contractors' trucks and work equipment. There should be tons of it somewhere nearby.

Tie up Bullard. Then go free Delaney and the two Emmas. He deserved to be the one to free them—that would almost make up for whatever hell Pepper was going to face in the legal system. So he'd need to find something sharp to cut those miserable tie wraps...

It was still way too damned dark. He groped his way along a trailer but didn't find a rope or anything else he could use to tie Bullard's hands and feet.

The police sirens were getting louder.

He reached a shipping container and pulled at its door; it was locked. He crossed a path—feeling the open space around him—as another hint of moonlight mercifully broke through, helping him locate another pickup truck. He crawled over the tailgate into the bed. At the very front, he found a big snarl of nylon rope. It was as thick as his pinky finger. It would be perfect. Pepper grabbed it and turned to climb down from the truck.

The next sequence unfolded in slow motion, like a nightmare.

Pepper saw the enormous dark form of Gus Bullard charge into the open space of the path. It was clearly him—the thin moonlight illuminated his muddy form, his bloody face and his extended arm, with something shiny in his fist. How could Bullard have regained consciousness so quickly? How had he found his handgun in the mud?

"I'm gonna kill you," shouted Bullard, lumbering toward where Pepper knelt in the back of the pickup truck.

Pepper gathered the big tangle of nylon rope to throw it at the man. Probably an empty gesture, but it was all he could do in his defense. Pepper had nowhere to go, and Bullard could get as close as he liked before pulling the trigger.

All this flashed through Pepper's mind in a second. His hands brought up the rope, turning to heave it at Bullard.

Bullard's mouth wide open and his ruined nose was a mass of red. The loony bastard was laughing—a broken, coughing howl. So close now. He saw the man's gun come up, reflecting silver moonlight.

Then Pepper saw a bigger glint in the night air, saw it descending toward Bullard. Saw it meeting Bullard's head with a soft, wet thud. He saw arms emerge from the shadows, then a person. Long hair. A woman.

Delaney Lynn.

He saw her axe rise again, less shiny than before. He saw it descend again, making the same wet, dull thud.

Pepper heard Delaney screaming, "Kill me? You'll fucking kill me?" Pepper saw the axe come up a third time, then down again into Bullard's body, now a still bulk in the mud by the front of the truck. Delaney continued screaming, her voice hysterical with rage. "Fuck you!"

A police car slid to a stop ten feet from her, flooding the scene with impossibly bright light. Its white high beams. Its light bar with swirling blue lights alternating with flashes of red. An inferno of brightness after all the dark.

The police car door opened, and a man was yelling at Delaney. Still kneeling in the pickup's bed, Pepper could see the officer's handgun pointed at her from behind the officer's car door. He saw her drop the axe, step back, fall to her knees in the mud.

The officer was still shouting. Delaney put her hands in the air but did not otherwise move.

Pepper stayed just as frozen. He was positioned off to the side and so was almost entirely hidden in darkness. The officer would have to look right at him.

Should he join Delaney on the path? Should he yell to the officer, announce his presence?

The police officer quickly had Delaney flat in the mud and cuffed, then led her to the back of the police car. Securing the scene, or so the officer probably thought.

Pepper didn't do either of those things. He just watched, trying to make sense of what had happened.

Delaney had still been mostly tied up in the oil delivery tank. She must have broken the tie wrap Pepper had tried to cut off her hands, then removed the duct tape from her legs and head. Somehow she must have had the strength to climb the metal ladder and escape.

But then, instead of running away, she must have armed herself with the axe, either to protect herself or to help her get revenge on the man who'd kidnapped her. And when she'd seen Bullard with a handgun yelling threats and running in her direction—Pepper's direction too, unknown to her—she had buried the axe in the man's damned head.

Shit, good for her. Bullard had snatched her, terrorized her and made her fear she would die when he had charged toward her with the handgun. The asshole got exactly the death he deserved.

Pepper climbed stealthily and painfully down the far side of the pickup truck, moving slowly because of his injuries and to make as little noise as possible. Staying low, out of the light.

He had a momentary impulse to step out of the darkness and identify himself to the officer. He wanted to get in the back of the police car and hug Delaney. To comfort her. She must be completely traumatized.

However, he couldn't do anything for her without destroying his own future. And his gut told him she would be fine, emotionally and legally.

Delaney would tell the police what she'd seen—Bullard advancing toward the spot where she hid, yelling that he would kill her. She'd likely never seen Pepper kneeling in the bed of the pickup truck. She'd acted in self-defense against the man who'd kidnapped her and now was advancing to kill her.

Her act was completely justified.

Reluctantly, Pepper left her. He slowly worked his way deeper into the maze of the Big Red Yard, away from the lights. Pepper soon reached the place where he'd climbed over the wall earlier.

What was he going to do now? He could barely walk, let alone scale a wall...

Pepper located a ladder on the roof of a panel van. He dragged it to the wall and extended it a few feet, which took agonizing effort.

Then he climbed to the top, sat on Angel's ruined blanket (still draped on the barbed wire!) and kicked the ladder away to the ground.

And there, waiting in *El Diablo* in the corner of the machine shop parking lot, was Angel. He'd come back for Pepper and the police sirens hadn't scared him off. What a buddy... But he was parked about ten feet forward of where he'd been earlier. Pepper had no choice except to jump off the wall.

The landing hurt him. Everywhere.

He eventually got to his feet and limped to the Camry.

"*Mano*, you're getting mud all over *El Diablo!*" complained Angel, as Pepper pulled himself into the passenger side. "And what's that, more blood? Good thing I'm already taking you back to a hospital. What the hell happened?"

As they drove away toward Hyannis, back toward the hospital, Pepper told Angel everything that had happened. About finding the Emmas and Delaney in the oil delivery truck. And that fake text message from Delaney's phone had lured them to the Big Red Yard.

He summarized his fight with the man who turned out to be Gus Bullard. He described the running battle through the contractor park and the intervention by Stinky the monster dog. And how everything ended, with Delaney putting an axe through Bullard's skull.

Pepper finished his story, and for once in the many years he had known Angel, his buddy was at a loss for words.

"So she...? Coach Bullard...? *Fuck...*"

CHAPTER FIFTY-THREE

The next day, Friday, was a long one for Pepper.

By luck or miracle, no one had challenged him for being away from his hospital bed during the night for almost two hours.

On Friday morning, the nurse found Pepper out of bed, foolishly doing stretching exercises. She predicted he would rip some of his stitches. Her prediction turned out to be right, or so the doctor thought as he sewed up Pepper again.

But Pepper's blood pressure had finally improved. He was young and strong. And the hospital was over-crowded. They discharged him around noon in a lot more pain than he would admit to anyone.

Mrs. Eisenhower and Zula drove Pepper home from the hospital because his dad and Lieutenant Eisenhower were up to their necks in the aftermath of the crime scene at the Big Red Yard. Zula and her mother didn't talk much, letting Pepper doze during the half-hour drive back to New Albion. He was grateful to them for that and relieved to be free of the hospital.

Before he got out of their car at his home, he remembered to thank Zula for gathering the research on Scooter McCord's two names, especially the death certificate. "That was impressive," he said to her. "You might be the real investigator in your family."

Zula had blushed and waved him off, seeming both embarrassed and pleased.

Pepper napped heavily all day.

That night, around ten o'clock, Pepper sat with Delaney Lynn in the sand on Dill Beach by a little driftwood fire. The fire was big enough to be romantic and give them some warmth, but hopefully small enough to avoid attention from Pepper's police colleagues or the neighborhood busybodies.

Delaney looked sensational in a peach tank top and white cutoff shorts. Pepper was just as casual in a blue T-shirt and jeans.

He had a little Bluetooth speaker going with a classic rock mix. Just loud enough, just sexy enough. They sat together, wrapped in a blanket. Because it was a little chilly, right?

Before long, Delaney was telling him everything she had gone through the day before, just like she'd told the police.

Gus Bullard had ambushed her in the Langham Arms parking lot as she returned home from visiting Pepper at the hospital. Bullard had overpowered her, tied her up and put a blindfold on her. Then he'd taken her somewhere.

Many hours later, Delaney felt Bullard start untying her. Maybe to rape her, she'd thought. The man stopped when she was partially free and left her alone for a few minutes. She broke a binding which held her hands, then finished freeing herself. She climbed out of the oil tank, trying to escape to freedom.

In the pitch blackness of the oil tank, she hadn't seen the two Emmas—she only learned later that they were in there too.

While escaping, she grabbed an axe from a random truck to protect herself in case she ran into Bullard.

She was sneaking along a muddy path, trying to find her way clear of the contractor yard, when she heard Bullard yell he was going to kill her. It was mostly dark, but she saw him running in her direction as he shouted.

So she used the axe to defend her life, like a farm girl would. Delaney explained it to Pepper just like that. Simple. Unapologetic. She shivered, reliving the moment.

"The thing I keep wondering," she said. "Why me? Why'd he grab me?"

Pepper wanted badly to tell her the truth. That she'd been bait to lure him to the Big Red Yard, so he would die there and get labeled the second half of the Greenhead Snatcher team. Bullard probably figured that the FBI would eventually reject the idea Flammia had acted alone and would look for a second, smarter person. A person with the missing $2 million.

Bullard must have planned to stage the scene to look like Pepper had worked with Leo Flammia on the kidnappings and Dennis Cole's murder, then had finally snapped under the pressure. Make it look like he'd killed Delaney and the Emmas, then killed himself like a coward. Everyone would wonder what Pepper had done with the $2 million, but the money would be gone forever. *Gone wherever Bullard ran off to...*

Pepper couldn't explain all of that to Delaney because he had to keep his name out of last night's events. Feeling terrible, he shrugged and said to her, "Bullard's dead, so who knows? But you were crazy brave. Really amazing. I wish I could have been at your side to help."

He meant it more than she knew.

Delaney snuggled closer. "Did the FBI figure out why they snatched the two Emmas? Did Flammia or Bullard have a particular reason to snatch them or was it all random?"

"My dad says they believe the kidnappings were mostly about Bullard. New Albion High forced him to give up coaching hockey one year short of his twenty-fifth season, a huge insult to Bullard, especially when the community didn't step up to support him. So he wanted to get revenge to the tune of $2 million, then disappear. By the way, the police found the money in a duffel bag shoved behind the front seat of the oil delivery truck."

Delaney squeezed closer to him. "But why the two Emmas? And the third girl—Leslie Holbrook?"

"The police and the FBI think Leslie Holbrook was random—a crime of opportunity. But the two Emmas' mothers attended New Albion High during the same years as Gus Bullard, and they were both very pretty and popular. Maybe the two mothers shot down Bullard in his high school days and grabbing their daughters was another part of his crazy desire for revenge. The detectives will try to figure that out."

Pepper added a log to their little beach fire. Sparks popped and disappeared upward, burning out in the smoke and darkness. He put his arms around Delaney and pulled her close.

It was time to change the topic. Pepper tickled her low on the side of her back. "So, are you finally going to tell me the story about your cool tattoo? The song lyrics?"

After a little convincing, Delaney told all. She explained that while growing up in Georgia, she'd fallen in love with the wrong guy as a teenager. A real asshole. He'd been abusive—physically and emotionally. He'd told her she was worthless, ugly, all that shit. Trying to control her.

She left Vidalia, Georgia, in the night, alone and with almost no money. She'd come to Cape Cod because there were lots of summer jobs. As soon as she saved up enough money, she got the lyrics of "American Girl" by Tom Petty and the Heartbreakers tattooed on her lower back to remind herself to never let a guy take advantage of her again. That's what the lyrics meant to her. However, she hadn't truly felt strong until last night in the Big Red Yard when she fought back against Bullard.

"I finally earned my tattoo. Unfortunately..." she said with a long sigh.

"No doubt," Pepper said, and he kissed her.

They sat quietly for a bit, mostly looking up at the stars but also very aware of how close their bodies were to each other.

Then Delaney said quietly, "I have some other big news."

"You've got another tattoo to show me?"

She laughed and elbowed him. "No, I decided this morning I'm making the leap. I'm actually moving to Nashville. I need to take my shot at making it in music."

"That's great!" Pepper said. "With your voice, you'll be a big star in no time!"

She laughed again. "We'll see. At least now I know I'm strong enough to do pretty much anything on my own. Although if you want to join me, we can give it a shot together." She leaned over and kissed him on the ear.

This was the toughest decision Pepper ever had to make, but sitting there in the sand he was finally seeing his situation clearly. The handcuffs he'd been fighting against all summer weren't put on him by other people—he'd put them on himself. He didn't need to run away from his situation on Cape Cod, or from his college plans. Or from anything.

No, Pepper finally needed to decide what was next for him, on his own terms. Finally be an adult. Stop blaming others for holding him back or imposing expectations. As hard as that might be. And in his heart, he knew the right decision to make.

"I'm sorry, Delaney. It'd be an amazing adventure with you, but I have to say no. I've made commitments already and I need to see them through. Going to Harvard. Playing college hockey. I can't walk away from all the hard work I did to get there."

Pepper had to give it his best shot, even if he flamed out...

Delaney hugged him, then looked away. "I understand. Well, this'll only be goodbye for now, right? Four years is fast. You'll be a college graduate, I'll be a country music superstar."

"Country music? Not rock?"

"You bet your ass."

So it didn't look like he and Delaney would live happily ever after, at least not yet.

"That's the story of my life," she said with a thin smile. Not exaggerating her southern accent this time. "Bad timing."

They sat in silence, both thinking. Then Pepper said, "But we're here now. How about we stay out here tonight? Watch the stars?"

Delaney laughed again, harder. "Watch the stars? How many girls have you used that line on? And what about getting eaten alive by those damn greenhead flies?"

Pepper hugged her close. "Nope. We had a super high tide…it knocks down the population. You never heard of a kill tide? Yep, we're done with those greenheads for the rest of the summer, I promise."

Delaney turned her head and studied Pepper for a long moment, then leaned in to kiss him. And he kissed her back. Pepper eased off her tank top and Delaney gently helped him out of his shirt, kissing her way down his chest…finding each bruise and wound… Making the pain go away. Which led to other things, finally, even better than Pepper had imagined.

The night was warm, and they spent it together, there on the Cape Cod sand, tucked away behind a dune, hidden from the rest of the world.

This one night was theirs—and they didn't waste a minute.

CHAPTER FIFTY-FOUR

Pepper's body hurt as he washed his truck, scrubbing away road dirt and grease.

It was the next afternoon and he was alone in his family's driveway. He'd retrieved his truck from his mechanic a few hours earlier. Before turning on the hose, he'd double-checked that the gas cap was on tight so he wouldn't get any more water in the gas tank...although he was pretty sure that'd been a dirty trick by Leo Flammia or Gus Bullard to slow him down.

The day was sunny and hot. It wasn't even the end of July yet, but Pepper's Cape Cod summer was almost over. He'd decided to drive his truck up to Harvard a few weeks early and was somewhat optimistic it'd get there without breaking down.

El Diablo crunched down the Ryans' long oyster-shell driveway and parked beside Pepper's truck.

"Hey, *mano!*" said Angel with his usual big, open smile. "Look at you back on your feet, doing menial labor! But you missed a spot!"

Pepper threw his sponge at Angel. Then he took a break to catch him up on the aftermath of the Greenhead Snatcher investigation.

When Pepper got to the part about Gus Bullard, Angel interrupted. "Did the FBI figure out why Bullard pulled something this crazy? Sure, he got canned as a hockey coach, but his response was pretty extreme!"

"They think he had a medical condition called CTE. Bullard had a lot of concussions in his old days in the East Coast League. It can totally mess up your brain and throw off things like memory, judgment and fear. They'll know for sure after the autopsy."

"If Bullard lived, his lawyers definitely would have used the CTE defense," agreed Angel. "A bunch of football players have. And that old wrestler... Superfly Jimmy Snooka?"

Pepper also filled in Angel about some other evidence the FBI had gathered which explained Bullard's plans. He'd basically used Leo Flammia as a pawn to grab the girls. He'd convinced Flammia the two of them and the three girls would escape Cape Cod together and start a new society in a remote part of the Great Smoky Mountains in eastern Tennessee. Like one big happy communal family.

"The FBI thinks Bullard's secret plan was to kill Flammia with a drug overdose in the oil delivery truck, then get the police to show up and find the girls. Meanwhile, Bullard would have disappeared with the $2 million. But I screwed up his plan when I killed Flammia."

It still didn't seem real to Pepper, even when he said it out loud. He'd killed someone...

Angel picked up the sponge and started cleaning the truck.

"And the Rhode Island police arrested Casper Yelle last night. He was at the Greyhound station in Providence, trying to catch a bus south toward Mexico. He also violated his parole by having child pornography on his laptop and by tampering with his ankle bracelet, so he's headed back to prison."

"Crazy!" said Angel, sponging dirt off a rear tire. "Speaking of bad guys who weren't *the* main bad guy, did you hear the news about Scooter McCord? He got picked up by ICE!"

Immigration and Customs Enforcement? Pepper hadn't heard they arrested the redhead, but he had passed along the info to Detective Sweeney about the death certificate for an eleven-year-old boy named Alastair McCord and the other suspicious info he'd learned along the way about McCord. Sweeney had been grateful for the hot tip. "Why?"

Angel let out a burst of his loud, contagious laugh. "He was from Scotland and overstayed his visa! He's been using some dead kid's birth certificate and Social Security number for years. His real name's not even McCord! It was on the news!"

Aha, thought Pepper. That explained the man's two names, the UK passport and why he had been acting guilty. McCord had nothing to do with the Snatcher kidnappings, but he had been desperate to stay out of law enforcement's spotlight.

"At least all's well for us, right? What're we going to do to get the hundred thousand reward for locating the two Emmas?"

And here it was. Pepper paused. "Angel...about the reward. We can't tell anyone it was us. We have to keep our names out of it. Sorry, pal, we won't be getting that money."

Angel looked confused. "*Mano,* when we explain the whole thing, they've *got to* give it to us!"

"That's what I'm saying. We can't tell them we were there. We have to leave it as anonymous."

"Jesus, why would we do that? It's one hundred thousand dollars! You know how many pizzas I'd have to deliver! And you're broke too. It'd be nuts!"

But that was the way it had to be, because Pepper couldn't tell anyone he was part of the crazy battle on Thursday night at the Big Red Yard. It looked like Pepper would get officially cleared for the brown van incident and the death of Leo Flammia. However, if Detective Miller learned what he did on Thursday night—and the many other sketchy things he had done that week—he could quickly end up in all kinds of legal jeopardy.

Which Pepper explained to his friend. "Angel, that's the way I have to do it. That asshole Detective Miller would ruin my life if he got a whiff I was involved. I'm sorry."

He had a second big reason he didn't tell Angel—he didn't want to get credit for solving a problem he helped create himself by killing Flammia so recklessly.

No, Pepper would stay anonymous as punishment for his rebellious actions and lies that week which could have led to the deaths of the two Emmas, Leslie Holbrook and Delaney Lynn. And his unprofessional gossiping which probably contributed to poor Dennis Cole's death.

Angel's face was flushed, and he was breathing hard.

"I wish we could take the credit, but we can't," said Pepper. "This one's got to stay buried. You need to trust me on that, brother..." He took the hose and rinsed the area Angel had been scrubbing.

Angel was silent for a good while. Studying Pepper's face. Looking like he would explode. Finally he let out a pained sigh and spoke. "*Mano*, with friends like you I'm never gonna get rich. I don't understand it, I think you're nuts. But if that's how it's got to be, then damn it—good enough for me."

What a friend.

Angel wrung out the sponge in the bucket. "This looks like a pre-trip washing," continued Angel. "The Ivy League calls soon, huh?"

"Yep. I'm heading up on Tuesday."

"You give 'em shit, kid. And don't worry about me—by the time you get home, I'll own this town."

Pepper didn't doubt it. If he could avoid getting kicked out of Harvard before the snow flew...

"You did good," said Angel. Then he gave Pepper a half-hug

and a punch on the shoulder. "You're finally all grown up, Pepper Ryan! And I think I did a great job raising you..."

Then Angel grabbed the hose and blasted Pepper with water, so Pepper chased him around the truck, laughing and cursing.

When they finished half-drowning each other, Pepper said, "I'll settle for just being a college kid for a while."

Angel gave his belly laugh again. "*Mano,* some people are called to greatness...and some people are called to trouble. We both know which kind *you* are. But don't forget us little guys down here on the Cape."

———

Pepper didn't learn the final punch lines to the Greenhead Snatcher case until he was at Harvard, up to his neck in his new life of studies and team workouts and trying to make a few new friends in all the chaos.

In early September, Pepper got a late-night phone call from Delaney Lynn. She said she was loving Nashville and was playing anywhere in town which would let her on stage. Paying her dues and finding her way. She sounded a little drunk and very happy.

Delaney told him she'd been writing a ton of songs about some Cape Cod guy she kinda used to be in love with. "Keep an ear out," she said. "Next time you hear my voice, it'll be on the radio..."

She also told Pepper she'd gotten a big surprise which was helping her survive financially in Nashville. For stopping Gus Bullard, the police had awarded her two-thirds of the $100,000 reward in the Greenhead Snatcher investigation.

The other third of the reward was given to a woman who'd called in information about the white van after the first kidnapping, which the police admitted was very valuable. The woman had apparently even made a watercolor painting identifying the kidnapper, Leo Flammia. That woman was grateful to get recognition of her efforts to help, but she donated her share of the reward to the Susan G. Komen charity. "Because she'd just beaten cancer herself," Delaney told him.

"Perfect," he said.

In mid-September, Pepper received another random surprise. It was a letter—the first piece of old-fashioned snail mail he had received at college. From young Zula Eisenhower, of all people.

The letter was a piece of paper cut down to the size of a napkin. It said:

You win, Pepper!

Good luck up there. Stay out of the hospital if you can. But I'm not counting on it, haha.

Your friend always, Zula.

Taped to the letter was a one-dollar bill, the amount of their playful bet.

Fricking Zula... The fourteen-year-old kid deduced that Pepper found the two Emmas before the police had? That the official story from the final night at the Big Red Yard had a hole in it? And how was she the only one?

He'd have to keep an eye on that Zula. She was a hot ticket...

But Pepper didn't find out that later-breaking news until weeks later, after his summer had ended.

Back on the Saturday afternoon in July that Pepper washed his truck and had the water fight with Angel, he eventually put away the hose and other cleaning tools. He was happy his truck looked decent again.

A while later, Pepper stood on the deck behind the Ryan family house. He noticed the deck's gray paint under his bare feet had worn down to the wood. His dad and his brother weren't home yet, so he was alone as night approached.

He stood in the warm breeze looking out across their small backyard, to the beach and the water beyond. Sailboats and motorboats carved silver lines on the surface of the bay. He arched his body in a big yawn.

Tomorrow morning, Pepper was going fishing with his dad and Jake. Jake had called in a favor from a buddy and borrowed a Parker 26 sport boat. They were going out for stripers. It was a chance for him to start rebuilding his relationships with his dad and Jake and to be a family again for a little while, before he got on with what life held next.

Pepper guessed the Ryan men would be more talkative than usual. They all knew that soon these family activities would stop for a while, or maybe longer.

Change. It only moved in one direction.

Pepper would make one request on the fishing trip—no talk about the Snatcher case. All of that was done. He needed time to heal and even forget a bit.

Especially the brown van incident. Pepper was the only person alive who knew what'd really happened that evening. It was a one-man secret, the only kind which ever got kept. He figured he'd have to keep the secret for the rest of his life. How he wasn't a hero for stopping Leo Flammia's brown van. That he was a fluke, and almost a total failure. *Wonderboy?* What a joke...

But Pepper didn't know yet that something else would happen to him on Cape Cod almost exactly eight years later, which would force him to relive the details of the brown van incident and to second-guess everything that had gone down, and why.

Standing on the deck looking out at the greenish blue water, Pepper realized he was finally excited for college. To drive over the Sagamore Bridge and head north to face his new set of challenges. Earning his spot on a Division 1 hockey team—a big step up for him. And proving he could compete in the classroom with Harvard's best and brightest. At least there'd be no kidnappings and dead bodies at college, right?

He'd give that new life his best shot.

Pepper stretched his arms overhead as far as he could, aggravating his injuries. All his little points of pain, every one of which he deserved.

He knew he'd changed that summer. Maybe he was still a bit too cocky for his own health. But he'd learned that growing up was about tackling problems, not about focusing on himself. It was a scary world which needed scarier good guys to step up and make sacrifices.

But I have less respect for myself now, he realized. And less faith in the world around me. Those truths hurt more than his bruises and stitches.

Pepper suspected life would get easier as he got older. Controlling his damned temper. Facing down fears. Bouncing back from failures.

And hopefully embracing his own complicated mix of strengths and weaknesses which made him who he truly was, deep down inside.

And the decisions too. All the people and things you decide to keep or lose along the way. It had to get easier. It made all the sense in the world to him, standing on the worn deck of his family home, watching the far edge of the Atlantic Ocean blend to nothingness against the evening sky.

But Pepper was only twenty years old, back then.

THANK YOU

Thank you for buying this book. Pepper Ryan and his friends (and some enemies) will be back for new adventures soon.

Can I share a little story about my writing? I have to admit, I was having a tough week recently as I dove into the outlining process for the next Pepper Ryan story. Life was grabbing me by the ankles and I couldn't shake it. Then, while taking a break, I read on Amazon a kind, enthusiastic new review of *Kill Tide*! It hit me like the caffeine rush of a great cup of coffee--I got back to outlining with a fresh burst of excitement. I was even whistling.

Your feedback can make a difference too! I greatly appreciate any honest reviews--even one or two sentences go a long way. If you need a second reason to act today--the number of reviews that this book receives greatly impacts its ranking in Amazon's A9 algorithm (the mysterious formula that determines which books are shown to shoppers and which ones stay hidden in the dark forever). So if you could be so kind, please take a minute to write a short review for me now on Amazon and/or Goodreads.

Email List and More

And do you like to stay in touch? To receive special offers, bonus content, and info on new releases, please sign up for my Readers Club email list at my website: timothyfagan.com.

Or if you have any comments or questions, don't hesitate to send me an email at: tim@timothyfagan.com. I'm always happy to hear from people who've read my work. I try to answer every email I receive. Be well and again, thank you!

ALSO BY TIMOTHY FAGAN

Another adventure in the Pepper Ryan Mystery Thriller Series available at select bookstores and Amazon.com.

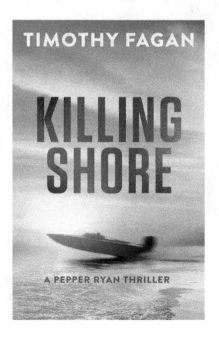